HARRY NAVINSKI

The Glass

First published by Harry Navinski Books 2020

First edition

ISBN: 9798667924340

This book was professionally typeset on Reedsy.
Find out more at reedsy.com

Contents

The Glass vi

Prologue – London, in the 1930s vii

Chapter 1 - Wednesday 14th January 2015 1

Chapter 2 5

Chapter 3 14

Chapter 4 19

Chapter 5 27

Chapter 6 34

Chapter 7 39

Chapter 8 45

Chapter 9 52

Chapter 10 58

Chapter 11 63

Chapter 12 70

Chapter 13 78

Chapter 14 83

Chapter 15 90

Chapter 16 96

Chapter 17 101

Chapter 18 105

Chapter 19 110

Chapter 20 116

Chapter 21 119

Chapter 22 123

Chapter 23 129

Chapter 24	131
Chapter 25	135
Chapter 26	141
Chapter 27 - Friday 16th January	147
Chapter 28	152
Chapter 29	157
Chapter 30	161
Chapter 31	167
Chapter 32	173
Chapter 33	179
Chapter 34	185
Chapter 35	191
Chapter 36	201
Chapter 37	206
Chapter 38 – Saturday 17th January	212
Chapter 39	219
Chapter 40	224
Chapter 41	231
Chapter 42 – Sunday 18th January	237
Chapter 43 – Monday 19th January	242
Chapter 44	246
Chapter 45	254
Chapter 46	259
Chapter 47	264
Chapter 48	271
Chapter 49	278
Chapter 50 – Tuesday 20th January	281
Chapter 51	285
Chapter 52	288
Chapter 53	295
Chapter 54	300

Chapter 55 304
Chapter 56 309
Chapter 57 314
Chapter 58 325
Epilogue – Monday 8th February 330
Reviews 335
Acknowledgements 336
About the Author 337
Also by Harry Navinski 339

The Glass

A Scottish Police Crime Novel
with Detective Chief Inspector Suzanna McLeod

by

Harry Navinski

Prologue – London, in the 1930s

Beside the Queen Anne-style armchair in which the elderly gentleman sat was a smouldering open fire, its radiance warming his legs. Classical music played quietly on the gramophone behind him. The lens of a magnifying glass glistened with the reflected light of the table lamps as the man twizzled it between his fingers. The recently polished brass rim glowed with reflected firelight. Its mahogany handle was intricately inset with ivory diamond shapes. But despite having evidently been cherished, the dents in its frame showed it had been a working tool, not just an ornament.

He set the object on the side table as he focussed on the task at hand. The man's piercing eyes looked upwards as if gazing through the ceiling, seeking guidance from the stars. He had his hands together, prayer-style - the tips touching his prominent chin. He'd led a risky life that included taking cocaine and smoking opium, and he'd been injured numerous times in his clashes with various criminals. It was amazing that he'd lived into his seventies.

A man was perched on the sofa opposite, his knees held together, and his briefcase laid on his lap, in use as a writing table. Unlike the old man, in his aubergine silk dressing gown, the younger man wore a pinstripe suit and white shirt with a dark nondescript tie. The solicitor awaited his client's instructions.

"As you know," the old man said, "I never married, so have no spouse to whom I can leave my assets, and I *certainly* do not wish my brother to inherit my estate. To my knowledge, I did not sire any offspring, but I do have a niece and a nephew. Despite my dislike for my brother, his children never wronged me. I prefer their offspring benefit from my estate, rather than the Government that I served throughout the last war. They've already had enough from me."

"My brother's children are middle-aged and possess sufficient wealth, so I am not inclined to make them richer. Even their children are now in adulthood and making their way in life. My estate, therefore, may go to *their* children."

"Excuse me, Mr Locke-Croft. Please offer further explanation of your desires, as it's not yet clear to me who should inherit your wealth?"

"Yes, of course! I had not finished. My estate will go to a descendant of my brother (note the singular, Mr Hicks), who, on reaching the age of eighteen, meets the conditions that I will set. Each child in my brother's line will be offered the opportunity to take a test, administered by your company. If passed, this person will inherit my entire estate. Do you understand?"

"Yes, sir."

"On my death, all my goods and chattels are to be sold. Proceeds from these sales are to be amalgamated with my investments and bank holdings to form my estate, which is to be placed into a trust fund. The only exception to these instructions is that this magnifying glass must not be sold." The old man held it up again for the solicitor to observe.

"It is to be retained in its cloth bag, along with a letter that I shall write. Your good company shall keep it safe until an entitled relative successfully analyses the scenario that I shall present. I will furnish your company with the solution to this mystery. At this point, your company shall pass the letter and magnifying glass to this person, along with the proceeds of the trust fund."

"If any of my brother's offspring fail the test, they will get nothing. If one generation fails, their children are to be given the opportunity, and *their* children, cascading downwards until someone with the right talent, intellect, and character solves the case. Have I made myself clear?"

"Yes, sir. I fully understand your instructions. Will the test and letter be ready for me on my return?"

"Yes. Now be off with you and return with the will and trust fund deeds before the end of the week. I do not know how much longer I will live." He picked up his pipe and lit it, retrenching into his private thoughts.

The solicitor rose and left as the smell of sweet tobacco drifted across to him. He knew from previous sessions with the eccentric old man that he would say no more and expect no goodbyes.

* * *

Chapter 1 - Wednesday 14th January 2015

The bank entrance door swung open, smashing into its stop with a crash as the two balaclava-clad men burst into the foyer. A shot rang out as the taller man pulled his pistol's trigger. "FREEZE. EVERYONE FREEZE. Hands in the air; NOW! Anyone moves towards an alarm, I'll shoot you. You two behind the counters stay still. You two," he ordered the people on his side of the counters, "move into the corner. NOW! DO IT! Do as you're told, and no-one gets hurt," he shouted threateningly.

A woman, shocked into inaction, was slow to respond. The robber slapped her and shoved her towards the corner he'd previously pointed to. She stumbled, landing on her knees, before falling forward onto all fours and bursting into tears.

The gunman threw a handful of large black cable ties at the customer services man. "Fasten one hand to that iron radiator, then connect yourself to that woman." The man did as he was told, but the lady continued to sob and didn't move towards the radiator.

"Shut up, you snivelling bitch," the big man shouted, kicking her in the ribs with the sole of his foot, knocking her onto her side, before booting her in the stomach. "SHUT UP, I said." She became silent, her eyes wide in shock. "Fasten the cable ties. NOW."

"Move to me now, before he kicks you again," the man whispered to the customer, having already connected himself to the radiator. She rotated onto all fours and crawled over to him, tears streaming down her nose and dripping onto the floor. He struggled to link himself to the woman, his finger trembling from fear of violence.

The second man had locked the entrance door, then turned and strode across to the counters. The smell of cordite hung in the air as he pointed his weapon at the first teller. "Keep your hands where I can see them. If you attempt to sound the alarm, I'll shoot you. Got it?"

The cashier nodded and froze. But unknown to the raider, he'd already hit the silent panic button on the floor. "Place *all* the money into these bags," the robber said, passing them through to the bank employee. "Do it carefully. No false moves. Do it NOW!"

In the bank manager's office, a red light started flashing. The manager moved into the general office to check the monitors. He could see that armed men in balaclavas were holding up the bank. He pressed the second hold-up panic-button, confirming the first signal. The control centre, now knowing it was not a false alarm, would contact the police.

The cotton felt smooth to the teller's fingers, and he noticed labels on both bags: *Freeset.*

"All the cash. I know you've just had a delivery. Don't short-change me, pal," the robber commanded. He emptied his till into the bag. It wasn't his money, after all.

"Now, bring them out here, carefully. If the alarm goes off, I *will* shoot you." He waved the gun to encourage the man to move. The teller opened the door and walked out carrying the bags, handing them to the gunman. "Move into the corner with the others and link yourself to them; NOW."

He did as he'd been told, as the gunman moved to the second counter. "Do the same and you won't get hurt," he said as he stared into the frightened eyes of the female teller and passed her two more cotton bags.

A tall bald-headed man emerged from the back office, catching the big man's attention. He swung his gun and pointed it at the new man's cranium, the manager at once raising his arms. "You," the robber said, staring at the manager, "over here, with the others, and link yourself using the cable ties. Do it NOW."

He did as instructed, calmly moving to the corner – no sign of fear on his face.

"Are there any other staff in the back office?"

"No. I was the only one," he responded, and the robber turned away to check what was happening outside the bank.

"Don't worry," the manager whispered, as he joined his staff and one customer, "the police are on the way."

The robber swung towards the captives. "No talking. Got it?" he shouted, staring at them intently, his facial muscles tense.

The manager linked himself with the others, his hands steadier than his staff's – his pre-banking experience in the Royal Navy apparently serving him well in this tense situation. He noticed that Joshua's palms were sweaty. He could sense the group's fright and see it in their bloodless, pale faces.

The second teller filled the bags, then entered the foyer, joining the others and linking herself with the zip-lock fasteners. The big man put away his gun and checked all the ties were secure, tightening any he thought were slack.

After leaving the bank, they ran across the road and got into a Ford, which sped off. They immediately turned off George Street, just as a police car swung onto the street further along. The get-away driver wove his way through the back streets of Edinburgh's New Town and out towards Leith docks. He drove smoothly to avoid drawing attention to their escape, but as speedily as the roads would allow. Once they were a few streets away, the two gunmen removed their masks.

On reaching Leith docks, the big man cheered. "Hey, guys. Just like I said. Straight in and out. Nae problem! I told you we could do it. What a team!"

"Yes!" whooped the others, punching air.

He shoved the four cotton bags into a backpack, ready for the next phase. They pulled into a quiet lane and stopped. All three got out of the car, the driver checking they'd not left anything behind.

"We'll meet as planned to divvy up the takings," the big man said, then walked off. The other two men walked a short distance before getting into another vehicle and driving off. The driver was grinning as he drove away. His financial troubles were over, for now!

By 09:20 am, on the Wednesday morning, it was all over – job done!

* * *

Chapter 2

Suzanna drove through the barrier, showed her card to the security man, and parked her black soft-top sports car in her designated slot. As she walked towards the building, she thought, for the hundredth time, how ugly it was.

The face was covered in clear and obscured glass panels, with vertical aluminium ribs, making it look like a stack of shipping containers. The taller building next door wasn't much more attractive. It was flat-roofed, as well, but constructed with metal-framed windows running around in rows, as if the filling in a stacked, redbrick sandwich.

On entering the building, she called out to the man on duty, "Morning Jack", and carried on walking.

"Morning, ma'am. A wee bit chilly out this morning."

"It certainly is, Jack. Have a good day." She was off up the stairs without a glance behind her.

Jack watched her as she marched up the stairs. She still looked good for her age – better, in fact. She could probably have been a model when she was younger, with her classical good looks. Sure, she had a few shallow wrinkles on her forehead nowadays, but she was still beautiful.

Passing through the open-plan general office, she called out to all: "Morning folks".

And many of her team responded: "Morning, ma'am", "Morning,

boss".

Suzanna entered her office and closed the door behind her, ready to start the day's work. On the door was her nameplate 'Suzanna McLeod, Detective Chief Inspector.' She checked out her appearance in the mirror, on the wall by the door.

Her hair looked as it did when she left home. She liked the new style, a blonde textured pixie cut with silver streaks. It was so easy to look after, but she wondered whether she should have stuck with the short, tousled bob she'd had the previous year. Some people had said it made her look like Cameron Diaz. The style had framed her high cheek-boned face, with its slim, turned-up nose and naturally full lips.

It had taken Suzanna nearly two decades to get where she was now – a position respected by both the team who worked for her and the bosses above her. She'd worked hard to achieve what she had, and fortunately, she'd inherited a talent for investigation. Naturally curious and analytical, she could also think creatively, putting herself into the mind of the criminals, and could piece together scenarios from the minutest evidence, not noticed by others.

Suzanna hung up her coat, fired up her computer, organised her desk and looped her handbag strap over the back of her chair, before heading back through the general office and onto the kitchenette; coffee was called for. As usual, she had on a dark suit and a white blouse. Nothing flash, just Marks and Spencer's office range.

She could smell tea brewing and the sound of the kettle about to boil as she entered the room. As normal, there was a small crowd making their morning hot drinks and chatting. "Morning, guv."

Suzanna smiled at Angus's use of the term 'guv' – he'd picked that up when serving with the Metropolitan Police in London. "Good morning, Angus. You've been back in Edinburgh nearly two years now, and you're *still* calling me guv."

"Sorry, guv... I mean boss. Just can't get it out of my head. I was there for four years, so guv's embedded in my brain."

"I thought you'd have wanted to delete the experience from your memory, given your dislike of the place?"

"Aye. You're right. London's a massive city full of strangers. I hated that no one greets you on the street, and everyone avoids looking at other passengers on the tube trains and buses. It's like they all want to hide away in their own little world, and they're scared of letting anyone in."

"Yes, well, it's a bit like that here, as well."

"Agreed. It's just more noticeable in London. Another thing I didn't like about the city was that English appeared to be a minority language. Almost every conversation that I overheard was foreign: Eastern European, Urdu, Somali, Bengali and Chinese, to name a few. Even when I did hear English being spoken, it was by an Aussie, Kiwi or South African, no doubt working temporarily in the UK, or on holiday. I never felt at home there, so I was glad to get back to Scotland... I'll try harder to ditch guv."

"No problem," she said, pouring her coffee, "it just seems weird hearing guv spoken with a Glaswegian accent, though!"

She took her coffee and returned to her office. It was a compact room – just enough space for three chairs, a bookcase, and a desk. Like the rest of the building, it was devoid of any character. The only item breaching the blandness was a picture of Suzanna with a young girl, both of them grinning, and beautiful mountain scenery in the background. Her computer was ready to log in to, so she placed her coffee carefully on its coaster – after first letting it warm her hands – then entered her login name and password.

Suzanna checked her calendar and confirmed that she'd be in court today, giving evidence in the McLaren case at 11:00 am. It always bugged her and her colleagues that writing reports, filling in forms and giving evidence in court took up so much of their time. She recognised, however, that the paperwork was essential to gain convictions, so gave it as much attention and effort as she did to chasing criminals. She encouraged her team to be just as diligent. Arresting a criminal was hugely satisfying, but gaining convictions were more important and gave her greater satisfaction.

Today's case was one that concerned her because the accused was a career criminal who she and her team had spent months trying to gather evidence on for a conviction. He'd gotten away with his crimes for far too long. But as was often the case with rich criminals, they could afford the best barristers. So, the notorious Stuart Young-Paterson would be cross-examining her – not something to look forward to.

She was also due to meet with the Superintendent at 3 pm, to discuss the annual appraisals of her inspectors. She was glad to have this opportunity to help shape the careers of her detective team and felt privileged to have this power, recognising it as a huge responsibility.

Even in the early 21st century, it was still unusual for a woman to be in her senior position; most DCIs were men. She was still young enough to make Chief Super, but probably not any higher. That didn't bother her, though, as she didn't especially want to get too far away from where the *real* work got done. She was politically astute, and regularly briefed senior police officers and politicians, but was not sure that she wanted to operate at the political level every day.

***

"OK team! Let's quieten down and get this over with, so we can get back to the work" Suzanna commanded, and the room quickly hushed. It was 9 am, and they had gathered for the usual daily catch up on progress of each open case. Nothing was dominating the team's work – no recent murders or major thefts, just multiple minor crimes to solve as best they could.

Many crimes, they all knew, would go unsolved. Some would be too minor to warrant the resources necessary to follow through on all the details and explore every possibility. But they did have some success, and it was always good to bring the worst of the criminals to justice.

"From the top then. Progress on your cases, please. Una, you first."

Una turned and looked her boss in the eye, her short chestnut brown straight bob and fringe framing her petite face. Her slimness was evident in features, as her cheek and jaw were prominent, her small and neat nose perched over full lips. She spoke with perfect diction but with a Scottish Highlands lilt. "OK, boss. We have more detail on the break-in at the pub on Infirmary Street. Mairi, please update us."

Mairi took the lead. She was a looker as well but looked nothing like her boss. Her hair was mousey and naturally wavy when she let it fall to her shoulder, but today it was tied back into a ponytail, exposing her ears, and emphasising her high cheekbones. If Una was Posh Spice, then Mairi was Sporty Spice. Her physique was muscular and her face fuller, probably from the extra weight she carried because of her indulgent party weekends. The team turned towards her as she spoke.

"The break-in was at the back of Tamhas's Bar. They gained access from a narrow road that leads only to the bar and a few other businesses and homes. They got away with a few crates of spirits and some wine. We knocked on doors in the vicinity and asked if anyone had seen or heard anything. One neighbour said she'd been disturbed at about 2 am and looked out her window. She saw a man loading boxes into the back of a van and then drive off. She thought it was a bit strange, but went back to bed without reporting it."

"The man appeared to be medium build and was wearing a dark-coloured, hooded jacket of some sort. She didn't see his face. The van looked to be white but could have been another light colour. She noticed there was a 05 in the registration plate, and a name on the backdoor – something like 'artner' – but nothing else."

"That could be Partner," Owen suggested. "The Peugeot Partner. They're quite common vans with small businesses." Owen was the team joker, always fooling around given the opportunity, but today he was unusually business-like.

"Thanks, Owen." Mairi noted the van's name in her book, then continued. "We compiled a list of vehicles that match the loose description but obviously it's a lengthy list. If we filter the list using the Peugeot Partner, that should help us reduce it somewhat."

"Has anyone reported a van stolen that might be the one, or has one been found abandoned?" Suzanna asked.

"Not yet, ma'am. I've asked the boys on the beat to look out for vehicles matching the description, and to let me know if they find one."

"Good work, Mairi. Anything else from your team, Una?"

Mairi smiled, happy that the DCI was pleased with her work.

"No, boss," Una responded. "The rest of the cases on our books are all minor. Rab was off sick yesterday, so there was no progress on his case. It wasn't urgent enough to assign it to someone else for just a day."

"OK. Thanks, Una." She turned to look at Rab. Although back at work, he wasn't looking his best. His mid-brown wavy hair, normally gelled on top, was messy today. Around his grey eyes, the skin was dark but the rest of his face was pallid. Even his short beard didn't look as neat. "Rab, you can update us tomorrow, when you've had time to follow up on the leads."

"Angus, you next, please." He turned and looked at Suzanna, his almost black, groomed eyebrows dipping slightly towards his nose, as he focussed on his response.

"We've been a bit quiet as well, guv. The only one worthy of mention is the mugging on St Giles' Street. Murray can give us the latest on that one."

"It has gotten nowhere, ma'am. The victim couldn't describe the attacker in useful detail – other than jeans, a black leather jacket and a dark-coloured crash helmet. No witnesses have come forward. Uniform found the bag half a mile away, with nothing of value left in it. We passed it to forensics, and they got some prints off it, but until we've had those of the victim, we won't know if they'll be any help. We're not hopeful, though, as it's believed the mugger was wearing gloves. There were no hits on the criminal records database for the prints found. Obviously, if the prints are of the mugger's this might lead to a conviction later if we pick them up for something else. That's all we can hope for at the moment."

"Has anything shown up on CCTV from the area that might help?"

"No, guv. We've not seen the assailant on any of the footage we've seen so far."

"Give it a bit more of your time, Angus, as you're not too busy. If you can spot the attacker anywhere else in the city, he or she might have their hood down, letting us see their face. Have we had any other recent reports of muggings where the assailant was dressed similarly or other common factors?"

"We had a similar attack two weeks ago, but the attacker had been on a motor-scooter with someone else, whereas in this last mugging, the guy ran away from the scene."

"Could he have run just a short distance, then joined up with his buddy on the scooter to leave the area?"

"Good point, guv. We'll have another look at the CCTV."

"Thanks, Angus."

***

The staff and one customer at the Lothian bank were relieved the robbers had left, and they were no longer under threat of death. "I can't believe that just happened." Jonathon, the deputy manager, said.

"You hear about these things but never imagine it could happen to you," the manager, Mr Silverton, agreed.

"It's like car accidents; it's always someone else involved. You don't think it will happen to you," the customer, Maria Cramlington, concurred.

"Or murders," Joshua, the first teller, added, "Everyone's shocked when one happens in their neighbourhood."

"Those men were scary," Maria said; "I thought that big chap was going to pistol-whip me or keep kicking me." She started crying again as the memory returned.

Hillary, the second teller, placed a hand on her shoulder to comfort her. "I agree," she said; "I thought one of us would get shot." She started sobbing in unison with Maria as she spoke about her worries.

"The police should be here shortly," Mr Silverton said, "and they will need to speak with you all about what's just happened. Once that's all over, you will be free to go home to rest for the rest of the day. You will need time to process the event and get over it. If anyone would like help to deal with this - perhaps you'd like to talk it through with a professional counsellor – just let me know, and the company will arrange it."

"That goes for you too, ma'am," Silverton said, looking at Mrs Cramlington. "I expect you will want to go home as well. Would you like me to call anyone for you?"

"No," Maria sniffled, "there's no need. I'll call my office in a minute. But thanks for offering."

The staff indicated their understanding voicelessly, then went back to chatting. "The guy that shot his weapon into the ceiling was a giant of a man, wasn't he?" Hillary said. "He was well over 6 feet, I reckon."

"Yeah, he must have been about six foot two. I have got a brother-in-law about the same height." Jonathon agreed.

They all looked up as a banging sounded on the entrance door. The uniformed policemen realised it was unlocked, so pushed the door open and walked in. Now the police work would begin.

***

A phone rang, interrupting the morning meeting, and Angus took the call while the meeting continued. He listened for thirty seconds, his face becoming stern, then hung up. "Excuse me, guv. We've just had a report of an armed robbery from Lothian Bank. It seems they might have gotten away with about £150,000. No shots fired, as far as we know, and no serious injuries. The chase is on to catch the thieves. Getaway vehicle is a black Ford Mondeo. Helicopter has been requested but is not overhead yet."

"OK, team. Meeting over. Angus, you take the lead on this one. I'm in court at 11. Brief me as soon as you're on the ground and know the full picture." Suzanna turned and strode to her office to report this latest serious crime to the Superintendent – he'd want to know about this one.

Chapter 3

Suzanna's mobile phone rang, disturbing her court prep. Angus's name appeared on the screen.

"Angus. What news do you have for me?"

"From what I've heard so far, two masked men entered the bank about a minute after the bank staff opened the doors and threatened them with pistols. One robber fired his gun into the ceiling as a warning. We don't know which one yet. One man kept his gun pointed at the tellers and the other herded the other staff and the one customer into a corner. The staff handed over all the cash from behind the counters and the robbers fled. They were in and out in a few minutes. No one was seriously injured, as we'd already been told, but they assaulted one lady."

"Any news on pursuit of the get-away car?"

"No. Our boys in blue never engaged with them. The car had left the area before they reached the scene, and the helicopter was away doing other work. So, by the time it got into the city centre, it was too late. My team's currently interviewing the bank staff and their one customer, to gather as much detail as they can. First impressions are that the robbers were in their thirties, lean and fit looking, and the way they controlled the situation suggests professionals of some sort – either experienced criminals or perhaps ex-military."

"Thanks, Angus. I've got to leave for court straight away, so please call the Super and brief him, as well. And if there are any further significant developments whilst I'm tied up in court, call him again. I'll check with you as soon as I leave the court to get the latest. OK?"

"Yes, guv. No problem."

Suzanna touched the red button on her phone, slipped it into her pocket, grabbed the documents she'd previously gathered together, and headed out to her car for the drive to the Old Town. She wasn't due in court for another hour and, hopefully, the drive would only take about 15 minutes, but traffic and parking could always be a problem and Suzanna made it a habit to never be late for such formal events.

Her BMW purred like a big cat as Suzanna cruised out of the car park and its engine growled quietly as she accelerated down Fettes Avenue. She swung a right, instead of the way her satnav would have taken her; there would likely be delays at this time of day in the central area of the city. She wove her way around the centre, avoiding the busiest roads, and approached the High Court from the south.

Having found a spot in a multi-story, she parked up, and paid for four hours – just in case, to avoid a fine for overstaying. 'Pay and display parking is such a rip-off,' she thought for the thousandth time.

The car park was typically grey concrete, with low ceilings and smelly stairwells. It reminded her of a prison. She walked away from the car park at a brisk pace. There was no rush this morning as she had plenty of time to reach the High Court, but she didn't know how to amble.

She glanced in the kilt-maker's window, as she passed by, and was reminded of a book she'd seen once in a gift shop, about yoga in kilts. It had stuck in her mind because the book was full of pictures of yoga poses with a bare-chested man in a kilt. Even more memorable, though, was the last page that pictured two men doing handstands, their kilts hanging down towards their heads and their buttocks bared. The picture had made her chuckle and still did when she remembered it.

Although Suzanna wasn't Scottish by birth – she'd married a Scotsman – she liked men in kilts. In fact, if Callum hadn't been wearing a kilt at her friend's wedding reception, she might never have noticed him and entered the relationship that led to marriage ten years ago. She was sad that the marriage had ended after eight years. Still missed him. But she also valued her independence and enjoyed casual relationships when she fancied some fun. Having been in love and been betrayed, she had no desire to get into another meaningful relationship – just yet.

When Suzanna reached the High Court, she still had thirty minutes to spare, so popped into the café and bar on St Giles to grab a coffee. The café had bare brick walls supporting an eclectic mix of ornaments sat in ornate frames. Aged wooden tables and chairs were scattered seemingly at random, and a fabulous open-plan wooden staircase turned its way to the upper floor, clinging to the walls. It was a warm and friendly place, where, if she'd had time, she would have stayed for a while.

"One skinny cappuccino to go, please; extra hot," she requested from the barista, then waited patiently for her drink. She always asked for extra hot because cappuccinos were almost always served warm, so they had to be drunk quickly to avoid tepidness. The hissing steam and gurgling noises of the espresso machine reminded her of the sounds of geysers at Rotorua, in New Zealand. She remembered her time in that town – the sulphurous smell of the lake, the queuing to watch a geyser demonstration, the out-of-work Maoris, hanging around the main street. New Zealand, for all its beauty, had its problems, like any country.

The aroma of coffee brought her mind back to the present. "Haven't seen you in here for a while," a second barista mentioned.

He was a handsome chap, with the looks that Suzanna normally went for. He was trim and sporty, dark-haired and had a four-day beard covering his chiselled face. But as he was about 15 years younger than her, she didn't give it a second thought. "No, it's been a few weeks since I last had to give evidence across the road."

"Why a regular at court? And giving evidence, you say. Are you a copper then?"

Suzanna realised that she'd given away too much by her casual conversation. She didn't want to be known everywhere she went as a policewoman. Fortunately, her cappuccino was ready, so she just ignored the question, said "Thanks" and headed out the door, feeling the barista watching her escape - awkwardness avoided.

Despite having seen the High Court multiple times, she couldn't help admiring the 17th Century, symmetrical Neo-Georgian classical styling. The chairs in the court waiting area were uncomfortable and not too clean either. She pulled her hand away from the seat frame with a look of disgust on her face as she felt the grimy stickiness. Suzanna hoped she wouldn't have to wait too long.

The coffee was tasty and not bitter, like some. It had been worth paying a little extra to get a decent coffee.

There was a commotion just up the corridor and she could hear the Right Honourable Young-Paterson raising his voice. But she couldn't catch what he was saying to the court official, who was looking like a sheep in a slaughterhouse.

Young-Paterson stormed out of the building, glaring at Suzanna as he passed. The official regained some courage and approached her. "Chief Inspector McLeod?" But before she could answer his enquiry, he went on, having already decided that she was the right person. "I'm afraid we have postponed the session. Judge Hilliard has been taken ill. We'll issue a new court date in due course. Sorry for the inconvenience. I did try to catch you at your office but was told that you'd already left."

"Thank you," she responded, rising from her chair. "Now I understand why Young-Patterson was just berating you."

"The man considers himself far too important to have a session cancelled. Actually suggested that the judge was a wimp for not turning up. He couldn't be more wrong. Judge Hilliard has the flu, not just a sniffle."

Suzanna detested people like Young-Paterson, full of their own self-importance and happy to put others down without a second thought. She remembered how her boss had shouted at her when she'd been a detective sergeant. She'd only made a minor error, but he'd humiliated her in earshot of all her colleagues. Suzanna was glad she'd survived that period of her career and moved on despite the treatment he'd dished out.

Realising that she still had over three hours of parking paid for and no other appointments, she left the building and strode off towards the New Town to see how the bank raid investigation was getting on.

Chapter 4

The constable manning the police cordon lifted the tape to allow Angus and his team into the Lothian Bank. It was 9:40 am. The uniformed officers, led by PC Stringer, were already taking statements from the staff when the detectives entered the bank.

Angus strode straight over to the PC and interrupted his conversation. "Excuse me, gents. I'm Detective Inspector Watson, from CID. I'd just like a quick chat with the constable."

"Of course, Inspector. I've got things to do anyway," the manager responded.

"I'll need to speak with you in a minute, once the constable has briefed me, so please don't make it too difficult for me to find you."

"No problem; you'll find me in my office, first on the left, through that door."

The manager went to his office and Angus turned to the PC. "Morning, Phil. How's it going?"

"Not bad, thanks, sir. As you can see, we've started gathering the evidence and talking with the staff. The robbers got the staff and the one customer to secure themselves with cable ties before they made their get-away, so we've bagged the ties ready to submit as evidence. The staff said one of the men fired his pistol just after they entered the bank, but no one saw any damage. We've had a quick look at the ceiling and can't see any bullet holes. Strange."

"Was there a shell case left behind?"

"We've not found one. The manager says he saw the big man pick one up before leaving."

"What did you get from speaking with the bank manager?"

"He said they'd just taken a delivery of cash from a security truck, which had left just five minutes before the raid. They'd just finished counting and organising the cash when they opened for the day. The raiders barged in shortly after the staff had unlocked the door, but not before one woman had entered. They locked the door behind them so no other customers could enter. The staff complied with instructions, filling four cotton bags with the cash – about £150k - and the men left with it, after securing them to the radiator in the corner."

"Was anyone hurt?"

"The customer, Mrs Maria Cramlington, was slow to react to directions, so the big man knocked her around. The paramedic examined her. She's got some bruising. No serious injuries. But they're all in shock, although the manager seems rather calm."

"Anything else you think I should know?"

"No, sir. I think that's about it. I take it that your team will take formal statements from all the employees. We've already got the manager to agree to allocate a room for that."

"Well done, Phil. Good job. Have you ever thought about joining our team?"

"I have, but I prefer front-line policing – being out on the streets dealing with situations. Maybe I'll apply for a transfer when I get too old for the running around and fighting criminals," PC Stringer said, flippantly.

"And you'll be taking up golf then, instead of football. Right?" Angus retorted in jest. "Thanks, Phil. If you and the others can maintain the cordon, my team will take over the interviewing of the witnesses."

"Will do, sir."

CHAPTER 4

Angus went straight to the manager's office, tapped on the door frame, and entered. "Bit of a shock this morning, sir?"

"It certainly was."

Angus sat opposite the manager. "I just need to take some details for my records, and so we can compile a formal statement for you to sign – my apologies if the constable has already done this."

"That's fine, Inspector. Fire away. Oh!" he paused, "That's not the best way of putting it, given this morning's events, is it?"

"Not to worry, sir. Let's start with your full name?"

Angus recorded the manager's details. Mr Fitzgerald's account of the robbery was in line with everything he'd been told so far but included details the others wouldn't have known.

"You say after hitting the second alarm, you went into the foyer?" Angus queried.

"Yes. I don't know why I did that, really. I suppose I should have just stayed put. But I was concerned for my staff and I just did it without thinking it through."

"OK! I understand they stole approximately £150,000. That seems like a lot of money to have had behind the counters?"

"Yes. We wouldn't normally have that much out front. But our delivery was late today, and we'd only just finished counting it. I instructed the deputy manager to put most of it into the safe, then returned to my office. It was shortly after that, the silent alarm went off; that light, above you, flashes when the alarm's activated, but there's no sound."

"Interesting..." Angus noted this in his mind. "I'd like you to think about the two men who robbed your bank," Angus continued. "Did they use any words or phrases that might have included jargon or dialect that would place them in a particular city or social group?"

Fitzgerald thought for a minute, recalling what they'd said. "The robbers didn't say much, but both came across as having been in positions of authority. They seemed to be used to ordering people around and expecting obedience. I did a stint in the Royal Navy before going into banking and in my opinion, the robbers were probably ex-military. It was something about their bearing, as well as their authority. There was no discussion during the raid; they clearly had planned it in advance and knew what was to happen, when, and how they'd deal with the staff. Yes, definitely a military-type operation."

Angus asked a few more questions about the men's appearances and details of the robbery. "Thanks for your help, Mr Fitzgerald. Could you please point me to the office that you've allocated to us for carrying out the rest of the interviews?"

"That would be this one," the manager responded. "It's the only separate office in the bank. The rest of the office space is open-plan. I'll move into the main office so you can conduct your interviews here."

"That's very kind of you, sir. Appreciated."

***

Angus took the manager's seat; it was black leather and comfortable. He played with the height and backrest controls until it felt right for him. 'Wish we had chairs like this at the station,' he thought. He leaned back and stared at the ceiling, the posture emphasising his spiky hair with 'Tin Tin' quiff, as he readied his mind for the next session. He set his things on the desk and went off in search of his next witness.

Owen was chatting with a man. Caitlin was talking to a woman in her forties, who looked somewhat distressed, and Murray was in conversation with another male witness. One member of the staff was sitting by herself, deep in thought, as Angus approached her. "Excuse me," he said, "I'm Detective Inspector Watson. I'm leading the investigation. Have you made a statement yet?"

"No. Not yet," she said, her voice quavering.

"Could I just get your name, please?"

"Hillary McColloch; Mrs."

"Right Hillary – do you mind if I call you Hillary?" She tipped her head as if to say that's fine. "Come with me, please. We'll take a seat in the manager's office to talk about what you've just been through."

Angus sat in the manager's chair again, and Hillary took a seat opposite. "Can we leave the door open, please?" Hillary requested. "I'm feeling rather shaken and anxious."

They went through the essentials of name, date of birth, etc. Angus asked Hillary to tell him about the raid.

"It was a shocking experience. I'm still somewhat phased out. I've never heard a gunshot so close before. In fact, I've only really heard gunshots on TV and in movies. I froze initially. Actually, that's what they told us to do, but I'd have frozen, anyway. Poor Mrs Cramlington – that's the other lady; she's a regular customer - she didn't move into the corner as fast as the tall gunman wanted her to, so he hit her and shoved her. She fell and hurt her knees. When she wouldn't stop crying, the big man kicked her and stomped on her – totally unnecessary!"

"After Joshua and I had handed over the money from our counters, the big man made us link our wrists to the others using cable ties. We had to squash up close. When we shuffled together, my skirt rode up and I think I flashed my knickers to Mr Fitzgerald. I saw him trying not to look, but I think he did a couple of times. It made me blush – a bit like the colour of my knickers. I'd especially put on red lacy ones because, Jim, my husband is due back off the oil rig today after ten days at sea."

Angus was content to let the woman ramble on, even though he felt embarrassed by her underwear revelation. Useful information may result from her spilled thoughts.

"Just before the robbers left the bank, the big man checked the ties for security and tightened the one around this wrist," she said, showing her left arm with a red mark on her wrist. "He was rather rough actually, and his hands were huge. It took the constable quite an effort to cut through the plastic without cutting my skin, as the wrap had squashed it up and it was wrinkly."

Tears came into Hillary's eyes as she recalled the experience. She started sobbing, relieving the built-up stress. As her sobbing subsided, Angus asked another question. "Did the robber have gloves on, Hillary?"

She took a few seconds to recover her composure fully before responding. "Yes. They were disposable ones, like doctors and nurses wear."

Angus noticed a box of tissues on the bookcase and passed these to Hillary. She took two, blew her nose and wiped her tears.

"What about tattoos? Did either of the men have any?"

"The big man had something on his right forearm. I couldn't see much of it."

"Please describe what you saw or draw it on this piece of paper."

Hillary took the paper and drew a pointed shape about one inch long.

"That looks like it could be the point of a dagger," Angus suggested.

"Oh yes! I see it now. I think you're right," Hillary agreed.

"Could you tell me about the clothes this man was wearing: colour, material, fit, style?"

"He was wearing dark blue jeans, a black sweatshirt and a black balaclava. He had on black trainers. The other man wore jeans as well, but they were black. He had on a dark grey sweatshirt and black running shoes. I remember they were running shoes – Adidas – because my Jim has a similar pair. He's a runner. He does the Park Run every Saturday, without fail, when he's not offshore – well unless he's not well, of course. But that's rare because he's a healthy man. He always eats healthily, and the exercise keeps him fit."

"Hillary, could you please tell me more about the robbery," Angus interjected. He wanted her to spill it all out but didn't really want her to go into her husband's habits.

"Sorry; I got carried away there a wee bit, didn't I? I don't suppose you need to know about my Jim. Oh dear! I just realised I told you about my knickers." She went red again, then started sobbing again. "I'm sorry. I don't know what's the matter with me."

"You've just been through a traumatic experience, Hillary. You're bound to feel upset by it all. Just take your time," Angus reassured. "So, what can you tell me about the two men?" Angus asked when she'd settled down again.

"The big man was barrel-chested, and his arms and shoulders were muscular. I reckon he does weight training. My Jim's fit, but he's rather skinny. The big gunman was massive by comparison with Jim; like a bull compared to a racehorse. The second man was slimmer but still muscular and lean. He certainly wasn't overweight. He reminded me of a footballer, rather than a rugby player. Did I say the big man looked like a rugby player? Well, he did. He had a large round head, as well."

"What about the way they spoke? Was there anything noticeable about their tone, accent, or words?"

"The big man's voice didn't match his large body. I thought he'd have had a deep voice, but it was much higher than I'd have expected. It was a rough voice; harsh. It sounded like he was always angry. The other man's voice was much smoother and deeper."

"Would you recognise their voices if you heard them again?"

"With certainty, Inspector. I'm good at recalling sounds. Our team always does well at the pub quiz, partly because of my good recognition of tunes and songs. I can even tell which dog on our street is barking. Mrs McIntyre's got a Jack Russell; it's a yappy dog."

"That's good to know, Hillary," Angus interjected. "When we identify them, I might call you in for a voice recognition identification."

"Come to think about it, I might have heard his voice before somewhere. But I can't place it."

"OK. Thanks very much for your help, Hillary. One of my team will get back to you to confirm the details you've given me and get you to sign a formal statement for the record. If you think of anything else, please get in contact with me," he said, handing her his calling card.

***

Angus returned to the bank's main office, then checked with the rest of the team to see how they were getting on. They'd all finished talking with the bank staff and were gathered around an empty desk, chatting.

"You all done with interviewing the witnesses?"

"Yes, boss," they chorused.

"Good. We can compare notes later. Caitlin, can you please get a copy of the bank's internal CCTV?"

"Ahead of you on that one, boss," she said, holding up a USB stick that Angus assumed held the videos.

"What time window does that data-file cover, Caitlin?"

"From 8:50 today until 09:15, so covering the entire period of the robbery."

"OK, great. If you could also get a copy of every day for the previous sixty days, that would be useful. We'll need to see if anyone looking like the robbers had been in the bank before to check it out. As the raid was just after the bank opened its doors, we should concentrate on the same time period every day for a first look, then widen the scrutiny further if nothing turns up."

"OK, boss. Will do." She rose and went in search of the deputy manager again.

"Owen, Murray. You two head off outside now and talk to the shopkeepers or anyone else you can find in businesses nearby that might have seen something."

The guys acknowledged their task and headed off outside. Angus returned to the bank manager's office to do some thinking and planning.

Chapter 5

Suzanna strode along George Street, its shops, businesses, and cafes separated by rows of cars parked in the central zone. As she neared her destination, a double-decker bus passed by, its backdraught buffeting Suzanna's coat. Her nose twitched at the unpleasant smell of diesel fumes. She looked across the road to the Lothian Bank.

It stood at the corner with Frederick Street, in the heart of Edinburgh New Town. It wasn't new any longer, of course, having been constructed in the late 1700s and early 1800s. But by comparison with Edinburgh Old Town, it was much younger, with some buildings being 200 years newer.

Unlike its neighbour on its left, the Lothian Bank sat in one of the original buildings, with its classical style and creamy stone still evident when looking above the first floor. At ground level, though, much of its frontage was plate-glass windows and doors.

The uniformed officer standing on guard at the taped-off cordon recognised her as she arrived. He lifted the tape and indicated that she should pass under it. "Good morning, ma'am," the constable greeted. "Inspector Watson is inside."

"Thanks, constable" Suzanna replied, not knowing his name (there were just too many to remember them all) and strode off to the bank entrance.

In the entrance, another constable stood guard. "Where can I find

Inspector Watson?" she asked.

"He'll be in the manager's office, I believe; interviewing staff, ma'am."

"Thanks," she responded and headed for the manager's office. She tapped lightly and opened the door a few inches until she caught Angus's eye.

"Hi, guv. Didn't expect to see you here. Come on in. We've finished the staff interviews."

"I wasn't planning to visit the scene; I'm not checking up on you, Angus. They cancelled the court session, so I thought I'd get some exercise and get briefed directly, instead of by phone. So what's new?"

"Owen and Murray are out talking with business people in the vicinity. Caitlin is going over CCTV footage, covering the period of the robbery and the preceding two months, in case either of the robbers had been in the bank before the raid, to gather intelligence. I haven't had feedback on the staff interviews conducted by those three yet, but I've already built up better descriptions for the two men who entered the bank."

Angus went on: "Both of the men were well built and confident. Their accents were from this area of Scotland, although one witness said there was a slight hint of Glaswegian in the taller man's voice. One was about 5 foot 10-11 inches tall and the other 6 foot 2. The bank's CCTV is quite good quality and will be a big help for us to piece together what happened in more detail, but of course no faces of the robbers because of the balaclavas."

"How's the public CCTV analysis going?" Suzanna enquired.

"Una's team has collected the footage and there's a team of three viewing it now. Rab's getting footage from private systems that might have picked something up: banks, ATMs, and petrol stations. What's puzzling me is why three guys put themselves at risk of going to jail for armed robbery just for a share of £150,000. It's just not worth it.

We get individuals with a knife or gun holding up off-licenses or post offices, but they're usually junkies looking for money to pay for their next fix. This was three, possibly ex-military guys, who planned this but got away with relatively little money. Strange!"

"Agreed Angus. We can thrash that one out later when we gather at the office. Do you have any more for me? And have you briefed the Superintendent yet?"

"No, on both counts, guv. I'll be interviewing for another couple of hours yet. Will you call the Super?"

"Will do Angus. Leave it with me. And well done on getting as far as you have already. I'll see you later." She turned and left the bank. Before walking away, Suzanna took in the scene, imagining the Mondeo parked outside and the public walking past to work, and to the shops. She stood for a while, just taking it in and letting her mind drift where it wanted.

A bus drove up Frederick Street and turned right onto George Street, away from the bank. She wondered whether one had done similarly at the time of the robbery, and who might have seen something. The nearest bus stop was just up the road so she checked the bus numbers on its board. Buses 10, 11, 12 and 16 dropped off and picked up at the Assembly Rooms stop.

She Googled 'Lothian Buses' then pulled up the timetable for the Number 10. There should have been two buses stopping around the time of the robbery. The Number 11 service also had two buses scheduled. So, there had been four buses full of people who might have seen something.

She went across the street, turned, and looked back. Just beyond the Bank of Scotland, she could see a card shop. Anyone leaving there might have seen the driver or the robbers getting in or out of the car.

Similarly, a customer leaving the Bank of Scotland or using one of its ATMs might have seen something. There could only have been a few customers who'd come and gone in the short time that the robbery was in progress, so it should be easy to get names from the Bank.

It was possible that someone might also be traceable from the card shop. Even though they might have just bought a greetings card for a couple of pounds, they could still have paid by credit or debit card, as many people nowadays were using contactless payments for low-value purchases.

There was also a café just to the left of the card shop, and she guessed that there could have been many customers buying their takeaway coffee on the way to work, so that would be worth a try as well.

Looking to the right, down Frederick Street, there were another two places selling tea and coffee that had outdoor seating. Not many people would have been sitting outside at 9 am in January, but it was worth a try. Perhaps Angus had already thought about tracking down customers from payment card records, but he'd not mentioned it.

She thought more about what Angus had said earlier. Professional criminals would have been after hundreds of thousands, not just £50,000 each. Perhaps this had been their first bank robbery?

It suggested to Suzanna that this was the action of men, one of whom perhaps owed money to a loan shark. If the lender was calling in his loan with menaces and they had no way of repaying it in time, that could provide a motive. This was little league, not big-time criminals at work.

She wondered, if she was right, who the loan shark might be? A man came to her mind. 'I'll have to have a quiet chat with him.' She thought.

***

Suzanna returned to the bank to pass on her thoughts to Angus and nearly bumped into him as she attempted to enter the building.

"Just popping out for a coffee," Angus offered as an explanation.

"Great. I'll come with you. There's one just around the corner."

CHAPTER 5

They entered the coffee shop and Angus went straight to the counter.

"Cappuccino is it, guv?"

"Yes, please Angus. Extra Hot, Skinny. My turn next time."

Suzanna sat at a table by the window. She could see across to the Lothian Bank from here, so another customer might have seen something. She wondered how many people spent time in the café at 9 am. Most custom would have been for takeaway at that time.

Angus was already placing their order. His black hair had recently been cut, going by the clean neck and gap around his ears. She thought the little quiff was cute – boyish even. But the inky shadow around his jaw and lip left no doubt he was a mature man. His nose matched his evenly balanced face, his dimpled chin jutting perfectly.

She noticed the barista wasn't paying much attention to his customers, being entirely focused on making coffee. He'd probably not remember much about this morning then, she thought.

A young girl screamed – not with fear, but with defiance. Her mum was trying to force her to put her shoes back on, but she wanted to run around in her socks. "Lucy; please sit still. We have to go now. You can't walk outside without your shoes on, can you?" her mother stated in a Tyneside accent. Suzanna smiled. It was typical behaviour from a three-year-old.

Her niece Athena was five now, and she remembered the tantrums when she'd been younger – not that she'd totally outgrown that stage yet. But her sister Charlotte said that Athena's rebellious outbursts were less frequent nowadays.

It had been a few months since she'd last seen her sister and her niece. Charlotte lived in Cockermouth, on the edge of the Lake District National Park. It was time for another visit. Not just to see her relatives, but because she loved the lakes and walking on the fells.

Last time she'd been there was in the Autumn when the burnt oranges and bronzes of the trees and shrubs on the track up towards

Walla Crag were glorious. When the sun shone in the Lake District – not often enough for Suzanna – she couldn't think of a more beautiful place in the entire world.

Suzanna took her phone from her handbag and WhatsApped Charlotte, 'Thinking of you and Athena. It's been too long. Can I come to stay for a weekend soon?' She pressed send and was putting her phone away when it chimed back to say she had a message. Charlotte must have been using her phone when Suzanna's message had arrived, given the speed of her reply: 'Agreed. Been 2 long. Free for next four weekends. Come any time. Just let me know when. Soon, please.'

Great. Just the response she'd been hoping for. She was just about to type a response when another message came in: 'Athena misses you.' Suzanna typed back: 'Will come soonest. Will let you know when.'

She looked up and saw Lucy leaving with her mother. She wondered what had brought the woman from Newcastle to Edinburgh – perhaps attracted to a Scotsman, like Suzanna had?

Angus arrived with the coffees, dragging Suzanna back from her ponderings. Cappuccino in hand, the cup's heat warming her palms, she shared her thoughts with him about the shop, cafés, bank and buses.

"Thanks for that, guv. The team will probably already have spoken with staff at the card shop and bank, but I didn't think to direct them to ask for customer details. I'll follow that up. I'll have a chat with the barista when we've finished here, then get Owen to follow up on any leads."

She sipped her cappuccino. It tasted smooth and strong. "OK, Owen's a good DC, so we should be able to trust him with that. What about the bus lead?"

"Yeah! I'd not thought of that angle at all. I'll get Caitlin to investigate that one. She should have finished getting the CCTV footage from the bank staff by the time I get back."

Suzanna wondered about sharing her thoughts on the loan shark pay-back motive for the robbery but thought better of it for the moment. She'd see what other ideas came up when they brain-stormed later. In the meantime, she'd also do some investigating into this possibility.

"When do you expect to reconvene at the office to get all the minds together? I'm with the Superintendent at 3 pm. It's inspectors' annual appraisal time, although I could get the meeting delayed."

"I expect we'll be tied up here until at least mid-afternoon, so the earliest I reckon we could meet would be at 5 pm. I'll plan on that, and let the team know, so they can let others know they're likely to be home late this evening."

"OK Angus. My meet with the Superintendent should be finished by 5 pm. A good result on this case would be great timing for your appraisal - due in two weeks' time. Hopefully, I'll be able to praise you even more for your effectiveness – but no pressure! I'll head back to Fettes now and update the Superintendent on progress and inform him about the planned meet at 5 pm. Anything else for me before I go?"

"No, guv. See you at five, then."

As Suzanna walked out, she noticed him approach the counter and start talking with the barista; good man, she thought.

Chapter 6

"Took your time, Owen; I've been back here for ages." Murray joked as Owen returned to the bank. They had systematically covered every business on the street within view of the Lothian Bank, but no further useful information had been forthcoming.

"Aye, well, you obviously didn't ask as many questions as me, then." The banter was always friendly within the team – especially between these two.

Angus noted their return and Caitlin reappeared holding something that was probably the CCTV video files. Angus called them into the manager's office.

"Anything useful come out of questioning the businesses?" Angus asked.

"We covered both sides of George Street," Owen said. "Me on this side, and Murray took the other. I only found one person who had seen anything useful – the guy in the bank next door, who had called 999. He saw and heard the men crash through the bank door and fire the pistol. He confirmed the car was a Mondeo and even noted the number plate. I called the number in, so Uniform could look out for it."

"Don't keep us in suspense, Owen. What's the number?"

"Sorry, boss. AB05 VJT."

They all noted the number. "Murray, how did you get on?"

"I also found only one person who had seen anything. The manager in the jewellery shop had seen the car arrive, then men run in and out and the car drive off. The number plate that Owen just reported fits with her recollection as well. She didn't get the whole number, but what she did recall, matches with the Bank of Scotland employee's report. Other than that, nothing of note."

"Thanks, Murray. Before we move on, the DCI's been in for a chat and she had some ideas. I know you've spoken with staff in the shops and the banks, but it's possible that customers may have seen something. I need you guys to go back to the Bank of Scotland and check whether they'd had any customers around the time of the robbery. And if so, who? We'll need to question them."

Angus continued: "Also, the card shop just beyond the bank; similar question. If a customer had paid by cash, we probably don't stand any chance of finding out who they are, but if they paid by card, we should be able to trace them. I've already asked the barista in the coffee shop around the corner and found that he'd served three people just before or around 9 am, and they'd paid by card. I've got their card details. Once you've done similar, we'll trace the customers and contact them. We can do that from the station."

"OK, boss. Do you want us to go straight away?" Owen said, standing.

"Don't be too hasty. I've not finished yet. We need similar enquiries carried out at the café next to the card shop and the tea rooms just around the corner."

"OK. Got it," Owen responded. "Shall we go *now*?"

"Just a minute; you *are* keen. We'll finish this session first. Caitlin, I see you're holding a USB memory stick. Does it contain all the footage I asked for?"

"Yes, boss. It's all on here. I started reviewing it straight away with the witnesses sitting by me. So far, nothing. But after they've had a break, we'll reconvene and continue the process. Hopefully, one of them will notice something."

"Let's hope so. But we might not be lucky. If nothing comes up, we'll need to think of another angle. I'll head back to the station soon and leave you to your work with the video footage, Caitlin, but before we do, I'd just like to go through the witness statements that you three took this morning."

"In fact, before we do that," Angus went on, "I've just remembered something else. Caitlin, I've another job for you. The DCI also noted that there were four buses scheduled to stop at the Assembly Rooms, just on the other side of the William Pitt roundabout. There are perhaps 200 passengers who might have seen something, plus the drivers. When you've finished with the video reviews, I want you to contact Lothian Buses and get contact details for the bus drivers: the 8:57 and 9:07 on the number 10 route, and the 8:59 and 9:09 on the number 11 route."

"Also find out when they're next on shift so we can catch them at work, or if they're off work, call on them at home. This needs done soon. Also, get some posters made up rapidly and dropped off with Lothian Buses for display on routes: 10, 11, 12 and 16. The posters should ask passengers to contact us if they saw anything at the time of the robbery. Lastly, contact the local radio station and ask them to publish this request."

"That's all good, boss, and I'll happily do it, but it might be some time before I can get onto it. There's a lot of footage to go through."

"OK. Good point. Owen, you handle the adjacent shop and bank queries. Murray, you get onto Lothian Buses. Here are the details of the buses I just mentioned."

"Thanks, boss, I'll get onto it as soon as we're done here."

"Good. I need your feedback on the bank staff interviews first. We'll start with the first bank teller who handed over the money. Who spoke with him?" Angus asked.

"I did, boss," Murray confirmed. "Do you want it word-by-word or just a summary of the key points?"

"A summary, please Murray."

"OK. His name is Joshua Kimble. He's been with Lothian for five years, and in this branch for the last two years. The timings he reported concur with everything else we've heard so far. His descriptions of the gunmen were clear. The first man, the one who shot his pistol, was about 6 foot 2, enormous chest and muscular, round head and gruff voice. He gave me more detail on the second man because he'd spoken directly to him and pointed his gun at him – tends to focus one's attention, doesn't it?"

"Anyway," Murray continued, "he said he was about 5 foot 11, almond-shaped head. Eyebrows were mid-brown and eyes – his recall on this was strong – a piercing green. Local accent. Authoritative in the way he spoke. No unusual dialect. Lastly, he felt that he'd seen him before – it was the eyes – but with the balaclava masking his features, he couldn't place him."

"Perhaps he'll notice something when he sees the CCTV playbacks?" Caitlin chimed in. "He was attentive when we were watching the footage earlier."

Angus continued, "So, that's two members of staff who recognised something about man number 2. One noticed his green eyes and the other his voice. We've even more reason to believe that he'd been in the bank before. Anything else Murray?"

"There was one thing: he noticed the brand of the cotton bags they used to put the money; it was 'Freeset'. Not sure if that will help, but you never know."

"As you say, it might be helpful. The second teller that I interviewed didn't mention the bags. I'm not sure if all four were identical. Please check with Hillary McColloch again, Murray, to see if she noticed the bags. Right, let's have a summary of the statement from the female customer."

"I spoke with her, boss," Caitlin stated. "She'd only just entered the bank when the robbers barged in. Her name is Mrs Maria Cramlington. She was traumatised by the incident so noticed little once they'd assaulted her and she'd landed on the floor. She'd cried initially, then just kept her head down until they'd left, hoping they'd leave her alone, so she couldn't tell us much about how the men looked."

"Thanks, Caitlin." He turned to Owen and looked directly into his grey eyes. His mid-brown wavy hair was long on top. It draped itself over his high forehead, hiding the receding hairline. His bulbous nose overshadowed his thin lips, putting his face out of balance. "Your turn now."

"The deputy bank manager is Jonathon Bilberry," Owen said. "He's been with the Lothian for twelve years, with five as the deputy manager at this branch. His recollection of the events and the robbers' characteristics are the same as the other staff; although he hadn't seen or heard either of the men before."

"I think that about wraps it up. Let's get onto the next enquiries and meet back at the station by 5 pm," Angus concluded.

Chapter 7

Superintendent Milne was engrossed in a report when Suzanna knocked on his door at exactly 3 pm. The noise and movement made him jump. "Afternoon Alastair, are you still good to talk through the performance reviews?"

Alistair's office was immaculately tidy; the only paper not in a tray being the one he was working on. His beech-wood desk was a 1970s classic, with smooth, rounded corners, and it appeared to have been unscathed by the four decades that had passed since its creation.

"Yes, Suzanna. Take a seat. This shouldn't take too long, should it? I have another meeting at 3:30," he said, putting aside the report.

Suzanna wondered how Alistair had managed to keep hold of his desk when all the others in the building had been replaced at least twice. She could smell the lavender-perfumed polish that must have recently been used to shine it. The only items that provided any personalisation to the desk were a framed picture of his two children, and his mug – with 'World's Best Dad' embossed on it – placed precisely on its coaster.

"No, we've only got two to talk through. They're both doing really well, although each in their own way and starting from different places. I'd like to talk about Una first if that's OK?"

Alistair nodded.

"You may recall that Una Wallace joined my team eighteen months ago, on promotion from sergeant."

"Aha."

"Well, as you know, she was still finding her feet at the higher level when we appraised her after her first six months, and she was showing promise but had a lot to learn. I'm pleased to report, and you've likely noticed, that her performance has been tremendous. Her confidence in leading her team has grown significantly over the last twelve months, and she's gained the respect of her team. Her briefings on case progress have become more succinct and informative, and her intuition has sharpened with the extra experience."

"Good to hear it."

"She's been receptive to my coaching and been willing to accept when she hasn't performed as best as she could. She has a positive attitude to learning from her mistakes or misjudgements, and has a great attitude – always listens to advice, consults peers, and is ever willing to help her colleagues. All-round, Una's developing into a great Detective Inspector and she's an excellent member of the team. I hope you agree?"

"Yes, yes. I also see her potential. And I recognise that her rapid development has been down to your coaching and leadership."

"I think she'd have done well whoever she worked for, sir. She'd be an asset to any detective team."

"Don't be modest, Suzanna. I know how well you lead your teams and get the best from them. I've seen numerous constables and sergeants leave your team on promotion. Your success rate is the best I've seen. In fact, better than I achieved," he admitted. "Una has a way to go before she'd be ready for the next step up the ladder, but it's good to see that she has the potential. It's now just a matter of time and experience, along with more of your coaching – provided you don't move on, that is."

"What do you mean?"

"Well, Suzanna, you know very well that you've been noticed in high places and it can't be long before you get promoted to superintendent. By the way, if I moved on, would you wish to stay at Fettes and take on my role?"

"I'd be thrilled to, Alastair. That way, I could continue to influence the development of the great people I've been working with and investing my time in. But I'm not so sure a promotion will come my way. The Chief Super doesn't appear to value my judgement or trust me."

"Good to hear you'd be happy here. If a move for me does ever come up, I'll mention your willingness to stay on. I shouldn't worry about Ewan Robertson. He's never overridden my recommendations on your annual appraisals. Although he interferes a little and doesn't always agree with the way you do things, he recognises your ability for solving crimes and your team's track record on convictions can't be argued with. He's due to retire within the year, so you'll not have to deal with him soon enough... Now, what about Angus? What are your thoughts on him?"

Suzanna paused momentarily as she absorbed what the Superintendent had said. "I've just mentioned how all my team are excellent detectives, and you've known Angus Watson for the last two years, so it will come as no surprise that I will be highly recommending him for promotion. His performance has been outstanding. His leadership is a pleasure to watch, with his team willing to support him all the way. He has their utter respect and trust. He's also become a competent coach, adding to my input, and developing his team. His detective work is thorough and effective. He abides by the rules – most of the time – only bending them marginally when essential, as it should be. His record of arrests and convictions is top-notch."

"I agree with you, Suzanna. I've seen all that in him, as well. He can sometimes be a bit familiar with superiors, though."

"Hardly! The banter goes both ways, but he knows where to draw the line and is never disrespectful."

"Fair enough, Suzanna. You'll probably lose him to another station if he gets promoted, though."

"Yes. I know - unless he were to move up into my job if it coincided with a move for me. That's all speculation, of course. However, if I have to lose him, so be it. The guy deserves to get his Chief and to take on a bigger team. I'd like to see – and certainly hope – that one of my sergeants might get promoted to Inspector to fill Angus's gap in the team. If that doesn't happen, I'll take whoever I'm given, as I always have."

"Good. OK. I'm happy to support your recommendation for Angus. Are we done?"

"Yes. Good to hear that you support my views." She rose and headed out the door.

"Oh! By the way, Suzanna, how's it going with you? No need to rush off just yet. Let's have a chat."

Suzanna turned back into the room and sat again. Despite the barrier of the desk, there was a relaxed mood, and the Super looked genuinely like he was interested in Suzanna, not just doing his duty.

"All's well in my world, Alistair. Thanks for asking. I've settled into single life again and got quite used to being alone in the evenings and weekends. Although I'm not at home that much, actually, as I've got numerous interests to keep me busy."

"Are you still keeping fit? You certainly look like you are."

"Yes. I run or go to the gym at least three times a week, and I still go to the local Judo club to keep up my combat skills."

"Great to hear it. I've known many a colleague who stopped exercising and went to seed once they'd got beyond 45. But I also have friends who are still exercising regularly in their sixties and seventies. And they're so much younger for it."

"Do you still play squash?"

"Rarely, nowadays. Some guys I used to play with have dropped out and, of course, I'm not as fast as I once was. I hate this ageing thing. It's easier to injure yourself once the fifties arrive, and it takes longer to heal from an injury. But I still get out for a jog regularly and Helen even roped me into playing badminton once a week with a group she's been playing with for years. They're quite a sociable lot, so I've been enjoying it. Funny to be playing badminton, though. I used to think it was a game for wimps – knocking around a lump of polystyrene with feathers on it. Compared to squash, it seemed easy, but since I've started playing the game, I've realised how energetic, skilful and challenging it can be."

They chatted for a while longer, talking about the Police Service's current recruitment and training policy, and various individuals they both knew who were or had been based in Edinburgh.

The Super paused for a moment. "You must come around for dinner one night soon. Helen would love to see you again; it's been too long since you and Callum came to the house. You could bring a friend if you like – do you have anyone in your life at the moment? You don't need to share if you don't want to."

"It's OK, Alastair. I'm over Callum; I've moved on. Not to another man yet, although there is one person who could become more than just a friend (James' face came to her mind). I'd love to come for dinner. Helen's such a marvellous cook," she said with a smile. "But it will probably be just me."

"Great. I'll have a word with Helen and suggest a couple of dates. Just realised, my meeting is due to start in ten minutes. We'd best leave it there, Suzanna. It was good to catch up."

"OK. I'll look forward to the dinner invite." She rose, turned, and left the office as the Superintendent grabbed some papers, a pen, and his glasses to prepare for his next meeting.

***

James was definitely a potential long-term, intimate friend. She'd met him many years earlier, at a friend's wedding reception, and found him to be likeable. He was handsome, an interesting conversationalist and at times funny, but a relationship had been out of the question as he'd had a fiancé. She texted James: 'Any thoughts for this weekend?'

Chapter 8

"OK, folks, let's get this done," Angus said, as he entered the meeting room with the DCI. "Owen, please summarise the results of the interviews with staff."

"We interviewed four members of the staff, three of whom had been in front-of-house when the robbery commenced." He went on to summarise descriptions of the biggest of the robbers. "He seemed to be the leader of the pair, as he was the one who shouted the initial orders and the one who shot his weapon on entering the building. No one could give us any useful information about his firearm, other than it looked like a standard pistol with a magazine in the grip."

"Have we found the slug he fired into the ceiling?" Suzanna asked.

"No, ma'am," Murray chimed in. "An extensive search of the ceiling found no entry holes or embedded slug. The man who fired it picked up the spent case before leaving. One witness, Jonathon Bilberry, said that the shell case was unusually shaped and after further questioning, I believe it must have been a blank."

"Interesting, Murray. What do you think this tells us about the criminals?" Suzanna asked.

"I think they wanted to shock the staff into action and command their obedience with the threat of being shot, but if they'd fully loaded their pistols with blank rounds, this would suggest they didn't want to risk someone getting shot," Murray replied.

"Good thinking, Murray. So, if Murray's correct, this tells us a bit more about their character. Maybe they really didn't want anyone to get shot and weren't taking the risk, so they had blank rounds in their weapons. It could also be a risk reduction for themselves. If caught with weapons that posed no risk to the lives of the staff, that might mean a reduced prison sentence. At this stage, though, what it means for us is we don't have any evidence to connect a gun to the crime." Suzanna surmised.

"And the second guy, Owen?" Angus prompted.

Owen described the second guy, then continued: "the two guys spoke with local accents, so they don't appear to be from out of town. They both had a military bearing and commanded obedience in the way you'd expect from a non-commissioned officer, or perhaps a commissioned officer."

Angus took over the narrative: "Our guess is that they were both ex-Army. They probably left as sergeants or similar rather than as officers. History tells us that officers tend to go on to excellent jobs when they leave and don't get into this type of crime. It was likely their first raid of this type."

"Why do you say that Angus?" Suzanna asked.

"Because they'd planned and executed the raid well, but no seasoned criminals would risk an armed robbery sentence for such little money. We're thinking these guys may have worked together in their Army days and they needed a cash injection to get them out of a situation. Most professional criminals would have been trying for big money to make them rich."

"Sounds right to me. Can't fault your logic there." Suzanna agreed. "We need to get onto the Royal Regiment of Scottish Borderers and get a list of names for soldiers who've recently left the Regiment."

"Agreed, ma'am. Owen will make the call straight after this meeting."

"I knew you'd already have thought of it," Suzanna affirmed. "What criteria will you be using for the search?"

Angus responded before Owen started talking, "We'll be looking for anyone who left in the last 5 years, at the rank of Lance Corporal to Staff Sergeant. Age range 28-40. We'll ask for any info on convictions for breach of Army Regs."

"OK. Great. But I shouldn't worry too much about charges for minor breaches of Army Regs, as most squaddies get into trouble at some time in their career. What else do you have?"

Angus took the lead again. "We need to profile these guys further. Thoughts on where they might live, type of employment and motives for the raid?"

Caitlin was the first to respond. "I'm thinking these guys might be in the security industry – bouncers, security guards, possibly security truck drivers, or even prison service. A lot of ex-Army guys move into these jobs, as it suits their skills. Statistics suggest that some of them move into building trades, such as bricklayers, plasters, carpenters, plumbers, and electricians, because the Army offers courses in these trades as part of their resettlement package. But I hear that the courses only prepare them to be trade assistants, not fully fledged tradespeople, so that would mean a big drop in salary. My feeling is security workers."

"Good thinking, Caitlin. Any other suggestions about day-jobs for these guys?" Angus asked.

They all looked like they agreed with Caitlin's assessment, so Suzanna asked another question. "Do we know anything about the driver?"

"Not much. He stayed in the car. So far, we've not interviewed any witnesses who could tell us anything about him... or her. The staff gave us the car registration number, so unless it's hidden away somewhere, we should soon find it. The car had been reported stolen, and we've already interviewed the owner. We don't think there's any connection between him and the raid. The car had been taken off his drive during the night. The thieves appeared to have got into his house through an open window at the rear, and the keys taken. Nothing else missing, so a targeted crime."

"Have you spread the net wide for the car search or targeted any particular areas of the city?" Suzanna prompted.

"We've put out a general bulletin for all beat officers and traffic police to look out for it."

"Does anyone have any thoughts on where they might have dumped the vehicle?" Suzanna asked.

"Well," Owen offered, "if I'd been them, knowing that a helicopter could be overhead in 15 minutes from the alarm being raised, I'd want to dump it within ten minutes. At that time of day, they could easily get caught up in school-run traffic. They'd need a route that would take them off the major roads with traffic lights – so along side-streets. I've already had a look at the map and plotted a few possible routes. Taking these routes and assuming a speed of twenty miles an hour and guessing they'd have dumped the car within ten minutes, I've estimated that they would have left the car somewhere in this zone of the city." Owen said, pointing to markings on the map he'd pinned to the board whilst speaking.

"Grand start, Owen," Angus said. "Have you done any further work to narrow down the search areas?"

"Not yet, boss."

"OK, let's have some ideas then, team."

They were all thoughtfully silent for a minute, then Caitlin spoke. "I reckon that they'd want to drop the car on a minor road or back alley to minimise the number of people who might spot them leaving the car, or perhaps an unused commercial area. They'd want to avoid anywhere with CCTV cameras. If we plot where known cameras are within the zone that Owen has identified and then find the quieter side streets and deserted commercial land, that should give us somewhere to start."

"Sounds good, Caitlin. Great thinking." Angus commended. "You and Owen work together on that as soon as we finish this session, and after Owen has made the call to the Army. You'll need to correlate the data on public CCTV locations, available on the Council Mapping Portal, with the locations of banks and petrol stations, as they all have CCTV nowadays. Let me know as soon as you come up with a shortlist of possible locations, then we can get Uniform to check them out."

"OK, boss." Caitlin acknowledged.

"Getting back to the driver. Any thoughts on his relationship with the other two?"

Murray was the first to speak this time. "He could just be any random friend but I think there's a high probability that he will also be ex-Army. There's a trust between soldiers that doesn't exist outside the military, except perhaps the Fire Service and the Police Service. I think they'd have wanted a known player in their team – someone they could rely on to not drive off as soon as there was a risk of getting caught. I'm guessing the two who carried out the raid may be single or divorced, because fathers are less willing to take risks that would impact their family, whereas the driver could be married because his role is less risky."

"Interesting assumptions, Murray," Suzanna commented. "There's definitely logic in what you said, but let's not get hung up on marital status. Good to hear that you have given it thought, though. When we apprehend them, we'll see if they fit your profiling."

"Agreed, boss," Angus said. "Anyone like a sweepstake on Murray's suggestion?" After a pause with no one taking him up on the offer, he moved on. "What about a motive for the crime?"

Caitlin opened the topic with her assessment. "We know the amount stolen wasn't enough to make them rich, so I'm thinking they were in debt or there was some other reason for them needing an inject of cash just to keep the wolf from the door."

"Talking of wolves," Suzanna chipped in, "loan sharks would fit that profile. I know someone who's into making short-term, high-interest loans, with a reputation for getting his money back from even the least able to pay. I'll have a quiet word with him and see if that gives us any names that would fit with the profiles of the robbers."

"Thanks, guv. I'll contact the Prison Service and ask the same questions. Once we have names that fit our profiling, we'll need to get back to the employers and check their work attendance at the time of the robbery; that should narrow the field down somewhat. We'll also check the wider list of names against the criminal records database for any matches. Anything else, team?" Angus asked.

They all shook their heads and looked ready to get up as Suzanna spoke again. "Well done, team. I'm encouraged that a lot of thought has gone into this. We need to get these guys sooner than later. If they get away with this robbery, they might do it again, only bigger. They'll have got a taste for it. Next time, though, someone could get seriously injured. Let's not let that happen. But don't work *too* late tonight, folks. You need to relax and get a good night's sleep, if your brain is to be any good tomorrow."

They all nodded and grunted agreement, then went off to get stuck into the work. It was already nearly normal knock-off time. Suzanna returned to her office, shut down her computer, tidied her desk – always a clear-desk policy for her – then left for home.

***

Angus pondered on what they had discussed in the brainstorming. The ex-military angle seemed likely, but they mustn't shut their minds to other possibilities. His twin brother, Hamilton, had joined the Army at eighteen and left when he was thirty. Having been a mechanical engineer, he'd got a job in a truck maintenance workshop as soon as he left. He'd never had a day unemployed and likely never would. But his brother had told him about guys he knew that had not transitioned to 'civvy street' as well as him. The infantry guys didn't have easily transferable skills, so sometimes struggled.

Angus took his boss's advice and followed her example, shutting down his computer and heading off home. As she'd said, they'd need well-rested minds if they were to catch the criminals. The others had already followed Suzanna's lead.

Chapter 9

The fire was crackling hot, and Suzanna felt cosy as a lamb before it had been sheared, as she sat on her sofa twirling a magnifying glass in her hands. The freezing Scottish mist of Edinburgh's January drifted past outside, like a passing cloud.

She had furnished the apartment with carefully chosen, artisan-made pieces, much of it decades old. There was no modern flat-pack furniture to be seen, as she knew it wouldn't last, and would soon become dated. Suzanna preferred solid wood furniture, made with loving care and beautifully finished.

She put the glass down carefully on the coffee table, got up and retrieved her laptop computer from the sideboard. As she passed the dining table, she ran her hand across it, enjoying the feel of the smooth finish, and she looked down at the lustrous grain beneath the lacquer. Both the sideboard and table always gave off a sheen after its weekly polish – she could still smell the perfumed, beeswax spray that she'd recently used. Suzanna was a tactile person and couldn't help but admire its gorgeous natural beauty under her fingertips.

Her sofa was not antique or even particularly old, but it had come from one of the better traditional manufactures from High Wycombe, in 'leafy Buckinghamshire'. She'd always wondered why they called Buckinghamshire 'leafy' because, when she'd lived in the area, she'd not seen more trees there than many other counties in England.

Many of her soft furnishings had come from Laura Ashley – tasteful and good quality, she'd decided. Well, certainly to her taste anyway, and they went well with the Georgian styling of the room, with the cornices, a large central, ornate rose and chandelier.

She fired up her laptop, pulled up YouTube on the browser and found what she was looking for. She curled up on her sofa, happy to be listening to Stjepan Hauser & Petrit Çeku playing Adagio in concert. The music was fabulous. Ceku's classical guitar playing and Hauser's extraordinary stroking of his cello were a brilliant combination.

As the music relaxed her, Suzanna's mind wandered off. She analysed the day's events, considered her colleagues' reactions to situations, thought about what the next day might hold, where she could go on holiday and with whom, and what her mother had said when they spoke earlier.

Her thoughts returned to the antique object that she'd laid on her table earlier: a four-inch lens, in a brass ring and with a wooden handle inlaid with ivory leaves. It had been owned by her great-grandfather's brother – a Londoner who'd become famous for solving mysteries. She imagined Victorian London, with its cobbled streets, gas lanterns and horse-drawn carriages. What must it have been like in those days? Those days of no television, no international flights, no internet and no 250 horse-power sports cars?

Leaving the music playing on her laptop, she turned to her smartphone and Googled her great-great-uncle's name. As Google searched for the data, she noticed an unread text icon and clicked on it.

'I'm free this weekend. Would u like 2 go out for dinner Friday?'

Suzanna responded to James, 'Love to. Where and when?' before switching back to Google.

There were multiple entries listed, including a sizeable piece in Wikipedia on the legendary man. It noted his birth in the mid-1800s and the many cases he solved as a 'consulting detective', sometimes working with Scotland Yard. He was known for his quirkiness and his strange ways, but also renowned for his ability to crack complex crimes that the police couldn't solve.

It still amazed her that after all the years since his passing, she'd been the one to receive his magnifying glass, and the financial inheritance that she was so glad he'd placed in trust. Who would have thought anyone would do such a thing – just another one of his peculiar ways?

Without the capital that had come her way, she wouldn't have been able to afford her lovely home and to live well. Her salary was OK, but it wasn't substantial, although she enjoyed her job immensely. Her colleagues were equally dedicated, and they all got immense satisfaction from their job – well, most of the time, anyway.

Suzanna felt fortunate to do what she did. Her passion was her job, and how many people could say that? She pitied the huge numbers of people who worked just to earn money. Work for them was merely a means to an end – a way to pay the rent or mortgage and put food in their stomachs. But for Suzanna and her colleagues, they had a sense of purpose, a reason to get up each day and join with their contemporaries as a team, and to make a difference to their city.

It was winning her great-great-uncle's magnifying glass in the test he'd set for all his brother's offspring that had inspired her to join the police. If, after many decades and numerous tests by his relatives, she'd proven to be the one worthy of the glass, because of her deductive powers, she reasoned, she must be naturally talented in detective work.

Susanna slipped her long, narrow feet onto the polished hardwood floor, discarding the tartan blanket, and gracefully moved to the kitchen to make a hot drink. The kettle was copper and brass, reminding her again of the glass she'd just placed on the coffee table. It seemed her thoughts would never get away from her beloved, unconventional relative. Would she ever be free of his legacy? Would she want to be?

She sipped at her coffee, savouring the Italian blend beans and just enjoyed the music. YouTube had run on to music played by Hauser and Sulic – known as the Two Cellos – now performing a Vivaldi piece in a concert performed the previous year.

As the cello concert ended, she noticed it was now past 10 pm, so time to prepare for sleep. Fortunately, Suzanna could easily get to sleep, even after late night caffeine. She shut down her laptop before the next video automatically started, rose, puffed up the cushions, then put her laptop and phone on charge, before putting her coffee mug into the dishwasher. She switched off the lights and headed to the bathroom to freshen up before bed.

Suzanna slept naked, not wanting to feel restricted by tangling bedclothes, as she turned in her sleep, and enjoyed the feel of the silky sheets upon her skin. She read for a while – a novel with some eroticism – and after a while became aroused. She put the book down. The thrill could wait for another day, and perhaps she could share it with a man? It had been a while. Suzanna drifted off to sleep with a tingle between her legs.

***

Thursday 15th January

In the morning, Suzanna filled her bowl with muesli and added some extra nuts, fresh fruit and skimmed milk, before sitting at her dining table to eat, whilst reading the news on her tablet. This was her morning ritual. She liked to eat healthily, to get the nutrition needed to maintain her energy, but also to keep her trim figure.

There was the usual mixture of disasters and politics in the news that morning: more people had died of Ebola in Sierra Leone ('where would it end?' she wondered); there were worries that billionaire businessman Donald Trump might become the next President of the

USA ('no chance, she declared to herself, then added God help us if he was'); and analysis of who was behind the Jakarta attack, the previous week — Islamic State connections, they reckoned.

Suzanna wondered whether there would ever be peace in the world, but immediately answered her own question. There never would be. The world has so many evil people, and always would have. Many of them used religion as their excuse to create murder and mayhem.

After breakfast, Suzanna cleaned her teeth, then returned to her bedroom and neatly made the bed, puffing up the pillows, smoothing out the quilt and laying some decorative cushions by the pillows, before laying a throw over the bottom of the bed.

She'd bought the throw in Calcutta during her travels. The Bengalis had re-named the city Kolkata in 2001, but when she'd visited, it was still known by the British version. They'd made the throw from 'pre-loved' saris, folded several times and hand stitched together. The multiple parallel lines of the Bengali traditional Kantha stitch reminded her of swimming pool lane markers. The work that had gone into making these throws was incredible, she thought. Best of all, she knew that her purchase had helped to keep a woman in work, who might otherwise have had to sell her body several times a day to customers in Kolkata's notorious Sonagachi red-light-district - reported to be one of the largest in the world, with an estimated 10,000 sex workers living and working there.

The small social enterprise, within this red-light area, was called Sari Bari – Bari being the Bengali for house or home. There were other Freedom Businesses, as they called themselves, working in the same area of the city, with the same mission: to provide alternative, dignified employment and support to women who had been trafficked into the sex trade. She'd visited two of these sister businesses: Love Calcutta Arts and Freeset. They were all doing a fabulous job, and she had great respect for the people who had founded and led these enterprises.

Her ex-husband, Callum, had never tidied the bed like Suzanna did every day. He couldn't see the point in it. In fact, he would just leave the bed unmade all day if Suzanna had let him. Although she missed Callum's company and his toasty body in bed on a chilly night, and the regular excitement of making love, she enjoyed her independence and not having to compromise on things that were important to her.

The apartment now tidy, she grabbed her coat and gloves, briefcase, and handbag before heading off to work. As she marched down the steps outside the tenement building, she noticed a youth with a rather pointy face. He looked out of place on this street, she thought, as she strode to her car.

Chapter 10

His heart was pounding in his chest, thumping fast like a bass drum in a rock song. Despite the cold, sweat ran in rivulets down his forehead and nose, dripping before he could wipe it away. His breathing was short as he sucked the frosty air into his lungs. Billy stood like a statue, trying to recover after his run, the bridge over the burn hiding him from his pursuer.

The adrenaline buzz of being chased heightened his senses and he could hear a blackbird chirping in a nearby hedge, and the burbling of the water over the small boulders and pebbles. He could see the dark water sparkling with the lights of multiple windows and could smell bacon being cooked in a nearby home.

Downstream, he could see one or two small logs discarded at the side of the flow, left over from previous rushes of water after heavy rains. A supermarket trolley lay on its side further upstream, spoiling the beauty of the spot. But Billy didn't care. Natural beauty was not something he appreciated.

Five minutes passed and Billy became restless; he hated having to be stationary and silent. He liked to be always on the move, doing something. His mum said he had "ants in his pants". As the adrenaline levels subsided and his pulse slowed, he turned his attention to his prize, taken from the tenement building on Drumsheugh Gardens.

The large shiny lens of the magnifying glass glinted in the light of the nearby streetlights, and the brass bezel glowed like antique gold in the yellow light. Its wooden handle was square and inlaid with ivory diamond shapes. It was heavy, and now it was his. He'd never owned such a beautiful object, and he decided this would be one item that he'd not sell on for a quick profit – it was so beautiful, he wanted to possess it, not profit from it.

***

Just half an hour ago he'd been wandering down the grey street with posh cars parked outside, when a smartly dressed woman in her mid-forties, hair slightly silvered, in contrast to her charcoal suit, emerged from one of the tenements. She'd walked off with purpose as if she had an important appointment to keep. The door to the three-storey house hadn't closed properly behind, but in her haste, she hadn't noticed that the closing mechanism had not done its job.

Billy, a seasoned opportunist, was through the door in a flash. He'd climbed the wide stone staircase, listening for any motion in the old building. Billy had stood still and listened, like a deer in a tiger sanctuary, before gingerly trying the first door to see if it would open. No luck there, so he'd moved on to the next door. He'd tried again, and to his delight, it had opened. Billy listened again before slipping inside with the speed of a huntsman spider. He'd surveyed the hallway, then moved swiftly into the living room with its tall ceilings, bay window and open fire. The mantelpiece was stone, like the building face, but its style was of no interest to Edinburgh's Artful Dodger.

A shiny object caught his attention just as the door slammed closed. The word "Fuck" leapt out of his mouth, as his body jerked like a startled cat. Instinctively, he'd grabbed the object, pocketed it, and ran out of the apartment, the door closing again with a loud bang.

As he'd reached the ground floor, a man had emerged and shouted at him, "Hey you! What are you doing?" Billy had taken no heed of the bald-headed, middle-aged man in his tweed jacket, and just kept on running, escaping the building without a backward glance.

As he'd leapt down the steps to the pavement, he'd nearly run straight into a passing copper, whose suspicion was raised by Billy's haste. The man he'd just passed reached the door and shouted, "Stop that boy," and the chase had begun – even though the policeman didn't know what the boy had done.

Although only thirteen Billy was fast, and he knew the streets well. He'd headed east up Drumsheugh Gardens, then zigzagged his route until he got to the water of Leith Walkway, opposite the historic Dean Village. He veered left, jumped the wall, then went right under the footbridge and stopped dead still. On reaching the bridge, he'd opened a good gap between himself and the copper.

***

The sun was finally rising from its mid-winter lie-in and was gradually brightening the morning's duskiness. Billy hoped the polis man would soon leave the area if he hadn't already. The smell of dog's mess invaded his senses – he must have stepped in some during the pursuit. "Pooh! That stinks," he said before shushing himself into silence again.

By now, his heart had slowed to normal, and his breathing had stilled. The sound of the burn tumbling over the boulders had relaxed him. He waited five minutes before deciding on what to do next. As he moved, his hand scraped against the rough brickwork of the bridge, grazing a knuckle, and he cursed for the second time since this venture had begun. 'No one could say my life isn't exciting, he thought.

Billy wiped the dog's mess off the bottom of his trainers onto a small rock, as best he could, then emerged cautiously from under the bridge and scanned the area for any sign of the copper. There was no uniformed person in sight, just people hurrying to work, so he headed off home to Leith, keeping a lookout for the copper who had chased him. It would be about a forty-minute walk if he didn't dillydally.

Fortunately, the copper had not seen his face fully, so he'd find it difficult to pick him out in a line-up, Billy reckoned.

Billy would have been mistaken in his thinking; he wouldn't easily merge into a crowd. His chin hung back in line with his thin lips. His forehead sloped backwards, and his eyebrows almost met each other above his long, pointed (almost witch-like) nose. Some would say that from the side, he looked like the front of an Intercity train.

Definitely memorable!

By the time he got home, his mother had gone off to work - cleaning houses for rich people. And his father must have gone to the job centre or betting shop, as he wasn't at home either. He let himself in with a key he'd had cut, without his parents' knowledge. He should have been at school an hour ago, but he couldn't care less. Billy didn't see the point of learning about history and other useless crap. He was a free spirit, finding his own ways to earn money, and looking forward to the day he could leave school.

Billy had the house to himself, so went to his bedroom, lay on his bed and studied his new treasure. It was a gorgeous piece. It looked to be expertly made and must have been expensive when new. The brass ring had smooth edges and the handle also showed signs of wear. He looked through the glass and the detail he could see through it amazed him. He could see the tiny flakes of dandruff scattered across his Hibernian football team duvet.

Billy was a firm Hibs supporter, mainly because the stadium wasn't far from his home in Restalrig. His father had taken him to the footy when he was just nine years old and he'd rarely missed a home game since, saving determinedly from his meagre income. He didn't get any pocket money from his parents as they never had any to spare, so he had to make money himself. Mostly, he would steal from shops and homes, or trade in stuff he picked up.

Normally, in his early morning wanders, he'd find stuff that people had chucked out, waiting for the recycling trucks to collect. Some of it was in great condition and he could sell it to mates or neighbours for a profit. It amazed Billy that so many rich people threw away quality stuff just because it was a little worn or they'd grown tired of it, and couldn't be bothered to sell it or even give it to a charity shop. It was great for him that they did, though!

He stashed his savings under a loose floorboard beneath his bed (he was on the bottom bunk), as he didn't trust banks and certainly didn't trust anyone in his family not to nick it. It was a hassle having to shift the rubbish that lurked under his bed to get at his money, and he could only do it when he was home alone, but at least the money should stay safe that way.

He wrapped the magnifying glass inside a sock and popped it into his school bag, then went downstairs and made some toast for breakfast. He'd be later than usual for school this morning, because of the chase, but he'd just spin the teachers a line that they'd likely believe. A gullible lot! he thought, especially Miss McKenna.

Chapter 11

"Hi-ya, Billy," his chum Cameron said, as Billy dumped his backpack on the desk next to him. "Where've ya been? You missed history and physics."

"I was busy doing more important things," Billy answered.

"Were you out on your rounds again, picking up stuff to sell?"

"Aye, I was. I did'nae get anything to sell this morning, but I picked up an awesome item – an old magnifying glass. Here – have a look." Billy took his sock out of his bag, but just as he was about to show Cam his treasure, the teacher, Mr Fraser, entered the classroom. "I'll show you later. OK?" Cam nodded, and they both sat down, ready for the lesson.

Maths was one lesson that Billy was happy to attend, as long as it was practical – not weird stuff used by science nerds.

Mr Fraser was busy writing sums on the board, so the chums continued to chat. "Has your dad got a job yet, Billy?"

"No. Not sure he wants one. He seems to have gotten used to picking up his benefits and spending most of it at the betting shop. He reckons he'll have a big win soon. But he's a mug; the only people who win from gambling are the owners of betting shops."

"That's no way to talk about your father, Billy. Even if you think it, you shouldn't say it out loud. He'd give you such a clout if he knew you were talking about him like that. I know my dad would."

"Well, he'll not know, will he, because I'll not tell him, and you won't either. So, there's nae problem then, is there Cam?"

"I suppose not," Cameron reluctantly agreed.

Mr Fraser stopped writing and turned to the class. "OK, boys and girls. Let's settle down, please." After a brief pause, he went on, "We're going to have a wee test. You'll see that I have written twenty sums on the board. There's nothing new about the type of question, but some are a little more complex than last time."

"What's complex mean, Billy?" Cameron asked.

"It just means more difficult," Billy whispered in response. Sometimes Billy wondered about his pal's intelligence. Even though Billy skived off lessons, he still did better than Cameron.

"William Boyd and Cameron McKenzie, perhaps you'd like to share with the class?" Mr Fraser enquired, pausing for an answer. "If not, please keep your thoughts to yourselves and listen to what I have to say, or you might miss something."

"Sorry, sir" they both chimed in response. But Billy added in a whisper, "Pratt."

School teachers were the only people to call Billy by his formal name. If he'd been posh or English, he'd probably be known as Wills. But Billy didn't want to be posh and certainly didn't want to be English. He was proud to be Scottish.

After the Hibernian Football Club, his next dedication was to the Scottish football team. If they got knocked out from a competition – too often annoyingly – Billy would support any football team playing against England, even if the team wasn't in the UK. He never thought of himself as British – only as a Scot. Although he knew nothing about politics, he'd wished the recent referendum had voted for Scotland to leave the UK.

He'd heard his dad say that the toffs at Westminster (wherever that was) ruled Scotland, when it should be Scots making their own decisions. When he was old enough, he would vote for the Scottish National Party. He'd seen the SNP's leader speaking on telly a couple of times, and she seemed like a clever woman.

"OK, then! There are twenty questions. You should be able to complete them in twenty minutes. So buckle down and get on with them straight away. No talking and no copying. When you've finished, put your hand up so I can see how you're all getting on."

The boys did as Mr Fraser requested, and Billy was one of the first to raise his hand after about fifteen minutes. Cameron just completed the questions as Mr Fraser spoke. "OK. Time's up. Make sure your name is written on the top. Skye, please collect up everyone's papers and bring them to me."

Whilst the students had been doing the test, Mr Fraser had written up additional questions. So, after Skye had collected the tests, he instructed the boys and girls to do these whilst he marked their test papers. Once the tests had been marked, he invited the children to collect their own papers.

Billy and Cam got their papers and returned to their desk, checked their scores, then conferred with each other. "What'd ya get Cam? Billy asked.

"60%. Not bad, eh! What about you, Billy?"

"95%. Brilliant," Billy responded.

"Last week, I beat you, so we're even then," Cameron countered.

"Aye, but that's because it was trigonometry. No point learning that stuff. But arithmetic is useful." Billy replied.

"Depends," said Cameron.

"On what?" challenged Billy.

"Well... I don't know... What career you want to follow, I suppose," he responded after a pause for thought.

"Just my point. I'll not be a scientist. I'm going to be a trader, so I need to know arithmetic, but what use would trigonometry be to me, or geometry and other weird stuff only geeks would need to know?"

"Good point," agreed Cameron, then went quiet as Mr Fraser looked up at him.

***

Billy survived the rest of the school day with no issues and wandered off home with everyone else. As expected, Billy's form teacher, Miss McKenna, accepted his excuse for missing the morning's registration.

"Hey Billy," Cameron said, "let's have a look at that glass of yours now."

"OK; in a minute. I just want to get out of the school gates first. I don't want anyone else to see what I've got." They passed through the arched gateway and moved off to the side as the other kids poured through the gates and headed for the pedestrian crossing. Billy fished out his sock.

"I hope that's not a used sock, Billy," Cameron queried, "knowing how smelly your feet can be."

"Course it's not. I'm not that daft. If I get sweat on the brass, it'll make it dull quicker. Talking about socks, at least mine don't have holes in them."

"That's because I've got holes in the soles of my shoes."

"It's about time your mum bought you new ones. My dad's out of work, but I don't have holes in my shoes."

Cameron looked sad that his chum had brought this up and went quiet. Billy unpeeled his sock, exposing the shiny lens and bright brass.

"Wow! That's one piece you have there, Billy," Cameron commented. "Let's have a proper look at it."

"OK, Cam, but be careful with it. And keep it hidden. I don't want any of the bigger boys getting to see it."

"Sure thing. Just give it here." Cameron took the offered magnifying glass. "It's brilliant, isn't it, Billy? Someone must have taken great care of it. Where did you say you got it from?"

"I didn't say, and I shan't be telling either. It's my secret."

Cameron looked through the glass at Billy's nose. "Wow, I can see the veins under your skin and the fine hairs on your nose; they're amazing."

"Yeah! It's a great lens, isn't it?" Billy replied.

"I think you're right about it being old and valuable. I bet it was Sherlock Holmes' magnifying glass. Perhaps we can become detectives now that we've got it?"

"What do you mean, we've got it? It's my glass, not ours. Here, give it back."

"Aww, Billy!" Cameron said. "Even though it's yours, we can still pretend you're Sherlock Holmes and I'll be Doctor Watson. We can solve mysteries together. And when we get older, perhaps we could become real detectives."

"Don't be daft Cam; how can we be detectives, like Holmes and Watson, when the police are my enemy? I'm the man of mystery that they'd like to catch. Why would I help them catch others like me?"

"But Billy, you might steal a few things but you're no murderer or international criminal, are you? Maybe we could be like that guy on the TV – what's his name? Hmm... Dexter. He works with the cops, but he's a serial killer. We could help the cops catch thieves but be burglars ourselves. That way, we'd know if the cops were onto us. They say it takes a thief to catch a thief, so you'd be great at that."

Billy considered what Cam had just said. It wasn't as daft as it sounded. Maybe he could be a detective when he grew up. But Cam could never be his Dr Watson because he had a crap memory and was useless at solving problems.

Just then Billy's older brother Jimmy turned the corner. "What are you two up to, then?"

Billy quickly replaced the glass into his sock and shoved it back into his bag, but his brother noticed that he was trying to hide something.

"What you got there, Billy boy?"

"It's nothing," Billy responded.

"I don't believe you," his brother responded. He grabbed hold of Billy, pushed him back and held him there, whilst he pulled the bag out of his hands. He took out the sock and extracted the magnifying glass. "What have we here then?" he proclaimed. "Where'd you get this from, you little thief? Bet you nicked it from someone."

"Give it back, ya bastard," Billy swore as he made a grab for it. But Jimmy was two years older and stronger than his younger brother. He elbowed Billy in the cheek.

"Don't you call me a bastard, you little shite." He pushed Billy back over the wall onto the ground, threw Billy's bag after him, and walked off with the glass. "If you tell dad, I'll tell him you nicked it. Then you'll be in trouble."

The elbow to Billy's face had split his lip, and he could taste blood in his mouth. He was angry and upset. He felt like crying but wouldn't let himself seem to be so weak in front of his best pal and the other kids who were now walking past. So he just muttered "bastard" again and told himself that he'd get his own back on his older brother – one day.

***

Jimmy was pleased with himself. He'd got the better of Billy again. Confirmed the pecking order in his household. As the oldest, he ruled the roost. Well, when his dad wasn't around. His mother was weak, so he didn't bother about her. If she got angry and hit him, it would just be with her slipper and it never hurt. He'd just laugh at her feeble attempts to discipline him.

His dad was different, though. He'd not cross him – especially if he'd had a few pints of beer down the pub, with whisky chasers. When he'd had a drink, he could be nasty. He'd seen him beat his mum a few times, leaving her with black eyes and bruised cheeks and arms.

His mother never complained to anyone about the beatings. She seemed to think it was her fault. Jimmy would like to have intervened, but he wasn't strong enough yet and was scared of his violent father. One day, he'd stand up to him when he had enough courage.

He'd won the battle with Billy, but now he wondered what he should do with the magnifying glass. It looked ancient – an antique, no doubt. Perhaps he could sell it to one of those collectibles' shops?

He stuffed the glass into his backpack, then ran across the road to get home before his brother and raid the biscuit tin – he was feeling peckish.

Chapter 12

"Angus," Suzanna said, turning to him. "Before we move onto the Lothian raid, do you have anything to report on the muggings?"

"Nothing at all, guv. Our focus has been entirely on the armed robbery, as you'd expect."

"Of course... Una," Suzanna said, turning to look her in the eye. "I'd like your team to pick that one up, please."

"OK, boss. Nae problem."

"Right. Angus, please update us on the Lothian raid investigation."

"Err, boss!" Rab interrupted: "Before we move onto the bank raid, I forgot to mention that we had a report just now, from the officer on the beat near your home. He saw a youngster coming out of a house near where you live, and a bald-headed guy from the building called out to him to give chase. PC Fleming ran after the youth but lost him after a few turns – couldn't keep up with the youngster, and in any case, didn't even know if he'd done anything wrong! Might have been from your building, boss. We're not sure."

"Thanks, Rab. What have I said about the need to keep fit, team? If the criminals can out-run us or fight their way out of an arrest, what chance do we stand of bringing them to justice? Glad to hear that it wasn't one of my team who didn't keep up! If you get any more details, Rab, please let me know."

"Will do, boss." Rab responded, glad that he regularly played rugby and should be able to meet his boss's expectations of fitness, if he had to.

"OK, let's move on."

"Right, guv," Angus started. "We have the results of a data search from the Army and there are a couple of hundred possibilities. But we've already narrowed it down to a shortlist of about twenty."

"How did you cut it down to the shortlist, Angus?"

"Most of the men were from other parts of Scotland, with just a third living in the Edinburgh area. That gave us about eighty to look at closer. Five have since died – road traffic accidents, mostly."

"That's a high proportion for young, fit men!" Suzanna commented.

"Yes, guv. But these guys have led adrenaline-charged lives during their time in the Army, and they tend to continue seeking thrills – taking more risks than the normal population. Three of the deaths were from motorcycle accidents. One was a rock-climbing fall, and the fifth was a car accident, where the guy wasn't at fault."

"OK, fair enough!"

"We've assumed that our criminals are likely to have come from the infantry, rather than those who were professionals at trades with a crossover to civilian jobs. Our thinking is that they're more likely to have found employment in fields similar to what they'd been doing in the Regiment. Whereas, the fighting guys' skills are with guns, camping and trogging long distances across moorland and mountain – less call for those skills outside of the Army."

"We've also assumed," Angus went on, "that they're likely to be employed in the security industry in one role or another or they might be unemployed. We found that four of them are living on the streets and have alcohol problems. Drugs, as well. They're well known to the guys on the beat. We believe that, given their circumstances, none of these guys will have been involved in this crime, because they'll not have the ability or mental capacity to plan or carry it out."

"OK, so what did that result in?"

"That left us with 41 ex-infantry guys from the Edinburgh area to focus on. Eight of these have since moved to other parts of the UK to work and another five have gone overseas. Of the 28 left in the list, seven were below 5 foot 7 inches tall, so don't fit with the descriptions of the robbers. It's possible that one could have been the driver, but we have nothing on him yet. We may bring these seven back into the mix later if necessary."

"Right, so that's 21 suspects to dive deeper into," Suzanna surmised. "I don't have any commitments, so should be able help you with that and subsequent interviews, if you like."

Murray walked into the room and Angus looked at him quizzically. "Glad you could join us," he said sarcastically.

"Sorry, boss. The Forth Road Bridge was closed this morning, and I had to drive right across to Falkirk to get around. It took me over an hour instead of twenty minutes. I've no idea why the bridge was closed."

"Fair enough, Murray. I'm surprised you're not held up more often, given that the bridge gets closed whenever there are high winds," Angus replied. "We'll need your input as soon as you're ready."

"I've another suggestion for you, Angus," Suzanna continued. "I think we should determine which security firm provides services to the Lothian Bank. The robbers would have needed to know when the cash deliveries are made, and how much is delivered, for planning the raid. Perhaps one of the robbers is a driver who's delivered to the bank."

"Good point, boss. I'll check with the bank to find out which firm delivers."

"Great. What about the get-away car? Has it been found yet?" Suzanna enquired.

"Yes, boss," Murray spoke up. "Uniform found the get-away car abandoned in a cul-de-sac in the Leith docks area. This is the place we'd identified as the likely dumping ground. They've taken it in, and forensics is checking it over for evidence. Chances are the guys would have worn gloves, but you never know your luck."

"So now we know the general direction they travelled in. Have you yet seen the relevant CCTV imagery?"

"Caitlin is handling the CCTV analysis, guv. How's it going?" Angus asked, looking at his sergeant.

"We guessed at the route they took, and we've already got video from six cameras that might have captured the car. So far, we've looked through four of the videos, focusing on the 10-minute time window after the robbery, and seen nothing. Una's team has been helping with that. We should have viewed the rest of the footage by lunchtime. Is it still OK to use Mairi and Zahir for this, Una?"

"Sure. No problem."

"If nothing shows up on these public camera videos," Caitlin said, turning back Angus, "I'll chase the files from the banks, etc. We've already requested copies, but they've not come in yet."

"Thanks, Caitlin," Angus said, turning back to Suzanna again. "There are no cameras near to where they'd abandoned the car, so we don't know how the criminals travelled away from there, yet. My thinking is that they would have split up and travelled independently to another rendezvous point, where they would count the takings and split the money. I doubt they'd have had time to do that in the ten-minute car journey."

"Agreed." Suzanna said. "So, we'll need to get CCTV data from all the cameras in the docks area and scrutinise it for the time when we suspect these guys were travelling away from the place where they'd dumped the Mondeo."

"Yes. Already onto it, guv."

"They could have gone on foot, but if they had used any vehicles, they'd have needed to park them in the area before the raid. That means it would be worth looking at footage earlier that day, prior to the raid."

"Good point, guv. Owen, another job for you. Get the footage as soon as you can, please."

"One other thing, Angus," Suzanna said, "if the public and bank CCTV footage doesn't turn up anything useful, you could ask Uniform to check out the roads most likely travelled by the get-away-car and look for home CCTV cameras. They might have caught something. I saw a friend's system the other day, and the imagery was excellent – far better than most banks and public cameras."

"OK, boss. I'll bear that in mind," Angus replied.

The Superintendent walked into the room. "Morning all."

The conversation paused, and they all responded with a "Good morning, sir."

Alistair Milne, as usual, looked smart and distinguished. His chocolate brown hair was grey at the temples, and there was a sprinkling of silver throughout his head. His crooked slim nose was evidence of a previous break, giving him the air of a man experienced in the rough and tumble of hands-on policing. In fact, a clash with an opponent on a squash court had been the cause.

"The Chief Super is looking for an update on the bank raid," he said, running his fingers through his hair. "What can you tell me?" Alistair's hair fell back naturally into its middle parting, as if sprung-loaded into style.

Angus responded, "We've got a shortlist of suspects, based on our profiling of the criminals, that we'll be working down today. We're still analysing the CCTV footage; nothing of any use seen yet. And we'll be speaking with employers of the suspects this morning, prior to interviewing any without work alibis, later today – if they're available."

"Right-o. What about criminals with a record of this type of crime?"

"We've got a few names from the database and some which came readily to mind that we'll be following up. Forgot to mention that, guv," Angus said, looking at Suzanna, before returning his attention to the Superintendent.

"OK. I'd like a report by the end of the day summarising progress, so I can brief up the chain when required," the Super requested, his Aberdonian origins still evident in his voice, despite having lived in Edinburgh nearly all of his adult life. "I'll leave you to it. Good work, so far." With that, he turned and walked out.

"I wonder why the Chief Super is specifically interested in this crime?" Angus said.

"Perhaps the bank manager is a friend from the Rotary Club?" Murray suggested.

"You could be right there, Murray. No harm in that, though. If you'd said Masons, I'd have been more worried – given that it's a secretive society. At least the Rotary Club's open to all and not secretive," Angus responded. "My Father's in the Rotary Club; they do loads of community and charity work."

"The Masons also do lots of charity stuff," Una offered.

"Yes, it's just the secretive stuff that bothers me," Angus concluded.

"Right then. Back to business team," Suzanna commanded. "Angus. Tell me more about the suspects with criminal records for previous armed robbery."

"There's only half a dozen that aren't in jail and could have done this job, but as we said before, they're not our prime suspects because they've history of doing it before but for larger sums of money. It's not likely that they'd lower their ambitions. However, the following are some possibilities: Rory McIntyre, Mungo Bruce, Gregor Munro, Hamish Stewart, Ewan Jamieson and Duncan Kelly."

"I recognise some of the names," Suzanna commented. "Didn't Bruce get charged with armed robbery about five years ago but got found not guilty?"

"That's right, guv. Had a good barrister. Evidence was only circumstantial. But, as mentioned before, why would he lower his ambitions? The raid he'd allegedly been involved with got away with £1.5m. Besides, he's not in his thirties or lean and fit!"

"Hmm... Are there any who might fit the descriptions?"

"Only one, guv. Ewan Jamieson. He's ex-Army, actually. We're trying to find out what his current situation is."

"OK. Keep me updated with progress, please, Angus."

"Will do, guv."

"Rab. Now you've had a day to investigate your case, I'd like an update please, starting with a reminder of the case."

"You may recall that it's a fairly trivial one. There have been a number of break-ins to people's homes around the city. There's never much taken. It seems that an opportunist thief, perhaps a youth, has just grabbed whatever he or she could and scarpered. There didn't appear to be any pattern, but piecing together all the reports of this type from around Edinburgh, it looks as if most of these crimes have occurred within a two-mile radius of Leith."

"Interesting. Go on."

"The robberies were all carried out between 7 am and 8 am, just after people had left for work, and before school start time. Perhaps our thief is a schoolboy or girl from the Leith area of the city – probably a boy, based on previous cases. I'm planning to knock on doors close to the scene of several robberies, and about the time that they'd occurred, and ask if the neighbours had seen a youth in the area that didn't look like he or she belonged. I'll also check out CCTV along the routes that the youngster might have taken from the crime scenes back to their home in Leith on the days of the robberies."

"You could also contact schools in the Leith area and get a list of kids who often turn up late for school or play truant."

"Thanks for the suggestions, ma'am. I'll do that."

"Great. Any other matters to discuss?" Suzanna queried.

There was silence and a shaking of heads.

"Right. Angus, please update me as you make progress in this case. Let's get to work, team."

Chapter 13

Suzanna swallowed the last mouthful of her Moroccan spiced couscous salad just as Angus knocked on the office door and walked in.

"Oh! Sorry, guv. Didn't realise you were still at lunch. I'll come back later." He noticed she had some food on her face but tried not to let on that he'd seen it.

"It's OK, Angus, I've just finished," she said, wiping off the offending food particle from her chin that she'd noticed Angus' eyes rest on momentarily. "What have you got for me?"

"Caitlin's finished her scrutiny of the video from CCTV cameras that could have been on their route to the docks. She saw the car pass one camera, and they'd removed their balaclavas, but the imagery was poor, and the car interior was in shade, so she wasn't able to identify any faces. She's extracted close-ups of the two visible faces and will get them enhanced. They should give us something to compare with other images later or when we see these guys in the flesh."

"OK. Now that we believe we have images of the vehicle in more than one place, we should be able to plot their route better, then deploy uniform guys to walk *those* streets and knock on doors when they see cameras. We might get some better imagery."

Angus continued: "Thanks, guv. We'll try that. Caitlin has also looked at the imagery for the period following the likely dumping of the car and she found images of a tall man leaving the Leith docks area about that time, on foot, who looked like he might be one of the suspects. He had a large backpack which could have held the money. There was only one sighting of him, but he might have caught a bus or got into a car, so we've no idea where he might have gone."

"Well, at least we've got some images that might help place one suspect in the area when we catch up with them. Tracking down home CCTV imagery in the area might also be worthwhile to help identify the pedestrian that Caitlin has seen. Any imagery we can get will help tie them in, even if only circumstantial. Did the other banks' CCTV files come in as expected?"

"Yes. Caitlin is looking through them now. Nothing to report yet."

"OK. Anything else?"

"Yes. We've already had feedback from the security truck companies about the rostering of drivers. Our 21 names are already down to ten because eleven of the suspects were at work. Of the ten left, six were off-shift drivers or sick. The last four are in work with other companies that we're not so likely to get help from – they're working as doormen for two different companies. But they're unlikely to get work alibis from their employees anyway because their work is generally in the evenings or overnight."

"So, what's next with these ten?"

"We'll track down all ten and question them. Find out whether they have any credible alibis and see what else we can extract that could help us narrow down possibilities."

"Good. Happy with that, Angus. With Caitlin tied up doing video scrutiny, would you like me to do some interviews? If we split the workload, we'll get the job done sooner."

"Great thinking, guv. If you'd like to come through to the office, we'll have a look at the shortlist and dish out work."

"OK. Let's do it."

***

Angus and Suzanna went through to the main office. The team were all sitting in front of their computer screens or in conversation. The desks were strewn with pieces of paper and pictures covering the Formica surfaces. Wires dangled from the backs of the desks, waiting to catch the stray, outstretched foot that might wrench it from its device.

Suzanna wondered why her request for cable wraps, to tidy the place up, had not yet been fulfilled, but she said nothing. She didn't want to distract Angus with health & safety stuff right now – it could wait until later.

Angus called the team together around the crime board, but Murray and Owen were deep in conversation and didn't respond to the call. "Murray; Owen. Can you please join us to go through the suspects?" Angus requested.

"Sorry, boss," they replied, before wheeling their chairs backwards and spinning to face the board.

"OK, folks, let's get down to business," Angus started. "We've got our list of suspects down to ten. The next step is to interview them, and we'll split up to do this for the first round. I'll run through the suspect list now and we'll allocate detectives to each person. Caitlin, I need you to complete your video analysis work, so we'll leave you out. That leaves the four of us to talk with ten suspects. That would be two and a half each! Obviously, that won't work. So I propose we take two suspects each. When you've talked with both of yours, or you've failed to get hold of them, let me know. I'll allocate one of the remaining two for you to visit. Hopefully, we'll get through all ten this afternoon or at least know where we stand. Understood?"

They all nodded in the affirmative, so Angus went on. "I've plotted all the suspects' homes on the map and allocated interviews geographically. Number one on our list is George Stevens, 36 and single. He left the Army as a sergeant and has been working for Scottish Security ever since. Lives in Bingham Place, Niddrie. Owen, you take him."

"Number two is Jeffrey Wilkins, 37, married, with three children. Lives on Edmonstone Terrace, Danderhall. Left the Army in 2014 as a staff sergeant. Worked for Boxall Security for a while, then moved to work for Scottish Security. Murray, that one's for you.

"Right-o, boss."

"Number three is Charles Sutherland, 35, divorced with two girls. Lives in a flat, Portobello, near the seafront. But his wife and kids stay in Leith. Left as a sergeant. Worked as a carpenter for about three months before taking up work with Scottish Security – that's three suspects so far that work for the same company. I'll take Mr Sutherland."

"The fourth suspect is Gordon Strachan, 32, married with one son. Lives in Longstone. He left as a Lance Corporal and went straight into work with Plumbing Central. He's still working for them. Could you take him, please, guv?"

"OK."

Angus went through the rest of the list, giving the key information about them. "All this detail, and more, is in the info packs on the table. Take those allocated to you and have a read through before speaking to them. I'll carry the extra two."

"Thanks, Angus," Suzanna said. "Sounds like a plan. Oh! By the way, what about Ewan Jamieson?"

"Good point, guv. We did some more digging. Turns out that he's now living on the Costa Brava. We checked with the UK Border Force and there's no record of him having returned to the UK recently, so I believe we can rule him out."

"Agreed, for the moment, Angus. It's possible he could have sneaked back into the country. But let's concentrate on our prime ten for now, anyway."

The team grabbed their respective info packs, then split up to prepare for the interviews. "It'll be good to get out of the office," Murray said to Owen. "I much prefer to be out asking questions."

"I agree, Murray, especially if the weather's fine, but where would we be without the work we get done on our computers?"

"True enough, pal, but I'm still glad to get outside." He grabbed his coat and walked out. "See ya later."

"Aye, see ya, Ginge," Owen responded, as he picked up *his* coat and car keys.

Murray frowned at being called Ginge. He didn't like people pointing out that he had ginger hair, particularly as so many people spoke about it in derogatory terms.

Chapter 14

A screech of tyres grabbed everyone's attention, and they watched as the silver Vauxhall Vectra skidded along the road, hitting Jimmy full on. There was a sound like a baseball bat hitting a pumpkin. The car swept Jimmy off his feet. He slid up the bonnet and onto the windscreen, cracking the glass, before slipping down again and being thrown onto the road in front of the now stationary vehicle.

There came a smell of burning rubber, and horror was written on many of the faces that had just witnessed their first car-pedestrian collision. Billy saw the car crash into his older brother and felt his brother's pain. Despite his just-moments-ago hatred for Jimmy, he ran to his side and his emotion got the better of him this time. Tears rolled down his cheeks as he asked, "Jimmy; are you all right? Speak to me."

Jimmy lay on the cold asphalt, unmoving and unconscious. Blood trickled from an ear and his right leg lay at a weird angle. Billy shouted louder than he'd ever done, even when arguing with his brother: "Help! Someone help my brother!"

The car driver emerged from his vehicle in shock, looking around for anyone that might listen to him. "I didn't stand a chance," he said. "The boy just ran out in front of me." He looked around again, hoping that someone would concur with his version of events and relieve him of his worries. It was true the boy had run out in front of him, but what worried the driver was that he'd had two glasses of wine with lunch and might be over the drink-drive limit.

An old gentleman, grey-haired but bald on top, and with a heavy moustache, clasped the driver's arm. "Come sit over here on the wall for a minute. No need to worry. I saw it happen, and it was definitely the boy's fault. There was nothing you could have done to avoid him. He should have used the crossing." After a pause, he asked, "What's your name, young man?"

"Donald." He replied. It had been a while since anyone had called him a young man. He didn't feel young or look it when peering into a mirror. What he saw in the mirror most mornings, as went to clean his teeth, was a wide forehead topped by greying wild hair that refused to hold any style. A broad, long nose ended abruptly just above his upper lip, with little space separating them. His lips lacked the usual waviness, running virtually straight across his face and were too wide for his narrow jaw. It wasn't a face he'd ever been happy with, since he'd started shaving and teenage hormones had made him self-conscious.

Despite the old man's reassurances and his own belief about the emergency stop that he'd just completed, he was still anxious. His eyes were wide and his mouth ajar; saliva trickled from the corner of his mouth.

The police would soon be here, and he'd get breathalysed. If he was over the limit, he'd lose his licence, perhaps even go to jail – even though it wasn't really his fault. His wife would undoubtedly find out about his long lunch with the female colleague and even though it had been an innocent meeting. She'd put two and two together and make seven as usual. He couldn't believe his terrible luck.

A taxi driver stopped his cab and took control of the situation, trying hard to keep the traffic moving. He waved his hands and shouted at people to "hold on there; yes, you come through now," waving at the car to proceed.

Meanwhile, a man in his mid-thirties went straight to Jimmy to help. "OK, lad. What's your name?"

"Billy Boyd."

"Do you know this boy?"

"Aye, he's my brother."

"OK. I need you to move back a wee bit so I can have a look at him. What's his name?"

"Jimmy."

"Hi, Jimmy, can you hear me?" the man said whilst lightly pressing on his shoulder; there was no response. "Can you open your eyes for me?" Still nothing. He shook the boy delicately and spoke to him again.

Turning, the man saw people milling around, gawping, and talking to each other. Some were taking pictures of the boy on their phones. They'd probably post them on Facebook and tell all their friends they'd just witnessed the accident. Perhaps they'd write stuff about how scary it had been to see the car hit the boy and to see him lying motionless in the road with blood on his head.

'Damn sightseers,' the man thought. "Has anyone called for an ambulance or the police?" There was no response. He scanned the crowd and selected a middle-aged woman who looked like she might be reliable. "Ma'am," he said, looking into her eyes. "Please call 999, now, and ask for an ambulance. Tell them there's been an RTA on Lochend Road, Leith, between Primrose Street and Restalrig Terrace. A teenage boy is lying on the road, motionless, with blood on his head. Got it?"

The woman nodded and started dialling, so the man turned again to the injured boy. His Army first-aid training had kicked in automatically: assess the situation – is it safe or are the injured person and yourself in danger? The stationary car and queue behind it were a good shield against any danger. Speak to the injured person and see if they respond. If no response, ask them to open their eyes. Maybe they can hear you and respond in this way, even if they're unable to talk.

He spoke to Jimmy again. "I'm just going to check you out. Speak to me if you feel anything." The man went through the ABC of assessment, first checking his airway by opening his mouth and peering inside to make sure it was clear, then his breathing. He observed the boy's chest moving and put his ear near the boy's mouth. He could hear air movement, so he seemed to be breathing fine – shallow and light. Fortunately, there were no gurgling sounds coming from his throat and no blood, so his lungs were likely uninjured.

Next circulation. The man checked for a pulse. It was strong and a little fast, so no worries there. Moving on, he looked for a source of the blood on Jimmy's head. He had a large bump on the side of his head and the skin had split with blood trickling from the cut. He felt carefully around the rest of his head and found nothing else of concern. He felt around the boy's neck for any abnormalities – nothing he could tell - taking care to not move him unnecessarily before shifting his attention to the obviously injured leg.

It looked like his right femur was fractured, as the upper leg was unnaturally twisted. He checked gingerly around the area for protruding bones or open wounds and found none. He could feel the end of a bone pushing against the skin on the inside of his thigh, though. 'Best not move him,' he thought or that could go through. 'There could be internal bleeding, so he noted the need to keep a close eye on his pulse and breathing, whilst waiting for the ambulance.'

The man checked out the rest of Jimmy's body, trying not to move him. He ran his hands tenderly over the surfaces that he could reach and found nothing else.

"Billy. Listen. Your brother has got a nasty bump and a gash on his head. That's why the blood is dripping off his ear. I don't think he's fractured his skull, so don't worry. He's also broken his leg, so we'll not move him. What I need you to do is just hold his hand and tell him he'll be all right. OK?"

"Aye," Billy replied... "Hi, Jimmy... It's Billy. You've been hit by a car, but you'll be fine." Billy chatted on and the man rechecked his breathing and circulation – still OK.

***

Donald sat next to the old man who had tried to comfort him, deep in thought - his mind continuing to analyse the accident. He wasn't thinking about the unconscious boy, but worrying about whether any blame might fall on him.

'If only the engine management warning light hadn't flickered on again just before the boy ran in front of me,' he thought. The light had distracted him and perhaps delayed his reactions.

'The bloody light had been playing up for weeks now, but the local garage was lost for ideas of why it was doing it,' he thought. A few months ago the warning light had come on steady and the car had stalled. The damn thing wouldn't start again, and he'd had to call out a breakdown service to rescue him. It had taken the garage two weeks to get the part delivered - a sensor of some sort - and replaced.

His mind returned to the scene as a siren screamed from the police car that was speeding down the wrong side of the road towards them. He could see an ambulance further up the road, also travelling with as much haste as possible in the difficult traffic conditions.

'I hope the boy's OK,' he thought belatedly. He wandered over to the scene and noticed a magnifying glass laying on the ground. He picked it up and studied it for a moment. It was evidently old but well cared for. He put it down again and returned to the wall where the old guy still sat.

Donald fretted again. 'Maybe I was breaking the speed limit,' he thought. 'Even if I was only just above the limit, they'll still charge me with driving without due care and attention and speeding. Shit!' It didn't seem like there was any way he'd get away with this. It was so unfair. 'Damned boy should have been paying attention and not run in front of his car.'

***

The police car pulled up on the pavement, leaving space for the ambulance to pull in close to where the boy lay. Two officers got out, donned their caps, and took control of the scene. One moved the bystanders back. The other officer went straight to the boy and spoke to the man who was monitoring him. "Have you done first aid checks on the boy?"

"Yes. He's stable at the moment and I've not moved him for fear that his broken leg might puncture an artery."

"Great. The ambulance will be here in a minute, so you hang on in there until the paramedics take over; OK?"

"Aye, that's fine."

"Who's this lad?"

"This is Billy Boyd, the boy's brother. The injured boy's name is Jimmy. There were loads of people around when the accident happened, so there'll not be a problem getting witness statements."

"OK. Thanks. I'll just try to get the traffic under control," and with that, the policemen walked off.

Billy's pal, Cam, pushed his way through the crowd. "Hi, Billy. Is he going to be all right?"

"Think so," Billy responded.

"Looks like you don't have to get your own back on him now – he's got his comeuppance."

"You bastard, Cam. Taking my glass and elbowing me in the face didn't deserve this punishment. Piss off. Go on. Some friend you are!"

"I did'nae mean it like that," Cam backtracked. "But if he'd not been mean to you and run off, he'd have never got run over."

Billy ignored his best pal and went back to talking to Jimmy. Cam backed away and drifted off towards home, wondering whether Billy would forgive him for being so crass and whether their friendship would still stand.

The man looking after Jimmy noticed the magnifying glass lying on the road next to the boy, and he picked it up. "Billy. Is this your brother's magnifying glass?"

"No, it's mine, but I lent it to him."

"OK. I'll just pop it into his bag."

The ambulance drew to a halt, and the paramedic went straight to the boy, seeing a man kneeling by the boy, the asked him what he could tell him.

"This is Jimmy Boyd," the good Samaritan said, "and this here is Jimmy's brother Billy. I've done the usual ABCs and checked out his body for breaks and bleeding. His breathing and pulse have remained steady. He's been unresponsive since the accident – it's been at least 10 minutes since we called it in. The blood on his head appears to be from a gash. He's got a sizeable lump there as well – probably from when he hit the windscreen. My main concern is his leg," the man continued, "which, as you can see, is obviously broken. But I've not found any protruding bones or open wounds."

"OK. Thanks for the briefing and for what you've done so far. Where did you get trained in first aid?" the paramedic asked.

"The Army."

"Great. I wish everyone was first aid trained. If you could just move away now, I'll check him over again." The paramedic started his checks, so the man moved back into the crowd and strolled away. He had business to attend to, and he'd done all that duty required. He didn't want anyone to suggest he was a hero, or have his name and picture in the newspapers.

Chapter 15

"Excuse me, ladies and gents. We'll need to talk with any of you who saw the accident occur, so we can be sure of the facts. Did any of you witness the accident?" PC White enquired. Three hands raised, and he asked each of them for their names and phone numbers. "If you can wait around a few minutes more, we'd appreciate it. It would be good if the rest of you could be on your way now. Thanks for your concern and do get in touch if you saw anything important. Otherwise, please clear the area so we can get things moving again."

Some of the crowd melted away, but many stayed on to watch the paramedic go about his work.

The PC turned his attention to the men sitting on the wall, one of whom seemed in shock. He approached them and introduced himself. "I'm PC White. Are either of you the driver of this car?" he questioned, whilst pointing towards the silver Vectra with the open driver's door.

"I am, officer," Donald admitted.

"And who might you be, sir?" PC White asked the older man.

"I'm Fraser McKenzie. I saw the accident and stayed to look after Donald here. The boy ran out right in front of the car and Donald did an emergency stop. There was nothing he could have done."

"OK. Thank you, sir. Could I just take your name, address and phone number?" Fraser gave him the details. "I'll need to get more detail of the accident if you can wait around a little longer."

"Happy to help," Fraser replied. I've no rush to be anywhere.

"What is your surname, sir?" the officer enquired, turning to look at Donald.

"I'm Donald Campbell... No, I'm not related to *the* Donald Campbell, in case you're wondering."

"I bet it annoys you being asked if you're planning to break the world water speed record again, eh?"

"It certainly does. I'm no relation to him at all."

"Right, sir. I need to take some details from you. Please show me your driver's licence and car registration and insurance documents."

Donald pulled his wallet from his back trouser pocket and extracted his photo driving licence, then handed it to the PC. "I'll just get my car documents from the glove box," he said and walked over to the car whilst PC White scrutinised the driving licence.

Donald returned a few minutes later with the car documents. "Sorry it took a while; they were buried under sweet packets and, would you believe, gloves?" He passed the insurance certificate and car registration document to the officer.

The constable checked the documents for validity and made a note of the important details.

"OK, sir. We have a few more formalities to go through. Firstly, and you probably already know, it's standard procedure to carry out a breath test of drivers after road traffic accidents." The PC passed the breathalyser device to Donald. "Blow into this tube here, sir, until I tell you to stop."

Donald put the device to his lips, his anxiety rising, along with his heartbeat. He took a deep breath and blew into the breathalyser until the constable said stop, then passed it back to him.

"Thank you, sir. OK; that's right on the limit for driving a motor vehicle. You'll have to come to the station with us and take another breath test. Do you understand?"

"Yes, officer. I understand. Am I under arrest?"

"Not at this stage, sir. If you fail the second test, then we will charge you with being in charge of a motor vehicle whilst under the influence of alcohol. Just stay here for now. We have to take some details of the incident scene before we return to the station. Just wait here."

Donald was now panic-stricken. His fear had been realised; he was over the drink-drive limit. If he failed the second test, he'd be in big trouble. His eyes widened and his mouth opened involuntarily. He'd lose his licence for sure. If the boy died, he'd get done for causing death by careless driving or whatever it was they called it. He'd lose his licence for longer, get a bigger fine and probably get sent to jail. He wondered how the boy was and walked over to see.

"Right Jimmy," the paramedic was saying, "we've immobilised your leg and your neck, so we'll now move you into the ambulance to get you to hospital. Don't worry about anything; we've got the best doctors in the country here and we'll soon be at the hospital. You're going to be all right. You just lie there, and we'll sort you out." Jimmy had yet to move or respond to anything, as he was still unconscious. But, to Donald, it seemed like the boy was complying with instructions. He felt somewhat relieved and went back to sitting on the wall.

The paramedic loaded Jimmy into the ambulance on the trolley and fixed it into place. He turned to Billy, who had followed them to the ambulance. "You'd better come to the hospital with us, young man. Come on, hop up here and strap yourself into that seat." Billy climbed in, his nose wrinkling as he breathed in the stink of disinfectant.

The driver started the engine, turned on his blue light and siren, then drove off.

***

As they travelled away from the accident scene, the wailing siren invading Billy's senses, the paramedic made sure, for a second time, that Jimmy was securely strapped to the stretcher and the stretcher to the ambulance. He turned to the equipment and hooked Jimmy up so he could better observe his condition. As he did so, a monitor illuminated and a moving graph started to show Jimmy's heart rate.

The paramedic continued to talk to Jimmy, hoping or expecting that his words might reassure the youth. "Right, Jimmy, we're on the way to the hospital now. We should be there in about twenty minutes. You're in expert hands Jimmy – we'll keep you safe until we get you to A&E. You're going to be fine, young man; don't you worry. I'm just going to have a chat with the hospital staff now, so you just hang on in there, pal."

Turning away from Jimmy, he pressed a button on his headset lead and spoke. Responding to a question from the doctor in A&E: "The lad's fifteen; name: Jimmy Boyd. Hang on a sec. Billy, is your brother's name James or Jimmy?" he asked.

"It's James, sir, but everyone calls him Jimmy."

"Thanks, Billy. OK. It's James Boyd. He's concussed and has a simple fracture of the femur. I've immobilised the leg, so it won't come to any more harm during the journey. I've left it for you to straighten out and set correctly."

"Breathing is shallow but fine and his heart rate is 110. Blood pressure's normal and temperature is 98.3. There doesn't appear to be any significant internal bleeding, judging by the vital signs. He has a large swelling and a cut on his scalp, but there's no sign of a fractured skull. We should be with you in about 10 minutes if the traffic keeps letting us through."

The doctor responded, then the paramedic replied, "Fine. All good. See you soon." Listening to this one-sided conversation reassured Billy. Although he often felt hatred towards his older brother, he was still his brother after all, and he'd stand by him now. Jimmy bullied both his younger brothers, but he also protected them from other, bigger boys. Within the family they might fight but family was important, and they supported each other.

"Hi, Jimmy. How're doing, pal? Can you hear me? Did you feel that?" the paramedic asked, as he pinched the boy's arm and then his cheek. Still no response, as expected. "Jimmy, did you know that you've got a lump like half a Cadbury's Cream Egg on your head? But you won't be able to eat it, pal," he said, trying to lighten the mood. "But it's nothing to worry about," he added so Billy wouldn't worry, nor his older brother if he could hear what was being said.

The paramedic turned to Billy again. "Are you all right, young man? You're looking a wee bit peaky."

"I'm feeling sick. I'm not normally travel-sick."

"It's probably because you can't see outside. Here's a bag. If you need to vomit, do it into the bag, please. We'll soon be at the hospital, so hopefully you'll survive the next few minutes. When we get into A&E, I want you to take a seat in the waiting area while I and the team from A&E move Jimmy into one of the examination cubicles. Take your brother's bag with you and just stay there for a while. Someone will ask you some questions, for the records, then they'll leave you alone again. So just sit patiently until you're called. OK?"

"Yes, sir," Billy replied, noncommittally.

The ambulance arrived at A&E and a team was ready to meet it, and they soon had Jimmy in the hospital. Billy did as he'd been told and took a seat as they moved his brother into a bay and pulled the curtain around him. He sat looking at the floor for about ten minutes, his mind wandering. Jimmy had always dominated his younger brothers but had also been their protector, even speaking up for them when their dad was being horrid to them – earning his dad's wrath instead.

Billy remembered the time when a group of boys had surrounded him after school, and they'd started pushing him around. When Jimmy had seen what was going on, he'd waded in pushing and thumping the boys, even though there were more of them. Faced with his anger, they soon scattered. Billy had been grateful for his brother's toughness then, but he wished he'd go easier on him the rest of the time.

A woman came and sat next to him, then took details of his and his brother's names, their address, parents' names, and phone numbers, then returned to her office. Billy was already getting restless. He still had Jimmy's backpack on his lap and remembered his magnifying glass was inside it. He opened the bag and took it out, slipping it into his own bag, before anyone noticed. At least he'd got his magnifying glass back.

Chapter 16

Charlie rang the bell of his former family home. He missed its old charm despite its compact dimensions. He was hoping his daughter would be home from school by now, and that Isla wouldn't be too nasty to him today. Isla opened the door. "What do you want?"

'There's one hope dashed then,' Charlie thought. "Good afternoon to you too," he said sarcastically, wishing he'd kept his voice emotionless.

Isla screwed up her face in reaction to his jibe. "I suppose you want to see the kids." She stepped back to let him in, her lips remaining pursed, reluctance written across her face.

"Christ, Isla! You don't need to treat me as an enemy every time you see me. We both need to be good parents to the kids, and it doesn't help when you act with animosity all the time. The kids pick up on it."

Isla went to bite back but bit her lip and said nothing, realising that there was some truth in what he'd just expressed. "Go on through," she said, then closed the door.

"Daddy," Alana screamed as he walked into the living room, then ran to hug him. "I've missed you, Daddy."

"I've missed you too, darling. Where's your brother?"

"Ethan's in our bedroom." Just as she said that Charlie's son barged into the room and slung his arms around his dad.

He hugged them both before releasing his grip. Alana grabbed her doll and brought it back to him. "Look Daddy, Adamina has a bun."

"Wow. You've done a brilliant job of tying her hair up. She looks beautiful with her hair up, doesn't she? But not as pretty as you, though."

Alana smiled at her daddy's compliment. "How's my wee young man, then?" Charlie asked, turning back to his son. "How was school today?"

"Boring!"

"What subjects did you have today?"

"Maths, history, English and sports."

"Did you enjoy sports?"

"Yes. That was the best part of the day. We had cricket practice."

"Cricket! It's January! Cricket is a summer sport."

"I know, Daddy. We practiced in the nets inside the sports hall. The teacher said it was too cold and damp to be outside today."

"Are you looking forward to the summer months when you can play cricket outside?"

"Yes. It's my favourite sport."

Charlie thought back to last summer when he'd watched Ethan at the tournament held at the Leith Links Cricket Club. He'd been standing just outside the boundary when another father spoke to him – an Englishman by his accent. "Is that your son batting at the moment?"

"Aye. That's Ethan."

"He's rather good, isn't he? A natural at the sport by the look of the way he's playing."

"Thanks. He seems to have taken easily to the sport. I never played cricket when I was at school."

"Looks like he might be good enough for the Scottish Cricket team when he's older, if he keeps it up."

"I suppose that's possible."

"It's funny when I think about what I just said. As you can probably tell, I'm not from around here."

"You don't say," Charlie said with a smile.

The father smiled back, then continued: "Well, last time I was watching a cricket match in England, I mentioned the Scottish cricket scene and the man I was talking to was astounded. He didn't think the Scots played cricket, let alone had a national team."

Ethan might be good enough for the Scottish Cricket Team, Charlie thought, remembering the words of that father again, but if I'm not around to encourage him, his talent may go to waste. Isla doesn't seem to care much about sport; her focus is on academic standards, alone. He wondered whether there was any hope for a reconciliation between them, but realised that it was too early to even think about it.

Just then, Isla entered the room and handed him a cup of tea. "Thanks," he said. Maybe there is some hope. At least she's being civil now.

"Daddy," Alana whispered in his ear, "when will you be taking me to Disney World?"

"Soon, darling. I've been saving all my pennies so we can go. I should have enough for us to go at Easter, if that will be OK with your doctor and your mum."

"Oh, Daddy. That's wonderful. I can't wait to go," she said, flinging her arms around his neck and nearly spilling his tea. He hugged her back, his cheek resting against the scarf covering her bald head. Ethan looked up and smiled but said nothing.

Isla looked at him sternly but waited until her daughter was playing with her doll again before speaking. "I hope you're not promising what you can't deliver. It'll really upset her if you let her down again."

"As I said, I have the money now. We need to talk about the dates and details so I can get things booked."

"Will you be taking Ethan as well?"

"Yes. I can't very well take Alana and not take Ethan, can I?"

Isla got up and moved to the door. "Come through to the kitchen."

Charlie joined her in the kitchen as instructed, hoping he would not get hassled about his decision.

"So, how come you've got enough money to take our kids to Florida? We never had enough when you lived here. Have you had a big win on the horses? You can't have earned it. That driving job doesn't pay enough. Why you had to leave the Army with its good money and all the perks, I don't know."

"You know full well why I left the Army, Isla. Let's not go over that again. There's more to life than money."

"Yeah, well, that's true, but you need money to live and we're just scraping by now, thanks to you leaving."

"I'm not getting into this topic again. If you'd seen so many colleagues and friends killed and maimed in Afghanistan, you'd have left. I stopped off and visited Drummond in Headley Court. You know he lost both legs in a road-side bomb explosion?"

Isla nodded but kept quiet.

"Well, I couldn't bear to see any more of my pals end up like him. Or for me to end up the same."

Isla's face puckered at the thought. "Point taken!"

"Look. I have to go. Wish I could stay longer, but I'm driving tonight. I'll call in again as soon as I can," he said, finishing his tea. "We need to talk about Florida. You do know I still love you, Isla?"

She crinkled her face. "It's too late, Charlie. What's done is done. There's no going back now."

Charlie left Isla in the kitchen and returned to the living room. "Come here, darling; give me another of your wonderful hugs." Alana hugged him vigorously, her cheek pressed against his, with an enormous grin lightening her face.

"I have to go to work now, darling. I'll come and see you again soon."

"Aww! Daddy, can't you stay a few minutes longer?"

"Sorry, Alana, I have to go, or I'll be late. You wouldn't want me to lose my job, would you?"

"No, Daddy." She released her arms and let him rise.

Ethan wrapped his arms around his dad and squeezed as hard as he could. "Come back soon, Daddy."

Charlie peeled himself away from his son's grip. "I will, son. I will. Don't you worry." Isla came to see him off and offered him a quick but warm smile before closing the door.

Charlie wondered whether that warmth might spread with time. He hoped so.

Chapter 17

After what seemed like hours of sitting around, bored, a nurse approached Billy. "William Boyd?"

"Yes."

"Please come with me." The nurse led him to a room with a table and three chairs. It looked like a place where the staff ate their sandwiches to save going to the canteen. They sat down and Billy asked: "How's Jimmy?"

"Jimmy's doing fine, Billy. He's had X-rays on his head and leg. He hasn't fractured his skull, and we can now see the condition of his leg. Your mum and dad should be here shortly, and Jimmy will go into surgery soon to have his leg reset."

"Will he be able to play football again? He's brilliant at footy."

"I'd certainly hope so. He's young and the fracture of his leg isn't too complex, so he should heal well. I can't say how long it will be before he's playing again, though. Just stay here for a while, Billy. I'll bring your parents in when they arrive." The nurse left him to track down his parents, then returned with them a few minutes later.

"Billy. Are you all right, Son?" his mum asked.

"I'm fine, Mum, but I'm worried about Jimmy. He's concussed and his legs badly broken. They're going to operate on him soon." Billy couldn't hold back his emotions any longer and started sobbing.

"Don't be such a wuss, Billy. Big boys don't cry," his dad said, scowling and unsympathetic.

Billy continued to sob, and his mum held him to her breast, looking across at her husband, as if to say: 'leave it; you'll just make him worse'. Billy's mum's clothes smelled of bleach and furniture polish, but Billy didn't mind. Her hugs comforted him. He knew she cared for him, even if his dad didn't.

He stopped crying after a couple of minutes, then sat silently, his mind drifting. "What happened to Jimmy, then? Did you see?" His mum asked.

His mum's question pulled his attention back to reality. "We all came out of school and Jimmy shot off towards home, as if he was in a hurry. Instead of waiting at the crossing, he ran across the road in front of a car. It skidded before it hit Jimmy." Billy paused, then went on. "He went up the bonnet, hit the windscreen, then slipped back onto the road. I think he hit his head on the windscreen."

"Bloody careless driver," Reg Boyd said. "He was probably going too fast. Just wait until I get my hands on him."

Morag Boyd gave her husband a dirty look. "There's no need to blame the driver. We don't know what speed he was doing. From what Billy said, he tried to miss Jimmy."

"I don't think the driver could have missed him, Mum; he didn't have any chance of stopping."

"I wonder why he ran out without stopping or looking," Morag thought out loud.

"I don't know, Mum," Billy responded, not mentioning the magnifying glass that Jimmy stole from him.

"Listen, son," his mum said. "Your pal Cameron is outside waiting for you. Why don't you get yourself off home with him? I'll phone his mum and ask her to feed you some tea. We'll have to stay here for a while until they've finished operating on Jimmy."

"OK, Mum." He wiped his eyes, then hugged his mum again. He

hoped Cam wouldn't notice the red rims of his eyes. "I'll see you later." He was glad to get out of the hospital – away from the germs and the boredom, and his uncaring father.

***

"Hey Billy," Cam called out and walked towards him. "Sorry I bad-mouthed your brother, pal. I didn't mean to. I was just sticking up for you."

"Aye, I know you were, Cam. I'll let you off."

"Thanks, Billy. How is Jimmy?"

Billy told Cam what he knew about his brother's condition. "My mum and dad will wait at the hospital until he's out of surgery. Mum said to go home with you. I can have tea at your house."

"OK. Great. Let's go." As they walked away, Cameron asked: "How're you feeling about what's happened to Jimmy?"

They walked out of the hospital – passing smokers in hospital gowns, sitting in wheelchairs or standing, with intravenous drips attached to stands, bearing the cold of winter to get their nicotine fixes – and walked off towards Leith.

Eventually, Billy responded to Cam's question: "You know I hate it when Jimmy pushes me around, but he *is* my brother, and he protects me sometimes from the other scum who try to bully me. I'm worried about him, Cam. You know how he loves his football. What if he can't play again?"

"I'm sure he'll be all right, Billy. The doctors are bloody brilliant. Have you seen that programme, Holby City? You should see what they can do nowadays."

"But that's fiction, not reality, Cam."

"Yes, I know it's fiction, but it's based on real life. Jimmy will be fine, you'll see."

A few minutes later, Cameron asked, "Did you get your magnifying glass back from Jimmy?"

"Yes. I took it from his backpack while I was in the waiting room."

"What will you do with it, Jimmy?"

"I've been thinking. Jimmy took it once, so he'll likely take it off me again. Before he gets out of the hospital, I'd better sell it."

"But you said you would keep it."

"I'd like to but there's no point, is there? May as well make a few pounds from it. I'll take it to a pawnshop and see what they'll offer me. It could be worth a lot. You never know. Will you come with me?"

"Not sure. Don't want to get involved in thieving."

"Thought you were my pal?" Billy pressed.

"I am. I'll think about it. OK?"

Chapter 18

Owen walked casually to George Stevens' door and knocked with his knuckles. Stevens came to the door, dressed in jeans and a t-shirt, his hair tousled. He would fit the description. He was taller than average, lean and muscular. "Mr George Stevens?"

"Who's asking?"

"Detective Constable Crawford, Edinburgh CID," he responded, showing his warrant card.

Stevens glanced at the ID card, then looked up again. "What can I do for you, Constable?"

"We're carrying out some routine enquiries. Can I come in for a brief chat?"

"Sure. No problem. Come on in. Would you like a brew?"

"That's kind of you, but this shouldn't take long."

"OK. That's fine, but let's go in the kitchen, anyway. I've got a tea on the go."

They drifted into the kitchen and both sat at the wooden table. The chairs were typical country tea-room style. Owen found these types of seats to be uncomfortable, as he couldn't get his hips fully into them. They seemed to have been made for skinny-hipped teenagers. He perched there as Stevens slurped his tea from a mug. "So, what brings you to Niddrie, Constable?"

"There's been an incident in the city that we believe might have involved someone employed in the security industry. We've already approached the employers and we have a shortlist of people that we need to talk with, to eliminate them from our enquiries, because they were not at work at the time of the incident. There's nothing to worry about."

"OK, fine. Ask away."

"Where were you at 9 am yesterday?"

"Oh! That's easy. I was at home unpacking and doing the laundry; I'd just got back off holiday, having had a short break in Aviemore."

"Were you skiing?"

"Aye, I was. As usual for the Cairngorm mountains, it was challenging stuff."

"Yeah, I know what you mean. I learned to ski there. It was probably – no, definitely – the toughest place I've ever skied," Owen replied, purposely being friendly.

"Aye, most of the fresh snow had blown off, leaving hard-packed snow and ice. One girl in our party slipped and dislocated her shoulder. Poor love."

"Yeah. It can be treacherous up there, can't it? The last time I skied there, I forgot the protocol for getting off Scottish T-bars. I was used to the Alps, so just threw the T-bar away and stepped to the side to do up my ski boots, when my wife shouted a warning. I turned just in time to see the T-bar whack me straight in the face."

"Wow. You poor bugger! I bet that hurt - having several kilos of hardwood and metal hit you at speed?"

"It certainly did! My eyebrow swelled up into a long bump with a gash down the middle. Sally said it looked like I had a second mouth on my face. I had to ski straight to the bottom to seek medical attention, and I spent the next two hours getting stitched up."

"Bloody hell! I've never had it happen to me, but I've seen loads of others get hit by a T-bar. I don't know why the Health & Safety boys let them get away with it."

"Nor me. There were three other skiers being treated for similar injuries while I was there. I wondered whether I should report it to the Health and Safety Executive, but lost enthusiasm for following up by the time I got home. Talking of home, when did *you* get home from *this* trip?"

"About 10:30, Sunday night. I dumped my gear and went to bed shortly afterwards; I was knackered after the whole day skiing, then driving home."

"If you'd let me have the names and contact details of the people you skied with, for corroboration, that would be great."

"No problem." Stevens found a piece of paper and noted the details, referring to his phone for contact details, then passed the piece of paper to Owen.

"Thanks. Now, is there anyone who can confirm that you were at home at the time of the incident?"

"I don't think so. Maybe a neighbour will have seen me hanging out the washing?"

"Did anyone come to the door, perhaps?"

"Now you come to mention it, I had a delivery. The courier called about 9:30 - I think."

"Do you have any delivery slips or anything that would help me confirm what you've told me? It would make it much easier to prove what you're telling me, then I'd not have to trouble you again."

"Sure thing. I think the slip is in the paper recycling. Should be near the top." Stevens stood up and went to the utility area, where the recycling bins were. "Here it is." He returned and passed it to Owen.

"Fantastic. Are you happy for me to take this with me?"

"Sure. No problem. Oh! Just a minute. I can do better than that." He picked up his smartphone, scrolled down, then opened an email and showed it to Owen.

Owen read the email confirming delivery of the package at 09:22 am on the day of the robbery. "That's brilliant. Just forward that email to me, so I can print it off at the station and file it. Then that should be the end of it. Here are my contact details. Thank you so much for your cooperation, Mr Stevens. Much appreciated. I'll be on my way then."

They both walked to the door and Owen exited. "Thanks again," he said as he turned and walked back to his car, combing his hair back off his forehead with his fingers. It felt fine to his touch, and he was tempted to feel its silkiness again, but he resisted. He remembered how his constant stroking of his hair in school used to drive his teacher mad. She'd sent him out of the classroom to stand in the corridor many times for ignoring her commands to leave his hair alone. He smiled at the memory, but at the time, it had been humiliating.

***

Murray found the five-storey building where Sutherland lived at the far end of the street, in Portobello, just before a bar. The shops below the flat had metal shutters pulled down, and there were large communal bins scattered around in front. It was a scruffy area, and it took him a while to find a place to park.

There was a single entrance and multiple bell push buttons, listed with A through to H – eight flats. He pressed the button for Flat G and held it for about three seconds. After a minute, he pressed the button again – longer this time.

There was still no answer, so he tried Flat H, then F and E. Eventually, a woman came to the door. She was about forty, with long, mahogany hair, bound into a ponytail – it made her features look harsh. The chubbiness of her face masked her small nose and high cheekbones.

"Yes?" she said, looking annoyed.

"Sorry to trouble you. I'm looking for Charles Sutherland. He lives on the top floor, but there's no answer. Do you happen to know whether or not he's in?"

The woman looked peeved that he'd disturbed her and she'd had to answer the door for someone else. "I don't think he's in. I got home just five minutes ago, and he was just walking down the stairs as I was coming up."

"Don't suppose you had any idea where he was going?"

"Probably for his daily run. He was in running gear and had his large backpack on. I think he's got bricks or some other heavy objects in it. He's super fit, you know."

"Oh! So, he might be back again soon?"

"Depends on what you call soon. He's normally out for about an hour."

"Oh! OK. Were you at home yesterday? Did you see him at all that day?"

The woman thought for a while. "I think I saw him about 10 am, coming in... Why are you asking, by the way?"

"Just routine enquiries; sorry I should have told you: I'm Detective Constable Docherty. Thanks for your help. No need to tell Mr Sutherland about our chat. I wouldn't want him to worry." Murray turned and walked away before she could continue the conversation.

Chapter 19

The terraces and semis, on Redhall Road, would have been built in the 1960s, going by their pebble-dashed boring style, although many had been improved by the addition of simple porches, the clean redness of their roofs giving away their young age.

Suzanna noticed a small white van directly outside Strachan's house, with *Plumbing Central* written along the side. She was pleased, as she'd expected him to be out fixing someone's blocked U-bend. She knocked on the door and after a few moments, a man dressed in striped pyjamas and a blue towelling dressing gown opened the door. "What do *you* want?"

"Sorry to trouble you, sir. Are you Gordon Strachan?"

"I am. But who's asking?"

"Chief Inspector McLeod," Suzanna responded, showing him her card.

"What can I do for you? As you can see, I'm not well," he said, wiping the drip from his nose with the sleeve of his dressing gown.

"My apologies for troubling you, but I have a few questions I need to ask you. Could I come in?"

"If you don't mind catching my cold, you're welcome to, but you'll have to excuse the mess." He stepped back from the doorway and Suzanna walked in.

"Just as long as you don't sneeze on me, Mr Strachan, I'm sure I'll survive."

Strachan led the way into the front room, which had a two-seater sofa and two easy chairs facing towards a large TV screen. The walls had been papered some years ago, and they were now tatty and drab. The seats hadn't been cleaned in a while, as there was food debris laying on them and empty snack packets lying around.

Suzanna brushed off some of the dirt from one chair, thinking she'd need to wash her hands at the earliest opportunity, and sat down. Strachan sat on the sofa, took a tissue from the box on the table and blew his nose.

"I just need to determine your whereabouts yesterday at about 9 am. I understand you weren't at work." Suzanna's eyes couldn't help being drawn to his hair, which was sticking up, pointing in random directions.

"I've been sick since Saturday. Can't seem to shake this cold. I was at home yesterday. That was my first day off work – in fact, the first time I'd taken a day's sick in three years." He sneezed; fortunately for Suzanna, into the crook of his arm, containing the spray.

"Do you recall what time you called in to work to let them know?" Suzanna asked, her senses detecting the smell of menthol mixed with stale beer. Strachan seemed to like a drink, but evidently, he couldn't be bothered to clear up spillages. Suzanna was glad she wouldn't be staying long.

"It would have been about 8:30. Why are you asking, anyway?"

"There was an incident that morning and our investigation has led us to a number of possibilities that we are trying to reduce, by eliminating as many people as we can. There's nothing to worry about. But you are on our list, just because you match a profile. Is there any way that you could prove you were at home at that time?"

"My boss should be able to confirm the time that I called in, and my wife can tell you I was in no fit state to go to work that morning if you ask her."

"I assume your wife left early, then?"

"Yes, she's a nurse at Royal Edinburgh Hospital. She started work at 7 am, so left home at about 6:30."

"Did you make the call to work by mobile or landline, Mr Strachan?"

"By mobile – the works phone."

"Would you mind if I had a look at your call records?"

"If it would help. I don't see why not." He handed over his phone, having selected the phone app and history.

Suzanna looked through the call log and noticed a call at 8:27 on the day in question. She noted the number he'd called in her notebook, along with the phone's number, then handed the phone back to Strachan. "What's the name of the man you spoke to at work that morning?"

"Gordon MacDonald. He's my line manager."

"Thank you, Mr Strachan. I think I've taken up too much of your time already. I'll let you get back to suffering alone."

They both rose and Suzanna left. "Thanks again for your time, Mr Strachan," Suzanna said, as she left the house. "I hope you recover soon." As she walked back to her car, she thought to herself, 'I reckon we can strike him from our list.'

Checking her phone before driving off, she noticed a text had arrived. 'Grand Café at the Scotsman Friday 7:30 OK?'

'Definitely. See you there,' Suzanna replied, smiling in anticipation of seeing James again soon.

***

The door to the three-story terraced house on Merchiston Grove was opened by a woman who might have been in her fifties. She had a cigarette hanging from the fingers of her left hand.

"Good afternoon. Detective Inspector Watson from Edinburgh CID," Angus said, showing his ID. "I'd like to speak with Stuart Forbes."

"Aye, well, he's not here right now."

"Do you know where I might find him, Mrs Forbes?"

"No, you'll need to call that agency he works for. They called him last night and asked him to do a shift today. No idea where he'll be."

"OK. Thanks. Could I just ask: was Stuart working yesterday morning?"

"No. He was home that morning."

"Was he at home at 9 am?"

"Aye, he was. He'd have just finished breakfast. He had a bit of a lie-in because he'd been working until gone midnight the day before."

"When you see Stuart, could you ask him to call me?" he said, handing her his card. "I just need to check a couple of details and reassure him that there's nothing to worry about. We're just carrying out routine investigations."

Mrs Forbes took the card, then took another drag on her cigarette, flicked the stub onto the pavement and closed the door.

Angus didn't think it was worth making a fuss about her littering. He stepped on the cigarette end and ground it out, then walked away.

***

Owen drove down Edmonstone Terrace, passing house after house of pebble-dashed, bland boxes. The houses looked like they'd been owned by the council at one time, but going by the tidiness of the road and the neat gardens, many had likely been bought by their occupants and were now being well looked after. Most of the owners had converted their front gardens into off-street parking, but cars still lined the road.

He parked the car outside the home of Jeffrey Wilkins and walked up to the front door. There was a neatly cut lawn and well-maintained fences, but there were no flowers or attractive shrubs in the garden. It was regimented by straight lines and clear edges to the lawn, but it was evidently not the home of a person with a love of plants.

Owen knocked on the door and a woman in her mid-thirties opened it, a toddler hanging around her legs, gripping her maternity slacks that covered the growing lump in her abdomen. "I don't need anything, thanks," she said, then went to close the door.

"Excuse me, are your Mrs Wilkins?" She opened the door again. "I'm not a salesman; I'm a police officer – Detective Constable Crawford from Edinburgh CID. Could I have a word, please?" He showed her his ID card, and she nodded after scanning the card.

"What do you want?"

"Just routine enquiries, Mrs Wilkins. I just have a couple of questions for you. Can I come in for a minute?"

She stepped back, "I suppose so," and let Owen into the house.

"Is your husband here?" Owen asked.

"No, he's at work. He should be back around six today if you need to speak to him."

"That might not be necessary. Could you tell me where your husband was around 9 am yesterday?"

"He was home, looking after this one. I had an early shift, and he didn't start work until the afternoon. They have a weird shift pattern at his company."

"Does your son not go to nursery, then?"

"He does if neither of us is off work. They charge by the hour, so we minimise the time he's there. They're quite flexible about it."

"That's unusual. My friends with kids of this age have to pay monthly, whether or not their child's at nursery. You've struck lucky there. What's the name of the nursery?"

"It's called Twinkle, Twinkle, for little stars, on Old Dalkeith Road."

"Great. I'll have to look into it for when I start a family."

"What's this all about, anyway?"

"There was an incident yesterday morning around 9 am and we're just trying to eliminate people from our enquiries."

"But why Jeff?"

"Oh, just because he's involved in security truck driving, and we think the crooks might have had inside knowledge of the deliveries."

"Ah! So that will be the bank raid on George Street I heard about?"

"Yes, that's right. As I say, we're just crossing people off our list, so we can focus on those that might have had the opportunity. Nothing to worry about. I'll let you get back to whatever you were doing. Thanks for your time, Mrs Wilkins."

When Owen reached his car, he used his phone to search the internet for Twinkle, Twinkle Nursery, got their number and called them.

"Twinkle Twinkle, Jenny speaking. How can I help?"

"Good afternoon, Jenny. Sorry to trouble you. I'm Detective Constable Crawford. I have a question for you about the attendance of one of your toddlers. He's the Wilkins boy. Could you tell me whether he was with you yesterday morning?"

"Well. You'll need to call in and prove your identity before I can release that information – Data Protection Act, you'll understand."

"No problem. Can I call in about five minutes? I'm just down the road"

Owen visited the nursery and determined what time Jeff Wilkins had dropped his son off before moving on to his next task.

Chapter 20

A silver Toyota Avensis passed in the other direction, as Murray drove along Mountcastle Crescent. He noted the number in his mind, then pulled over before reaching the house where Andrew Stevenson lived. A quick check of the registration number confirmed it had been the suspect's car. He performed a rapid three-point turn, then drove off in pursuit of the Toyota. At the end of the road, he looked both ways and saw the suspect's car to his left, so quickly turned and followed it, closing the gap a little as he followed the car. He didn't notice the yellow box at the side of the road.

He followed Stevenson for two miles until he stopped outside a house that looked like a small castle, its grey stone face foreboding in the drizzle. Murray assumed he was there to collect a customer, so he pulled up just beyond the Toyota and walked back to it. Stevenson had his head down, engrossed in something. Murray knocked on the driver's window and bent low, so he could speak with the driver.

Andy wound down his window and looked up at the detective, not having noticed that he'd just got out of the vehicle in front. "Sorry pal, I'm already booked, and in any case, I can only take passengers who book via the Hail-a-Ride App."

"I don't need a ride, thanks. I'm Detective Constable Docherty. Are you Andrew Stevenson?"

"Yes, I am."

"Good. I just need to ask you a few questions. Can you spare me a couple of minutes?"

"Well, I'm supposed to be taking a customer to the local hospital; if she comes out, I'll have to end the conversation and take her to where she needs to be."

"Fair enough. If that happens, I'll follow you to the hospital, and we can carry on our conversation there. I'm just carrying out some routine queries into the whereabouts of various people that fit a certain profile. There's nothing to worry about. Could you tell me where you were at 9 am yesterday morning?"

"Why do you ask?" Stevenson said.

"There was an incident that occurred at that time and we need to rule out the people on our list. Where *were* you at 9 am?"

"I was travelling to my first pickup of the day. I have to work ten hours a day for Hail-a-Ride, then work evenings as a doorman, to bring the money in."

"Fine. That's *what* you were doing, but *where* was the pickup and drop-off?"

"I picked up a woman in Portobello and took her to the hospital. Got there about 9:20."

"Seems like you make a lot of hospital journeys! I take it that the Hail-a-Ride log will confirm this?"

"Aye, it will."

"Great. Can I just take a look at your log then, please?"

At that point, the customer arrived and got into the back seat. "Good morning. I'm running a wee bit late; can we get a move on please, or I'll miss my appointment."

"Sure thing." He turned back to the constable. "Sorry, I'll have to go now."

"OK, sir. I'll see you at the hospital, then."

A few minutes later, Murray pulled up next to the Toyota and lowered his off-side window. Stevenson also wound down his window. "Let's pull into the car park for a few minutes to finish our chat. OK?"

"Sure," Andy responded.

"Join me in my car, please, Mr Stevenson. It's too chilly to stand around outside." Murray drove into a slot in the car park and Stevenson found a slot nearby, then walked over to Murray. He got into the passenger seat and offered his phone to the constable, with it open to the Hail-a-Ride driver's log page.

Murray took the phone, then scrolled through the log for Wednesday. He had indeed picked up a fare from Portobello and taken the customer to hospital, but the journey started later than Stevenson had suggested.

"I see the journey didn't begin until after 9:30. You said 9:20."

"Aye, well, the customer was late. They often are, unfortunately, and us drivers lose money sat around waiting for them."

Murray noted the relevant details in Stevenson's logbook and jotted down his Hail-a-Ride registration number before handing the phone back to Stevenson. "That's all good, sir."

Andy got out of the car without delay and returned to his Toyota, then drove off without picking up another fare.

Chapter 21

Suzanna rang the bell of the house on Saughton Mains Place for a third time and banged on the door just in case. Still no answer. She gave up and walked back up the path, but as she crossed to her car, a woman and little girl turned into the path and approached the front door.

The girl must have been around six years old. She had long chestnut brown hair tied into plaits. Her mother looked to be in her early thirties. She looked dishevelled, her blonde hair, although tied back into a ponytail, was straggly. Suzanna turned back and strode up to the house, just as the woman and her daughter were entering. "Mrs Kirstine Jones?"

The woman turned and noticed Suzanna approaching. She looked like an official of some type, so she instructed her daughter to go on in and find something to play with. "Yes. I'm Mrs Jones. And who might you be?"

"I'm Chief Inspector McLeod of Edinburgh CID. I'd just like a quick word if I may? It won't take long."

Mrs Jones looked perplexed. 'Why would a chief inspector want to talk to me?' she thought. "Come on in. It's too cold and damp to talk on the doorstep."

Suzanna followed Mrs Jones into the hallway of the mid-terraced house. It was as gloomy as the weather, with grey paint covering the hall walls, scarred from many years of wear and tear. It seemed dark and narrow – depressing. They went into the kitchen, where Mrs Jones filled the kettle and switched it on before turning back to Suzanna.

"We're carrying out routine enquiries about an incident that occurred yesterday morning. Could you tell me where your husband was at 9 am?"

"Why do you ask? He'll have not done any wrong. He's a good man. Never been in any trouble."

"I'm sure he is Mrs Jones. But his name has come up on a list and we just need to check where he was so we can cross him off the list and concentrate on the others."

"Oh! OK. He'd have been dropping Molly off at school. She starts at 9 am. I was already at work."

Suzanna found out which school Molly went to, then drove straight there. The school was probably 20-30 years old, single-story, and designed by an architect whose brief would have been to minimise build costs. She found the admin office and spoke to the receptionist. "Good afternoon. Chief Inspector McLeod from Edinburgh CID. I'm hoping you can help me."

"I'll certainly try."

"What time does the School open its doors for pupils in the mornings?"

"Well, school starts at 9 but someone's here at 8:30, for any early arrivals."

"Is there any way of knowing if a certain child was dropped off early and at what time?"

"If they arrive after 8:45, they'll just stay in the playground until it's time to start, and we don't log the children in at this stage, as it wouldn't be practicable, but we do have two members of staff in the playground to monitor them. If any child arrives earlier, they have to be taken into Classroom 1, where they're handed over to the duty teacher and logged in the register."

"Would the register record who brought the child in?"

"No, but the teacher is likely to recognise them."

"I'd like to see the records for yesterday, if possible, so we can just check on one specific child."

"Sure, that shouldn't be a problem. Give me a minute."

The receptionist, Gillian Smythe – according to her name badge – brought the record to the counter and let Suzanna check it. Molly had been dropped off at 8:35 am on the Wednesday.

"Lovely. I'd like a copy of the register if that's OK?"

"Suppose so. I'll photocopy it for you. Can I ask what this is in connection with?"

"Sorry, I'm not at liberty to tell you. But I can say that we're just trying to determine the whereabouts of certain individuals that fit our profile of suspects."

"OK. That's fine. I was just concerned that the school may need to be aware of something about one of the children."

"There's nothing to worry about, I can assure you."

Suzanna took the offered register, thanked Gillian, then turned and walked out of the school.

Gillian watched her leave, then went back to her duties. 'She was a pleasant lady. Nothing like I'd have expected a Chief Inspector to be,' she thought.

Suzanna drove back to the Jones' house and knocked on the door again. When Mrs Jones answered, she looked surprised to see the Inspector again, so soon. "Hello again, Mrs Jones. I just realised that I do need to ask Hugh a couple of questions. Do you know where he'll be now?"

"He'll be at work, as he is every weekday. He works from ten in the morning 'til seven in the evening."

"OK. Thanks. I'll have a chat with him later, then." She walked back to her car and got in, watched by Mrs Jones, who by then had a phone to her ear.

Suzanna Googled the number for Scottish Security, then pressed call.

The receptionist answered after just two rings. "Scottish Security. How may I help you?" she said, cheerily.

"Good morning. This is Chief Inspector McLeod, Edinburgh CID. I need to have a quick chat with Hugh Jones; it's just routine enquiries. Can you tell me how I could meet up with him?"

"Good morning, Inspector. I take it this is in connection with the enquiry we had about which drivers were on shift at 9 am yesterday?"

"Yes, we're just following up on that. Hugh Jones was not at work, so I just need to check with him about his whereabouts; then I can eliminate him from the enquiries."

"That's fine, Chief Inspector. Let me just check his schedule." After two minutes, the receptionist had found what she needed. "He doesn't have any breaks between now and finishing his shift, so I can't suggest anywhere that you could meet with him. He should be back at the depot about 6:40 pm, if that's any help?"

"That's a bit late for me. I'll try to catch him at home in the morning, instead. Thanks for your help." Suzanna broke the connection, then called Angus to check on progress.

Chapter 22

Angus rang the bell of the maisonette in Forester Park Grove. There was no response, so he rang again and a minute later walked away. He was twenty metres up the path when he heard the door open and a man called out. "Hello. Did you ring my bell?"

Angus turned and walked back, noticing that the man was shorter than the two prime suspects. "Yes. Are you William Hunter?"

Hunter was dressed in blue jeans and a light grey hoodie, with white training shoes. "Aye. What can I do for you?"

"I'm Detective Inspector Watson. I'd just like to ask you a couple of questions if that's OK?"

"Nae problem, come on in."

They climbed the stairs and went into the living room. "I've got tea in the pot, if you'd like one?"

"That'd be great. Thanks. White, one sugar, please."

"Grab a seat if you can find one. I'll be back in a minute."

Angus looked around while he waited for his tea. The only soft furniture was a chocolate brown, frayed sofa with saggy seat cushions. It sat on a dirty carpet almost as brown as the sofa, opposite a large wall-mounted TV – its cables hanging untidily. The rest of the small room was taken up by a Formica-topped desk and a basic swivel chair. Documents and ring binders covered the desk, and some clear-plastic-bodied pens lay scattered around.

Hunter returned from the kitchen and passed him a steaming mug. Angus cupped his hands around it, welcoming the warmth, and smelled the tea, then took a sip. “Ah! That’s great.” Angus remarked.

“So, what brings you to my door, Inspector?”

“Just routine enquiries. Could you tell me where you were at 9 am yesterday morning?”

“That’s easy. Same as every day. Here.”

“I thought you were employed by Centre Guards?”

“Yes, I am. But it’s a small company. We don’t have an office. All our employees work on customers’ sites. I work from home, checking in on them from time to time and allocating people to locations. If we have anyone go sick, I move someone from another location, if I can, or call on one of our agency workers who fills in when we need them. If we’re really desperate, I fill in gaps myself.”

“I just need proof that you were here at that time, so I can cross you off our list of potential suspects in a crime. You fit the profile we’ve built.”

“9 am yesterday, you say? That would be the bank raid, then. It was on the news last night. Sounded like a professional job... I think I understand why you’d be checking up on people like me – ex-professional soldiers.” Hunter commented. “I started work at 8 am, because I had a few people call in sick and had to do my juggling act. I made a cup of tea around 9 am.”

“But is there any way that we can verify that?”

“Unfortunately, the teapot doesn’t have a memory feature,” he quipped.

Angus smiled.

Hunter thought for a minute and drank the rest of his tea. “There was no-one here to confirm that I was at home, but I guess my phone records would prove I was making calls a few minutes before nine. You’re welcome to have a look at my phone log, if you’d like?”

"Yes please. That would be helpful."

Hunter thumbed the screen until he had his phone history on display and passed it to the Inspector. Angus looked through it, noting numerous calls in and out between 8:03 am and 8:52 am, then a gap until 09:11. "Would you be happy for me to call the people who you spoke with at 08:52 and 09:11, just to confirm?"

"I'd prefer you didn't, as that may start rumours running. I've not been in this job that long and I need to watch out for my reputation. But if it's *absolutely* essential, then I guess I could live with it."

Angus noted down the phone numbers for the two calls and the number of Hunter's phone. "I'll tell you what. I won't call them if I can avoid it. And if I do, I'll be tactful."

"I'd appreciate it, Inspector."

Angus finished his tea and handed back Hunter's phone. "Thanks for your cooperation, Mr Hunter. Hopefully, I won't need to trouble you again."

Hunter escorted him out of his home, closing the door before returning to his makeshift office.

***

Angus's phone rang, and he picked up. "Hello, boss. How are you getting on?" He was pleased that he'd remembered to call her boss for a change.

"I'm done with my two suspects, Angus." Suzanna said. "Would you like me to take on a third?"

"That'd be great. I've just finished with the William Hunter enquiry. I've not heard from Murray or Owen."

"How about we meet up at by Union Park, near the Post Office, so you can hand over the info pack on Ross Gibson? It would be on the route for me to Corstorphine."

"Sounds like a plan. See you in a few minutes."

***

Angus parked up on Saughton Road and waited for Suzanna to arrive. He dug out the info pack, ready to give to her, then looked in his rear-view mirror and noticed Suzanna's BMW approaching. It didn't seem to be slowing. Angus braced as the car closed the gap, then stopped just in time. Relieved, Angus got out of his car, as Suzanna open her car door.

"You had me worried there, guv. I didn't think you would stop in time."

"Sorry Angus. I didn't mean to scare you," she said. Looking directly into his hazel eyes.

"Aye, well; perhaps I was worried more than most would have been, because I've already had one whiplash injury."

"Oh! I didn't know. How did that happen?"

"It was about seven years ago, when I was travelling to work on a January morning. There was snow on the verges, but the road seemed clear. It was wet, not icy. I came up behind a slow-moving van and decided to overtake, but what I didn't know was the next section of road was like an ice-rink."

"That's strange. Why the difference, do you think?"

"It was a bridge. I'd never heard before but now know that because bridges have air under them, the temperature of the surface will be much colder on a winter day than the road that's been laid on the ground."

"That makes sense when you think about it."

"Aye, it does. With hindsight, I shouldn't have overtaken. But, as I said, I had no knowledge of it at that time. I just wished the council had put warning signs up, saying 'Road Liable to Icing'.

"What happened when you hit the ice?"

"I lost the back end of the car. It just swung off to the side. I steered into the skid, but the car just swung back the other way and I ended up going backwards along the road at 40 mph. The car went off the road, up a bank, mowed down a wooden fence – that's when my neck got wrenched backwards – and dropped upside down into the adjacent field about fifteen feet below."

"Wow. That must have been frightening?"

"It certainly was scary. I'd thought I would die. It was a surprise when I found myself hanging inverted by my seat belt, apparently unscathed. I remember releasing the seatbelt, dropping to the roof, and crawling out of the smashed windscreen. There was a smell of fuel around, so I got clear fast. The car went up in flames about a minute later."

"That was a close call, Angus. I didn't know you'd had such a near encounter with death."

"I've been grateful to be alive ever since. You just never know when your number's up," Angus said. "Actually, that wasn't the end of it. The van driver had stopped, and he helped me up the bank into the warmth of his van, before calling 999. The nearest emergency vehicle was the local uniformed policeman, so he came out and took me to the hospital to get checked out. But, would you believe it, on the way, his car collided with another car by a bridge? It was one of those treacherous mornings."

"Incredible! Does your neck trouble you routinely?" Suzanna enquired.

"Aye it does. I regularly get neck-ache; especially if I'm looking down at a laptop screen for a while."

"Is your work computer set up OK? Or do you get neck-ache at work, as well?"

"It's OK, thanks, guv, but I could do with a better chair."

"I'll see what I can do."

"Now, how did it go with the first two suspects?" Angus said, changing the subject.

Suzanna updated Angus on her interviews with Strachan and Jones, then Angus shared about his talk with Forbes's mother and with Hunter.

"Sounds like we've made good progress on this. I wonder how the other two guys are getting on?"

"We'll find out soon enough, guv. Just one interview each left, then we can get back to the station and confer with Owen and Murray. I expect Caitlin will also have an update for us by then. Here's the Ross Gibson info folder."

"Thanks Angus. I'll see you back at the station, then."

Chapter 23

The three-story, stone terraced house where Gibson lived, unlike its neighbour, had been split into four flats. Railings separating the property from the pavement were showing signs of neglect, with the black paint blistering and peeling because of underlying rust. The house's stone façade had been greyed over decades of coal burning. In contrast, the attached house appeared to be a single-family home. It had unblemished black railings, fronting a neatly trimmed hedge and its stone face had recently restored to its clean sandy coloured origins.

Suzanna pressed the bell-push to Gibson's flat, but there was no answer. She rang again, but there was still no response. So, she tried other flats until someone buzzed her into the building. She climbed the stairs up to Number 3, where a bare-chested young man stood at an open door, dressed in pyjama bottoms. "Who are you?" he said grumpily.

"Sorry to disturb you. Were you asleep?"

"I had been when you rang the bell, but I had to get up, anyway. What do you want?"

"I'm Chief Inspector McLeod, Edinburgh CID. Do you know Ross Gibson from Number 4?"

"I see him coming and going occasionally, but I know nothing about him... He lives with his girlfriend." He said, as an afterthought.

"This is an unusual time for you to be rising from sleep; do you work a night shift?"

"Yes. I work at the Airport. The shift starts at midnight and ends at 8:30 am, after I've briefed the day shift about ongoing issues."

"What time do you normally get home then, sir?"

"I'd normally be home by ten to nine and in bed shortly after that."

"When you got home yesterday, did you happen to see Mr Gibson?"

"I did. He was leaving as I was coming in."

"And that would have been at the normal time, about 8:50 am?"

"Yes; there'd not been any issues with the hand-over, so I got away on time."

"Thanks very much for your help. Could I just take your name for the records?"

"Sure; it's Jamie Brown."

"Thanks for your assistance, Mr Brown; appreciated."

Suzanna let herself out of the building's main door. The gate's hinges squeaked as she pulled it closed behind her. It had been a productive afternoon.

Chapter 24

"How did the interviews go today, guys?" Angus asked as the team met back at the station.

"Interesting," Owen and Murray said in synchronism, then looked at each other and grinned.

"Are you guys secretly twins?" Suzanna asked.

"No way," Owen replied. "How could I be a twin to gingernut, here?"

"There's nothing wrong with ginger hair. At least my hair doesn't fly around and get in my eyes every time a wind gets up." He scrunched his face as he looked at Owen.

Before either of the pair could continue, Angus interjected. "OK guys, that's enough. Owen, how did your investigations go?"

Owen immediately switched into serious work mode, but Murray still looked peeved. "George Stevens was at home and he had an alibi for the time of the robbery. He'd taken delivery of a package at 09:22. I've seen the evidence of the delivery. So, I reckon that rules him out - unless he's mates with Scotty from Star Trek and he beamed him up from the docks and into his home within a minute?" Owen said, grinning.

"It sounds convincing. However, it's possible that someone else was home and signed for the package. I think you need to speak with the couriers and find out who actually took delivery."

"OK, boss. Will do."

"What about your second man, Owen?"

"I spoke to Jeffrey Wilkins' wife, and she said he was at home looking after their son. But when I checked with the nursery, where the lad goes when they're both at work, they told me that Wilkins had dropped the boy off at 7:30. So, he doesn't have an alibi, and he's keeping secrets from his wife. I need to speak with Mr Wilkins himself and ask him why his wife thinks he was at home, and where he was yesterday morning."

"Hmm, suspicious! I think you and I should pay him a visit tomorrow morning. If he doesn't convince us, we'll bring him in for questioning," Angus directed. "Murray; what were the results of your enquiries?"

"Sutherland wasn't in, but I spoke to one of his neighbours, who said she'd seen him entering their building around 10 am on Wednesday. So I'll have to go back another time and find out where he'd been that morning." Murray said.

"And your second suspect?" Angus prompted.

"It took a while to track down Stevenson, but when I eventually caught up with him, I confirmed from his Hail-a-Ride log he'd been in Portobello at 9:35 am but I don't know where he was before then. He reckoned he'd been waiting for his customer at 9:20. If that's true, he couldn't have been in Leith docks at that time. I'll try to get more details from Hail-a-Ride."

"OK. Thanks, Murray. I think he should remain on our suspects' list, for the moment," Angus said. "Guv, I know you've already updated me on your first two, but if you could just share with the others about all three of your investigations, that would be great."

"Sure. Strachan was sick at home yesterday. I just need to check his phone records and get the phone company to confirm his mobile's location when he called into work. My feeling is, though, that he's not one of our men."

"I confirmed with the school," she went on, "that Jones dropped his daughter off there at 8:35 am that morning. The chances of him having done that then getting to a rendezvous with the other two by 9 am is extremely unlikely. Again, I don't think he's one of our men, but I will call into his house in the morning for a direct chat about his whereabouts."

"Lastly, I spoke with a neighbour who saw Gibson leave at 08:50. There's no way that he could have been at the Lothian Bank by 9 am," Suzanna concluded.

"Thanks, guv," Angus took over. "I visited the home of Stuart Forbes, and his mother confirmed that he was at home having breakfast around 9 am. I've asked her to get her son to call me, so I can have a chat. I don't suspect him, though, unless his mother's a natural liar and had prepared her answer before my visit; that's highly unlikely."

"William Hunter was at home when I called, and it seems he was working from home at the time of the robbery. I need to check some phone records to confirm where he was at the time. If that's confirmed, it will eliminate him. Lastly, Lachlan Russell was at his mother's in Dunfermline on Tuesday and didn't leave her home until nearly ten, Wednesday; so he's not in the frame for the raid. That's all ten covered," Angus concluded. He paused, then spoke again: "Caitlin, how did you get on with the CCTV imagery from the banks in the area?"

"Thought you'd forgotten, boss," Caitlin said, grinning cheekily. "I've checked out all the footage provided, covering the relevant period. We don't have comprehensive coverage, but from what I've seen, there's nothing useful for us. The ATMs outside the banks on George Street caught glimpses of a black Mondeo driving past, but it was impossible to get any identification of the occupants or even confirm that it was the get-away car."

"That's disappointing. Oh well, let's call it a day, and get together as soon as we're all back from our house calls in the morning... Oh! Just one more thing. Murray, did you question Hillary McColloch about the cotton bags used by the robbers?"

"Yes, boss. Initially, she couldn't recall, but when I showed her the Freeset logo, it jogged her memory, and she confirmed she'd seen the label on at least one of the bags, and the bags looked to be identical."

"Right. So it seems that all four bags were the same. When you get time, please do more research to see if you can find out who sells that brand."

"Will do, boss."

"Just a minute; did you say Freeset?" Suzanna interjected. "I visited their factory in Kolkata when I was on my travels there. They're a social enterprise that gives employment to women who have been trafficked into the sex trade. They sell their bags and T-shirts through Fairtrade shops. So, you'd best check out the Fairtrade shops first, Murray."

"OK. Thanks, ma'am."

The team grabbed their coats and Suzanna went back to her office to finish off a few things. There had been excellent progress on the bank raid, and Angus had impressed her again with his leadership and deductive abilities.

Chapter 25

It was a gloomy night with clouds covering what little light might have come from the heavens, as Suzanna headed home. Although there was no frost, it felt icy. She shivered and pulled her coat tighter around her, shielding herself against the Northerly breeze's attempt to suck away her body's heat.

It had been a busy day, dominated by the bank robbery. Fortunately, there had been little else to demand her attention. Just a couple of burglaries reported. Someone had left their back door unlocked, stupid man, she thought; and the other had left a key on the inside of their back door, in which there was a cat flap. Crazy. The burglar only had to push the key out onto the floor and retrieve it through the cat flap.

It amazed her that so many people made it easy for criminals. Some might say they invited burglary, but no one actually invited burglars into their house. Homes become tainted by the unwelcome presence of strangers. But, despite the trauma of burglary, many people were complacent and careless with their security.

She strolled to her convertible car. Whenever it was sunny, she relished dropping the roof and driving with the wind in her hair. But on a chilly, damp night, the roof stayed firmly in place.

Suzanna drove home to Drumsheugh Gardens, which wasn't far from where she worked. Occasionally, she walked to work, but she often needed to use her own car for business, as there weren't enough police cars for every detective to utilise simultaneously. And on dull, damp, wintry days, she preferred to be cocooned in her car.

Living in the city meant she had to park her car on the street and walk a short distance to her apartment, rather than being able to pull up onto her own driveway, but it was worth it to have easy access to the city's amenities and be near her circle of good friends.

***

Suzanna's gym was only a few minutes away and today she planned to change swiftly and head straight there to burn some calories before dinner. She exercised regularly, not only to keep fit, in case her job demanded it (detective chief inspectors had to chase villains occasionally!), but she believed in exercise to stay healthy and live a longer, better quality life.

She crossed the road, ascended the steps to the building's front door and opened it with her key. Stepping inside, she paused as she heard a shout from behind her. Turning, she saw that the guy from one of the ground-floor apartments was waving at her and calling out. She recalled his name and responded to his hailing. "Hi Kennedy; what's up?"

"Glad I caught you," he said, entering the building and closing the door behind him. "This morning, as I was leaving, a door slammed twice on the 1st floor. Shortly after, a young urchin came hurtling down the stairs – nearly knocked into me – and ran out of the door before I could stop him. There was a passing policeman, and he gave chase after I called for him to stop the boy, but I've no idea if he caught him or what he might have been up to, as I went straight off to work. I thought I'd better let you know."

"Oh! That doesn't sound good. I'd better check my apartment straight away. Thanks for telling me." Suzanna turned and marched up the stairs. She tried her key but found it wouldn't turn. On operating the handle, however, the door opened. 'How could the door be unlocked?' she thought.

Suzanna checked around the door for signs of forced entry, but there were none. She must have forgotten to lock the door this morning, but she was normally diligent about locking up. 'Had something distracted me this morning,' she wondered.

She entered the apartment quietly, listening for movement in case there was still an uninvited guest. Moving stealthily and ready to react, she cautiously checked the rooms leading off the entrance lobby before entering the living room. There was little light coming from outside, despite the large bay windows. She switched on the lights and surveyed the room. Nothing appeared to be out of place.

There was nothing of great value on the walls or furniture tops. She had lovely pieces, but none of the stuff had any real value if sold. The 42-inch TV was the only exception, but it was still attached to the wall above the Edwardian fireplace. She checked the cupboard where she stored her cameras. Her digital 35mm SLR was still there, along with its lenses. Moving into the bedroom, she checked her safe and found it still attached to the wall within the fitted wardrobe. It evidently hadn't been tampered with. Nonetheless, she shifted the clothes out of the way and opened the safe.

Her passport was still there, along with her cherished jewellery; some she'd purchased herself or Callum had bought for her, but she'd also inherited pieces from her grandmother. The beautiful turquoise opal on its platinum ring was still in its leather box, enveloped in silk. The one-carat diamond ring Callum had bought her during their trip to Cape Town was also still in its blue leather box; he'd not dared ask for it to be included in the shared wealth calculations when they'd split up.

Satisfied that the thief hadn't broken into the safe, she moved into the kitchen, filled the kettle and pulled out the cafetière. She'd have a coffee and contemplate for a while, before going to the gym.

***

As she sipped her strong, smooth black Sumatran coffee, it occurred to her how condemning she'd been of others, burgled because of their carelessness. Yet here she was sitting in her apartment knowing that she must have been equally careless, but apparently got away with it – by luck. She'd have to change her attitude and be more understanding.

Her mind drifted as she sat on the comfortable sofa. She'd had a brilliant time in South Africa with Callum - a romantic holiday that he'd suggested. They'd spent time on safari in the rugged Kruger National Park, next to the Mozambique border, where they had spotted the 'Big Five'. The Stellenbosch wine lands, with its Dutch colonial influence, had been relaxing and Suzanna had enjoyed tasting their red wines – particularly their pinotage.

She remembered the stinky penguins of the Cape Peninsula, and the fog-blanketed Table Mountain; unfortunately, they didn't see a thing from the top. And there had been the ring purchase – bought to mark their fifth wedding anniversary. The ring was the loveliest in her small collection, and the one she'd cherish for years to come, despite having fallen out with its giver.

The two years since Callum had left had passed swiftly; she'd been so busy. They had been together for 10 years and they'd not rushed into sharing accommodation; it had been eighteen months of dating before they had reached that stage, and a further six months before they'd married.

Life had been good with Callum. She loved how he'd courted her, with flowers and treats and words of endearment. She knew that their love had been true. It's a damned shame that he'd spoil it by giving in to temptation at an office party and falling into an affair. She'd discovered his unfaithfulness by chance and, when confronted about it, he soon caved in under her skilful interrogation, and admitted it. He'd promised to end it, not wanting to lose what they had, and repeated how he was still madly in love with her. But the damage had been done!

Even though she still loved him, she'd never be able to trust him again. If he'd ever worked late or had to go away on business, she'd wonder whether he might be with another woman. Their relationship would never be the same again. She couldn't live like that.

Faced with the truth that there was no future for them, Callum left that day. The affair hadn't become a long-term thing. The temptress wasn't looking for a relationship, just some exciting sex – fired by the risk of getting caught. She didn't care that she'd wrecked a marriage – the selfish bitch.

Suzanna wasn't yet in a long-term relationship with anyone. She missed the companionship of marriage and the regular lovemaking, but she wasn't keen to repeat the experience that she'd just had with Callum. Perhaps James might fill that gap but there was no rush.

She turned on the TV just as the news was starting. The presenter read out the headlines:

"Over three million people have taken part in marches across France, following the death of seventeen people over three days in Paris, related to the satirical magazine Charlie Hebdo. In Mexico, protesters have demonstrated over the disappearance of 43 students from a Teacher Training College. They accuse the police of handing over the missing students to criminal gangs who murdered them and burnt their bodies. In the Middle East, ISIS has released a video, which it claims shows a boy about ten years old executing two men who have "confessed to being Russian spies". It comes just a day after another video showed a child aged around fourteen apparently carrying out a suicide bombing in the Iraqi province of Salahuddin. Back home in the UK, a father has been jailed for mistakenly sending his toddler to his nursery with a bag of drugs and knives instead of his packed lunch. And on the economic front, a major supermarket is to cut 500 jobs."

Why was there rarely any good news? It was always depressing. She turned the TV off again, finished her coffee and quickly changed into her sports gear before heading off to the gym. She'd still not figured out whether the intruder had taken anything from her apartment. Maybe she'd been lucky?

Chapter 26

The smell of sweaty bodies permeated the hall, filled with devices of torture. Voluntary masochists were on nearly all the machines, working their bodies hard and fighting the pain to the sound of whirring wheels. At least, that's how some less-active people might have perceived it. To those training on the equipment, however, this was pleasure. It was a time to focus on their physical needs and to switch off from the worries of work and home as they concentrated on keeping fit.

There were many muscle-bound men and a few women in the weights' area, who seemed to favour bulky limbs. Suzanna rarely saw these people exercising aerobically and wondered whether their focus on muscle-building was good for them. She had never been one to train merely for body shape. She wanted to be fit for life, her sport, and her job. And it helped keep her from putting on weight.

Forty minutes into her session on the cross-trainer, Margo arrived at the gym. Suzanna wouldn't need to knock on her door later. She waved at her neighbour and Margo came over for a chat.

Margo had on long Lycra pants with pink and white training shoes and a pink top. Her hair was long and wavy but tied up into a bun, perching on her head like a giant fluffy doughnut. She had a broad face, with a small nose and substantial lips – perhaps they'd had Collagen treatment.

"How're you doing, Margo?"

"Good, thanks, Suzanna. How's it going with you?"

"Not bad, thanks. I'm glad I bumped into you here, as I wanted a quick chat, anyway!"

"Oh! What about?" enquired Margo.

Suzanna shared about the scruffy boy seen leaving the building and the police chase. And about finding her own apartment unlocked. "I wondered whether he might have been into another apartment and thought of yours. Have you been home yet?"

Margo was astonished at this news. "Yes, I've been home. My door was locked, so I assume he's not been into my apartment. I can't think why the lad might have been in our building, especially at that time of day, and running out in haste. But perhaps there was an innocent reason?"

"I hope so," replied Suzanna. "Can't stop thinking what might be missing, and why I left my door unlocked today."

"Hope it turns out to be nothing. See you later." Margo responded as she moved off to start her exercise regime.

Suzanna continued working on the cross-trainer. She favoured this device, as it exercised her legs, upper body, and arms simultaneously, reducing the number of hours each month she'd have to spend on keeping fit. The more Suzanna thought about the break-in, the less convinced she was that she'd left her apartment unlocked, although she couldn't actually recall locking it.

As she stood in the shower later, the hot water caressing her body, it came to her. When she'd taken her coat from the hall cupboard just before she'd left, she noticed a scarf belonging to Callum hiding behind her Barbour jacket. It looked similar to the one that Callum had bought her on their last Christmas together, but she realised it was definitely his scarf.

She'd been thinking about the need to contact Callum and arrange its collection, or perhaps its posting, as she was leaving the apartment. Just after she'd closed the door, she'd dropped her phone. The distractions had must have caused her lapse in attention to the job of locking up. At least that puzzle was solved.

***

Suzanna sat in her lounge, reading a novel. It was about an Edinburgh-based, hard-drinking, smoking, make-a-mess of everything - but eventually get his man - detective. He was the opposite of Suzanna in character - their only similarity was that they were both successful. Suzanna, however, was clean-living, well-respected and liked.

She loved her job but didn't let it dominate her life. She put in long hours when necessary, when the team needed to follow a warm trail after a murderer, but she managed to get her work-life balance right. Many detectives seemed to be married to the police, and their relationships often failed because they were rarely at home to maintain the bond with their loved ones. Suzanna prided herself on being dedicated to her work, but *not* at the expense of her relationships. She was convinced it hadn't been her fault that her marriage had failed.

Silently, she thanked her great-great-uncle for his legacy that inspired her to become a detective. She looked at the coffee table where she'd last placed the magnifying glass but couldn't see it. Weird, she thought, she was sure she'd left it there... "Ah! *That* could be the answer to what's missing?" She searched the flat, looking everywhere she could have moved it to, and found nothing.

Damn! she thought. It wasn't the monetary value that concerned her; the glass was a family heirloom, and it had sentimental value. It was symbolic of the change in her life's direction – it had changed her fate and steered her to become what she was. It took her back to that day she received the letter confirming her inheritance.

She had unhurriedly opened the sealed envelope with a knife, taking care not to tear the ancient, yellowed and somewhat crumpled document. The flap had been sealed with red wax and embossed with S&P, surrounded by a laurel wreath. It was the seal of Somerville and Peacock, solicitors – the company that had contacted her on her 18th birthday and summoned her to London, all expenses paid.

It was Mr Wrightson, a partner at this company, who had administered the test set by her great-great-uncle, and it was his covering letter that she had read prior to picking up the 60-year-old envelope that she now had in her hands. She had delicately extracted the letter from its envelope, gently unfolded it and read.

Dear Relative

I cannot know to whom will receive this letter, as I will probably have deceased many decades before it is read. If you do not already know, I spent many years on dangerous assignments in the service of His Majesty's Government during the War of 1915–18. It surprised me to have still been alive at the end of this challenging period. I dedicated the remainder of my life to the pursuit of England's most clever criminals – those of which Scotland Yard would probably never have caught without my help.

It has been said that I have a brilliant mind, but also that I am intolerable. I cannot help the way that I am but have lived by the only code I know – my own. Fools who profess to know what they are doing annoy me intensely and there have been many occasions when I have had to knock them down a peg or two.

But to you, dear relative, I give my sincere congratulations. You are obviously no fool because you have passed the test I set. Well done sir, or madam. I trust you will enjoy the inheritance that you will now receive. You may have heard that I came from a wealthy family and expect to receive a fortune, but I must confess that I never owned a property and spent most of my inheritance. What little was left at my death will now be yours but should still be substantial.

With your inheritance, perhaps you could purchase a property or travel the world. But I earnestly hope that you will not relax in your small wealth. Instead, you will use your superior intellect to pursue a worthy career. You have proven yourself to have great insight and analytical talent. Do not waste these. I would be delighted to think your natural abilities would be used to put criminals behind bars, following in my footsteps, but whatever career you choose must be your own destiny.

When you hear about my exploits, and the disparagement of my condemners, I hope you will see through the clouds of disapproval and know that, even though different from most others in my approach and manner, I am still a man of honour and courage. I wish you well for your future and that of your offspring, should you have any. May you and they live a better life because of my gift.

Your Unanticipated Benefactor

Suzanna had noticed the detailed signature of her great-great-uncle. From the flowing mix of strokes and loops, she'd never have been able to decipher the name had she not already known it. She'd placed the letter back on the table and re-read Mr Wrightson's letter.

I write to congratulate you on passing the test set by your distant relative and to inform you in detail about the impact of your success.

It is with great pleasure that I pass onto you the four objects left by your great-great-uncle, with his specific instructions that you should receive them. The first is the test he set, a copy of which you have already seen. The second is the solution to the mystery, so you may understand, not only the answer, but his deduction that your analysis must have mirrored. Thirdly, a letter from your relative for your eyes only and lastly an object, in its cloth bag – his remaining singular possession, which he wished you to have and cherish.

I will transfer the trust fund, that he set aside, into your name. You may withdraw funds from the trust whenever you wish by contacting this office. Please note that, having been wisely invested over the last eight decades, the funds held in the trust are substantial. If you wish to receive financial advice on how best to invest and manage these funds, our company will be happy to assist.

After re-reading the letter, Suzanna had picked up the cloth bag. She'd found it to be weighty, and initially puzzled by its shape, but she'd soon realised what it was, even before seeing it. She'd undone the cord holding it closed, stretched the end until fully open and delved into the thick cotton mouth. Withdrawing the object, its glass and brass had sparkled as it caught the light. The magnifying glass was a beauty, a real artisanal piece. She'd loved the inlaid ivory but frowned when she'd realised that poachers would have ruthlessly killed an ancient, tusked elephant to steal the off-white material.

Suzanna had wondered how many crimes the glass may have helped solve, using it to examine detail not seen by unmagnified sight. She'd thought of her potential future now that she had been blessed. He had hinted at world travel, and she'd already had the longing to explore far-flung places. Now she realised it would be possible for her to go to locations that she would previously have thought beyond her budget, travelling further and for longer. But not until she'd graduated from university. It hadn't occurred to her before that catching criminals might be a career to take, and she'd wondered if her great-great-uncle's desire would be realised.

Now, over twenty years later, she was leading a team of detectives, tracking down criminals and gaining justice for the victims. Suzanna sat, stony-faced, saddened that she'd lost the magnifying glass. She was annoyed that she'd not locked up that morning – the first time she'd ever failed to. What would her family think of her for losing the glass? She'd become its guardian, and she'd been careless. She must get it back, no matter what.

Chapter 27 - Friday 16th January

At 8:30 am, the next morning, Suzanna parked her car on Saughton Mains Place and went straight to Hugh Jones' house. She rang the bell, and a thirty-something, fit-looking man, dressed in a vest and jeans, holding a spatula, opened the door. A sizzling sound could be heard, and the smell of frying bacon wafted out through the door, confirming he was cooking breakfast.

"I hope you're not thinking of attacking me with that weapon, Mr Jones," Suzanna opened.

Hugh smiled at her joke, "I guess you're the police inspector that Kirstine said had called, and my manager mentioned?"

"Yes. I'm Chief Inspector McLeod. Can I come in for a quick chat?"

"Sure, but you must excuse the mess and the chaos – I'm trying to get my daughter ready for school."

"No problem."

Suzanna followed Hugh into his kitchen, where he returned his attention to the sizzling bacon and eggs. He switched off the gas and dished up an egg and two rashers of bacon to his daughter, leaving his food in the pan to stay warm. "I hope this will be quick. It takes all my military training and planning just to get us both fed and Aimee to school for nine."

"It shouldn't take long at all. Could you just tell me what time you started work on Wednesday?"

"Aye; it was my usual 10 am start. I'd have got there about ten-to. I always like to arrive early, so I'm never late."

"And what time would you have left home that day?"

"It's normally about half an hour to get to work, so I leave at 9:15 if Kirstine's on late shift because she can drop Aimee at school. But that day, she was on earlies. I took Aimee to school and went straight to work."

"And you say you arrived at 09:50?"

"Yes."

"But school starts at 9 am, so if you drove straight to work, you'd have got there at 9:30, latest, wouldn't you?"

"Aye, I suppose I would, but, actually, that morning I dropped Aimee off early – just after 8:30, so I had ninety minutes to get to work. I needed some time to myself that morning," Hugh said, moving closer and lowering his voice. "Truth is, we'd not had a good weekend. We'd had a blazing row and Kirstine had threatened to leave me. After I took Aimee to school, I went for a walk up Corstorphine Hill. I sat at the Viewpoint looking over the Golf Course contemplating our relationship."

"Would that be the Rest and Be Thankful Viewpoint?"

"Aye, that's it."

"And did it help you clear your mind and see a way forward?"

"It did, that."

"Can anyone confirm you were at the viewpoint?"

"Well. No one who I could name, but there were other walkers on the path, and a few were at the Viewpoint during my time there."

"Where was it you parked your car for the walk up the Hill?"

"At the end of Balgreen Road, near to Corstophine Road. There's on-street parking allowed there."

"What time would you say you parked up?"

"It would have been about 8:45. I left there around 9:30 to drive to work."

"I'll need your car make and registration number, Mr Jones, for verification of your story."

"It's not a story. It's what I did that day."

Suzanna ignored his pleas and awaited details of his car.

"My car's a Seat Leon. The reg number is WE55 REG."

"It must be easy to remember that number – having WE REG in the registration number!"

Hugh couldn't help smiling, but he said nothing. Suzanna made notes in her book and turned to look him in the eye. "Mr Jones, do you know the Lothian Bank on George Street?"

"Yes, of course; it was the one that got robbed on Wednesday morning," Hugh replied, realising that was why he was being questioned. "You don't think I had anything to do with that robbery, do you?"

"We have to consider that possibility, Mr Jones, given your background, your employment and your availability."

"There's no way I was involved in that robbery. I've never stolen anything in my life."

"What, not even a pen from work?"

"That's not what I meant. Everyone uses work pens for their own use occasionally, don't they? But I'm no criminal. I don't steal from others."

Aimee looked up at her dad, her breakfast plate now cleared of food, looking worried. "Daddy," she spoke, attempting to defuse the situation, "it's nearly time to take me to school." Even at her young age, she sensed there was conflict, and she didn't want her daddy arguing with this strange lady.

"Don't worry, Aimee. There's still time for me to eat breakfast and get you to school. You go and clean your teeth now and get your shoes on."

Aimee left the room, as instructed. "Thanks for your time, Mr Jones.

I doubt I'll need to speak with you again about this. Sorry to have interrupted your morning routine. I'll let myself out."

As she closed the front door, she could hear a spatula lifting the contents of a frying pan onto a plate – back to normal life for Hugh Jones. She returned to her car and drove to the station. All she had to do was get the CCTV checked for Balgreen Road. She felt confident that it would provide validation of Hugh's story.

***

The bus doors opened, and James stepped on board, scanning his bus pass before taking a seat by a window. He liked to look out at the traffic, buildings, and people, unlike most passengers who all had their chins on their chests as they played with their smartphones. No one spoke to those around them anymore. James wondered why everyone was caught up in the virtual world of phones, tablets, and computers. They had their place in today's life but instead of just being communication tools, they seemed to dominate. Blotting out the real world. James was no technology dinosaur. Far from it, but he made sure the devices served him, rather than the other way around.

Despite his dislike of smartphone-itous, he removed his gloves, pulled his phone from his coat pocket, and texted the woman who he was expecting to meet that night. He tucked the phone away again and peered out of the window.

He noticed a woman step out of her front door and nearly slip onto her posterior. There had been a frost again during the night and some surfaces were slippery. It reminded James of when he'd first tried ice skating. His legs had been totally out of control to start with and his bottom had soon become wet and bruised from falling onto the ice multiple times. He got the hang of it after a while, but his ankles ached for the rest of the day once he'd taken the skates off.

It had been ages since he'd last tried skating and wondered whether a trip to the ice rink might make a suitable date night. It would provide an excuse for holding hands and perhaps hugging. He'd have to ask her.

Chapter 28

Angus met Owen in Danderhall and walked together to the Wilkins' home. "How are you this morning, Owen?"

"Apart from freezing to death, I'm fine. I wish this frosty-fog would move away and give us back wet and mild weather."

"Do you not have heating in your house?"

"Of course! But the bloody car heater's bust. The fan stopped working, so it's also difficult to keep the windscreen clear on these chilly damp mornings."

"You will buy Italian cars. They're not suited to Scottish weather," Angus teased.

"Have you never been to the Italian Alps? It's always below zero in the winter, and there are loads of Fiats there. Of course, they're made for the cold."

"I didn't know you'd been to that part of Europe. Was it to ski?"

"Aye it was," Owen replied. "I try to avoid Scottish skiing nowadays, on account of the dangerous ski-tows and atrocious weather."

"Do you need some time out to get the car into the garage?"

"Actually, I meant to call you last night about this. I've booked my car into the garage this morning. If you could follow me there after we're done talking to Wilkins, then take me into work, that would be grand."

They reached the Wilkins' house and Angus pressed the bell-push.

He heard a tune playing somewhere in the house (ding dong, ding dong, ding dong, ding dong) then footsteps approaching, followed by the door opening. Jeffrey Wilkins appeared in the doorway. "What can I do for you?"

Angus held up his warrant card. "Detective Inspector Watson, Edinburgh CID; this is Detective Constable Crawford. We just need to ask you a few questions."

"Oh yeah! The wife said you called yesterday when I was at work. Come on in."

"Thanks; we could do with getting out of the cold. Crawford here is shivering."

"Would you like a tea or coffee? The kettle has just boiled."

"Seeing as how you're offering, yes please; mine's coffee, black, no sugar; the constable will have a white coffee with one sugar."

"I see you guys know each other well. It reminds me of my Army days. All the guys in the troop knew exactly what the others liked to eat and drink. I miss the camaraderie; I have to say. By the way, this wee chap is Owen. Say hello." His son said nothing and looked at the strangers warily.

"Hello, Owen. My name is Owen, too."

The boy's face brightened a bit. "Did you go to Twinkle Twinkle yesterday?"

Little Owen nodded. "Did you have a nice time playing with your friends?"

"Yes," the three-year-old responded. "I played with Sally and Emily." Then his face darkened again, and he looked towards the ground as he recalled something. His large sticky-out ears reminded Owen of Dumbo. "But Robert kept taking our toys. He is four."

"Oh dear! That's not nice, is it? But I expect there were lots of other toys to play with. Plenty for everyone."

"Yes, but we were playing with them first, and he took them. He pushed Emily over, and she bumped her head."

Jeffrey placed two steaming mugs on the table in front of the detectives. "There you go, gents... So, what was it you wanted to speak with me about?"

"Your wife said you were at home yesterday at 9 am, looking after Owen. We just needed to confirm facts with you because she wasn't here to verify this." Angus stated.

Owen looked around as Angus led the questioning. The kitchen lacked cupboards and was cluttered with crockery and appliances. He wondered how they managed to prepare food as there was hardly any surface free to work on. It had likely been fitted out in the 1980s and was well overdue for an upgrade. The worktop by the sink was swollen from water that had penetrated the chipboard, and there were several places by the cooker where the Formica was burnt and blistered.

"Oh! I see," Wilkins responded. "You'll have spoken with the nursery staff and know that I dropped Owen in at 7:30 instead of 12:30, as planned."

"Correct. Care to tell us where you were that morning, then?" Owen asked.

"I went fishing."

"So why does your wife think you were home, looking after Owen?"

"Well, to be honest, we've been having some issues lately. My wife's not happy about the wage I'm bringing home and the weird shifts I work. She misses the Army life more than me: the secure base, with lots of other Army wives to socialise with, the Sergeants' Mess, the cheap housing and good wages. Things are tight now, and life's not so good."

Angus and Owen just listened and sipped their drinks. The black coffee tasted bitter; it was no doubt made with instant coffee powder. Angus regretted asking for black, no sugar. He should have had white with sugar, to mask the poor-quality coffee.

"I really needed some leisure time," Wilkins continued, "and I like to fish because sitting by the water waiting for the float to bob is meditative. Catching a fish isn't important; it's just my way of relaxing. The reason I didn't tell Lindsay was because it cost us money to have Owen in the nursery, so I could go fishing, and I knew that she'd not approve, as money's so scarce. I understand her concerns, but I have to have time out or I'd go mental."

"I know what you mean. Leisure time away from your partner is important for a relationship. I heard that mentioned on the radio just this morning, actually," Owen commented.

"Is there any way we can verify that you were fishing at 9 am? And where did you go fishing?" Angus asked.

"I was at Duddingston Loch. The fishing's not bad. There's a few perch, roach and carp to be had there."

"Did anyone see you at the Loch?" Angus enquired.

"There were other people around, but no one that I could name."

"OK, sir. We'll see if we can find anyone to corroborate your presence at Duddingston Loch. If we do, then we'll not need to visit again," Angus stated. "But if we don't, you'll remain on our suspect list and we may have to return."

"I hope you find someone, then. I wouldn't want Lindsay to know about the fishing, and me spending extra money on the nursery."

"Daddy went fishing, and I went to Twinkle Twinkle," little Owen said.

"Blast it. I forgot there was another pair of ears in the room. I hope he doesn't repeat that."

"Good luck with that one, sir. We'll be on our way. Thanks for your time. And best of luck with sorting things out with the wife," Angus concluded.

Angus had been in a long-term relationship, but they'd split up after five years together. That's why he'd taken the London job – to get away from her and the reminders of the break-up bitterness. He still couldn't figure out why she'd become so distrusting and unjustifiably jealous. Every time he'd worked late, she'd thought he was staying away because there was someone else that he'd prefer to be with.

He'd loved Aimee from the moment they'd met, but her possessiveness had become almost psychotic and she'd become violent. When his colleagues had questioned him about the facial bruising, one day, he'd had to lie. It took nearly a year of abuse before he left her.

Outside, the detectives conferred. "I reckon he's telling the truth. What do you think, boss?"

"I agree, Owen. But we need evidence, rather than just a feeling that he's a likeable chap and a good dad, who's having a relationship issue with his wife. Let's just check with some neighbours in case any of them saw him that morning."

Chapter 29

Angus and Owen split up and knocked on doors either side of Wilkins' home. "Good morning, ma'am, I'm Detective Inspector Watson. Could you spare me a minute?"

"Sorry, Inspector, I don't even have a minute. I'm late for work and will miss the bus," she said, pushing past him and closing the door after her. She strode off up the path to the road, leaving Angus to follow.

"Oh well! I guess I'll try the next house then!"

Owen rang the bell of the house across the street and a woman wearing an apron opened the door, and he could smell bread toasting and brewed tea. "Yes."

"Sorry to trouble you, ma'am. I'm Detective Constable Crawford. We're carrying out routine enquiries. Could you spare me a minute?"

"It will have to be just one. I'll be leaving for work in fifteen minutes and I've yet to feed the kids."

"I wondered whether you might have seen any of your neighbours on Wednesday morning?"

"Wednesday; hmm. I saw Jeff Wilkins taking his son to the nursery. At least I assume that's what he was doing."

"What time would that have been?"

"7:20, I think. I thought it was strange, as Owen doesn't normally go to nursery until the afternoon, because Jeff's usually at home in the mornings."

"Is that right? Did you see any other movements that morning?"

"What's this about, officer?"

"I'm sorry, ma'am, I'm not at liberty to say, but anything you can tell us could be important. Did you see anything else that morning?"

"I saw Jeff again when I left home, about 8 am. He was heading off out by himself."

"Was he carrying anything? Do you recall?"

"Just a small backpack, I think."

"And how was he dressed that morning?"

"Jeans and a dark jacket, as far as I recall."

"Is there anything else you can remember about that morning?"

"No, that's all I can remember."

"Thanks for your help, ma'am. Could I just make a note of your name?"

"It's Shirley Higgins."

"Thanks Ms Higgins. I'll leave you to get back to feeding the kids."

"Its Mrs Higgins, actually."

"Noted. Thanks for clarifying that. There are so many couples living together nowadays that I never assume they're married."

"True," she said, then closed the door.

***

They tried a few more houses, but no-one could recall anything useful. There was no sighting of Wilkins carrying a fishing box out to his car. But that still didn't mean that he hadn't gone fishing. His kit might have already been in his car.

"I wish we had something to corroborate Wilkins' going fishing story, as I believe him. But he matches our profile. He's the right height and build for the big man in the robbery, and he appears to have had the opportunity. We'll go to Duddingston Loch and ask around. But first, let's get this car of yours into the garage. You lead the way."

***

Owen dropped his Fiat at the garage and got into Angus's car, who drove them to Duddingston Loch. "It's 8:30 now, so if anyone saw him fishing around this time on Wednesday, that should rule him out from involvement in the bank raid. I'll head along this way. You take that bank, Owen," Angus said, pointing in the direction he wanted him to take. "I'll meet you back here in thirty minutes, max."

"OK, boss. I'll see you soon. The path doesn't go far in either direction. I'm looking forward to getting back to the station for a decent cup of coffee."

They split up and walked along the Loch's banks, talking to anyone who they could find.

Twenty minutes later, they met up again. "Did you find anyone who'd been here on Wednesday morning, Owen?"

"No, boss. Did you?"

"Yes. See that chap over there? The one with the grey, shaggy beard and quilted jacket?"

"Yes."

"He's retired and regularly fishes here. He says it's his way of getting some peace. If he stays at home, his wife loads him with jobs to do. I've heard that one a few times!"

"Me too."

"He was here about seven on Wednesday morning and didn't leave until after 9:30. He says you have to get here early if you want to catch anything. Anyway, he's certain that there was no-one matching Wilkins' description here that day. In fact, he was sure there were no other anglers at all. So, it looks like Wilkins was lying to us, and his wife, about where he was. Let's head back to the station and discuss this with the team. But it's looking like we'll need to bring him in for formal questioning."

"I agree. I could do with warming up before we head off out anywhere again, though."

***

The morning rituals of greeting everyone and grabbing a cup of coffee over, Suzanna went through to the uniformed sergeant manning the desk, and reported her magnifying glass stolen. Pete Reilly, the sergeant on duty, logged the theft, noting time, date, location and the supporting documentation. "I'll pass the info up to your department, ma'am," Pete said. "I guess it will add to the growing evidence of multiple break-ins that have been occurring. Might help your team find a pattern?"

"Yes, Pete. Can you give me the case number, please, so I can give them the heads-up at the morning briefing?"

"Certainly, ma'am. It's 3478652."

"Got it, Pete. Thanks. By the way, how's that teenage daughter of yours getting on? What's her name? Bridget, isn't it?"

"Aye, that's right. She's doing well thanks, ma'am. She seems to have pulled through her anorexic phase, and is back on track, eating properly and able to concentrate at school. They say we'll have to keep an eye on her, though, as she's almost as liable to turn back to her old ways, as an alcoholic is to the drink."

"Good to hear that she's eating well again, Pete. I'd best be getting back to the office. I don't want to be late for the briefing. See you around."

"That you will, ma'am. Thanks for asking about after Bridget."

Chapter 30

There was a hubbub in the office, with multiple conversations going on, as Suzanna entered. "OK, team, let's get underway." The morning briefing was later than normal because of the early morning house calls. "You first, Angus. Bring us up to date on developments in the bank raid case."

"Well, we've now questioned almost all ten of the short-listed suspects and eliminated most of them. Owen and I paid a visit to Jeffrey Wilkins this morning, and we came away believing him to be off the list. His alibi, however, was that he was fishing at Duddingston Loch, but we visited the Loch and found a man who had been there that morning and was certain that Wilkins wasn't there. So we need to question him again... Guv, please update us on Hugh Jones."

"I'd say Mr Jones is off our list. But I just want to check CCTV for where he said he'd parked, to be sure that his story holds up. Una, could one of your team do that for me, please?"

"Sure, boss. Zahir, one for you, please," she said, looking across at the newest member of her team. Zahir's family had migrated to Scotland from Bangladesh. He was dark-skinned and had almost black straight hair. His eyebrows nearly touched above his small, narrow nose. At just 25, he was still fit and slim.

"OK, boss... What was the location, ma'am?"

Suzanna wrote the location on a piece of paper and passed it to Zahir.

"I'll get onto it straight away."

"Thanks," Angus said. "I checked on Hunter's phone records and got a rough location from the phone company for where he'd made the calls. This confirmed he was at home around 9 am on Wednesday. So he's out of the picture."

"So of the ten on our shortlist, we have Jeffrey Wilkins, Andrew Stevenson and Charles Sutherland remaining as suspects," Angus summarised.

Suzanna noticed Una had reacted to hearing the name Charles Sutherland. She wondered why.

"Stevenson wouldn't match the description of either of the robbers," Angus continued, "as he's only 5 foot 8 inches tall. But he could have been the driver."

"Stevenson doesn't have an alibi for the time of the robbery," Murray added. "And he lied to me! He said he was in Portobello, waiting for a customer at 9:20 am, but I checked with Hail-a-Ride and they confirmed the customer didn't request the ride until 9:30 am, and when Stevenson took the booking, he was already in Portobello. In fact, he was on the street where Sutherland lives. Suspicious, I'd say!"

"Definitely suspicious," Angus concurred. "Sutherland matches the general description and profile for the second robber – the one that held the gun on the teller and took the money. Wilkins could be the big man in the robbery because he is of similar height and build, and it would seem that he had the opportunity. But we have nothing to place him in the Leith Docks area or George Street yet, or to connect him with the other two guys."

At that point in the meeting, PC Graham White popped his head around the door, "Excuse me, ma'am, I was passing the office earlier and noticed the suspect photos on the board. I recognised one of the pictures – Charles Sutherland."

"Interesting," Suzanna commented. "Where do you recognise him from?"

"I attended a road traffic accident yesterday afternoon, and when I arrived, Sutherland was looking after the injured boy. He'd dealt with the situation, got someone to call in the accident and carried out first aid on the lad. After he briefed the paramedic, he slipped away without leaving his details."

"A bit of a humble hero, it seems," Angus suggested. "Graham, as you saw him recently and may remember his body shape and walking action, and heard his voice, I'd like you to have a look at the video footage from the Lothian. Perhaps you'll recognise him?"

Una briefly smiled, as she heard Charlie described as a hero, and Suzanna locked this second reaction into her brain for later.

"Happy to do that, sir. Shall I pop back in about 20 minutes?"

"That'd be great. Murray, please look after Constable White when he returns." Murray nodded to acknowledge the tasking.

"I think we need to widen our net of suspects," Suzanna suggested. "The only person on the list from the Army who met the physical description we had of the apparent leader – 6 foot 2 inches tall and built like a rugby player is Wilkins."

"Agreed. We definitely need to question Wilkins again – formally this time. Although he came across as a decent guy and wouldn't have beaten up the female customer, you never can tell. Some people are excellent actors. I'll bring him in for questioning. But if Wilkins isn't our man, we need other options," Angus continued.

"Can anyone think of someone who might meet the description and profile but who is not on our list from the Army? Maybe they've been out of the Army a bit longer than we projected?" There was no response from the team. "Murray, please run a search for anyone on the criminal database who might meet that description. If they've been arrested or were a person of interest in a violent crime, that would be another indicator to focus on."

"Will do, boss." He swivelled his chair to start searching while the meeting continued. But then swung back. "Boss, before I forget, I thought you'd like to know. I identified shops in the city selling Fairtrade goods, then asked uniform to pop in when passing and ask about any recent sales of Freeset cotton bags."

"Any response from the shopkeepers?

"Yes. One remembered selling four bags to a fella last week. He remembered because the purchaser was a tall, military-looking guy. He wasn't the normal type of customer who would have bought cotton bags in his shop. Most of his customers are women, either hippy-styled with nose-rings or mature middle-class. I'll pop into the shop as soon as I can and show him pictures of the suspects, to see if it might have been one of them."

"Great. Well done, Murray." Murray spun his chair away again to start the search.

"Another thought for you, Angus," Suzanna offered. "We could be looking for an ex-Marine or RAF Regiment man. Perhaps someone from those forces may have left and returned to Edinburgh?"

"Good point, guv. I'll get the team to contact the Air Force and Marines," Angus responded. "Caitlin, any news from forensics regarding evidence from the crime scene or the get-away car?"

"Yes, boss. We have possible DNA evidence from the car: hair and skin particles on the seats, along with wool fragments that could be from the balaclavas. If we get our hands on the woollen headgear, it might match to that found in the car. We need to get the car owner's DNA checked so we can eliminate their hair and skin particles from those found. There was also a partial fingerprint on the door, which could be the driver's."

"We'll need to get the suspect's DNA when we pull them in to see if either matches with the skin and hair evidence from the car. If we get any matches, we'll have our physical evidence tying them to the crime,"

Suzanna suggested. "As long as White confirms the identification of Sutherland, I think we'll have sufficient circumstantial evidence to justify a search warrant for his home."

"Agreed," Angus stated and turned towards Caitlin.

"I'll sort that out, boss, as soon as PC White has completed his review of the video footage," Caitlin offered before being asked.

Owen re-joined the conversation, having checked his messages. "Boss, there's been an interesting development that definitely puts Stevenson into the frame for the bank job. He's just paid cash into his bank account - £5,000, and he's paid off his credit card bills in cash. One card had nearly £20k outstanding! He'll have a hard time explaining that when we bring him."

"Thanks, Owen," Angus responded. "Good to hear. The evidence is growing rapidly."

"We've also got Sutherland's accounts under scrutiny, so we'll see if anything flags up on them." Owen turned and went back to his desk.

"Caitlin, make that two warrants, then. Stevenson and Sutherland. Hopefully, we'll have the warrants by early afternoon, so let's plan on bringing in the two suspects in at 15:00 and organise a simultaneous search of their homes."

"Would you like us to get the car owner's DNA for you?" Una offered.

"Yes, please, Una, that would be great."

"Are we done on the bank raid?" Suzanna asked.

"There was one thing that just came to mind, ma'am," Owen said, after swinging back into the conversation, on his office chair. "I recall the bank manager said he'd instructed his deputy, Mr Bilberry, to put most of the recent cash delivery into the safe, but he didn't do that. He was sitting at the customer services desk when the robbers burst into the bank, and all the cash from the delivery was still behind the counters."

"OK, go on," Suzanna prompted.

"Well, when I interviewed Bilberry, he told me he'd been at the George Street branch for five years as deputy manager, but I picked up some resentment in his voice. He sounded peeved that they'd posted a new manager into the branch two years ago, instead of promoting him to the job. Maybe he collaborated with the robbers to get back at the bank? He could have purposely ignored his boss's direction to ensure there was plenty of cash for the robbers to take?"

"Interesting idea, Owen. Good thinking. We'll make a detective out of you, yet!" She turned to Angus to encourage his thoughts on the suggestion.

"We'd best bring Bilberry in for questioning. See if he cracks under the pressure of a formal interview. Owen. It was you that came up with this line or query, so you bring him in and conduct the interview."

"Will do, boss." His face brightened, obviously pleased to have been acknowledged and given the reign to follow up.

"I think we've got enough to be going on with now," Angus concluded.

"Right then, you guys crack on with your investigation. We need to see more progress. Una and I can follow up on her team's work after a comfort break."

Chapter 31

Suzanna re-entered the office and noticed Owen still at his desk. "Owen. Aren't you supposed to be on your way to Lothian Bank?"

"Yes, ma'am. Just leaving," he said, standing and moving towards the coat hooks.

She turned back to her other DI's team. "Una. Please update us on the series of minor thefts."

Una just turned her head and looked at Rab, who responded to the unspoken invitation to brief on his case. Una's expression reminded Suzanna of her mother. That look could make people feel they'd done something wrong, even if they hadn't.

"Mairi and I visited the locations where the thefts had taken place and knocked on doors near the scenes of the robberies, around the time that they'd occurred. We found two people who'd noticed an unknown boy in their neighbourhood close to the time when the robberies had taken place. They'd thought nothing about it before but when questioned, they both realised the likely connection."

"The one I spoke with," Mairi interjected, "didn't get a look at the lad's face but described him as wearing jeans and a hoody sweatshirt, and Converse-style shoes."

"Why did she say Converse-style?" Suzanna enquired.

Her mind wrenched back to the present by the DCI's question. Mairi responded: "she knows the brand logo because her son has Converse shoes. These looked similar but didn't have the Converse star logo on them."

"Fair enough!"

"The neighbour I spoke to," Rab re-joined, "didn't get a good look at the lad's face either, but she noticed his nose was long."

"That sounds like more than a coincidence," Suzanna commented. "The boy I saw outside my apartment had a long pointy nose. If I'd been at school with him, the kids would have nicknamed him Concorde. I guess it's worth me mentioning now that Sergeant Reilly will soon pass you further information about this case. He's just doing the formalities now. You'll remember the mention about the chase of a youth from near my home? Well, it would appear that he *had* been in my apartment and stolen my main treasure: the magnifying glass that I inherited from my great-great-uncle."

"He stole your magnifying glass!" Murray exclaimed from the other side of the office. "How will you be able to solve crimes without it, ma'am?"

"Hilarious, Murray. I didn't realise the glass was missing at first. Nothing else had been taken. I can only assume that something had disturbed him, so he grabbed the glass and ran for it." Murray went back to his work without another word, realising that he'd perhaps overstepped the mark.

"So, you think this lad might have been the one you saw outside your building who'd seemed out of place?" Una asked.

"Based on the pointed nose description, we've just heard from a neighbour near one of the other burglaries, most likely. The glass is a family heirloom. I need you to focus on getting it back for me."

"After the meeting, could you spare half an hour to get a facial composite done, ma'am?"

"Yes, of course, Rab. It should be easy to do an e-fit, given his unusual features. I've brought in documents and images of the magnifying glass that should make it easier to identify when it's found."

"Thanks, ma'am. I'll get the images and descriptions sent out to Uniform and get some PCs to call into pawn shops in Leith, as a priority. After that, we can spread the word further around the city. I've got PC Fleming coming in this morning, so I can quiz him about the boy he chased. I'll show him the facial composite and see if he recognises the boy."

Rab continued, "I'll get forensics to visit your flat and check it out for fingerprints. Perhaps we might get a match that, when we find the boy, will prove he'd been there?"

"Did you check out CCTV for sightings of the youth?"

"We made a start on it but have seen nothing yet. Again, once we have the E-fit, that should help us spot the lad if he shows up on a camera."

"Have you checked out truancies and late arrivals in Leith's schools?"

"We contacted all the schools and asked for the information. The school administrators agreed to email us the data. A couple have responded already, and we're expecting to get the rest of the data in this morning. If it isn't forthcoming, we'll chase them up."

"Good. OK. I think we have one more case update to do. Zahir, what do you have for us on the muggings?"

"I studied CCTV footage from around the city and saw someone dressed like the mugger in three of the clips. One clip was from near to one of the mugging locations. It was recorded around the time of the mugging, so that places him in the area."

"What about the other two clips, Zahir?" Suzanna enquired.

"He was wearing similar but not identical clothing in the other two video clips. In one, he was riding pillion on the back of a scooter, and the helmet matches the one seen in the first clip. The third clip shows him carrying his helmet and the scooter riding off. I'm pretty sure it's the same guy. In the last clip, we got a partial facial shot. He looks to be of Middle Eastern descent."

"Any other thoughts on this one from anyone else?" Suzanna opened to the team.

Mairi responded: "My understanding is that the muggings have mostly been bag snatches and usually from women or girls. How about we deploy a woman police officer, dressed in civilian clothing, as bait, where most of the muggings have been taking place?"

"Are you offering to be the bait, Mairi?" Una asked.

"Why not! If he tries to take my bag, I'll floor him."

"Very commendable, Mairi," Suzanna commented. "But we'll have to ensure you have back-up close by to come to your aid if it gets nasty. Although there's no history of it yet, he may carry a knife to ward off any attempts to apprehend him. The last thing we'd want is you getting stabbed."

"I am well practised at disarming knife attackers, ma'am."

Suzanna knew Mairi was stronger than the average woman and was fit and agile. Her favoured sports were hockey and tennis, so there was always one to keep her engaged throughout the year. But she didn't take part in any fighting sports, and her only combat experience came from occasional police training sessions.

"In theory, you are, Mairi, but you've only done it in training so far, and real-world combat doesn't follow the neat scenarios our trainers use to practise the techniques. So, I'll remain cautious about putting you out as bait."

"Ma'am," Mairi said. "I've got data on sums stolen by date over the last three months."

"Does it tell us anything?"

"What I see is that the total stolen each month has been about £500," she responded. "That might keep a drug habit going."

"Or perhaps enough to pay the rent for a shared flat in the city," Zahir suggested.

"So, where does this get us? If the robberies are feeding a drug habit, we'd draw a blank because we can't go around asking the drug dealers to rat on one of their customers. What we haven't seen yet is an unnecessary use of force used by the mugger. A drug addict wouldn't be so restrained. If the muggings were just to pay his rent, he'd need other income to live on. It seems extreme to carry out multiple muggings every month just to pay the rent. Besides, anyone who can't pay their rent because of a lack of income can apply for housing benefit... Ah! just supposing this guy is an illegal immigrant who can't claim benefits to help pay the rent. That could be the answer?"

"Excellent point, ma'am; that would fit with Zahir's suggestion that he appears to be from the Middle East. Most of the illegal immigrants are from that region of the world, and from North Africa." Una said.

"A lot of illegal immigrants work in the lowest-paid jobs. Zahir, please get the image of the mugger circulated around Uniform and ask them to look out for anyone working at a hand car wash who looks similar. Oh! And to look out for a motor-scooter parked nearby," Suzanna directed. "Make sure they have a copy of the scooter on the CCTV still image."

"Will do, ma'am."

Mairi continued, "What I also see in the data is that the next mugging is likely due within two to three days. If we're to catch him, we need someone, or a team, on the streets in plain clothes keeping an eye out for the mugger."

"Agreed," Una said.

"I also agree, Mairi," Suzanna said. "From what I've seen in the data, it suggests the crimes take place early afternoon and, as Mairi mentioned, the victims are always women."

Moving to the city map on the office wall, Suzanna carried on: "If we draw a line around the sites of the muggings, we can see that they were all carried out in the Old Town area of the city. Assuming that the mugger observes his victims before stealing from them, and bearing in mind the time of day, I'd suggest he might hang out around one of the fast-food restaurants or coffee bars."

"Thanks, ma'am, so we should plan on a Monday stake-out in that area, then?" Una proposed.

"Agreed. Let's do it."

Chapter 32

Murray tapped on Suzanna's open door. "Excuse me, ma'am, I've just spoken to Strachan's boss, and he confirmed Strachan had called in sick around 8:30 am on Wednesday, sounding full of cold. The phone company has provided a geo-fix on the phone, for around the same time on Wednesday. As you expected, he was telling the truth. He must have been at home in Longstone."

"Thanks, Murray. That's another door closed, then. Did PC White come back to look at the bank CCTV footage?"

"Yes, ma'am. He's looking at the footage now. I'll let you know how it goes."

***

"How's it going, Graham?" Murray asked as he got back to the computer screen that PC White was staring at.

"I've re-run the video clip five times now and the more I watch and listen to it, the more convinced I am that it is the man who provided first aid at the accident. Obviously, without a face, I can't be 100% certain."

"What confidence do you have that the guy in the video is Sutherland?"

"I'd say 75-80%."

"That's good enough for me. We'll log that as a positive identification, caveated that it was by body shape, motion and voice, but not facial recognition."

***

"Ma'am," Zahir said to catch her attention.

Suzanna looked up from her computer screen. "Yes, Zahir?"

"I've checked out the CCTV and it shows Jones' car parked at Balgreen Road when he said it was."

"Great. I thought it would be. I appreciate the speedy work on that one, Zahir. We can close that potential lead now and focus on the others."

"Thanks, boss. No problem." Zahir headed back to his desk, happy that the DCI was pleased with his work.

***

At 11:15, Suzanna and Angus joined Murray and Wilkins in the interview room. Wilkins sat back from the table with his right ankle resting on his left knee and his hands loosely gripping his horizontal leg. His casual manner gave the impression of innocence, or perhaps it could have been over-confidence.

"Mr Wilkins. Thank you for agreeing to come in and speak with us. This interview is formal and is being recorded. If you wish representation by legal counsel, please speak up before we continue the interview," Angus stated.

"No need for lawyers. I've nothing to hide and have faith in you guys to do your job."

"OK. Then we'll get underway." Angus switched on the tape.

"Mr Wilkins, you are here to answer questions in relation to involvement in the robbery that took place at the Lothian Bank on George Street two days ago. Do you understand?"

"Aye, I understand."

"Please explain where you were at 9 am on the day in question."

"As I mentioned before, I was fishing at Duddingston Loch."

"But you cannot provide any evidence to support that claim."

"No. I was by myself. I didn't see anyone I knew who could confirm that I was there."

"Did you see anyone else at the Loch? If so, please describe them and where they were."

"I couldn't be specific. I saw several people in passing."

"Were there any other anglers near to where you say you fished?"

Wilkins thought for a while. "I saw someone about 100 yards away, but I never went near him and I've no idea what he looked like."

"Did you catch any fish that morning?"

"I caught a couple of small fish. Nothing to brag about."

"And what fish would they have been?"

Wilkins did not immediately answer, evidently having a slow recall or taking time to think up an answer. "One was a perch and the other a roach."

"Tell me about the equipment that you took with you that day."

"I had my fishing box that acts as a seat and holds all my gear."

"It must be a sizable box, Mr Wilkins. Where do you store this box when you're not using it?"

"In the shed, out back."

"Was that the case on Wednesday?"

"Yes. I always stack it in the shed, to avoid the wife complaining."

"The problem we have, Mr Wilkins, is that you say you were at the Loch at 9 am that day, but you can't describe anyone at the Loch who might have seen you. You say you used your fishing box, which you keep in your shed, yet we have witnesses who saw you go to your car, carrying merely a small backpack. Please explain how the fishing box got from your shed to your car."

After a brief delay, Wilkins responded. "I took the box out to the car early that day before I made breakfast. The witness you have must have seen me later, when I was going to the car, having already loaded it."

"What time would that have been, Mr Wilkins?"

"About 7:15, just before I took Owen to the nursery."

"So, did you leave Owen unattended in your house, whilst you loaded your fishing box?"

"No. We left as soon as I'd loaded it."

"That's interesting because we have a witness who saw you taking Owen to school and there was no mention of you loading a box into your car." Angus let that sink in for a few seconds. "What did you have in your backpack that morning, Mr Wilkins?"

"I had my sandwiches and a bottle of water."

"Do you know a man by the name of Charles Sutherland?"

Wilkins thought before answering. "I've heard the name before somewhere, but I don't know him."

"What about Andrew Stevenson?"

"Never heard of him."

"How would you explain the payment of £26,000 into your bank account yesterday, sir?"

"Bloody hell! You seriously think I was involved in this robbery, don't you? This isn't a 'clear up a few facts' discussion, is it?"

Angus was silent.

"Look. I paid the money into my account by cheque. You'll be able to trace it back to the solicitors that sent it to me. It was a very welcome inheritance from my deceased uncle. I didn't know I was getting anything until I received the cheque."

"I imagine you were over the moon to receive the money, given that you had a credit card balance of over £9,000!"

"You really have done your digging, haven't you?"

"It's our job, Mr Wilkins."

"Well, I'm not sure I want to say anything else. It seems like you're trying to pin this on me."

"We're just seeking the truth. You served in the Army for a long time, I believe?"

"Eighteen years. It was an excellent career, even given the two tours in Afghanistan – maybe that's where I heard the name of the guy you mentioned, Sutherland, wasn't it?"

"Perhaps it was. And perhaps you knew Charles Sutherland and met up with him again after your discharge, and perhaps he suggested the bank raid. The money would certainly have helped with your debts, wouldn't it?"

"I told you. The money was an inheritance. You'll find out if you check."

"Oh! We will, Mr Wilkins. We will. The thing is: you fit the profile for this job. You served with other suspects. You had the opportunity. You needed the money and you've just received a substantial sum into your bank account, *and* you fit the description of one of the robbers."

"That may well be, but you've no other evidence."

"They are the words of a guilty man!" Angus stated. "The trouble is, Mr Wilkins, we know you're happy to lie when the circumstances suit you, as you did to your wife. So why should we believe you when you tell us you were at the Loch? We've spoken to a man who was at the Loch that day and he categorically stated that no one matching your description was there at the time you said you'd been."

Wilkins thought for a while, weighing up his response. "OK. I'll tell you the truth."

"That would be good, sir."

"About five years ago, I had a brief affair with the wife of a colleague. It was unplanned, and it quickly fizzled out. But it resulted in her having a baby. The husband still doesn't know, and my wife doesn't either. If either of the spouses got wind of our affair and its result, there would be two marriages wrecked. That morning I went to visit the mother of my daughter, Ailsa. Catriona's husband was at work. If he were to find out I was there, he'd put two and two together and the result would be all hell let loose."

"So, if we added two and two, what would it make? Are you still having relations with this woman?"

"The truth is, I'm in love with her and the sex is fantastic. But I also love my Lindsay, and Owen, of course. I daren't risk them finding out about my affair. It would be disastrous. That's why I lied. Please don't tell my wife."

"Thank you for this additional information. I just wish you'd been honest with us in the first place. Given your willingness to lie to us, though, we will, of course, need to confirm what you've just told us, with the woman that you've been having an affair with. Name and address, please, sir."

"OK, but I need you to promise that you'll be sensitive about how you gain the confirmation, so no one else finds out about this."

"We'll do our best, sir. We have no wish to wreck homes. Whether this happens now, though, because of this investigation, or not, it's bound to get out, eventually. Secrets don't always stay secret."

"I know. Every time I've been with Catriona, I've felt guilty and worried that we'll be found out. But the excitement of the affair being clandestine and risky is like a drug."

"Time for rehab, then sir?"

"You may be right, Inspector."

"We'll leave it there for the moment, but if this latest story turns out to be untrue, you will certainly hear from us again. Please provide contact details for your lover to the constable. Interview terminated at 11:47 am."

Chapter 33

Owen walked into the office, accompanied by the deputy bank manager, and went straight into Interview Room 1. Bilberry looked worried. "Good," thought Angus. "He's more likely to spill the beans if he's anxious."

***

The doorbell tinkled as Caitlin entered the hairdresser's, reminding her of the brass bells traditionally attached to the doors of local general stores. But this one was an electronic imitation.

"Mrs Catriona Taylor?" Caitlin asked as the manager – a thirty-something Jennifer Aniston look-alike – gazed at her quizzically. She had blonde straight hair, cut in a short bob, and her make-up had been skilfully applied to enhance her natural good looks, without being over-the-top.

"Yes. Can I help you?"

"Not me personally, but perhaps you could help Jeffrey Wilkins?" she said in a hushed voice. "I'm Detective Sergeant Findlay."

Catriona looked around to see if anyone might have heard what the sergeant had said. She was sure that Blair would be earwigging, even though she appeared to be concentrating on applying dye to Mrs Walker's hair. "Let's go through to the office," she suggested, holding a door open for Caitlin to enter. "Go straight through."

"Blair," Catriona raised her voice. Blair turned, feigning a lack of interest in what was going on. "Please hold the fort. I have to speak privately with this lady." Blair nodded and mouthed, "OK!"

The office was compact; it had just enough room for a small pine, knee-hole desk, a two-drawer filing cabinet, with a printer sat on top, and two chairs. Caitlin sat in the chair closest to the door, and Mrs Taylor took the other behind her desk. Despite its size and likely little utilisation, it was neat and tidy (like the manager). Caitlin could smell polish, and she noticed the desk was streak-free and had a fresh sheen; it felt silky to her touch.

"So, what's this about Jeff?"

"You do know Jeffrey Wilkins, then?"

"Yes. He's a good friend."

"How long have you known Mr Wilkins?"

"About five years now. What's this about?"

"We're carrying out some enquiries and your friend's name has come up in connection with a certain event. We're just trying to clarify his situation, to see whether we need to follow up on the lead we have. It's nothing to worry about."

"OK. Go on."

"How would you describe your relationship with Mr Wilkins?"

"As I said, he's a good friend. We see each other a couple of times a month."

"Is his wife included in these get-togethers with Mr Wilkins?"

"No. It's normally just the two of us."

"Would you say that your friendship with Mr Wilkins is a secret?"

"Yes, it's very much a secret. Mrs Wilkins isn't aware of our friendship."

"You know that he's married then. Does it bother you?"

"No. I don't mind sharing him with his wife. He's dedicated to his son and doesn't want to leave Lindsay. I can live with that."

"If Mrs Wilkins was to find out about his affair with you, do you think she would leave him?"

"It would cause a massive falling-out, but whether she'd leave him, I couldn't say."

"How would your husband react if he found out you regularly meet with Mr Wilkins, in secret?"

"He'd likely shout the house down, slap me and walk out, then go and beat up Jeff."

"Would you mind if he left you?"

"Yes. I do love him, despite also being in love with Jeff. It's hard loving two men and challenging to keep up the two relationships. But I just can't let go. Jeff's the father to my daughter, Ailsa."

"When was the last time that you spoke with Mr Wilkins?"

"We spoke last night, briefly, about our next date. Jeff suggested we get a weekend away somewhere."

"Have you seen Mr Wilkins this week at all?"

"Yes, he was with me on Wednesday morning. I don't open the shop on Wednesdays. So, I was available and so was Jeff. His wife and my husband were at work. He came to my home, and we had some quality time together."

"What time would that have been?"

"About 8:45 am, I think."

"And he stayed until when?"

"Jeff left about 11 o'clock. He needed to get ready for work."

"Thanks for your time, Mrs Taylor. I believe I have enough information to progress my case. I'll likely not need to trouble you again." Caitlin rose and Catriona also stood.

"You won't need to involve my husband or Jeff's wife in this investigation, will you? It would wreck both our marriages."

"I don't expect that will be necessary, Mrs Taylor. We're not in the business of wrecking marriages. But sometimes the truth comes out and there are consequences to our actions. I hope, however, that your relationship will continue to be a secret for now. It's always the children that suffer when relationships break down, isn't it?"

"I suppose it is. Thanks for your concern, Sergeant. If you'd like a re-style, you can have it on the house."

"That's kind of you to offer, Mrs Taylor." She thought about what the offer implied. She'd let her straight, dark chocolate hair grow out over the last year or so, and now had it tied back in a loose bun at the back of her head. "Do you think my hair needs re-styling?"

"It's really neat as you have it, and no doubt very practical for work, but with your Halle Berry features, you'd look exceptional with a short bob."

"Thanks for the compliment. Halle Berry is beautiful. But I don't see her looking back at me when I look in the mirror."

"Maybe you would if you had her hairstyle. Think about it..."

***

Owen emerged from the interview room, his face giving nothing away. "How did it go, Owen?" his boss enquired.

"Bilberry didn't admit to anything. He said it wasn't his fault that the delivery was late that morning. And the money would have been locked in the safe if it had arrived on time,"

"How did he explain ignoring his boss's orders?"

"He said he was conditioned to opening the bank on time and when he saw Mrs McCulloch at the door and checked the clock, he automatically opened up, naturally taking his seat at the customer services desk. But, in any case, he didn't recall his boss telling him to put the money into the safe. He said the manager would normally have done that."

"Sounds feasible, I suppose, but it's still possible he might have been involved."

"He did sound genuine. Although he'd initially been nervous, once he understood why I was questioning him, he became relaxed and showed no further signs of stress. As you say, we need to keep him in mind as a collaborator, though. I'll run some background checks on him and look out for any unexplained deposits over the next few days," Owen finished.

***

"How did it go this afternoon, Caitlin?" Angus asked as the team got together for another catch-up.

"We still don't have warrants to search Sutherland's and Stevenson's properties. The duty Sheriff is off sick (probably man flu). They're trying to find another official to stand in. It could take a while. We might not get the warrants signed until late afternoon now."

"Why did you say man-flu?"

"All men are the same. As soon as they have a sniffle, they go to bed and complain they're dying of the flu. If men had to have babies, the human race would soon die out."

"I didn't realise you were so biased in your thinking, Caitlin. I could say that's such a typical woman's stereotyping of men, but I'd be guilty of the same for saying so," Angus responded, then swiftly changed the subject back to work. "What about Wilkins' alibi?"

"Mrs Taylor, Wilkins' lover, confirmed that he was with her that morning. It didn't appear that Wilkins had warned her about a visit from the police. So, his alibi stands up. That leaves us with no third man suspect now."

"True. Oh well! Did the tech team get back to you with enhancements of the get-away car CCTV imagery?" Angus asked.

"The enhancements of the two men sat in the front of the get-away car, are clearer than the originals and I believe they're good enough to identify the suspects, but might not provide sufficient proof to stand up in court," Caitlin said, as she passed him the images.

"I see what you mean, Caitlin," Angus responded, as he looked at them and passed them to the rest of the team.

"Those guys look remarkably like my two suspects," Murray said.

Chapter 34

As Suzanna was leaving the kitchenette, coffee in hand, Una arrived. "Hi, Una. How's it going? Any progress tracking down the young thief?

"Good thanks, boss. Yes, we've had Forensics' report in from their checks at your apartment. Rab's got the results." Una quickly poured her coffee from the recently boiled kettle, so they walked together back into the main office. "Rab," Una raised her voice to get his attention.

"Yes, boss," Rab responded, then realised why Una had commanded his attention. "Ah! Ma'am. Forensics have recently reported back on the testing they did earlier. They've got an unknown partial fingerprint on the lounge door frame and one smudged fingertip print on the coffee table, where the magnifying glass had been. If we bring the lad in for questioning, hopefully, we'll get a match to the prints."

"That's good news. Are you any closer to identifying suspects?"

"All the schools responded with lists of late arrivals and absences on the days of the robberies. There appears to be some pattern, with three boys from different schools being late or off school on some of the days when the robberies occurred, but nothing definite yet."

"Any further progress with the CCTV analysis?"

"Yes. We took the E-fit that you helped develop to the man who lives in your building - the one who had asked for the boy to be chased. He confirmed the E-fit was a reasonable likeness, so knew we were on the right track."

"We've since checked CCTV on routes from the crime scenes to the Leith area and have spotted a potential suspect. He turned up on-route to Leith on three occasions when robberies had been committed. Although it seems to be the same lad, going by the long nose, because of the CCTV angles and the lad's hoody, much of his face can't be seen. So although we're quite confident that it's the same lad, we're not sure it would be enough to provide strong circumstantial evidence in court."

"We'll need something more tangible than that, then. Perhaps there will be evidence in the boy's home or school when we catch up with him? As we have partial prints from my flat, that might be enough to get him for at least one break in?"

"We have DNA evidence from two of the other break-ins. As you say, we just need to identify him and see if the hard evidence supports the circumstantial evidence that proves he had the opportunity, means and motive that we're assuming."

"What's your next move then, Rab?"

"I spoke with the administrator at the schools where the suspects are from and gave them the rough description. From the feedback I've had, I think we might have identified the youth. I'm planning to go out and have a word with him this afternoon. As he's only thirteen, I'll need to inform his parents and have one of them present when I formally interview him. But initially, I was planning to just have a casual chat, to see what he has to say for himself and to see how well he matches with the E-fit."

"As you say, Rab, be careful with questioning without cautioning and a parent present."

"Of course, ma'am."

"Oh, by the way, Una," Suzanna said, "what progress on the pub robbery?"

"Not much, boss. We interviewed the van owners, as discussed.

Clark is the only one with previous form for robbery, so was my prime suspect. We visited him at work this morning. He was angry that we'd contacted his manager, then showed up at his place of work. Said he'd served his time for the previous robbery and we were hounding him unjustifiably – not quite in those words if you know what I mean! I'll let you know if we get any further."

"Thanks, Una. I'll let you run with that one, so I can focus on the bank raid. Just let me know when you've made the arrest."

Suzanna's phone beeped as she entered her office. She glanced at it, noticing who it was from. 'We are still on 4 2nite?' Suzanna responded with 'Yes, see you there.' She didn't like text speak but could see the need for it in certain circumstances. Even her 95-year-old great-aunt Amelia was using it! She was hard of hearing and didn't speak to anyone by phone nowadays; her eyesight was failing, and her fingers had lost much of their dexterity, so abbreviating texts made it easier for her to communicate. But Suzanna still used words when she texted, instead of the numerical substitutes.

She thought ahead to what was in store for her tonight, when she would meet with her man friend, and smiled. She was becoming fond of James.

***

The phone rang, and Suzanna picked it up. "DCI McLeod."

"Suzanna. It's Chief Robertson here. I need to speak with you in my office about a matter of discipline within your team."

"Who do you need to speak about, sir?"

"Never mind who; I'll give you the details when you get here." The Chief Super hung up.

Suzanna rose, almost knocking over her office chair in her haste, and strode to his office without delay. She didn't like the Chief Super's tone. Within two minutes of receiving the call, Suzanna knocked on his door frame and walked in, then sat in the chair opposite him as he finished a phone call, looking perturbed at Suzanna's intrusion.

"That was quick, Suzanna."

"It sounded important, sir, so I didn't want to keep you waiting," she said, suppressing the actual reason for her rapid reaction.

"Well, it is important. I've had a report that DC Docherty was caught speeding in his car whilst on duty. We can't have police officers breaking the law. It brings the Force into disrepute. We need to make an example of him, so the others don't think they can get away with flouting the law."

"I don't think there's a need for making an example of him, as you say. I'll get Angus to have a word with him."

"No. That's not enough. You're too soft with your team, and so is Inspector Watson. I've noticed how the sergeants and constables get away with insubordinate comments. I believe we should suspend Docherty for a week. Inspector Ferguson would have made sure his DCs didn't get away with transgressions like this. I think you're losing your way, Suzanna."

"Don't talk to me about Inspector Ferguson." Suzanna raised her voice. "He couldn't keep his private life separate from work. He was a heavy drinker and irrational, and he treated his team awfully. Crimes got solved, but he left a swathe of misery behind him to achieve it. I believe in the power of the team, not the prima donna intellect of a single detective."

Suzanna thought momentarily about her own great-great-uncle's style, then continued. "I believe in inspiring the best from my team, giving them free rein to have ideas and follow their own leads, even if, occasionally, this leads to a dead end. I believe in developing, encouraging, and empowering my staff, so one day they'll be able to step into my shoes."

"If we step on our staff to gain promotion, we crush them. That's wrong for the person, wrong for the department, and bad for Service.

And would be a gift to the criminals, who would be more likely to get away with their crimes, because of a poor performing department, here at Fettes Avenue."

The Chief Superintendent was knocked back by Suzanna's rant. He understood her thinking and mostly agreed with it, but he was astounded by her passion about leadership styles.

"You know what, sir, when I first became a detective, I nearly gave up on it. I considered resigning because I hated the way my boss had treated me. He had no interest in developing me; just used me as someone to do his bidding. He never sought my thoughts and ideas on the case in hand, and he never shared his with me. I wasn't allowed to follow my own leads and when I tried, he stamped on me, humiliating me in front of my colleagues. I will never do that to anyone on my team."

"You say Murray needs to be bought into line, and I agree he shouldn't have broken the law, but I'll do it my way. I'll bring him in and talk to him with Inspector Watson present - talk him through the results or potential outcomes of his actions. I agree we can't have officers of the law breaking the law. Obviously, if he'd been involved in a collision with another car or worse still hit a pedestrian, he would have been guilty of causing death or injury by dangerous driving. And it would be bad for the credibility of the Police Service."

Suzanna drew a breath, then continued. "But I believe he made a mistake. I don't believe he blatantly broke the law. If I make an example of him, I'll lose him. He might comply with regulations and procedures and try harder not to transgress for fear of the consequences, but he'll become demotivated, and I'll lose his loyalty. We're all human; we all make mistakes."

"Okay, Susanna, you've made your point," the Chief Super responded, the wrinkles on his forehead now very prominent. "I'll leave you to deal with this in your own way, but I expect results. If he transgresses again, I'll deal with him myself; *got it*?"

"Yes, *sir*." Susanna turned and walked out, still annoyed by the attempted interference in the management of her team.

***

The Chief Super stared at the empty doorway as Suzanna marched away. He thought about how things had changed over the last three decades. He would never have spoken like that to his chief superintendent. Respect for rank seemed to have eroded over the years. It was just as well that he'd not see any more cultural changes in his remaining time in the Force... It would be good to have extra time to play golf and potter around his garden and spend more time with Maureen.

He thought back to Suzanna: her attitude, her methods, and her record for putting criminals away. He couldn't deny that she got results, but her way of doing things was different from what he was used to. Maybe he should retire early?

Chapter 35

PC Grant Silvester was sure he'd seen the chief inspector's magnifying glass in the hands of one of the young ruffians who had just left the pawnshop. The owner of the shop had just called him and said he suspected the glass was the one he'd seen in the picture that Grant had just given him.

The PC challenged the youths who ran off, so he gave chase. Grant had kept himself fit, so could keep up with the youngsters, but he couldn't gain ground on them because his heavy police equipment constrained his speed. He kept them in sight as they wove through the streets, but after turning a corner, he could only see one of the lads – they must have split up. Grant started following the one that he could still see, but as he reached the next junction, he noticed the other youngster, motionless, just 25 metres away.

The bicycle was leaning up against the lamppost – amazingly not locked to it. It was one of those old-style bikes: handlebars that turned towards the rider, rods that connected the brake handles to the brakes, fat tyres and mudguards front and rear, and just three gears. Its paint was a rich, smooth, dark blue colour, and the saddle was light tan leather with large springs supporting it.

Cam was at first transfixed by the beautiful, old-fashioned machine, but quickly snapped out of it. He needed a bike to get away and here it was, unlocked and waiting for him to borrow. As he grabbed the handlebars, he noticed the policeman. He swung his leg over the frame, stamped on the peddles and rode quickly away.

Grant saw him riding off on a bike and knew there was nothing he could do to catch him. He couldn't follow two people going in different directions, anyway, so he ran in the direction that he'd seen the other one heading. The lad was still in view, and he hoped the youngster would slow after a while. Grant often ran long distances – 10km or more – so, had no concerns about his own stamina, it was just his lack of speed that had so far hampered him.

Around the next corner, he lost sight of the youth – he'd just disappeared. He stopped and surveyed the area. He couldn't see anywhere that the boy could hide except the park across the street, so he walked over and entered the park. There was a bank of swings hanging from a rusty blue-painted tubular frame: two for older kids and two for toddlers. One swing was moving, having been recently disturbed. A seesaw sat motionless beyond the swings, its red paint also peeling and looking unkempt. There were other play pieces in the park, but none of these could offer a hiding place.

As he moved towards the hedgerow at the back of the park, there was a sudden movement and the youth ran off again, emerging from some bushes. As the PC ran towards the boy, he tripped and fell badly, bashing his knee on the pavement and yelling with pain. He grimaced and held back tears as the dagger-like pain hit his senses.

Billy sprinted away. Seeing the copper trip spurred him on. He wouldn't pass up this opportunity to escape capture. What luck! After taking a few turns, he was confident he'd shaken off his pursuer, so slowed to a walk. So far, the magnifying glass hadn't brought him any luck – quite the opposite. Perhaps his luck had changed by leaving it behind in the bushes. He'd just leave it there. As nice as it was, it was jinxed.

***

By the time Grant looked up, the youth had gone. His pain transfigured into anger that he'd missed the opportunity to catch the thief – anger at himself for not having avoided the trip hazard. The youth had tired and needed to hide, to recover from the chase. He could have had him, his superior fitness winning through. But he'd thrown it away by tripping on something. He should have been more careful.

***

The bank-raid team met in the concourse of Edinburgh Waverley train station. It was packed with people on their way to a platform or hanging around waiting to find out where their train would leave from. The magnificent Victorian glassed doom with the surrounding skylights flooded the covered gathering point with natural light. They had chosen it as a venue to meet and split the money, so they could merge with the crowd in case any of them were followed.

The big man passed out a bag each to them. "Don't spend it all at once, guys," He said light-heartedly.

They placed the bags into their own backpacks. Then the big man spoke again. "I've been thinking. The job we just did was helpful in keeping the wolf from the door. But we could do another and set ourselves up for life; get some payback for the years we served Queen and Country on low pay, living in crap accommodation and putting our lives at risk."

One of the men said, "I'll leave you guys to it. I couldn't get involved in another raid." He turned and walked off without waiting for a response from the others.

They watched him go before returning to the subject. "I could certainly do with the money but I'm not sure I want to do another job with you, after the way you treated that woman in the bank. She'd not done anything to deserve a kicking like that."

"You have to show the rest that you mean business. She won't have been injured much. I needed to shut her up so I could concentrate on the task. She'll probably just be off work for a couple of days, with a few bruises."

"I'm still not happy with what you did. She's somebody's sister, wife, and mother. How would you feel if someone treated one of your loved-ones like that? It was unnecessary violence."

"As I said, we had to show that we meant business."

"I think we demonstrated that when you fired off the round."

"Oh well, belt and braces, as they say. Two demonstrations are stronger than one."

"I don't agree with you and there's no way that I'll work with you again unless you can assure me you'll not use violence unless it's *absolutely* necessary and measured."

"Yeah, yeah. Of course. I take your point. I'll keep it in check next time. Can we move on?"

"What do you have in mind?" the driver said, breaking the tension.

"I was thinking of a different target and bigger money. Enough money to make it our last job. We're a bloody talented team. We've got the skills and professionalism to pull it off and not go to jail. It just needs good planning and execution."

"Yes, I agree," said the driver. "Let's do one more and make it a good'n. Pay off the mortgage, put some money in the bank, buy a nice car, and perhaps a villa in Spain. That's my vision."

The second man pondered the idea for a while, and the others left him to his thoughts. "OK, I'm listening. Give us some more detail on your idea."

***

Grant Silvester hobbled back to the police station, buying some painkillers from a pharmacy en route, and reported his failure to the sergeant.

Later that day, after he'd finished his shift, a thought crossed Grant's mind, so he diverted from his normal route home. He parked his ten-year-old silver Peugeot on the road just across from the park where he'd recently tried to arrest the youth, then wandered across and into the bushes where he'd seen him emerge.

Grant couldn't believe his eyes: the magnifying glass was hanging there from a thin twig that penetrated its wooden shaft. About to take it off the twig, he thought again. He should use an evidence bag to collect it, as there could be fingerprints on the object that would provide evidence of the thief's identity. He pulled an evidence bag from his pocket and was about to envelop the glass and remove it when it occurred to him that there might be another way of catching the thief. And next time he'd not trip over anything.

He went back to his car to wait, with the optimistic expectation that the culprit would return for his prize. Hopefully, he wouldn't have to wait too long, but he called his wife on his mobile to let her know. "Hi, Lizzie. How are you doing? Have the kids been good today? ...Great. Good to hear it. Did you go around to your mum's today? ... Yeah. OK. Good."

"Listen: I'll be late home this evening. I have an opportunity to catch a thief and if I do, it could help me get a transfer into CID. It's a slim chance, but if it pays off, it should be worthwhile. Remember me telling you that the Chief Inspector's magnifying glass had been nicked? Well, I chased the thief this afternoon."

"He gave me the slip when I tripped up, but I found that he'd hidden the magnifying glass in the bushes, so I'll wait to see if he comes back for it. Hopefully, he won't notice me sitting in my car... Thanks for your understanding, love. I'll see you later; and don't bother keeping anything for me to eat, I'll grab a sandwich from the local shop. OK. Brilliant. Love you."

Grant ended the call and put his phone down and prepared to experience a lesson in patience – one that he'd undoubtedly have to repeat many times if he made it as a detective constable. It was three hours before there was notable activity.

***

Connor had recently become of age but still felt like a teenager sometimes. He regularly went to the nearby playground and sat on the swings when no one else was about. Some would say he was living in the past, frequently reminiscing about his boyhood. But Connor was in employment as an admin assistant with the local council and was no longer living with his parents, even though his home was a rented, shared flat.

He had pals and got drunk occasionally, almost always regretting his overindulgence. He recalled the first time that he had thrown up after a drinking session.

At only sixteen, he'd not got a taste for beer, Chardonnay or Cabernet Sauvignon. He liked cider for its appley fizz, its cheapness and its alcoholic content, but it was his introduction to rum and blackcurrant that had taken him over the edge.

He'd been living at home, and the next morning his mother was furious when she saw and smelt the thick, purple stain on the wall beneath his window. She stormed into his bedroom at 7:30 that Saturday morning shouting at him, "Connor, what the hell is that mess on the wall outside your window? You're a disgusting boy".

Connor hadn't yet slept long, because it had been a late night, and his head was pounding from dehydration; his mouth tasted like someone had vomited in it. It must be himself, he realised, and remembered hanging out the window.

"You can get out of that bed right now and wash off that awful mess," his mother went on.

"But Mum," he winged, "I'll do it later."

"No way, young man, you'll do it now," and she left, returning quickly with a bucket of hot soapy water and a scrubbing brush. "Right get up now."

He slipped out of bed just wearing his boxer shorts, and snatched up his dressing gown, to cover his body - embarrassed to be almost naked in front of his mother, with a semi-hard penis pushing against his boxers.

"I'll leave you to it, but make sure it's done right or there will be no breakfast for you."

The dried blackcurrant-coloured vomit was difficult to remove, and hanging out the window to scrub at it made him feel more unwell. Connor promised himself that he'd never drink rum and blackcurrant again. He learned from that experience but not so well that he didn't get nauseously drunk again on other drinks.

He got off the swing, the park quiet now in the late evening. In the nearby houses, nearly all the lights had gone off. First downstairs with the lights flicking on in the bathrooms and bedrooms before each house became unilluminated as if their lives had been extinguished.

He liked this time of day when there were few people about – perhaps an occasional dog-walker taking their hound for a last pee before bed or a uniformed woman heading off to start her night shift in the hospital, but few others. He felt a peace drifting around the playground, owning the space; no threats, no one to order him around.

He knew this time would soon have to end because he needed to get up in the morning for work. "I'd best go." he thought, but as he turned, the sparkle of something caught his eye in the bushes.

The leaves, more yellow because of the glow from the sodium streetlights, were overlapping, as if trying to hide whatever laid within. When close, he could see something trapped in a branch. It was just hanging there as if a present on a Christmas tree, waiting to be plucked. He reached in and wrapped his smooth, delicate fingers around the stem of the object. It felt hard and square-edged, intriguing him. As the sparkling round section emerged from the greenery, he saw the glass lens and realised what it was – a magnifying glass.

"Fantastic," he thought. "What a wonderful object." He twirled it in his hand, noticing the smooth dulled brass ring and its inlaid wooden handle. What a lucky find, he thought, not knowing how wrong he was. He could use it to look in detail at the stamp collection he'd collated in his younger years. Connor pocketed the glass and turned for home.

"Hold it right there, young man," said the uniformed policeman who'd appeared from nowhere. "Walk over here into the light, so I can see you properly. What have you got in your pocket? I saw you put something in it. Come on, take it out."

Connor shook with anxiety. He'd had no dealings with the police, and he didn't want to have either, When younger, his mum had often threatened she'd call the police to put him in prison when he'd been naughty.

He stuttered, "I-I found this i-in the bush," he said, pulling the magnifying glass from his pocket.

"Aye, right! Drop it in this bag" said the policeman as he held out an evidence bag.

Connor did what he was told, worrying about what would happen to him. He had done nothing wrong, yet he felt like a criminal. He felt guilty just because he'd been accused and caught with the glass in his hand.

"I saw you hide it earlier, then run off before I could apprehend you, and I've been waiting for you to retrieve it."

"What do you mean? I've only been here half an hour, and I've never seen that thing until just now."

"So you say," said the PC, "but you'll need to come to the station with me. That's a valuable treasure that was stolen just last week. You're in big trouble, young man!"

"Right, sir. I am arresting you under Section 1 of the Criminal Justice (Scotland) Act 2016 for the theft of a magnifying glass. The reason for your arrest is that I suspect that you have committed an offence and I believe that keeping you in custody is necessary and proportionate for the purposes of bringing you before a court or otherwise dealing with you in accordance with the law. Do you understand?"

Connor nodded his head. "Do you understand?" Grant repeated.

"Yes, officer."

"You are not obliged to say anything but anything you do say will be noted and may be used in evidence. Do you understand?"

"Yes, officer."

"I require you to give me your name, date of birth, place of birth, nationality and address. You have the right to have a solicitor informed of your arrest; and to have access to a solicitor. These rights will be explained to you further at the police station."

"What's your name, young man?"

"It's Connor. Connor Mitchell."

"Do you have any ID on you?"

"I've got my Council ID card... Here it is," he said, handing it to the officer.

Grant noted the details on the card before returning it to Connor, then took down all the other necessary details about his date of birth, address, etc.

"Thank you. Now turn out all your pockets, one by one."

Connor did as he was told, still not believing this was happening to him. Grant checked the belongings of each pocket as it was emptied and satisfied that there was nothing of consequence or threat, allowed Connor to return the items to his pockets.

"Given that you ran off when challenged earlier today, I need to place you in handcuffs."

"But I didn't run off. I've never seen you until a few minutes ago."

"Don't argue with me. Turn around and place your hands behind your back."

Connor did what he was told and felt the cold metal of the cuffs tighten around each wrist.

"Right. Sit there on the bench, while I arrange transport to the station."

Connor sat as instructed, his worry increasing. He thought about what the policeman had said. 'He could request a solicitor if he wished, but who should he call? Maybe he should call his dad (not his mum – she wouldn't believe him and would just give him a load of hassle). Yeah, he'd ask to call his father.'

"Hello, Sarge. Its Grant Silvester." The sergeant interrupted him, then he responded, "I know Sarge, I finished shift four hours ago but I've just apprehended a suspect in the theft of the Chief Inspector's magnifying glass." Another pause as the sergeant spoke to him.

Connor heard what the PC had said: the magnifying glass had belonged to a Chief Inspector, and it worried him. From what he'd seen on TV crime series, the police were like a family. If you crossed one of them, you crossed them all.

"OK, Sarge. I've arrested the suspect and require transportation for us both to the station. We are in the play park, on the corner of Sloan Street and Iona Street. OK. I'll wait here. Fifteen minutes, you say. OK, fine." It would be a late night tonight, but it should be worth it. He was sure the Chief Inspector would put in a good word for him, for apprehending the culprit and recovering her heirloom.

Chapter 36

The police car, manned by one of PC Silvester's colleagues, turned up a quarter of an hour later - as expected. The driver emerged and walked across to where Connor sat, and Grant stood guard.

"Hi, Phil. How's it going?"

"Good thanks, Grant. What are you doing hanging around here four hours after your shift finished?"

"I chased the youth who'd stolen the DCI's magnifying glass, and he dumped it in the bushes before escaping, so I waited around for his return and nabbed the lad, red-handed."

"That's dedicated of you. Are you after a transfer?"

"Well, why not?"

"Fair enough, pal. Each to his own. I'm not planning on leaving my uniform at home when I go to work. Anyway, let's get this lad to the station for processing. I'll take him in if you want to follow in your own car."

"Thanks, Phil. I'll see you at the station."

***

Phil Stringer took Connor into the station and was just finishing the booking formalities when Grant Silvester arrived. Grant placed Connor into an interview room, then went back to ask for someone to sit in with him, whilst he questioned the suspect further.

The sergeant allocated PC Fleming to the task. "Hi, Grant. I hear that you've caught the boy who nicked the DCI's magnifying glass. You must be faster than me. When I chased the lad from outside the DCI's home, he gave me the slip."

"I'm not sure I'm faster, but I have the stamina for a chase; I run regularly as part of my fitness regime."

They went into the interview room together, but when Dave Fleming saw the boy, he took Grant's arm and gently pulled him out of the room. "You say that's the boy who took the DCI's magnifying glass?"

"Aye. He's the one."

"But that's not the same boy who ran away from her flat. This one's taller and older, for a start!"

"Well, I caught him red-handed with the glass, emerging from the bushes with it, after I'd staked it out all evening."

"Tell me how this came about, pal."

Grant explained how Connor's arrest had been made. "You say the young man didn't run away when you challenged him?"

"That's correct."

"Yet the youth I chased, and the one you chased earlier today, was not one for giving himself up!"

Grant frowned. He pondered what Dave had said before speaking again. "But even if he's not the same person, he had the magnifying glass when I caught him."

"True. But maybe he's telling the truth? Did the youth you chased earlier look like he was twenty years old?" Phil queried.

"No," Grant paused. Another good point. "The lad I chased looked about fourteen or fifteen years old."

"So, you chased a boy, then arrested a young man. He can't have aged five years in four hours, Grant, can he?"

Grant twisted his mouth and pursed his lips as he considered the obvious fact that the boyish man he'd arrested was much older than the youth he'd chased earlier. Perhaps he'd got carried away with his success of capturing him. "Well, now I've brought him in, I'd better question him, anyway. Either he'll incriminate himself – perhaps he's friends with the youth – or clear himself."

"OK. Let's get it done then."

They re-entered the interview room, started the recorder and went through the usual preamble. Connor had by now calmed down. He knew that he'd done nothing wrong, so needn't worry. The PC who had arrested him started the questions: "As you know, you have been arrested in connection with the theft of an antique magnifying glass. So, where were you at 07:50 am on Tuesday this week?"

"I was having breakfast in my flat. I start work at the council offices at 9 am."

"Can anyone verify that?"

"Yes, my flatmate was also at home. We both work for the council."

"His name and contact number, please."

Grant noted the flatmate's name and phone number. "We will, of course, have to speak with Mr McIntosh. Where were you at 5 pm today?"

"I was at work. My normal hours of work are 9-5:30. In fact, I remember taking a call around that time from an irate Council Tax payer whose bins hadn't been emptied that day; he wanted a rebate on his Council Tax, would you believe? We get loads of people like him. Just because the council doesn't provide the service they expect, they think they can get a rebate on the tax they've paid. Some people even withhold payment and get taken to court for their failure to pay the tax."

"Who can I speak to at the Council, to verify that you were there at that time?"

Connor was feeling a lot more confident now that he'd answered the questions. He had alibis for times when the PC thought he had been involved with the crime. He gave the PC the contact details for the

Council Tax Manager.

"OK. Thank you for the details. We will contact your manager to confirm your alibi. Now, please explain to us, Mr Mitchell, how the magnifying glass came into your possession."

"I told you before, I was chilling out on the swing when I caught the glimpse of something in the bushes reflecting the light of the streetlamp. I went into the bush to investigate and found the glass. When I emerged from the bush, you were standing there."

"And you say you'd never seen the glass before?"

"That's right. It amazed me when I found it hanging from a twig in the bush. It never occurred to me that the glass might have been stolen."

"The fact is, though, the glass had been stolen, and it was in your hand when I caught you." Grant could feel this one slipping away from him; no glory for having caught the DCI's glass thief, after all. It seems he'd given up his evening for nothing.

"Right, Mr Mitchell. We will follow up on the alibis you've given us. If they confirm your whereabouts at the specified times, we'll not charge you with the theft of the magnifying glass. It remains possible, however, that we might charge you with possession of stolen property. Do you understand?"

"Yes."

"OK. You're free to go. We will be in touch with you again once we've followed up."

"Can I get a lift home, please? It's quite late."

"I'm sorry, Mr Mitchell, but police resources don't allow us to work as a taxi service," PC Fleming said.

Grant was feeling guilty, though: "Look. I'll be heading in your direction soon. If you can wait five minutes, I'll give you a lift home." It might provide an opportunity to speak with Connor's flatmate before he could prime him.

"Thanks; that would be good. I'll wait for you."

"I'll be back shortly."

The two PCs left the room. "What do you reckon then, Grant?"

"I guess he's telling the truth. I'll follow up on the alibis, but suspect they'll confirm what he's told us. Could you log the magnifying glass as evidence for me, so I can get off home? I'll contact Rab Sinclair in the morning to brief him on what happened today. He'll no doubt get his boss to identify the glass. At least I'll have recovered it for her. That's something!"

"You're right, pal. It's a pity you didn't get the right man though, eh? I'll finish off the paperwork for you – nae bother."

"Cheers, Dave. I'll get Connor Mitchell home, speak to the flatmate if he's in, then explain to the missus why I stayed out all evening for nothing, instead of being home to help put the kids to bed."

"Good luck with that one, pal."

Chapter 37

"Can I help you, ma'am?" a waiter asked as Suzanna entered the Scotsman Hotel Grand Café and looked around, quickly spotting her date. James was in his late forties but looked ten years younger. From the distance, he looked handsome enough to be the owner of an Aston Martin and be known as 007.

"I'm meeting a friend. He's already here," she said, indicating with her eyes where he sat. The waiter turned and noticed a man waving at the woman.

"Please go ahead. I'll be over shortly to take your order."

"Thanks," she said as she stepped away.

James stood up as Suzanna approached. Close up, she still thought he looked like he could have worked for MI6. He had an uncanny resemblance to Sean Connery. Even his voice had that deep, growly accent that Connery had become famous for.

"Suzanna. Bang on time, as usual. It's great to see you." He kissed her on both cheeks, and they sat opposite each other. Couples and small groups surrounded them, enjoying an early evening meal and drinks. No children, youths, students, or scruffily dressed people could be seen. The Scotsman required high standards.

"How's your day been, Suzanna?"

"Frenetic. We've been chasing down the villains who robbed the Lothian Bank on Wednesday morning."

"Oh! I guess there's pressure on you from up the chain, as it was *an armed* robbery?"

"Yes," Suzanna whispered. "Well, we've identified two suspects and expect to make arrests as soon as we have enough evidence."

"You're confident they'll be arrested?" James responded equally quietly.

"Yes. The circumstantial evidence is strong, but we need some tangible evidence to be sure."

"Good to hear." He paused, then raised his voice to its normal level. "And what are your intentions for the weekend?"

"A lazy Saturday. No alarm. Breakfast in PJs and a catch-up with the news. Maybe some shopping later. What do you have planned?"

"I was thinking of a day out to the Lake District for a walk." He paused for a few seconds. "I wondered whether you might like to join me, but I can understand your wish for a lazy day if you've had an intense week."

"Now you've set me a dilemma. I love the Lake District, and like nothing better than walking the fells, but it is a long way to go for a day trip. I'll need some time to consider the suggestion."

"Fair enough. I did drop the idea on you at the last minute. I'll understand if you say no. What would you like to drink?"

"I'll have a chardonnay, please."

James signalled to the waiter, then placed the order. "Excellent choice, the Chardonnay. I find some Australian Chardonnays can be a little harsh but the one they serve here is more like a Chablis – refreshing, a little fruity but not too acidic."

"You're so right, James," Suzanna agreed after tasting her wine. "Cheers," she said, holding up her glass for a chink. "Here's to a lovely evening and a great walk in The Lakes tomorrow," she said with a smile.

"Cheers," James said smiling back, delighted Suzanna had already agreed to join him for his day out in one of the UK's most beautiful locations, despite the lengthy return journey.

***

Their meals finished, James excused himself and went to the gents. Suzanna looked around. The Grand Café was elegantly appointed. Light oak panelling surrounded it, and it had carved balcony supports in the same wood. A giant, white-flowered arrangement stood on a plinth, reflected by the mirrored wall behind. Looking up, an enormous crystal chandelier hung in the centre, its mock candles subtly illuminating the tables, and multiple, intricately carved panels framed each of the smaller chandeliers. It was opulent.

She thought back to her time in Calcutta when her friend had taken her to the famed Flurys Bakery on Park Street. It had seemed opulent to her then, but Edinburgh's Grand Café was much classier. Suzanna wondered if she'd ever return to the 'City of Joy', as Calcutta had become known. And she pondered, again, how such a dirty, hot, humid, and polluted city, with widespread poverty, could ever have become known as a joyous place.

With the atmosphere of the café, Suzanna felt relaxed, and in no rush to go home. James returned to the table. "Would you like another Chardonnay?"

"No thanks. Two reasons. One glass is my limit when driving. And I prefer red wine after eight. White is great as a 'sun-downer' but red's my normal tipple when having a cosy time."

"Are you a Merlot girl? Cabernet or perhaps Shiraz? I should know, shouldn't I, but it's been too long since we last had quality time together."

Suzanna was giving nothing away, teasing him into trying other wines that she might acknowledge as her favourites. James tried again: "If I recall correctly, you're a Châteauneuf-du-Pape woman?"

"Well done, James. I'm also partial to a good South Australian Shiraz, though."

"Could I interest you in a bottle of Barossa Valley Shiraz, a comfy sofa, a cosy log fire and some easy-listening, classical music?"

"You are a tempter, Mr Stewart. I have to warn you, though, that I find it difficult to rise early after a late night and a bottle of wine," she said provocatively, hinting at the intended overnight stay.

"I can live with the disappointment of a missed walk if it means spending more time with you tonight. Shall I get the bill?"

"Yes, please. Let's go."

***

James switched on table lamps, lit candles, and turned off the overhead light. The mood was set. The sofa was as comfortable as he had promised, the wine exquisite and the cello music he'd selected perfectly to her taste. They chatted and sipped wine, getting to know each other better as they relaxed.

It was good that they shared an interest in walking in the mountains and they were both sporty. She liked her men lean and fit, although didn't mind if they had a tiny belly. But she didn't find men with double chins and rotund abdomens attractive. Fortunately, James definitely fitted into the lean and fit category.

They evidently enjoyed the same music, and James' taste in furniture was to her liking. The flat was nothing like her own – more masculine, of course. The sofa on which they sat was soft grey leather, luxurious to the touch. His furniture was contemporary light oak and ornaments adorned the surfaces, bringing colour and texture to soften and brighten the room. A charcoal grey pair of ceramic cats perched on the mantelpiece hinted that he might have a fondness for animals. She approved.

They sat close, their eyes locked on each other's, as they chatted. James studied her face: short blonde hair streaked with silver, framed her high-cheek-boned face. Her nose was slim and turned up just a little at the end. Her lips were full, but not artificially bloated like many 21st-century women chose. He touched her lips with his forefinger and gently circled their periphery. Her mouth parted slightly as he withdrew his finger.

The kiss was inevitable, magnetic forces drawing their lips together. It was luxurious, warm, and erotic, like sticky toffee pudding with brandy liqueur. He cupped her head in both hands, his fingers fondling her ears as he drew her close. Their tongues touched and danced together fleetingly before he pulled away. When he kissed her neck and tenderly nibbled her earlobes, a glorious sensation ran through her body, like mild electricity, travelling all the way down and making her squirm - there was no turning back.

She offered no resistance, as James slowly undid the buttons of her blouse and slipped his hand inside, caressing her breast before releasing her bra strap. He circled a nipple with his finger, barely touching her skin, until it stood fully to attention, then squeezed it gently and rolled it between finger and thumb. Suzanna just melted. As his mouth took over from his hand, he could smell her arousal and it turned his firmness rock-solid.

James took her hand and led her into the bedroom. He undressed her unhurriedly, kissing her soft skin as he exposed her flesh, before discarding his own clothes and climbing onto the bed beside her.

Satisfaction for them both came minutes later, and they collapsed beside each other, replete with sex, wine, and food. It had been too long! She'd almost forgotten how wonderful making love could be – with the right man. They lay silently for several minutes, relaxing after the excitement of making love.

She thought back to her first experience of intercourse. She'd been at school in Colwyn Bay when she'd met Aiden. He was another student at the co-ed independent school she was attending. She was only 17. They'd walked up the hill from the town and sat on the grassy bank looking out across the Irish Sea and drank cider from an enormous bottle that Aiden had bought in a supermarket. They'd laughed so much. They'd kissed passionately, and he'd touched her breasts. She'd been so excited. They rolled down the bank together, tumbling hysterically, then walked back to her accommodation hand in hand.

Aiden had sneaked into the dorm house through her bedroom window. Fortunately, most of the staff and students were out shopping or just enjoying the sunshine. They kissed more and this time, she let him explore her flesh. She'd discovered fresh, wonderful sensations. She hadn't planned to go all the way, but the alcohol had lowered her inhibitions, and her excitement had hit new highs, so she'd let him take her virginity. Afterwards, she felt guilty. If her parents got to know she'd had sex before marriage, they'd have found it devastating – being ultra-religious, as they were.

Suzanna felt no guilt *now* as she lay in James' arms – only satisfaction, warmth and perhaps, dare she say it, love.

"Suzanna. Maybe your idea of a lazy Saturday would be better than my walking in the Lake District?" James said, dragging her thoughts back to the present.

"Agreed, but we must go to the Lakes together soon. Rather than laze around all day, though, how about a walk to the peak in Holyrood Park? If we park down by Duddingston Loch, the walk up to the peak will at least get our hearts working."

"Definitely, on both counts," James concurred before drifting off to sleep.

Suzanna draped her arm across James's chest and snuggled up to him. Some men *could* be trusted. Perhaps James was the right man?

Chapter 38 – Saturday 17th January

The next morning, Suzanna rose first and showered, before dressing in her clothes from the night before – at least they'd been clean on when she went out the previous evening. She slipped out the door, leaving James sleeping, and walked to the nearest coffee shop. Fifteen minutes later, she was back at James' apartment and let herself in with his keys.

"Ah! there you are, gorgeous. I thought you'd done a runner."

"Just a brisk walk up the road and back," she said, placing the coffees and pastries on the breakfast table. James must have woken when she'd left the apartment, as he was looking clean and ready for the day. He'd already dressed in walking clothes.

"You still up for a walk in Holyrood Park, then?" Suzanna said with a questioning tone.

"I certainly am. Not quite Scarfell Pike, but it will have to do."

"To be honest, I'm not sure I would have wanted to climb Scarfell today, anyway. I've lost some of my fitness. I was thinking more like Cat Bells fell and a walk around Derwent Water. It would have been wonderful today, as the forecast says there'll be blue skies and sunshine."

"Oh well! Let's get our diaries out after breakfast and plan in a trip to the Lake District as soon as we can."

"I see you've picked up some newspapers, as well as coffee. Are you a Scotsman girl or is it the Telegraph?"

"Either."

They both drank and ate, enjoying the excellent coffee and food. "Hey, look at this on Page 2 of the Scotsman. The headlines are 'Police Close to Apprehending Bank Robbers.'"

"Where did they get that information from?" Suzanna went slightly pink in the face. "Surely, no one could have overheard what I said to you at dinner last night?"

"They'd have to have supernatural hearing if they did, as I could only just hear what you said, and the nearest person to us was twice the distance away from you as I was. They've not attributed it to you, so I wouldn't worry."

"But someone has told the press how the case is progressing. It could jeopardise the forthcoming arrests if the criminals read that headline and decide to scarper over the weekend. I'll need to contact Angus and make him aware."

"Are you worried that this leak could affect your career?"

"It's not that James. I'm concerned that they could escape justice, and it's bringing criminals to justice that drives me. But I am likely to get it in the neck from the Chief Super or Chief Constable if we miss arresting them because of this leak. Obviously, it would not be good for my career." Suzanna looked at her watch: 8:33 am. "Excuse me, James. I need to make a call."

She moved into the corridor, selected the contact, and hit the call button.

"Good morning, guv."

"Good morning, Angus. Have you seen the Scotsman this morning?"

"Yes. I thought that would be why you were calling. I've checked out the other papers, and there's no mention of it in any of them. So just one journalist has got to hear that we have two firm suspects."

"I'm concerned that if the suspects see those headlines, they'll leave the city and potentially escape arrest."

"I shouldn't worry too much about that. Never known petty criminals to read the broadsheets; they're more likely to read the Daily Star or the Record. The Scotsman's too highbrow for most of them."

"I hope you're right, Angus. But, even so, we'd better not hang around."

Suzanna returned to the kitchen, where James was still chewing on his croissant.

"All sorted?"

"I've talked it through with my DI and we're hopeful that the leak won't affect the case. Anyway, where's my coffee? I hope it hasn't gone cold."

Suzanna sat at the dining table and picked up her coffee.

"Just curious, Suzanna. What led you to becoming a police officer and a detective?"

Suzanna paused for a few seconds before responding. "The journey started when I was 18. I got a call from a firm of solicitors in England, who were acting on behalf of a distant relative. He'd died back in the early 1930s but left a legacy. He was my great, great uncle."

"That must have surprised you. What did the solicitors have to say?"

"My relative didn't have any children or anyone else that he wanted to leave his money to, so he had his estate put into a trust fund. The fund was to be paid to the first of his relatives (children of his dis-liked brother) who could pass a test he'd set."

"A test! What type of test?"

"He'd been a detective for the biggest part of his life, working as a consultant to the Metropolitan Police, cracking major crimes that the Met couldn't solve. The test was one of deduction. He set out a lengthy scenario, describing a crime and suspects. The test was to work out who had committed the crime. I got the right answer so inherited his estate!"

"Wow! That's fantastic. He sounds like an amazing man to have done that. So, you were set up for life from just 18!"

"Some would describe him as idiosyncratic. Others in more derogatory terms. But yes, he was an astounding character – infamous, actually!" Suzanna paused. "The inheritance was substantial, but not enough to make me rich. It paid for my travels after uni, bought this apartment and gave me some reserves to draw on. I also inherited his only possession that hadn't been sold off – a magnifying glass. Annoyingly, the glass was stolen this week from my apartment – I'd carelessly left my door unlocked. It's quite a special piece; an antique, and of course a family heirloom."

"Sounds like something that Sherlock Holmes would have had."

Suzanna smiled. "Yes. It does, doesn't it?"

***

After breakfast, Suzanna rethought their plans for the day. "James. I was just thinking: if we left for the Lake District within the next hour, we would be there by early afternoon. We could catch a bite to eat at a café in Portinscale, then climb Cat Bells. If we drop into the valley near the lake's end and walk back parallel to it, it will take less than three hours."

"True. We could drive back to Edinburgh in the evening."

"This might be a bit premature in our relationship, so tell me if you'd prefer not to, but I was thinking we could overnight at my sister's house in Cockermouth."

"Taking me to meet your family so soon after our first night together. Wow!"

"Look, I don't mean to scare you and I'm not trying to tie you down already - I'm not sure, myself, whether I'm ready for another long-term relationship yet. But my sister said my niece was missing me, and it would be rude to go all the way to Keswick and not go the additional ten miles to visit her."

"Hmm! I had planned to play golf on Sunday morning, but I like the idea of not having to rush back to Edinburgh after our walk. If your sister can put us up, I'll cancel the golf appointment. I can play with my brother another time – nae bother."

"Right. You're on! I'll call Charlotte straight away. You'll love my niece. She's so cute."

***

The sun's glow and warmth lifted their spirits as they got into her car. Suzanna needed no prompting from James to drop the roof of her car. She smiled at the prospect of the forthcoming drive and turned to James as if looking for approval. He smiled back, silently confirming that he was also expecting the drive to be enjoyable. They donned hats and scarves to ward off the chill of the January day, then Suzanna slipped the car into Drive and pulled away.

They emerged from the city onto the A702 for Carlisle, with the sun on their faces. It felt good to be leaving the city. As they moved out into the countryside, where petrol and diesel fumes didn't hang in the air, it smelled fresh. Suzanna felt an urgency within her. She'd been constrained by Edinburgh's speed limits for too long, with many of them being restricted to 20mph. The open road enticed her. As she came out of a bend, behind a long truck, she saw the highway straighten, heading off into the distance, and no traffic coming towards her. She pressed the throttle to the floor. The BMW boomed into life – its engine made for these scenarios.

The auto gearbox changed down, and the car accelerated, its velocity building swiftly. She passed the truck doing 70 mph but didn't lift her foot. There was no traffic and no junctions; why slow down? The thrill of travelling fast relieved her frustrations. She glanced at the gauge: 95, 100. 'Whoa!' She thought, 'best slow down.'

As she dropped over a slight rise, she saw a lay-by ahead, with a car parked there and a man stood looking in her direction with an object in his hand. "Shit," she said and braked hard. She knew she'd still be over the speed limit – significantly.

The man in his Day-Glo yellow jacket and black uniform waved her down, and Suzanna pulled into the lay-by just beyond the police car. She stopped, applied her brake and switched off the engine, then waited for the officer to arrive. She looked at James. "Don't say anything."

James wisely showed no disapproval of what she'd just done.

"Good morning, ma'am. In a hurry today?"

"What speed was I doing, constable?" she asked.

"I have you at 87 mph. You realise the limit is 60 mph?"

"Yes, constable. I'd just overtaken a truck and hadn't noticed the speed build until I looked down at the gauge."

"Your licence please, ma'am."

Suzanna dug her driving licence out of her bag and passed it to the officer.

"McLeod, Suzanna, Amelia," the officer read aloud, whilst noting it in his book, including the licence number. As he handed it back to her, he said: "You're not Detective Chief Inspector Suzanna McLeod, are you?"

"Guilty, as charged, constable."

"Can I see your warrant card, please, ma'am?"

She passed him her police ID card, and he perused it before passing it back and responding. "Ma'am. Good to meet you. You're a legend in the Edinburgh Force. I wish we'd met under better circumstances. You realise that I have to write you up for this?"

"Of course, constable. I've broken the law and have to take the consequences."

"Afraid so, ma'am."

Suzanna was wondering how the Chief Super would react to this one. He'd been mad when Murray had been caught speeding in the city. He'd be livid when he heard that she'd been caught doing nearly

30 mph over the limit. Just 3 mph faster and it would have been an automatic driving ban. 'Damn,' she thought, 'what an idiot.'

The constable wrote the speeding ticket and passed it to her. "Please drive carefully, Chief Inspector. Have a pleasant weekend." She started up and drove away, accelerating gradually until she was doing 60 mph, then set the cruise control. Best to let the computer control her speed, rather than her right foot. James still sat unjudgementally silent. 'Good man,' she thought. She hoped they could still enjoy the weekend. Keswick beckoned.

Chapter 39

Angus decided to stretch his legs and visit the gents. He stopped off at the water dispenser on the way back to the office and found Caitlin topping up her glass. She was looking shabby. "Good morning, Caitlin. A bit late in this morning, I noticed, and you don't look well. Are you all right?"

"Sorry, boss. I went to a friend's party last night and stayed out too late. I had a bit too much to drink, as well. Not feeling too good this morning."

"I know you like to party, Caitlin, but I really need you to have a good brain when we're working on an important case, like this."

"Agreed, boss. I wish I could turn back the clock. I hadn't intended to get drunk or stay out late, knowing I had to come into work today. But I met an old friend that I used to hang around with when I was chalet hosting in Méribel, in my gap year. It brought back awful memories, and I tried to counter the depression with alcohol. It won't happen again."

"Come with me, Caitlin," Angus said then walked through to the DCI's office, waited for Caitlin to enter, then closed the door behind them. They both sat, and Angus invited Caitlin to share about the dreadful memories that she still found depressing a dozen years later.

"I was only eighteen. I fell in love with this wonderful guy, who was training to be a ski instructor. But one day, when we'd both been drinking a lot, we had a blazing row. He stormed out. That was the last time I saw him alive. He'd angrily strode off towards his flat and decided to take a shortcut but fell down a cliff, landing at the bottom unconscious. Someone saw him in the morning. He'd laid there all night and died from exposure." Caitlin burst into tears at recalling the memory.

Angus leaned across and placed his hand on her shoulder. "Wow! So sorry to hear that. No wonder you were upset last night." He stopped speaking and let Caitlin sob for a while until the emotion subsided.

"Have you ever spoken to a professional about how this affected you?" He waited patiently for an answer.

"No, never," she said, trying to stop herself from crying again.

"I know this happened before you joined the Police Force, but I'm sure I could arrange for you to have some time with the PTSD therapist if you'd like."

Caitlin went even redder in the face and looked at Angus with her facial muscles tense. "I don't need a shrink," she said and stormed out, slamming the door behind her.

Her response shocked Angus - he'd never understand women. He went back to the main office but ignored Caitlin for a while and waited until he could see she'd settled down before speaking again.

"Caitlin, did we get any feedback yet from the bus drivers or passengers – I take it the posters went up on the routes yesterday?"

Caitlin looked in his general direction when she answered, but failed to make eye contact. "Yes, I gave the posters to the manager at Lothian Buses yesterday and he assured me they would get displayed on the buses and at the relevant bus stops. Murray spoke with the drivers, but they saw nothing. That's not surprising, as they'd have been concentrating on manoeuvring around the roundabout. We've had one phone call so far - from a passenger."

"Did they see anything that might help us?"

"Surprisingly, yes. The lady who called us, Mrs Eileen Brody, had just got off the bus and was walking towards the Lothian Bank when a car turned off George Street onto Frederick Street, just as she was crossing the road. The passengers were wearing balaclavas. Fortunately, she got a good look at the driver. Mrs Brody is coming in this afternoon to give us a statement and a description."

"Excellent. Let me know how it goes."

***

The striking scenery of the fells awed them as they travelled westward from Penrith into the Lake District. "It's always the same when I drive down this section of the A66," Suzanna stated. "Once I see this view, I know I've arrived, and I'm always reluctant to leave."

"It's a wonderful landscape, isn't it?" James agreed. "I considered taking out a second mortgage to buy a holiday home in the Lakes."

With the mention of loans, Suzanna remembered a job she'd not done and pulled over into a lay-by. "Sorry, James; I've just remembered something that I urgently need to do. It should only take a few minutes."

"No problem, Suzanna. I'll just admire the view."

She retrieved her phone from the depths of her handbag and called Erskine Jamieson.

"Erskine here."

"Mr Jamieson, Erskine; how are you?"

"Would that be a gorgeous detective chief inspector on the line?"

"Chief Inspector Suzanna McLeod speaking, Erskine. I haven't seen you in a while. How's business?"

"Not so bad, not so bad. Ups and downs. You know how it is."

"Yes, Erskine. It's a risky business you're in, but it can be lucrative, can't it? How's your wife Maureen doing? Are you looking after her well?"

"Of course. She's doing fine, thanks. I'm just heading home now to see her."

"Give her my regards, Erskine."

"Will do, Suzanna. How can I help you?"

"I was just wondering whether you might have had any recent large repayments that have made you smile?"

"Well, it's always hard work getting my money back, as you know. I did have a good response today, as it happens."

"I wonder if you'd mind sharing with me who it was and how much they repaid?"

"That's confidential information. You'd need a warrant if you want me to divulge that."

"I'm sure I can arrange that if that's what you'd prefer, Erskine. It might be worth asking for the divulgence of all your loan records while I'm at it. I'm sure I could find a reason to persuade the judge."

"There'll be no need for that lassie, but tell me one thing: if the money he paid to me today had been stolen, would I have to return it?"

"What's done is done, Erskine. You took the money in good faith in repayment of a loan. I can't see how anyone could chase you for its return."

"In that case, I'll be happy to divulge. He owed me 25 grand. I think he'd got himself in a spot of bother with the Black family, so came to me for a loan to keep them off his back."

Suzanna made a note of the name Erskine gave her.

"I guess he saw you as the least of two evils, Erskine."

"Now, now. No need to call me evil. It's just business. The borrowers know full well the terms of the loans when they take them out. The interest is high, but it's their choice to take a loan. I don't go around forcing people to take my money."

"OK, Erskine. I'll let you get back to your business. Thanks for your cooperation. I'll see you around."

Suzanna texted Angus with the name of the man who'd just paid off the large loan, to add to the evidence he was gathering, then started her car and accelerated back onto the road.

***

"Sir," Caitlin called quietly across the office. There was no response. "Boss." She said again, raising her voice. Angus turned.

"Sorry, Caitlin, I was miles away. I was contemplating what we have so far, and just thinking if we had another witness, that would be great."

"You must be psychic, boss. I just took a call from a man who left the coffee shop and was heading towards the jewellers opposite the bank. He saw the two men jog over to the car, and it drive away. He also got a look at the driver. Bad news is, boss, that he was wearing a face mask. A caricature of Simon Cowell!"

"Great," Angus said with a sarcastic voice and rolling eyes. "So, the lady off the bus who said she got a good look at the driver will describe the chief judge on the X-Factor and Britain's Got Talent!"

"It would seem so."

"So much for the good news earlier, eh?"

Caitlin acknowledged the unwelcome news with a tilt of the head, then spun back to her computer screen just as her phone rang. "Detective Sergeant Findlay."

"We've got a visitor for you, Caitlin," Sergeant Reilly informed her.

"Thanks, Pete. I'll be down in a minute." She hung up and marched out of the office, thinking, 'this will be a waste of time then.'

Angus noticed a message on his phone and, seeing it was from the DCI, opened it immediately. 'Now that is useful info,' Angus thought, having read the message.

Chapter 40

The café in Portinscale sat next to the road leading towards the Cat Bells walk starting point, so they didn't have to waste time diverting from their route. There were a few tables and chairs outside on the paved area, with people sat chatting, their walking boots showing signs that many had already done a walk in the fells. Bicycles leant against the wall near a group of people wearing Lycra gear that hugged their slender bodies.

They took a seat at a table next to a closed French window and devoured their lunch, packing in the calories for the forthcoming climb – it was too chilly to sit outside unless you'd already exercised. "I've never seen a fat club cyclist," James commented.

"Nor I. Cycling must be a huge calorie-burning exercise. I cycle occasionally, but I could never do it for hours at a time in packs like these clubs tend to," Suzanna responded. "Talking of exercise, it's about time we got moving, James."

They drove to Brandelhow, parked up, then took the summit path up the ridge. The sun was pleasantly warm on their faces as they climbed. They stopped occasionally to take in the views across Derwent Water and the town of Keswick. As they gained height, the views became more extensive.

Suzanna could see Lake Bassenthwaite in the North, as it led her eye to the wind turbines on the ridge, beyond which lay the Solway Firth coast and the mountains of Dumfries. They pressed on, knowing that in January, the sun would set about 4:30 pm, and they didn't want to be walking in the dark.

They scrambled up the ridge, the rough rocks roughening their skin, then stood erect again for the last few metres of the climb. On the summit, they rested and took in the 360-degree views. Derwent Water lake lay below them to the east. Little Town sat in the valley to their West, the fells masking their view to the distant Crummock Water.

"James. Did you know that in the Lake District, there's only one lake?"

"Of course, there's not. I can see two from here."

"Actually, you can see the only lake in the National Park: Lake Bassenthwaite. All the others are called meres or waters. Buttermere, Crummock Water, Lowes Water, Derwent Water, Thirlmere, Windermere."

"OK. I get your point. I'd never thought about that before. Lakes or not, though, they're all beautiful, especially with the fells as their backdrop."

"I never tire of looking at the splendour of the Lake District, particularly when the sun shines like today. I can't think of anywhere more stunning."

"The Scottish mountains are spectacular as well. We have plenty of beauty spots in our home country. Have you driven up the A9 to Inverness?"

"I have. I've toured Scotland extensively over the last two decades, and you're right. It's a great drive through the Cairngorms. The views are splendid, but it's a rugged beauty. There's something about the mix of lakes and mountains that makes this place really special. Why did you mention that drive, particularly?"

"I'm from Forres, so have driven it hundreds of times returning to my hometown."

"I didn't realise you were a small-town boy from Morayshire. You've never said you're 'going to the shoppie'! Thought you'd always lived in Edinburgh."

"So much for your brilliant deductive powers! Not everyone from Forres adds an 'ie' to the end of nouns."

"You'll never guess where I went to primary school."

"Not Forres, surely?"

"Warm."

"Elgin?"

"Colder."

"Inverness?"

"Warm."

"Nairn, then?"

"You got it. My father was in the Royal Air Force, based at Kinloss, but our home was in Nairn. I went to Rosebank Primary for two years before the RAF posted him again."

"I've never heard you say 'shoppie' either. Nor 'play piece'"

"I only lived in the Highlands for those couple of years. When I left Nairn, I'm told I had a Scottish accent but soon lost it once I'd been living in Germany for a while, mixing with military kids from all over the UK."

"Have you ever been back to Nairn?"

"I passed through once, in my twenties, but not since."

"Perhaps you might like to visit with me sometime when I head up to Forres to visit family?"

"I'd like that."

"What were we talking about? Oh yeah! Have you ever been to South Island, New Zealand? It's supposed to be spectacular, isn't it?"

"True. I'd put it on a par with the Lakes," Suzanna said. "Did I ever tell you about the tandem free-fall parachute jump I did while I was in Queenstown?"

"No. I didn't even know you'd been there, let alone jumped out of an aeroplane."

"I can't think of a better place to do a parachute descent than over Lake Wakatipu."

"So, you're saying it's more beautiful than the Lake District?" James questioned.

"No, but it must be one of the best places in the world to do a jump. There's no tandem jumping carried out in the Lake District. The nearest skydiving centre is in Grange-over-Sands, on the southern coast of Cumbria. They say you get brilliant views of the South Lakes and the Lancashire coast, but they don't sky-dive onto a spot right on the banks of a lake like they do in New Zealand."

"Did you get to Arrowtown while you were there? My father lives there now. He's re-married to a Kiwi."

"I didn't know your parents had divorced." Suzanna paused momentarily. "I did go to Arrowtown, just for a day trip. It's really quaint and, as they say down-under, historic because it dates back to the late 1800s."

She looked like she would continue talking about New Zealand and beauty spots, so James interjected. "We'd best continue this conversation on the move, as the sun's heading towards the horizon and we need to get down into the valley while we still have sufficient light."

Suzanna looked around. Unusually, there weren't many people on the peak of Cat Bells, and she couldn't see anyone climbing up. There were many heading down the track, though. "True. Let's go."

Halfway down the fell, Suzanna saw a ferry cruising along the lake towards Keswick. "Have you been on one of the Derwent Water ferries?"

"Not yet. I'm not sure I want to. It looks weird. From this angle, it looks like a water-borne bus pushing a rowing boat."

"I see what you mean. Strange! It doesn't look like that when you get closer. Perhaps you'll see for yourself one day."

By the time they reached the car, they were feeling weary. Normally, such a low mountain – just 451 metres above sea level – and a quick walk, would not have challenged them. But they had climbed rapidly and walked down fast, because of the limited daylight hours.

"Enjoyable walk, James?"

"Yeah. It was great. It's wonderful here. Although I love Edinburgh, I actually thought about moving to the Lake District, rather than just having a holiday home. But I'm just not sure there'd be enough demand for my skills in this area. It's mostly tourism industry work around here."

"I don't have that problem in my job. There are criminals in every part of the country. I've thought about it many times. Edinburgh's a great city, but I just feel so at home here. Maybe one day, I will move."

"Not too soon, I hope. I'm only just getting to know you," James responded.

"I can't see it happening anytime soon. It's good to hear that the idea of me moving away worries you, though," she said with a smile. "Come on. Let's go to Cockermouth to see my niece."

***

"Come this way, Mrs Brody."

"Call me Eileen, dear. Everyone does."

"In here, Eileen; please take a seat. Can I get you a cup of tea of coffee?"

"A cup of tea would be lovely, dear; white, no sugar, please."

Caitlin popped back into the office. "Owen, could you bring a cup of tea into Interview Room 1, please.? I've got the lady from the bus in to make a statement. She'd like it white, no sugar."

"Sure thing, Sarge. I'll just be two minutes."

Caitlin returned to the interview room and sat down opposite Eileen

Brody. She must have been eighty-ish. Her hair was mostly grey and fluffed out, probably by using hair rollers. She wore a raincoat, covering a dress which had daisy flower prints over a dull green background.

"Now then, Eileen. You believe you might have seen the driver of the getaway car from the raid on Lothian Bank on Wednesday morning?"

"Yes. I was crossing Frederick Street on the zebra crossing when the car sped around the corner. The driver didn't stop for me. Gave me quite a shock, as I was just about to step off the traffic island onto that side of the road. Made me pull up short."

"Please describe the vehicle for me."

"It was a black Ford Mondeo. I'm certain about that because my neighbour has a similar car. I didn't get the number plate, though."

"What can you tell me about the driver, Eileen?"

Owen entered the room and placed a cup of tea on the table near Mrs Brody.

"Thanks, lad." She turned back to Caitlin. "He had a large head and prominent features. His hair was inky, almost black, and brushed back."

"Did he remind you of anyone you'd seen before?"

"Come to think of it, he looked a wee bit like that fella on the X-factor. Simon Cowell."

"That confirms it, then. We've had another witness mention that the driver looked like Simon Cowell. But he was certain it was a mask. Perhaps that would explain why the driver's head seemed rather large?"

"Oh! I'd never thought of that. Perhaps it was a mask?"

"That's fine, Eileen. What can you tell me about the two passengers?"

Eileen took a sip of her tea. "Wow, that's a rare cup of tea, that... One passenger was sat in the front of the car with the driver. He was wearing a dark balaclava. It could have been black, but most likely it was dark blue."

"Is there anything you can tell us about the other man?"

"Not really. As I said, he was in the back of the car."

"If you think of anything else, please call me," Caitlin said as she handed over her card. "I'll just make a note of your contact details, Eileen, so we can get in touch again if necessary. Is that OK?"

"Yes, dear; no problem."

The interview ended, and Caitlin escorted Mrs Brody out of the station.

Chapter 41

"Auntie Suzie," Athena shouted excitedly, as she ran along the path to towards the road. Suzanna crouched down; her niece leapt into her arms and hugged her. She had her mother's small, turned-up nose and golden hair. But unlike Charlotte's flowing, shoulder-length waves, Athena's hair was in pigtails.

"How is my favourite niece?" Suzanna asked, not really favouring her over others – she was her *only* niece. "Wow. You've grown so much since I last saw you. Such a big girl now. You're definitely catching up with your mum fast."

"There are a few years to go yet, Suzanna," Charlotte chimed in. "Come on Athena, let go of your Auntie Suzie for a minute. I want to say hello."

James stood back, observing the reunion. Mother and daughter were both pretty, and he could see the resemblance with Suzanna. The path led to a 1990s, mock-Tudor, compact detached house. Down the side of the house, beyond the fields that bordered its back garden, he could see distant views of the fells. Charlotte and her husband had chosen well. The garden, despite its winter bareness, was neat and tidy, suggesting a pride in its appearance.

Charlotte and Suzanna hugged briefly before Charlotte turned to James. "So, this is James," she stated. "I'm glad to see your tastes have moved upmarket," she said, looking him in the eye and smiling.

"Welcome to Cockermouth, James."

"Thanks, Charlotte. Good to meet you," he said, offering his hand. "Suzanna has told me loads about you on our way here. Good to put a face to a name."

"What's she been saying?"

"All good, I can tell you. Is this Pete?" James said, quickly changing the subject.

Pete stepped forward and shook James' hand. "Good to meet you, James. Welcome. How was the walk? I bet it was glorious up Cat Bells today."

"Brilliant, thanks. Yes, the scenes were spectacular from the top – in fact, from everywhere we stopped to look around."

"Come on in, you two," Charlotte suggested, "It's too chilly to stand around outside chatting." They removed their small bags from the car boot and followed their hosts inside. "We've only one spare bedroom, as you know, but they are single beds. You can push them together if you wish," Charlotte said, not knowing where Suzanna and James were in their relationship. "Dinner's in the oven. Should be ready in about half an hour. If you'd like to get showered and changed, feel free."

They both took advantage of the offer to shower, as they'd worked up a sweat climbing Cat Bells, despite the low temperatures.

***

"Boss," Caitlin said as she entered the team office. Angus swivelled his chair towards her. "I've got the warrants to search Sutherland's and Stevenson's homes."

"Glad to hear it; It's breakfast calls on Monday, to bring them in, then. We'll need to start early to catch them unawares. Let's aim for knocking on their doors at 7:30 am."

"Did you not want to go for it tomorrow morning?"

"I thought about it, but we need time off if we're going to keep sharp at this job. If we brought them in tomorrow, we'd be here all day processing them. And the Chief Constable might not be happy with all the overtime he'd have to pay for."

"Even with the leaked news in the Scotsman this morning?"

"Aye. The DCI called me about that. She was concerned they might do a flit. But the way I see it, I think we're safe to go for a Monday arrest."

"OK, boss. Your call. I could do with a lie-in tomorrow and some relaxation. I'll instruct Owen to meet you outside Sutherland's flat at 07:20 and get Murray to meet me at the same time. I'll also organise two search parties to go through their homes and cars. The guys have already been given a heads up that we would probably need searches done, so I don't expect it will be a problem."

"Thanks, Caitlin. Good to see you've thought ahead. As discussed, we need to make sure they both see that the other has been brought in for questioning."

"OK, boss. We can coordinate that when they're both in the station. Oh! By the way, Murray spoke with the shop owner about the cotton bags and he identified Sutherland as the man who purchased four of them last week."

"Excellent news. More circumstantial evidence to support the case against him."

"One last thing, boss... Sorry about my outburst earlier. I'll take you up on the offer of help if you can arrange it?"

Angus nodded. "I'll certainly try. Have a good rest tomorrow, Caitlin. We need you fresh on Monday."

***

"It's bedtime, boys," Lindi called out to the youngsters sitting huddled on the sofa watching a movie on their iPad.

"Aw, Mum! Can't we just see the end of this film?" the boys sang in synchronism.

"No, you can't," Andy said as he entered the living room. "It's a school day tomorrow, and you need your sleep."

"Come on boys, you know the deal. Pause the movie; you can finish watching it tomorrow."

The boys reluctantly did as they were told and walked up the stairs, with serious faces and heads bowed, sulking at having to stop the video. "iPad, please, Adair; you know it doesn't go up to your bedroom when it's bedtime."

Adair handed the iPad back to his father. 'Why Lindi insisted we buy them an iPad, I don't know,' Andy thought. 'Any tablet would have done the job, but she has to have the best all the time.'

"Get your teeth cleaned boys and into pyjamas. No time wasting."

Andy sat on Archie's bed while he was waiting for the boys to return. The recent injection of cash would help for the moment, but he knew he couldn't live up to Lindi's expectations, without further boosts to his wage. He hoped Charlie would go ahead with another job. But, like Charlie, he didn't trust Jack to minimise the violence.

"OK, boys, let's get into bed," He said, closing the curtains.

"Dad. How did the moon get into the sky?" Archie asked.

"Good question, son," Andy responded, as he tucked the boys in, then sat on the bed. "Some say it was a mountain that broke away from the Earth and got stuck in orbit around the Earth."

"What's orbit, Dad."

"That's difficult to explain. Let me tell you a story that might help."

Both boys looked at their father expectantly. He was good at telling stories.

"If we go back to the beginning of time on Earth, it's written in the Bible that God created the Garden of Eden. Then he created Adam and Eve – the first humans. After some time, Adam said to God, 'Lord, sometimes Eve needs to get up at night to pee and she can't see where she's going. Please, could you give her a light after the sun has gone down at night?'

'Aha! Adam, you want a nightlight. Just a glow. Enough so you and Eve don't bump into things at night. Have I got it right? God knew that Adam also needed to go for a pee at night, sometimes.'

'Yes Lord, that's exactly what we want.'

'OK, leave it with me.' So, God took a gigantic mass of rock and moulded it in his hands into an enormous ball that he put into orbit around the Earth, to reflect the sun's light when the sun was asleep. It was the perfect distance and speed to match its mass with the gravitational pull of the Earth, so it wouldn't spin off into space or get drawn to the Earth and crash into the planet because that would have destroyed the Earth.

The next night Adam said, 'Thanks so much for the Moon, God. That's perfect.' But after a few days, the Moon's light faded until one night there was no light at all. Adam called to God and said, 'Lord, I'm very thankful for the Moon. On the lightest nights, I can see very well but on some nights, I can't see a thing, and on cloudy nights it's also difficult to see where I'm going. Can you do anything about that for me?'

God chuckled and said, 'Sorry, Adam, you'll have to wait a while for the solution. Electricity is the answer, but its inventor will not be born for a few thousand years. I'm afraid I can't trust you with electricity yet – you haven't even learned to control fire.'

So, Adam was sad that he didn't get his way, but was still thankful that on most nights, he and Eve had a little light to show the way."

The boys looked at him quizzically. They appeared to be thinking up further questions.

"That's it, boys. Time for sleep now."

They both parked their curiosity, knowing their father wouldn't be distracted by more questions at bedtime. He ruffled their silky hair and kissed them both on their foreheads. "Good night, boys. Sleep tight. Tomorrow is another day to look forward to. Who knows what's in store for us?"

Andy turned out the light, leaving their night-light glowing, and lightly pulled the door closed.

***

"This hotpot is gorgeous. What did you say it's called?" James asked as he breathed in the herbal aromas of the dish.

"Halloumi Casserole. It's one of my favourites."

"The flavour is incredible. What's in it?"

"Baby potatoes, cherry tomatoes, green olives, sweet potato, leaks, shallots, veggie stock, pesto and, of course, halloumi."

"It's a fantastic combination of flavours and textures. Is it your own recipe?"

"No. I can't claim that to my credit. It was off the internet."

"I don't remember the last time I had such a fabulous meal," James concluded. Charlotte smiled at the compliment.

They chatted the evening away, quaffing three bottles of wine between them, getting to know each other, and drifted off to bed around midnight.

Suzanna and James made love – quietly, given the proximity of the other bedrooms and the thin walls. It was a fabulous end to a superb day out together. She was thankful James had suggested they push the single beds together as she cuddled up beside him in the after-sex glow, ignoring the gap between the mattresses that later might swallow her.

Chapter 42 – Sunday 18th January

In the morning, Suzanna and James went downstairs to join the family, who were just finishing their breakfasts. It was a glorious day: blue skies and sunshine, with the occasional wispy high-level cloud.

"Good morning Suzie," Charlotte said, looking up from her bowl of breakfast cereal. "Morning James. I hope you slept well. What plans do you two have for today?"

"I slept wonderfully, thanks," James responded. "The mattress was so comfortable."

"Glad to hear it. We bought the memory-foam mattresses after Suzie's last visit."

"I'm so glad you did," Suzanna responded. "They're a massive improvement on the old ones. I think they were the mattresses we'd slept on as teenagers."

"They were. Mum and Dad passed them on to me. I hadn't realised they were so bad until you pointed it out on your last visit. When I checked them out, I could feel all the springs and not much padding. We couldn't let you sleep on them again."

"Thanks, Sis. Appreciated."

"So, what are your plans for today, guys?" Pete reminded them of the earlier question.

"We need to head back to Edinburgh this afternoon, and we'd like to do another walk before we leave; I was thinking of the trail around

Buttermere," Suzanna replied.

"That's a wonderful walk. One of my favourites," Pete responded.

"Would you like to have lunch with us before you go walking?" Charlotte asked.

"That would be nice, but we still have to drive back to Edinburgh after our walk, so I think we'll have to decline. Besides, the forecast is for cloud and possibly some rain to arrive this afternoon; and of course, the days are so short at this time of the year. As you know, I'm a fair-weather walker. I don't enjoy being blown about and soaked."

"OK. Fine. We'll be heading off to church soon if you'd like to join us?"

"You know I don't do church anymore, Charlotte."

"I know you've stopped attending, and I don't blame you. The traditional Anglican service that Mum and Dad used to force us to attend was enough to put anyone off church unless you were over 75. We go to a contemporary church. It's really casual; the pastor doesn't wear a dog collar or frock. There's no organ music and you don't have to juggle pieces of paper and multiple books to follow the service."

"You've mentioned that before Charlotte, but it's not just the service and cold, damp, gloomy buildings that put me off, it's the hypocrisy of so many, holier-than-thou, prim-and-proper, judgemental, church-goers." At the thought of cold, damp, gloomy buildings, something clicked in Suzanna's mind – something to follow up on Monday, back at work.

"Are you calling me a hypocrite, Suzanna?"

"Not at all. You're different from the rest."

"I know what you mean, Suzanna. As you know, I stopped going to church as soon as I escaped to Uni. But that's where I met Pete and he introduced me to real Christianity."

"What do you mean, *real* Christianity?"

"I mean people who have been born again, who are followers of

Christ and try to live how Jesus would wish them to. People who worship Christ with enthusiasm, rather than merely dutifully. And people who serve Christ every day of their lives – not just attend church on Sundays."

"Yeah; you've mentioned this before, but I still don't get it."

"Perhaps if you were to attend an Alpha Course like I've suggested several times, you might find out for yourself."

"I'm too busy to give up one evening every week for ten weeks."

"I know you have a busy job, Suzanna, but the course includes a shared meal, coffee and chatting about each of the subjects they cover. No one I've known has regretted attending the course. And it could change your life."

"I'm not sure I want my life changed thanks, Charlotte. I'm happy with it the way it is."

"OK. I'll say no more. You know how I feel about this. It's such an important thing. I hate to think you'll not come to find the peace and sense of purpose that I have since becoming a Christian."

James sat in silence, diplomatically not joining in the conversation between these two sisters, on such a controversial subject. He had strong views on religion, but now was obviously not the time to share them with Suzanna.

"Athena. Get your shoes on, please, Darling. It's time for us to go to church."

Athena obediently found her shoes. Charlotte and Pete also got up to get ready. "I'll leave you two to have breakfast together, then. The Sunday papers are on the table. Bread for toasting is in the bread bin. Butter, jam and spreads are on the counter and cereal can be found in this cupboard," Charlotte said, indicating where.

"We'll be fine, Sis. Enjoy your time in church. We'll let ourselves out."

They all hugged. "When will I see you again, Auntie Suzie?" Athena asked.

"I'm not sure, sweetheart. Hopefully soon. I'll let your mum know when I can get away again."

"Can you come for longer next time?"

"Yes, you must stay longer next time, Suzanna," Pete added.

"I agree," Charlotte said. "We haven't had any girl time together for ages."

"I'll try. Go on. Off you go. See you next time." Suzanna concluded.

***

After breakfast, Suzanna and James headed out of Cockermouth for a walk around Buttermere and Crummock Water.

When they'd entered the town yesterday, they travelled through the Georgian main street with its multiple pubs, restaurants, and independent shops, on their way to Charlotte's house, which was buried at the far end of a large housing estate. This morning though, they exited the town on a road cutting under the A66 bypass, through the Lorton villages and on, deep into the northwestern Lake District for their walk around the area's most picturesque lakes.

The journey home was a bit of an anti-climax, with them both sad to leave the Lake District, and knowing that they had to be at work in the morning.

Suzanna pulled up by James' flat and got out. He took his bag from the car boot, and they hugged. "Thanks for a great weekend, Suzanna. I hope we can do it again sometime."

She kissed him on the cheek. "It was good, wasn't it? Fantastic weather, marvellous views, fresh air and exercise, and delightful company," she said, smiling. "What more could we want?"

"You're so right about your niece; she really is cute, isn't she? And the meal last night was incredible. Your sister's a splendid cook."

"Yes, but sorry about her Christianity lecture."

"No bother. I liked what she had to say, actually! At least she cares for you and wants you to be saved as well."

"Saved from what?"

James didn't answer; just looked at her quizzically.

"Oh well! Best go. Are you free next weekend?" Suzanna asked.

"I could be. Do you have something in mind?"

"I'll give it some thought and call you. See you, James."

"See you."

Chapter 43 – Monday 19th January

The doorbell rang continuously, and there was a thumping on the door. It was 7:30 am precisely, on another chilly, damp day. Andy was having breakfast with his kids. And his wife was upstairs showering. "What the bloody hell!" Andy exclaimed. He strode to the front door and opened it, about to give whoever it was a piece of his mind, but was shocked into silence when he saw the detective that had spoken with him two days before, along with a woman and two uniformed policemen.

The detectives immediately barged into the house, grabbed Stevenson, and cuffed him. "Andrew Stevenson?" the woman said. "I'm Detective Sergeant Findlay. You are being arrested on suspicion of armed robbery. We have a warrant for your arrest and to search these premises. Constables read Stevenson his rights and take him into custody.

Caitlin handed Stevenson over to one of the constables, then she and Murray moved into the house, with Murray heading up the stairs. "You can't go up there. My wife's in the shower." Stevenson called out, as he was being led out the door. Murray hesitated, and Caitlin indicated they should swap roles. Caitlin headed up the stairs and Murray went into the kitchen where Stevenson's children sat with spoons of breakfast cereal lifted halfway to their mouths.

"Hello, boys. What's for breakfast this morning?"

"Who are you? Where's my Daddy?" Adair demanded. Archie burst into tears, shocked by the commotion and strange men coming into his home at breakfast time, uninvited.

The uniformed officers led Stevenson to the squad car, placed him on the rear seat and closed the door. He looked back at his home, worried about his wife, and his two boys – his square face and chiselled jaw set hard. An intense frown created new wrinkles on his forehead.

"Daddy's got to go to the police station this morning. Don't you worry though," Murray said. "You'll get to see him again soon. Mummy will be down in a minute."

As he finished saying this, Lindi Stevenson flew into the kitchen, her hair still wet from the shower and, tying the belt of her dressing gown, went straight to her boys. She hugged Archie to her chest and reached a hand across to Adair's shoulder. "It's all right, boys. Don't worry. Daddy's gone with the policemen. No one will do us any harm."

Archie sobbed into his mother's towelling gown; his tears quickly soaked up. As his hand pulled on the gown, Lindi's left breast became exposed. She smelled enticingly of lemon but, despite his base instincts, Murray quickly averted his eyes, not wanting to cause Mrs Stevenson further distress.

"Ma'am, you'll need to stay here with the boys while we conduct a search of the house," Murray stated. One of the uniformed officers returned just then. "Constable Stringer will stay with you. Please carry on as best you can while we complete our business." Murray moved into the living room, where searched through the cupboards and looked under the chairs and sofa.

Caitlin searched the main bedroom first, emptying drawers and replacing them when there was nothing of interest. None of the dressing table drawers offered anything, so she turned to the wardrobe and emptied their clothes onto the bed, taking care not to crumple them unnecessarily. To her knowledge, Mrs Stevenson had done nothing to deserve this intrusion, and she didn't want to see her punished because of her husband's actions. She'd suffer enough anyway when Stevenson got put away.

Having found nothing there, either, she checked under the bed, in the plastic boxes that had been crammed in, holding spare sheets and old shoes - still nothing.

She checked the pockets of every coat and pair of trousers but found merely a few bits of crushed paper: card receipts from fuel purchases, parking tickets and a bus ticket. None of them seemed relevant. She'd run out of places to look so moved into the only other bedroom, where the boys evidently slept.

There were bunk beds with quilt covers themed to the children's likes. The youngest lad's bed, Caitlin assumed, had the dogs and machines of the Paw Patrol kid's TV series covering it. A wine and white checked quilt, with multiple heart-shaped motifs of the Hearts premier league team, covered the other bed.

Murray completed his search of the living room and moved on to the toilet. It was an old-style WC, with a high cistern and a long pipe down to the toilet bowl, with a chain hanging from it to operate the flush mechanism. He closed the wooden toilet seat and stood on it to check inside the cistern.

Caitlin looked in and under the bunk beds, then in the chest of drawers and the built-in wardrobe. Alongside the boys' clothes, there were toys squashed into this recess and she pulled them all out. Lying beneath a pile of crumpled pyjamas, she could see something thin sticking out and when extracting it found a plastic mask, with a piece of elastic connecting both extremes.

There was a crash and yell from downstairs; Caitlin immediately left the bedroom and went down to find out what had happened. She found Murray on the floor of the loo, one leg inside the toilet, his leg gashed on the broken toilet cover and a polythene bag in his hand. She couldn't tell if he was grinning or grimacing.

"Found this inside the cistern," Murray said, holding the bag out to Caitlin.

Caitlin took the wet bag and realised that there was a thick wadge of money inside. She put it in an evidence bag before slipping it into her coat pocket, then laid the mask on the sink whilst she dealt with Murray.

She helped Murray off the floor and held onto him as he pulled his injured leg out of the toilet. He placed it gingerly on the ground, pausing for a few seconds to regain his stability and test the leg's strength.

"Thanks, Sarge," Murray said. "I see you found the mask then."

Caitlin turned to where she'd placed it and, staring back at her, was Simon Cowell.

Chapter 44

Angus and Owen rang Sutherland's doorbell at 7:30 am. He didn't answer immediately, so Angus rang it again and thumped on the door.

"All right, all right. Give me a minute." Angus heard from inside the flat just before the door opened. Sutherland had on running gear but didn't look sweaty or tired.

Charlie saw two men dressed in smart civilian clothing and two uniformed policemen. He looked puzzled, and Angus could almost see his mind working: 'Surely they haven't tracked me down for the robbery. How could they have? Why else would they be here?'

"Charles Sutherland?" Angus asked.

"Yes," Charlie confirmed, his basil-green eyes staring straight at the Inspector.

"Detective Inspector Watson. Edinburgh CID. I have a warrant to search your premises and take you in for questioning. These officers will go through the formalities. I'll need the keys to this property and your car, please, sir."

Charlie turned as if to let the officers in, then slammed the door shut with a crash. He grabbed his coat, phone, and car keys, then headed out the back door onto the fire escape. He went down the stairs two-three at a time, the metal steps clanging underfoot, despite his soft-soled training shoes, and sprinted away out of the alleyway that led onto the Portobello seafront.

The tide was in and a strong wind swept across the promenade, whistling through the railings of adjacent gardens, but Charlie didn't hear the wind nor notice the air movement, as he sped along the front like an antelope running from a lion.

Glancing back, he saw one uniformed policeman and another in plain clothes following him. He turned the next corner so they would lose sight of him, then doubled back towards his home, before turning again, away from the seafront. Charlie knew Portobello as well as he knew the workings of the rifle he'd stripped and re-built hundreds of times whilst in the Army. He'd run these streets daily and could map every alley and side road.

Gradually he circled round, like a platoon attacking from the flank until he was back at Bath Street. The police must all have been chasing him or inside his flat. His car was unguarded, so he unlocked it with his key – not the remote, as the car beeped twice if opened that way – slipped in and drove away without squealing its tyres.

Angus had entered Charlie's home by force with the help of a constable equipped with a door ram and was searching the flat when he heard a car drive away. He regretted his soft approach to the arrest, avoiding the aggressive tactic of breaking the door down and armed police rushing in, with the risk that someone might get shot. But he now questioned his decision.

Angus looked out of the window overlooking the street and saw Sutherland's car travelling away from the flat. 'Clever,' he thought, then pulled his radio from his pocket to inform the chase team. He called in details of the car and occupant to get a pursuit underway, then went back to his search.

Owen arrived a few minutes later, breathless. "That Sutherland is one fit man. We couldn't keep up with him."

"I know, Owen. The DCI won't be happy to hear that. But I'll stand up for you. Sutherland is way fitter than the average man of his age, or any age, actually."

"Thanks, boss. I keep fit, as the DCI encourages, but that guy is outstanding. Have you got a motorised pursuit in operation?"

"Yes. Let's get this search completed, then get back to the station. I've already covered the living room, bedroom, and bathroom, so there's just the kitchen to search. You call in to get a door security contractor out here as quickly as you can, so we can lock Sutherland out if he returns and keep the scene safe. I'll crack on with the search and when you've organised that, you can give me a hand."

"OK, boss. Will do."

***

Charlie wove his way through the city's thoroughfares, travelling as fast as he dared. His mind was in overdrive, thinking ahead to where he should go and how he would stay out of the police's reach. He had friends to the north of Edinburgh, across the Forth Road Bridge, but Portobello was on the southeast of the city and the bridge on the northwest. He decided to head out of the city to the south, then circle around before heading north. 'I'll go out to Falkirk, then Stirling, before heading to Perth,' he thought. He stayed near the coast, driving into Musselburgh, before turning for Monktonhall, to route through Old Craighall and Millerhill, avoiding the Edinburgh Bypass.

As he was passing Danderhall, driving smoothly to avoid bringing attention to himself, he caught sight of a police car. It turned in his direction and the blue lights started flashing. "Shite," he said out loud.

He turned right onto The Wisp and sped up, noting that the police car had followed him but was not keeping up. Charlie was glad he'd bought the ST version of the Ford Focus. Its acceleration wasn't supercar class, but it could see off most cars, with a 0-60mph time of under seven seconds. He turned right again and soon regretted his decision when he hit the first of a series of speed bumps. The humps didn't extend fully across the road but left gaps to enable slow-moving vehicles to avoid them. Charlie was not moving slowly. He clipped the edge of the first bump, jolting the car.

A parked car beside the next speed restrictor forced him to mount the bump, throwing the car off track momentarily. Charlie soon recovered the car using the skills he'd learned from doing motorsports in his Army days. When he reached the school and its road-narrowing, traffic-calming measures, he had to slow to let a car pass in the other direction before he accelerated away again. He glanced back and saw the police car, a Vauxhall Astra, maintaining the same gap, despite his superior acceleration. He wished he also had a blue flashing light.

The long straight had allowed him to open up the gap from his pursuer, but as he approached a mini roundabout, he noticed blue lights on a car coming towards him. He swung a right at the roundabout and accelerated again, knowing that he now had two police cars to lose. Wrenching the wheel to the left, the car's tyres squealed as they fought for grip. Left again before swinging a right. He bounced over more speed bumps and when checking his rear-view mirror noticed that the second car was keeping up with him. It was a BMW, so faster that the Astra.

He turned left, then followed the road round to the right, pressing on the throttle pedal as the car emerged from the bend. The Focus's handling was superb, and he initially opened up a gap from the BMW.

Another right bend came up, then to his shock, he saw the Astra heading straight towards him in the middle of the road. He didn't know this part of Danderhall well, but evidently, the police did. His only option was to turn right, but as he swung the car into the road, he saw a woman pushing a buggy across it. He swerved to avoid her and the child, crashing into a wall.

Charlie was not one to give up so easily, so exited his car without delay and sprinted off down the road. It was a cul-de-sac, so he couldn't have escaped in the car, anyway; but there was a path at the end of the road. He took it. One police car had followed him into the road and one of its occupants chased him on foot. The policeman couldn't compete with Charlie's fitness, so he pulled further away. He knew he could keep this up for a long time.

He crossed the road that he'd recently driven down and ran onto the green field in front. Charlie leapt the fence and hedge at the far side of the field and found himself in an area that was likely used by local dog walkers – paths weaving their way around the green field.

Turning right, he powered off down the field, swinging left and exiting it onto a track, with shrubs and small trees lining both sides. Turning right again, he sprinted along the track, over a footbridge that crossed the A7. He looked back over his shoulder and couldn't see anyone following him but didn't slow down.

Further down the track, Charlie leapt a gate into a field where a sign saying Public Footpath pointed. He started to run again but at once fell into slippery mud. Up again, he set off across the field, but it had been ploughed recently and the footpath churned up. He tripped on a ridge and fell again. As he rose, he heard the throb of a distant helicopter. Charlie assumed it would be the police and that they would soon see him floundering in the muddy field. "Fucking farmer," he swore, "why did he have to plough the bloody path?"

He saw a cluster of trees close by and made best speed into it, slipping frequently, his feet caked in sticky clay that clung to his shoe's soles. Charlie just had to hope that the chasing coppers would run past the gate he'd hopped over, and that the trees would hide him. He entered the coppice and dived into a large shrub. Although he had masses of stamina and in good conditions could outrun the police on foot, the helicopter brought a new dimension to the chase.

The regular thud of rotating blades became louder as the police helicopter neared his hide. 'They'll undoubtedly have infra-red sensors onboard, so they'll soon identify my location.' He could hear at least three voices shouting to each other as they progressed down the lane towards the gate.

The helicopter now hovered overhead and must have been guiding the officers to the woods, as the voices became louder. Then one voice stood out above the others. "Charles Sutherland. We know you're in there. You may as well come out now. Give yourself up, man. It's over."

Charlie thought the officer was probably right. Whilst he could win in combat with each individual policeman, fighting off all three would be a bigger challenge and if he injured them, he'd no doubt get a longer prison sentence. Besides, he had no wish to cause them harm. They were professionals, doing their duty as he'd done in the Army. Unlike his opponents in war zones, where it was kill-or-be-killed, these guys were committed to upholding the law, not to harming him.

He stood and walked out of the thicket. "I'm here. I'll not run anymore." He staggered back across the ridged, slippery field to the gate, then offered his arms for cuffing and sadly accepted that his escape attempt had failed.

***

As Suzanna entered the station, she heard her name being called by the Chief Superintendent. She turned and responded, "Yes, sir."

"What progress on the bank raid over the weekend?"

"Angus and his team worked through Saturday and obtained warrants to arrest two of the prime suspects. They should be bringing them in now."

"Why didn't they bring them in on Sunday?"

"Angus's assessment of the evidence and circumstances was that it didn't merit a Sunday morning raid."

The Chief Super went red in the face and raised his voice. "These men had been involved in a robbery, brandishing firearms, and your team thought it was fine to leave them until after the weekend. Well, it's not good enough, especially as someone in your team leaked to the press. Did you see the headlines in Saturday's Scotsman? DI Watson should have brought the suspects in yesterday. It wouldn't surprise me if they've already fled the country."

Suzanna went to speak, but the Chief Super continued. "And where were you at the weekend? You should have been here providing direction to your team."

Suzanna responded in kind – her emotions raised by her boss's tone. "And were you at work over the weekend to supervise *me*? How far up the chain does it have to go? Angus is a fine Inspector and I fully trust his judgement. If it turns out these men have escaped justice because he delayed their arrest by one day, I'll review my opinion of him. But judge us by our results, sir. Not by comparison to how you or some other officer might have handled it. Besides, you always complain when the overtime bill is too high. Now you're complaining because we haven't spent money on overtime. You can't have it both ways." She stared him in the eye, showing she wouldn't back down on what she'd said.

The Chief Super turned 180 and marched off, huffing.

"Angus had better bring both suspects in this morning, or I'll have to eat humble pie," Suzanna said silently to herself, as she headed to her office.

***

After thirty minutes of searching Sutherland's flat, they gave up having found nothing of relevance. Angus's phone rang and Suzanna's name appeared on the screen. He answered. "Yes, guv?... You say Sutherland's in custody. Brilliant news. I assume his car is also being brought in... Great."

"What's that?... You say the Chief Super's not best pleased that we left it until this morning to make the arrests?... OK. I'll try to keep out his way, but as we have both suspects in custody, I'd have thought he'd be OK with my decision... We'll see. I'll head back to the station now."

***

The team gathered in the office for a quick chat before interviewing the suspects. They went over the evidence they had so far, recognising that they still didn't have Sutherland's gun or his balaclava. Suzanna suggested they check his work's locker and Angus tasked Owen with doing that, whilst the interviews took place. The only fresh evidence they had was that Stevenson and Sutherland had made multiple calls to each other during the two weeks leading up to the raid. And immediately after Stevenson's warning about the police interest, Sutherland had called a number that appeared on both phones. It was listed as Jack.

Chapter 45

Rab entered the school foyer and his nose crinkled at the smell of disinfectant from the recently mopped floor. He nearly tripped over the sign warning that the floor might be wet. He thought the wet floor signs should be more prominent and also say watch out for this trip hazard!

Rab tapped on the glass of the admin office window to announce his arrival. A woman looked up and smiled, then walked over to him. As she approached, he noticed she was good-looking and her long, wavy, auburn hair glistened in the lights. Sliding the window open, she spoke: "How can I help you, officer?"

"Is it that obvious?" Rab responded.

"Well, I knew you were coming, so I was expecting an officer of the law and assumed that you would be him – by your dress and demeanour."

"Well done. Mrs McGuire, is it?"

"Yes, that's me. We spoke on the phone. Come through to the office. The door's just around that corner," she said, pointing.

Rab entered the office. "Please take a seat, Detective."

"Billy Boyd's class should finish their lesson in about ten minutes. I'll get a message to his teacher to have him sent to the office. Would you like a cup of tea while you're waiting?"

"That would be great. Thanks. White, one sugar, please."

Mrs McGuire re-boiled the kettle and made two teas before sitting down again. "That Billy Boyd's a right scamp. Is he in a lot of trouble?"

"I can't discuss the nature of our business with young Boyd, but I will be taking him in for questioning, as he's suspected of several crimes."

"He's only thirteen. I just hope that any action you take will help put him back onto the straight and narrow."

"We can but hope, Mrs McGuire."

"Call me Sally."

"OK, Sally. Thanks."

Rab sipped his tea. She'd brewed it just right, but she must have heaped the teaspoon too much, as it was on the sweet side.

"Most of the kids at this school are a good lot, but we have a few rascals. Mischievousness comes naturally to some of them, but we don't have many who are bad, through and through."

"Good to hear it. I guess that's the same in all schools. There'll always be a few bad eggs - some perhaps violent - and a range of other behaviours from angelic down to the disruptive." Rab thought back to his own school days. He'd always tried to behave well and the disruptive boys, who spoiled the experience with their attention-seeking antics, had annoyed him immensely.

The school bell rang noisily, then a multitude of childish voices echoed down the corridors.

"Oh, goodness! There's the bell already. Billy will be here soon. I'll just get the paperwork ready for him to leave school early. His mother is due soon."

Just then, there was a tap at the window, and a dour-looking woman peered into the office. Her hair was unkempt, and her face prematurely aged by smoking, he reckoned.

"I guess that will be Mrs Boyd."

Billy's mother wore the same clothes she used in her cleaning job.

Her hair looked unwashed and tied back in a style that suggested she had no money for hairdressers and no time to look after it.

"Aye, that's her." Sally walked to the window and slid it open. "Good morning, Mrs Boyd. Billy should be here soon. If you could just wait there until he does, then you can both go into the Headmaster's Office, along with Sergeant Sinclair," she said, motioning to Rab, who was sat at her desk with a cup of tea in hand.

Mrs Boyd silently acknowledged what Sally had suggested but frowned when she realised that a seat and a cup of tea were not on offer.

Rab noticed her expression and thought: 'There's someone who believes life's been unfair to her – that everything is stacked up against her, and life will always be a struggle.' Although from a working-class background himself – his parents still lived in social housing – he couldn't help thinking her situation was likely of her own making. But she probably blamed everyone else for her predicament. He'd seen it in so many of his neighbours when he'd lived with his parents.

"Ah! Here he is now. Let's go through to the Headmaster's Office. He's expecting you all."

"Thanks for the tea, Sally," Rab said, holding the empty cup up in a salute, before placing it carefully back onto its saucer.

"This way, Sergeant."

Sally led the way out of the admin office, collected Mrs Boyd and Billy, then led the way down the corridor. She tapped on the door and entered without waiting for a response, but hesitated in the doorway to check the coast was clear, before moving in fully and inviting the others to join her.

Mr Farquhar rose from behind his desk. "Sergeant Sinclair, I presume." Rab nodded. "Mrs Boyd. Please come in. William, you can sit there." He indicated a chair off to the side of his desk. "So, Sergeant Sinclair, I hear that you have business with young Boyd here?"

"Yes, sir." Rab turned so he could face the Headmaster, Mrs Boyd and Billy. "There have been several crimes committed around the city over the last few months and the evidence we have has made William a person of interest," he said, looking at Billy. "I can't be more specific. You'll understand."

Billy looked defiantly back.

"I need to take William to the station for formal questioning about these crimes. Obviously, as a minor, he needs a responsible adult present during the questioning, hence my request for the school to contact his parents."

"Well, you got the right one of us then, Sergeant, because his father's an irresponsible bugger. I'm the only one who keeps the family together and a roof over our heads," Mrs Boyd said.

Billy looked annoyed at the public mention of his father's inadequacies.

Mrs Boyd continued. "I hope this won't take too long, as I need to get back to work. I'm losing money every minute I'm away."

"Sorry to inconvenience you. We'll try to make this as quick as we can but I'm afraid there are a lot of questions that William will need to answer. If he can be straight with us, we'll be able to get the questioning finished earlier."

Mrs Boyd looked at her son. "You'd better come clean, Billy. I can't afford to waste my time listening to you telling lies. Can we go now?"

Rab rose from his seat. "I'm ready if you are Mrs Boyd." She got up as well and Billy followed suit.

Sally passed a form to Mrs Boyd. "Please sign here to acknowledge that you're taking Billy out of school early."

Mrs Boyd looked at Sally as if to say: 'It's not me taking him out, it's this copper.' But she just signed the document and handed it back. "Can we please go?"

Rab led the way. "Did you come by car, Mrs Boyd?"

"Don't be daft, lad. I can't afford a car."

"Then you can ride with William in the police car."

As they emerged from the school, Billy looked furtively around, wondering whether he could do a runner. But the idea soon passed, as he realised there was no point because he had nowhere to run to. His mum read his mind and gave him a clip around the back of the head, looking at him sternly. "Don't even think about it."

"I wasn't doing anything," he said.

"I know what you were thinking, lad. Don't give me any back-chat."

They got into the car, and Rab drove off, Mrs Boyd still glaring at her son.

Chapter 46

Once back at the station, Rab sent word to the DCI that William Boyd was in the building. As they were entering the interview room, Suzanna took a quick look and indicated to Rab that this was indeed the lad she'd seen outside her apartment the morning of the magnifying glass robbery. She returned to her office, relieved that the case seemed to be coming together, and her guilt at losing the glass might soon dissolve.

Rab took William's fingerprints, along with a photograph, before he sat at the table with him and his mother. After the pre-interview formalities, Rab started the questioning. Mrs Boyd had said there was no need for a solicitor. If her son had done wrong, he'd admit to it and take the punishment.

"Right, William. Let me tell you why you're here today. Over the last few months, there have been several robberies from homes around the city. All these robberies were committed between 8 am and 9 am on weekdays, and they were all carried out within walking distance of your school."

Billy sat expressionless.

"We've interviewed several neighbours, from properties close to where the crimes were committed, and their descriptions of the unknown youngster, seen around the time of the robberies, fit you. We checked with your school and they confirmed you had been late to school on each of the days of the robberies. Also, we have CCTV images of you en route from the crime locations to your school in the period shortly after the robberies had been committed."

Rab went on. "You have a reputation at your school, for always having things to sell at prices well below what they'd be worth. If we track down the individuals that bought these items from you, I'm sure we would find they match the description of the items stolen from the houses. What do you have to say about this, William?"

"I didn't do it."

"Tell the sergeant the truth, Billy," his mum commanded. But Billy said nothing more.

Rab laid pictures onto the table one by one, noting the location the CCTV systems had captured them, and the time and date. After he placed each picture, he asked Billy: "That is you in the image, isn't it?" Billy nodded but kept silent and Rab commented on Billy's reaction, for the audio record.

"Last Thursday, you were seen outside the home of a policewoman in Drumsheugh Gardens. On that morning, her apartment was entered, and an item was stolen. Do you recall what item that was, William?"

Billy said nothing.

"It was a magnifying glass. An antique, of great value because of its heritage."

Billy looked quizzically at the Sergeant, not sure what he meant by heritage.

"It had been the possession of a famous detective; he'd worked with the police in London during the late 1800s when Queen Victoria reigned. That's why it would be worth a lot of money."

Billy's face changed, showing that he now understood what the copper had been talking about.

"We took fingerprints from the apartment and when the forensics team report back, later today, I expect they will confirm that it's your prints on that door frame. So, why don't you save us all the wait and tell us what happened that morning?"

Billy offered no response. Mrs Boyd gave her son a push. "Answer the policeman, Billy. Was it you that took the magnifying glass? You may as well tell him now if it was."

"I don't know what you're talking about. I haven't taken no magnifying glass and you can't prove it."

"We can if your prints are the ones found in the apartment. We also have the statement of a man who lives in the same building. He heard a door slam and saw you running down the stairs and out of the door. He called to a passing policeman, who gave chase. Both these men have described you, and when we put you in a line-up, they'll be sure to pick you out."

"Not only that but you were seen trying to sell the magnifying glass in a pawnshop in Leith. Another policeman chased you and your accomplice. He will undoubtedly be able to pick you out as well."

Mrs Boyd turned to her son. "Your accomplice? You haven't dragged young Cameron into this, have you?"

"Cam didn't have to come with me. He wanted to." He immediately clammed up, realising that he'd just admitted having been to the pawnshop to sell the glass and that he'd taken Cam with him.

"This Cameron. Does he have a surname?"

"That'll be McKenzie. Cameron McKenzie. He and his mum live in the same block as us. Cameron and Billy are best pals."

"Would Cameron's father be Jack McKenzie, by chance?"

"Aye, that's his father. He's no good, that'n."

"OK, William," Rab continued. "You've just admitted that you went into the pawnshop with your pal, Cameron, and attempted to sell the magnifying glass. You know that there are several people who can pick you out of a line-up and that the prints we found in the apartment where you took the glass from will prove to be yours. So, why don't you just tell us about the thefts?"

Billy's continued silence exasperated his mum. "Right, Billy Boyd. Start talking. It'll be easier on you if you admit it, rather than keep denying it when the evidence is already stacked up against you."

"OK," Billy responded, then started talking. He gave details of all the houses he'd burgled, as best he could remember, and what he'd taken.

Thirty minutes later, Rab asked, "Is that all, William?"

"Aye, that's it. I've not done any more robberies. Just them."

"Interview terminated. Thank you for owning up. William. As your mum said. You will be dealt with more leniently because you have. Given your age, I'll now contact a children's reporter, who'll decide whether your case should be heard by a children's hearing or be sent to criminal court. We will allow you to go home with your mum and return to school. The children's reporter will contact you soon, Mrs Boyd." Rab concluded. "Take this as a lesson in life, William. Keep out of trouble. OK?"

Billy nodded.

"Let's get you back to school, Billy. I just hope your dad's not been drinking when we get home and tell him about this. He'll be furious, but at least if he's sober, you might get away without a beating," Mrs Boyd whispered to her son.

Billy looked worried. He'd seen what his dad had done to his mum when he wasn't happy and had been drinking.

***

"Ma'am," Rab said, taking Suzanna's attention away from her computer screen. "Young Boyd has owned up to the robberies, including the theft of your glass."

"Excellent. Any word on where my glass might be?" Suzanna asked hopefully.

"Sorry, ma'am, I should have mentioned earlier. We had word that the PC, who chased Boyd from the pawnshop, recovered the glass. It's logged as evidence in the case."

Suzanna's face brightened, relief lifting her spirits; guilt gone. "I'm so glad to hear that. Thanks, Rab." She refocused on her report as Rab walked away, but further movement caught her attention. "Mairi. Zahir. Before you go, I'd like a word," Suzanna called out as they passed her office door.

"Yes, ma'am," they chorused, as they reached her door again.

"It occurred to me over the weekend that when we studied the map of the city centre the other day, right at the centre, was the Cathedral. It might be worth staking out cafes around St Giles' Cathedral before trying any others."

"Good point, ma'am," Mairi said, turning to Zahir for concurrence. "We'll start our surveillance there."

Chapter 47

"Right guys. Time we brought the suspects up for interviewing," Angus said. "Caitlin, as discussed, you bring Stevenson to Interview Room 2 and I'll get Sutherland and take him into room 1. We'll do it at the same time and make sure they see each other."

As the group passed through the office, focussed on their destination, Una tried not to show a special interest in one of the suspects, but Suzanna noticed.

As Charlie was being led to the interview room, he noticed Andy entering another room down the corridor and rolled his eyes. Suzanna was pleased - just the reaction they'd hoped for.

"Una." Suzanna raised her voice to catch her DI's attention. "Please come through to my office in half an hour. I need to have a chat with you."

"OK, ma'am. Will do."

***

"Please sit Mr Stevenson." He sat. Andy was used to obeying orders.

Caitlin went through the standard pre-interview formalities and asked Stevenson whether he wished to have legal representation. Andy thought about it for a few seconds before answering: "I think I'd better."

"OK. That is your right. Do you have a solicitor to call or do you want us to call in the duty solicitor?"

"The duty solicitor, please."

"It could take two or more hours before he or she gets here?"

"I've nowhere to go, have I?" Andy mumbled.

"Interview suspended. Duty solicitor to be called," Caitlin said for the benefit of the recorder, before stopping it. "Owen, please call the duty solicitor... Phil," she said, addressing Constable Stringer, the uniformed officer, "please get Mr Stevenson a cup of tea. Would you like tea or would you prefer coffee?"

"A cup of tea would be good, thanks."

"White, two sugars?"

"Yes, standard NATO, please."

Phil left the room to make the tea. Caitlin studied Stevenson as he looked around the room, avoiding looking at her. "Look, Andy, we're not being recorded and anything you say would be inadmissible as evidence but I just wanted to let you know how this is going to go."

Andy looked at her silently. "We have evidence that puts you in the car at the time of the robbery and we found cash hidden away in your WC cistern. In your house, we also found the mask you'd worn when driving away from the bank. Phone records show that you and Sutherland are pals and, as you'll have noticed, he's in the cell next door. When the forensic evidence gets processed, we'll have the hard evidence needed for a conviction and you'll be charged with armed robbery."

Andy stayed silent.

"Do you know what the sentence is for armed robbery, Andy? It's a minimum of four-five years and could be a life sentence."

Andy's eyebrows closed the gap between them, creating deep crevices in his face as he absorbed what he'd just been told. "I'm not saying anything until I've spoken with a solicitor," he stated.

"Fair enough, Andy. I respect that," Caitlin said, still trying to convince him she wanted to help him. "You seem like a decent chap.

You've got kids, haven't you?"

"Yeah, two boys." Caitlin smiled, partly because she'd got him to speak and partly to show him she cared about children and fatherhood.

"What are the boys' names, Andy?"

"Adair and Archie. Adair's seven and Archie's five."

"Both at primary school, then." Andy nodded. "Five and seven are grand ages for kids, aren't they? They're so full of enthusiasm for everything. Keen to learn and keen to play. Do your boys play football, Andy?" "Aye, they're both pretty good, although Adair's more skilled, being two years older."

Caitlin smiled as she noticed Stevenson relaxing. "I remember my younger brother when he was seven. He was so full of energy. He couldn't sit still for a minute. My mum said he'd got ants in his pants."

Andy grinned at that expression. He'd not heard it used since he was a kid and his mother had been talking about him to her neighbour. "That's Adair for you. He's just like that. He never stops talking and can't sit still unless he's engrossed in a movie."

Phil returned with the tea and placed it on the table. "Here you go, sir. I hope it's not too strong."

"It looks fine to me. I'm used to strong brews."

"Phil. There's no need for you to stay. We're just having a chat, whilst waiting for the solicitor. Could you just check with Owen, please, to find out when we can expect them to arrive?"

"Will do Sarge." Phil left the room again.

"You were in the Army, weren't you, Andy?"

"Aye, I was. The Royal Scots. But they changed it a few years back to the Royal Scottish Borderers when the Government merged us with the King's Own Scottish Borderers."

"How long did you serve?"

"I was in for twelve years. Joined when I was just a boy."

"Was it a good life, Andy?"

"Aye; I wish I could have stayed in, really."

"So, why did you leave?"

"My wife was fed up with me always being away. She especially hated it when I deployed to Afghan. She was worried sick that I would get killed or crippled."

"I guess your wife's concerns were based on knowledge, not just unjustified worries."

"Aye. True. I lost a few mates to roadside IEDs and several ended up with limbs blown off."

"IED, that's Improvised Explosive Device, isn't it?"

"Aye. The bastard Taliban are cowards. They plant bombs and wait for us to walk or drive past. That's what I hated about being there. We couldn't make use of our combat skills much. We just patrolled the area and got picked off by bombs or snipers."

"So, in a way, I suppose you were glad to leave the Army, after all?"

"Aye, I was, but since leaving, I miss it. I miss the camaraderie, the banter, the teamwork, the sense of value and purpose."

"How do you feel about the work you've been doing since leaving?"

"I tried doing some construction work. the Army Resettlement Service trained me in bricklaying and concreting but it didn't work out."

"Why was that, Andy?"

"The training was only for one week and all I knew at the end was the basics. I had to work as a brickie's apprentice. It was crap pay, and they treated me like rubbish, so kicked it into touch."

"So, what have you been doing since then?"

"I got work as a bouncer and, as you know, I drive for Hail-a-Ride."

"Does the Hail-a-Ride work pay OK?"

"Not really. The rewards are pretty rubbish, but it's flexible, so I can work it around my security commitments. Basically, I can drive whenever I want to, or not. No one tells me I have to, so that's great."

"There's been some talk lately about Hail-a-Ride drivers and other people working in the gig economy being made employees and entitled to sick pay and holidays. What do you reckon to that?"

"Well, it'd be great to have sick pay and paid holidays, but if we got that, Hail-a-Ride would no doubt want to control us and tell us when we had to work. So that wouldn't work for me. I just wish the rewards for driving were higher. They could keep their holiday pay and sick pay then."

Owen entered the room. "The duty solicitor is on her way. Should be here in about ten minutes."

"Wow, that's amazing, Owen. You're lucky, Andy. I expected it would be another hour or two before she'd be here. Ms Robinson's a lovely lady, Andy. She'll look after you. Owen, please ask Phil to come back in until the solicitor turns up." Owen left the room. "Look, Andy, I'll leave you to finish your tea. If you need to go to the loo, let the constable know. OK?"

"Sure. Thanks."

"Your solicitor will want all the facts, which will take a while. I reckon the next interview will have to wait until tomorrow. It will be a formal interview and I won't be able to chat. But I just want you to understand that I think circumstance has dragged you into this enterprise, and you're not a bad guy. I don't want to see you go down for ten-twenty years because of the other two's actions. Just think how old your kids would be when you got out of prison. You'd miss them growing up! If you come clean, it would go well for you in court and you'd get a more lenient sentence. Just think about it. OK?"

Andy nodded his head and Caitlin left. 'Job done,' she thought.

***

Una knocked on Suzanna's open door and entered, taking a seat without being offered, as she knew the DCI would wish.

"Close the door please, Una," Suzanna requested. Una rose, closed the door and sat again, puzzled at why the door needed to be closed.

"So, Una. How do you know Sutherland?"

Una's face paled and her eyes widened. "What makes you think I know Charlie?" Una said, realising immediately that by using his informal first name, she'd given herself away, anyway.

Suzanna tilted her head to the side and looked at her knowingly, but said nothing.

"OK. You're right, ma'am. I do know him," Una confirmed.

Suzanna waited silently for further information, and Una continued after a momentary pause. "I had a brief relationship with him about three months ago. Just a few dates and an overnight stay. He's a likeable guy. When I first heard his name, I thought Angus must have been talking about another Charles Sutherland. I couldn't believe he'd have been mixed up in anything like that."

"But why did you not mention it at all?"

"I'm sorry, ma'am. I know I should have said something but once I realised the suspect was the Charlie I'd been with, I was too embarrassed to raise the matter."

Suzanna stared at Una for a full minute, her eyes boring into her mind. "I understand, Una, but never withhold information about a suspect again. As it turns out, your silence didn't hamper the investigation, but it might have done. You're not a constable. I expected openness and honesty from a DI. You let the team down, and yourself, by not speaking up." Suzanna concluded.

Una acknowledged that she'd done wrong and promised not to repeat her mistake. "Apology accepted. I'll not say anything to anyone else. It's between you and me. But I won't be so kind if there's a next time."

"Understood, ma'am. Thank you." Una rose and returned to the main office, giving a wonderful impression of a dog with its tail between its legs. She continued on to the kitchenette and made herself a coffee before returning to her desk, where she woke her computer, then stared at the screen, pretending she was reading an email.

Una thought back to their last evening together. He'd been caring, polite, loving, and sexy, but she'd felt there was something wrong as if he were holding something back. They'd made love and slept together afterwards. She had become very fond of Charlie and thought it was the start of a long relationship. He was confident and athletic, and there were many things that they both liked: karaoke, keeping fit, playing sports, adventurous travel, music, and food. And they were compatible in bed.

But Charlie had called her the next day and said they should take a break. He had too much troubling his mind and it wouldn't be fair on either of them to get too close to each other until he'd sorted things out. This had disappointed her, but she'd reluctantly accepted the suggestion, telling him to call her when he wished to see her again.

She hadn't been planning to wait around for him, but if no one else had filled the gap, she'd have been willing to try again. Now there was no chance of that. She wondered what on earth could have led to such a decent chap going off the rails and condemning himself to years in prison. Una would probably never know.

Chapter 48

Angus led the way into Interview Room 1. "Take a seat, please, Mr Sutherland."

Charlie sat and waited. Angus started the recorder and went through the formalities. "Mr Sutherland, you know why you're here. So, why don't you tell us how it went down at the bank on Wednesday morning?"

"I don't know what you're talking about. I didn't go to a bank on Wednesday morning."

"Where *were* you around 9 am on Wednesday, Mr Sutherland?"

"I went for a run along the front at Portobello."

"Really? Then how would you explain this image, taken by CCTV in Leith Docks shortly after 9 am?" Angus said, throwing the photo onto the table in front of Sutherland.

"Ah! That was later. I went running first thing."

"And why were you in the Leith docks area that morning, Mr Sutherland?"

"I met with a potential employer about a new job."

"What time did you meet with this potential employer?"

"It was at 9 am."

"So why didn't you say so when I asked you?"

"I just got the times muddled up."

"How long did this meeting last?"

"About fifteen minutes."

"Then what did you do?"

"I went home again."

"How did you travel to the area and return to Portobello – that image isn't of you alone in your Ford Focus?"

"I got a taxi there and back again."

"Why did you do that, Mr Sutherland?"

"Because my car's engine wouldn't start."

Angus passed a piece of paper and a pen to Sutherland: "We'll need the name and contact details of this potential employer. Write them on this piece of paper, please."

Sutherland hesitated, then started writing – they hadn't thought through this situation before and worked out viable stories. He passed the piece of paper to Murray, who read it out for the audible record: "Mr Jack McKenzie, the Chain & Anchor, Ferry Road, Phone 0131 072 177."

"We will, of course, contact this Mr McKenzie. What was the job on offer?"

"He said he might need some help with security at the bar when they have events on – doorman duties."

"Why did you not meet at the bar, then?"

"He had to be in the Leith Docks area for some other business and it was the only time and place when we could get together that day." Charlie was making a reasonable job of making it up as he went along, but he still wished that they'd planned for this. He wondered how Jack would react when they questioned him.

"What resulted from this meeting?"

"He said he'd let me know if he needed help. It would only be occasional jobs."

"That all sounds plausible, Mr Sutherland, but how would you explain this image, which shows you with the same driver, but in a different car? This was at 09:11 am, en route from George Street to Leith Docks."

Charlie looked at the image, which was grainy. "It looks a little like me. I can see why you'd think it, but I wasn't in that car and this image doesn't prove it."

"We'll return to the car later, Mr Sutherland," Angus said, wrapping up that line of questioning. "We know you got yourself into serious debt from gambling." This amazed Charlie. 'How could they know?'

"We also know that you recently paid off a debt of £25,000 in cash. Care to explain where you got your hands on that amount of money?"

The revelation dumbfounded Charlie. His face paled a little, and he paused before answering. "That's my business. It's not against the law to take out loans and repay them. It's confidential information."

"So, you are refusing to explain how you paid off £25,000 in cash shortly after the bank raid on Wednesday. How do you think a jury will interpret that refusal, Mr Sutherland? If you had nothing to hide, and there was a good and legal answer to the question, you'd be happy to share it with us, wouldn't you?"

"No comment."

Angus ignored the no-comment response and continued: "Mr Sutherland, we have CCTV imagery from the bank that, although not showing your face identifies you as being involved in the raid – a man's body shape, mannerisms and movements are also unique." Angus nodded to Murray to start the video playback.

"Please look at the monitor, Mr Sutherland." Charlie looked up at the screen. "You will see yourself walking around the room, pointing the gun at the teller, and handing over bags for the money to be placed in. You can't deny that the person on the video is you."

"It's not me. It could be anyone who looks similar in height and build."

Angus continued, "Another means of identification, is voice. We all have our own idiosyncrasies in dialect, accents, and vocabulary. We'll play this recording to the bank staff, along with several other recordings, and I'm confident the staff will identify your voice."

"That's rubbish. You can't convict someone of a robbery just by their voice."

"If we were to rely on the staff alone, you might be right – although five or six people, all picking your voice out from a selection of recordings, would be quite convincing. But, Mr Sutherland, the bank's recording equipment also has good quality sound recording, so when our technical experts compare your voice from this interview recording with that taken at the crime scene, I'm certain there will be an irrefutable match."

Charlie said nothing in response but sat staring ahead, giving nothing away by his expression.

Angus continued: "We also tracked down the supplier of the cotton bags you used in the raid. The teller noticed the label on the bags. It's a rare brand, sold at only one shop in the city. The shop owner remembers selling four Freeset bags to a man matching your description and he recognised you from photos of suspects we showed him. This is further evidence that you were the man that held the tellers at gunpoint and forced them to place the money into these bags."

Sutherland sat silent and stony-faced.

"Let's recap shall we?"

One. We know the raid was professionally planned and orderly. This suggests military training, and you are ex-Army.

Two. It would require some knowledge of bank operations and cash deliveries, and you drive for the security firm that delivers to the Lothian Bank.

Three. The CCTV imagery makes it plain that you were the man in charge of the raid, controlling the hand-over of cash, whilst your sidekick handled the staff.

Four. You've admitted that you were in the Leith docks area at the time when the get-away car was driven to the bank and returned.

Five. The CCTV imagery shows you in the front seat of that car on the way back from the bank, just after the raid.

Six. You recently paid off a substantial debt with cash that you cannot or will not account for.

Seven. There's no viable explanation for you coming into that money legally. The money didn't come through your bank accounts – yes, we've accessed those and can see that you're still in debt.

Eight. The cotton bags used in the raid were a rare brand, Freeset, and we have evidence that you purchased four of these bags from a Fairtrade shop just last week.

"Nine," Angus concluded. "We have proof that on your journey from Leith docks to Portobello, you shared a car with a Mr Andrew Stevenson. Does that name ring a bell with you, Mr Sutherland?"

'Charlie paused before answering. "I've heard it before."

"I'm sure you have since you served with him in the Royal Regiment."

"Aye, ... I think he was a corporal in my regiment."

"So, you admit you know Mr Stevenson. Don't tell us it was just a coincidence that he happened to drive the taxi you were riding in that day."

"No comment."

"Another thing Mr Sutherland: Stevenson doesn't drive taxis. He drives Hail-a-Ride cars that have to be ordered by their app. But he wasn't on an official journey at that time because we've checked. So you've been lying to us. You said you took a taxi, but that's not true."

Angus let the accusation hang for a minute, then continued. "We also know that Stevenson was the driver of the getaway car because we have his prints on the car and he was wearing a Simon Cowell mask – a mask that we found, with his prints on, in his home," Angus stated.

Charlie kept his face blank and said nothing, but he was thinking what a bloody idiot Andy was for not having disposed of the mask.

"Not only that, we know from your phone records and Stevenson's that the two of you have been communicating regularly for some time now and that there have been multiple calls in the last couple of weeks. It's no good you pretending you don't know him."

"What if I do? That proves nothing."

"Mr Sutherland. Let's be frank: I've just mentioned nine reasons that, together, would lead a jury to conclude that you carried out that raid and to put you away for an extremely long time. Added to those nine reasons is the fact that when I came to arrest you, you tried to escape justice by running, requiring the resources of patrol cars and a helicopter to apprehend you. That is not the action of an innocent man. Do you know what the sentence is for armed robbery, Mr Sutherland?"

There was no response. "The minimum you could expect for a small robbery, where the threat of violence was low would be four years, but for a robbery that included the discharging of a firearm and the physical assault of an innocent woman, the sentence is likely to be over ten years and could be '*Life*'."

Angus let this hang for a minute to give Sutherland time to absorb it. "The leader of an armed gang is likely to get the longest sentence, so you can expect twenty years."

"I wasn't..." Charlie stopped himself, having nearly said he wasn't the leader. Jack was.

"Look, Charlie," Angus said, becoming more informal and friendly, "If you weren't the ringleader it would mean a lesser sentence. If you were to come clean, admitting your guilt, the sentence would be significantly less, because the justice system likes to encourage shorter trials, saving everyone's time and money."

Charlie sat motionless, his mind churning. He didn't know what to do and wished he'd requested a solicitor. He'd been a fool to think he could handle the detective by himself. "I want a solicitor."

"Interview adjourned. The suspect has requested legal representation." Angus closed off the recording with the usual formalities, then switched the device off.

"Do you have a solicitor in mind, Mr Sutherland?"

"Aye. There's a company I'm dealing with about my divorce; they also do criminal defence work."

"OK. Give the details to the constable, and he'll allow you to make a call, to arrange representation. Then it will be back to the cells." With this, Angus left.

Chapter 49

Mairi walked into the coffee shop and went to the counter, casually looking around the room as she went. Like most other cafes in the city, it had bare floors, square wooden tables and chairs, newspapers folded into a rack near the door. The counter displayed brownies, cookies, and cakes, enticing customers to treat themselves to something to go with their hot drink.

The coffee aroma was gorgeous, and the smell of toasting sandwiches enticing. It made her feel hungry. She ordered a cappuccino and panini. After some gurgling of the espresso machine, the barista handed her the coffee and said he'd bring the panini to her table when ready. She took a seat near the window with a view of the door, so she could monitor movements. Zahir was in another coffee shop nearby, doing similarly.

She sat glancing at the newspaper, pretending to read, but was actually watching the activities of every customer, especially men who might fit the general description of the mugger. An hour passed, and Mairi had seen nothing suspicious, so she WhatsApped Zahir to suggest they swap locations to avoid being noticed. Zahir agreed, so she left the café and wandered off down the street. Just as she was rounding the corner, a man wearing a crash helmet appeared and made a grab for her handbag.

Mairi resisted, and the man smashed his helmeted head down on her unprotected forehead. It knocked her back. Her left eyebrow split and blood immediately poured from the wound. The pain from her injured nose caused her to stumble. With Mairi off-balance, the man snatched the handbag from her, and she fell to the ground.

Despite her injuries, she quickly recovered and jumped up, just as the attacker turned to run off. She saw Zahir running towards them, but so did the mugger. He turned and ran in the other direction, back past Mairi. By now, she was back on her feet.

She went to grab her attacker, but he fended her off with a straight arm, pushing her backwards again. Mairi was not so easily deterred, though. She agilely spun in the direction the mugger had pushed her and was quickly back in action as he ran away from her. She took off after him as if the starter's pistol had just sounded for a 100-metre race. Zahir caught up, and they ran side by side, momentarily, until Zahir pulled gradually away, closing on his prey.

Mairi didn't slow. She wanted this man. He was guilty of multiple violent robberies, and now he'd even attacked her. She'd let her attempted rapist get away with his crime when she was young, and she was determined not to let this guy get away. Besides, it was her idea to be the bait – and he'd bitten. They had set the trap. Now they must reel him in. She sped ahead resolutely, closing the gap.

The mugger turned down a lane and continued to sprint away, but the weight of his helmet slowed him and when he glanced back, he could see Zahir getting closer. Just then a motor-scooter came up the lane towards them. He braked to a halt just ahead of the mugger, who jumped on the scooter and it sped off.

Zahir leapt at the mugger, grasped his arm and wrenched him from the scooter. The scooter wobbled, but the rider regained control just as Mairi grabbed the man and dragged him sideways to the ground. The scooter skidded across the tarmac, stopping when it hit a wall.

Zahir wrestled the mugger onto his stomach and dragged his arms up his back, the man yelling in pain. Despite having fallen off his scooter, the other man fought off Mairi and attempted to run off, but she rugby-tackled him, and he went face down onto the hard ground. If it hadn't been for the helmet, he'd likely have broken his jaw.

Zahir cuffed the mugger and knelt on him, freeing his hands to call in support. As Mairi clambered up the body of the scooter-rider, he tried to kick her off, but a passing member of the public went to her aid, pushing the man down and holding him there for Mairi to get her cuffs on him.

"Thanks for your help, sir. Can I ask your name?"

"Glad to help catch scumbags like this. It's Burns, Lewis Burns."

"Could you write your contact details in here," she said, passing him a notebook, "in case we need to contact you to give evidence?"

Lewis took the book, wrote his details in it, and returned it to Mairi. "There you go."

"Thanks," she said, checking his details were legible, "And thanks again for the help."

"Nae problem," he responded and walked away.

Zahir and Mairi looked across at each other and smiled, but refrained from punching the air, despite their desire to do so. Zahir couldn't believe that their operation had been a success on their first attempt – brilliant! That's the value of intelligent stakeouts. Perhaps if he told his father about the arrest, he might be proud of him for this success. He could only hope.

Chapter 50 – Tuesday 20th January

The team gathered together in their office. There was a buzz in the air this morning.

"Morning all," Suzanna said, as they gathered for their morning meeting. "Angus, please brief us on how the interviews of the two suspects in custody went yesterday and thoughts on the third man."

"I interviewed Sutherland after we eventually brought him in. For those who haven't yet heard, Sutherland did a runner – literally. First on foot, then in his car, then on foot again. Uniform finally apprehended him after the helicopter found him hiding in woodland on the edge of Danderhall. Despite all the evidence against him, he wouldn't admit to his involvement and he asked for a solicitor. We'll interview him again later today when his solicitor arrives. We now have more evidence against him, and I hope he'll realise it would be better for him to confess."

"How did your interview with Stevenson go, Caitlin?" Suzanna prompted.

"I had a friendly chat with him after he requested the duty solicitor. I built a rapport with him and told him I thought he was a decent guy, but that circumstance had led him astray. And he'd be better off confessing. Although the solicitor is likely to advise against that initially, I've sown the seed," Caitlin offered.

"Well done, Caitlin. Good tactic. We'll see how it works out later,"

Suzanna said. "How close are we to identifying the third man?"

"Owen has been interrogating the crime database and analysing possible matches to the description of the third man."

Owen rotated his chair towards the gathered detectives without further prompting. "I've got a few matches for build and height of people on our database, with a record for violence."

"Let's hear them then, Owen."

"First one is Alban Campbell, convicted for Actual Bodily Harm two years ago. He did three months in jail. I've not heard anything about him since his release. Second is Bryce Kennedy; arrested last year, for affray and cautioned. Again, nothing reported on him since that incident." No one commented on these suspects.

"Third is Ewan Christie. He was brought in for beating up his wife, but after a night in the cells was released as his wife didn't want to press charges. Fourth is Jack McKenzie. He has been questioned three times in connection with assaults, but there has never been enough evidence for a conviction. There were hints that he also beat up his wife whenever he got drunk. The Army kicked him out after a spell in the Military Correction Centre at Colchester for assaulting his commanding officer."

'That's the man I had in mind,' Suzanna thought.

"How come he wasn't on our original list of suspects?" Angus queried.

"I guess because he would have left the Regiment before our trawl dates and discharged by the Army from Colchester?"

"That would make sense," Suzanna said. "I've come across Jack McKenzie before. He's a nasty piece of work."

"Me too," Rab piped up. "I was involved in one of the three times he was questioned about assault. The victim named him as the attacker and we charged him, but he was bailed. The next day, the victim called to say that he'd been mistaken and would deny his statement if called to give evidence. Suspicion is that McKenzie warned him off with a threat of a worse beating or perhaps a threat to his family."

"Sounds interesting, this McKenzie," Angus commented. "His name came up when I interviewed Sutherland. Sutherland said he'd been meeting McKenzie in the Leith Docks area on Wednesday morning, regarding a potential job as a bouncer at the bar McKenzie runs on Ferry Road. That was his excuse for being in the area."

"What else do we know about him?" Suzanna asked.

"He lives in the flat that goes with the bar. His ex-wife lives in one of the tower blocks behind Lochend Avenue."

"That's a coincidence. That's where William Boyd, the young burglar, lives," Rab commented.

Suzanna acknowledged the comment about a potential connection and stored it for later.

"We'll have to find out where he was when the robbery took place," Angus said. "But we also need something to tie him to the robbery, other than this supposed meeting with Sutherland. Let's deal with the other two suspects first and see what comes out of those interviews. In the meantime, some research into what McKenzie's been up to lately: bank and credit card records, for instance, and find out who he's working for. Owen, see what you can unearth after we finish this meeting."

"Sure thing, boss."

"Any more names, Owen?"

"Just one more, boss," Owen said. "A bouncer named Gregor Henderson. He got over-enthusiastic in ejecting an abusive, drunken punter. Uniform questioned him under caution, but they didn't prosecute him, as his colleagues said the force used was appropriate, and the CCTV evidence supported this." "OK! Thanks. Obviously, Jack McKenzie is the most likely candidate for the third man." Angus concluded. "Owen, please let me know as soon as you have the background info on McKenzie."

"Will do, boss."

"Well done, team. It looks like we're getting near to closing this one." Suzanna concluded.

Chapter 51

Angus rang the doorbell of the Chain & Anchor bar but got no response. It was too early for the bar to be open, but he thought staff would be around, getting things ready for the lunch trade. He rang the bell again. Still no response. His smartphone came up with a phone number for the bar, so he called that instead of ringing the doorbell again.

The bar's phone was answered on the sixth ring. "Chain & Anchor."

"Good morning. This is Detective Inspector Watson from Edinburgh CID. Am I speaking to the manager?"

"Yes. I'm the manager. What do you want?"

"I need to speak with you about a security matter. My colleague and I are at your door. Can you please come down and let us in? It would be much better if we could meet face to face."

Jack recognised the inspector's name. Watson. A police sergeant by that name had interviewed him a few years back. He wondered whether it could be the same man. "Aye. OK. I'll be down in a minute. But it'll need to be short, as I have to open the bar soon."

A minute later, Jack opened the door and let the officers in. They sat around a table, and Angus rested a hand on its surface but quickly withdrew it. Despite the table looking clean, it was sticky. He wiped his hand on his trousers, as he addressed Jack: "How's the bar doing nowadays, Mr McKenzie?"

"It's been doing fine since I took over managing it. But what's it to you?"

"Have you had any security issues lately?"

"None that I can't handle myself."

"So, you're not recruiting for a doorman at present?"

"No. Why would I need to employ someone when I can handle it myself?"

"Do you know a man by the name of Charles Sutherland?"

"Why do you ask?"

"We've recently interviewed Mr Sutherland over a certain matter and your name came up."

"Yeah; well, I do know him. We were in the same regiment."

"Have you met recently with him?"

"I saw him a few days ago," he said noncommittally.

"And where would that have been, sir?"

"He came to the bar."

"May I ask where you were at about 9 am on Wednesday?"

Now Jack was concerned. He knew exactly where he'd been, but there was no way he'd be telling the copper. "I was here, of course. I live on the premises, and there's always something to do."

"So, you weren't in the Leith Docks area at that time, then?"

"Who says I was?"

"Mr Sutherland, actually."

Jack thought, 'What might Charlie have said?' "No. As I've already told you, I was here on Wednesday morning. I've no reason to visit that area of the city."

"Were you perhaps in George Street on Wednesday morning? Only you appear to fit the description of someone that we'd like to interview in connection with an incident that occurred there."

"No. I've already told you. I was here," Jack said, raising his voice as his worry and anger rose. "Look. I've got a bar to open. I can't sit around here being questioned." He stood up. It's time for you to leave.

At 6 foot 2 inches and broad-shouldered, he looked menacing and a close fit with the description they'd had. There was not yet enough evidence of his connection with the robbery, though. Angus rose and left. "Thanks for your time, Mr McKenzie. I believe we will need to talk again soon," he said as he walked away, and Jack closed the door behind him.

"Bloody coppers," Jack said. "How the hell did they get onto them so quickly?"

***

While Angus was making himself a mug of coffee – back at the station – Owen stepped into the kitchenette. "Hi, boss. How did it go with McKenzie?"

"He denied meeting with Sutherland in Leith or having anything to do with the robbery. But he doesn't have an alibi. I'm fairly sure he's our man, but we don't yet have enough evidence to arrest him or search his flat, yet. Was anything found in Sutherland's car?"

"Nothing, boss."

"How did you get on at Scottish Security's depot?"

"You'll be delighted to know I had success. Sutherland will have to wriggle hard to explain what I discovered in his locker."

"Good to hear it. Let's go back into the office and you can show me what you found."

Chapter 52

Caitlin was deep in thought when she heard Owen call her name.

"The duty solicitor is here."

"OK, Owen, thanks. Bring Stevenson up from the cells and into Interview Room 2. She's entitled to a few minutes with her client. Show her in and leave them to it."

"Will do."

After about 15 minutes, Caitlin and Owen enter Interview Room 2. "Hello Ms Robinson. Good to see you. We met just last week when you were representing the man who'd beaten up his wife."

"Yes. Sergeant. I remember it."

"Are you ready to proceed?"

"There's been too little time to discuss in any detail my client's defence. If you wish to go ahead, you shouldn't expect to make much progress."

Caitlin started the recorder, then began questioning. "Right, Mr Stevenson. Let's recap. On Wednesday 14th January, there was a raid on Lothian Bank in George Street around 9 am. The suspect nodded," she stated for the record.

"During the raid on the bank, a shot was fired, and a woman assaulted. A sum of £150,000 was stolen from the bank and the culprits were seen driving off in a black Ford Mondeo, licence plate: Alpha, Bravo, 05, Victor, Mike, Tango. A pedestrian saw the people in the front seat of that vehicle as it turned into Frederick Street, as did another witness across the road from the bank. The driver was wearing a Simon Cowell mask, and the passenger had on a balaclava. Are you following me?"

Andy nodded again. "The suspect has nodded. The driver and passenger were later captured on CCTV without masks to cover their faces." She passed the CCTV still image to Stevenson. "That's you driving the car, Mr Stevenson, isn't it?"

"No comment."

"You do realise that when evidence from this interview is given in court, the jury will realise you have something to hide by just saying no comment, Mr Stevenson. If you wish to deny you were driving the car, why don't you say so?"

"No comment."

"OK. We know that you transported Mr Sutherland to the Leith Docks area in your car and later took him back to Portobello. We have CCTV imagery of the two of you together in your car." She passed the next still image to Stevenson. "That is you in the car with Sutherland, isn't it?"

"No comment."

"Mr Stevenson, making no comment doesn't change the fact that this image is of you transporting Sutherland away from the area where the get-away car was dumped, and at precisely the time that it would have been dumped. Your connection to Sutherland is not in doubt."

Andy said nothing.

"Following your arrest on suspicion of armed robbery, we searched your house and, as already stated, found a mask similar to the one worn by the driver of the getaway car, along with a large sum of money wrapped in a polythene bag and hidden in the downstairs WC cistern. Would you care to tell us where this money came from?"

"No comment."

"Further, on checking your bank accounts and credit card accounts, we know that you recently paid more than £20,000 into those accounts. Please inform us where this money came from."

"No comment."

"If you fail to answer these questions when in court, in front of a jury, this lack of explanation will be seen as suspicious. I repeat the question: where did the money come from that was in your cistern and paid into your accounts?"

"No comment."

Mairi quietly opened the door and indicated to Caitlin that she needed to speak to her. "Interview suspended whilst Sergeant Findlay leaves the room." She paused the recorder and walked out. "Excuse me, please. This won't take long."

"Caitlin, we've just had word from forensics that the partial finger-print on the get-away car is a good match to Stevenson's right index finger."

"Brilliant. Thanks, Mairi. Let's see if he'll crack now."

Caitlin re-entered the interview room and started the recorder again. "Interview recommenced. Sergeant Findlay now present... Mr Stevenson, I've just had word from forensics that a fingerprint lifted from the getaway car is a match to your right index finger. What do you have to say about that?"

"No comment."

"Right then Mr Stevenson. I'll give you one more opportunity to admit to the crime before I formally charge you and send you back to the cells. Did you, or did you not drive the get-away car to and from the Lothian Bank on Wednesday 14th January around 9 am, at which a robbery was carried out, a firearm discharged, and a woman assaulted?"

"No comment."

"Mr Andrew Stevenson. You are hereby charged with involvement in the armed robbery of the Lothian Bank on George Street, in that you drove the vehicle to and from the scene, conveying those persons who carried out the robbery. You will be held in custody and remanded before the court on this charge. Take him back to the cells, please constable."

"Just a minute. I need to have a word in private with my client," Ms Robinson interjected.

"As is your right, ma'am. OK, guys, let's leave the duty solicitor to speak with her client." They filed out and shut the door behind them.

"How do you think that went, Caitlin?" Owen asked.

"As expected, Owen. The duty solicitor was bound to instruct him to say nothing at this stage; it's the standard way of keeping criminals from incriminating themselves. I've set him up for our next session, when I hope he'll see the sense of admitting to the crime and getting a lighter sentence, because he'll get convicted, anyway."

"I hope you're right, Caitlin. That would make things easier all around."

***

"Interview of Charles Sutherland, in connection with the robbery of Lothian Bank...." Angus completed the formalities then got into the questioning.

"Mr Sutherland. You have now had the time to consider your position and I invite you to describe to us your involvement with the robbery at the Lothian Bank last Wednesday."

"I've told you before, I wasn't involved with the robbery."

"When last interviewed, you admitted you had been in the Leith Docks area about the time of the robbery, and where we found the get-away car from the robbery. You said you were there to meet with Jack McKenzie, about a potential job working with him. That's correct, isn't it?"

Charlie nodded. "The suspect has nodded his head. I put it to you,

Mr Sutherland, that the job you would work on with Mr McKenzie was the robbery of the Lothian Bank on George Street that very morning. You met Mr McKenzie in the Docks along with your friend Andrew Stevenson, who drove the three of you to the Lothian Bank, where you and McKenzie carried out the robbery."

"No. I told you. I was just meeting him about working for him as a doorman."

"Mr Sutherland. I spoke with Mr McKenzie this morning and he stated that he had no need for a doorman and had not met with you in Leith. You are lying, Mr Sutherland. The reason you were there was to team up with colleagues and to rob the Lothian Bank. Isn't that the case?"

"No. I've already told you. I didn't rob the Lothian Bank."

"If we are to believe you, you need to explain to us how you came across £25,000 in cash to pay off a debt?"

"No. I have nothing to say about that," Charlie said, looking for confirmation in the face of his solicitor.

"Perhaps you might change your mind when I tell you that, since we last spoke, we have gained access to your locker at Scottish Security and have found certain items."

Charlie's face went pale. He'd not expected that.

"In that locker, we found this pistol," Angus said, laying a polythene-bagged gun onto the table, "along with a box of ammunition and a stack of cash, totalling approximately £10,000." Angus also laid these on the table.

The solicitor leaned towards his client and whispered into his ear.

"They're mine, but I've not fired the gun in months and the rounds are all blanks. It's just for training with friends out in the wilds, away from the city. We get together occasionally just to keep our hand in."

"And the cash?"

"I won it at the races."

"You can prove that you won the money from gambling on horse racing?"

"No. I don't have any proof."

"Mr Sutherland, do you have a licence for this weapon?"

"You'll know that I don't have one."

"How did you come to possess this weapon?"

"I brought it back from Afghanistan when we pulled out. It's a Browning HP - Hi-Power."

"So, you illegally imported a weapon into the UK."

Charlie looked across at his solicitor, who shrugged his shoulders – there was no getting out of this. "I never thought of it as being illegal. Everyone was bringing back weapons they'd picked up on the battlefield – the spoils of war. They're souvenirs of our time there and some compensation for having put our lives on the line for Queen and Country."

"I understand the reason for soldiers bringing weapons home with them, but it *is* illegal, Mr Sutherland."

"We have analysed the CCTV footage from the bank, and we're convinced that the weapon held by the leader of the crew that raided the bank was a pistol like this one. This is further evidence that you are that man, and the gun used in the raid was this one in front of us."

"You can make all the assumptions you want, but there's no evidence."

"Well, funny that you should say that, Mr Sutherland," Angus said, as he picked up a piece of paper and lowered it onto the table in front of Charlie. "This is a forensics report. The DNA testing has concluded that your DNA is a match for the skin fragments taken from the getaway car used in the bank robbery. From the passenger seat where we can see you sitting in this image." He passed the CCTV still to Sutherland again. "The skin fragment was dandruff from your head that had been dislodged when you removed the balaclava, after leaving the scene... You should have used *Head-n-Shoulders* shampoo, Charlie." Angus said with a grin.

This news shocked Charlie. They'd found his gun and cash and now had evidence to place him in the get-away car. How could he possibly get out of this one? He whispered to his solicitor, Steven Hardcastle, who turned to the Inspector. "I'd like a few minutes with my client, please."

"Interview suspended... OK, guys, let's leave them to talk for a few minutes. The constable will be outside the door. When you're ready to reconvene, just let him know."

Chapter 53

"So, Mr Sutherland, what would you like to tell us now that you've had time to talk this through?" Twenty minutes had passed since Angus and Murray had left him to speak with his solicitor.

Hardcastle answered the question: "Mr Sutherland would like to make a statement admitting his involvement in the robbery, but wishes to make it clear that he was not the leader of the raid and he in no way encouraged or condoned the use of violence by the other member of the team who was actually the leader."

Angus forced himself not to smile at this news. "I'm glad that you've seen sense, Mr Sutherland. Let's start from the planning of the raid, through to the cash distribution. We'll need the names of your two accomplices."

The interview went on for over forty minutes, with the detectives clarifying points and seeking facts for the record.

"Thank you for confessing to the robbery, Mr Sutherland. Just one last question: how did you know there would be £150,000 behind the cash desks that morning? That wouldn't normally have been the case. You couldn't have left to chance," Angus prompted.

Charlie thought for a moment, saying nothing. "I've delivered to the Lothian many times and know how they operate. I knew which truck and driver would make the delivery that morning, so I let the air out of one of the truck's tyres the night before the raid, to delay the driver leaving the depot. It bought us just enough time to make sure the delivery was made before we arrived, but enough to delay locking the money away."

"Do you know the deputy bank manager, Jonathon Bilberry?"

"Not really. I've spoken to him a couple of times in the bank, but that's all. Why do you ask?"

"Oh! It's nothing. Just tying up some loose ends," Angus replied. Sutherland had seemed genuine during his response, and his explanation appeared to be feasible, if risky, so it looked like Bilberry was off the hook.

Angus left the room, happy that they'd got a confession and had sufficient evidence against Stevenson for a conviction. Just the last man to reel in now.

***

"Boss. We're just about to re-interview Stevenson. How did you get on with Sutherland?" Caitlin enquired.

"Sutherland has just admitted his part in the robbery," Angus responded. "He's named Stevenson and McKenzie as the accomplices. I've left Murray writing up the statement."

"We'd better let the DCI know. She's out somewhere."

"Agreed, Caitlin. I'll call her."

***

Feeling peckish, Suzanna decided to stop off at a supermarket in Leith, to get something for lunch. She noticed Mrs Boyd entering a shop, so parked and followed her into the small supermarket, thinking she might have a quiet word with her about Billy. Having grabbed a few items, she joined the queue behind Mrs Boyd and another woman. They were both unkempt, their clothes smelled like dirty ashtrays and their skin pallor was grey and wrinkled.

The second woman turned to Mrs Boyd. "How's your Jimmy getting on Morag?"

"He's on the mend now. Was unconscious when they took him into the theatre to work on his broken leg, but he came around once the general anaesthetic had worn off. He was still befuddled, though. The doctor said it was temporary amnesia. She reckons that his memory will come back slowly, although sometimes with trauma cases like his, he may never remember the actual accident."

"How long will he have to stay in the hospital?"

"They couldn't tell me for sure. They need to make sure he's got no permanent brain damage – he took quite a knock on the head. You should see the huge bump he has, and they say that there was also a deep and long cut to his scalp. But at least he didn't crack his skull open. So they're expecting he'll be fine. I need to check in with them later, in case they can let him out."

"When he gets released, I suppose he'll not be able to go to school for a while, what with his leg in plaster?"

"That's my worry, Isla. Jimmy's dad will have to take care of him, but Reg is not the most reliable of men."

"I feel for you, Morag, having four boys to look after."

Morag thought about what Isla had said and held back her response until she'd gotten over her annoyance with Isla for calling her husband a child. She was right. Reg had never grown up and accepted his responsibilities as a father and husband but she didn't want anyone else saying so, even her friend and neighbour.

Suzanna watched as Morag started unloading her trolley. The process was taking too long for Suzanna's liking, and she was getting impatient. She'd only popped into the shop for a couple of things, and it was taking ages to get served. She resented having to hang around so long to buy just a sandwich, a banana, and an apple. Most of the other supermarkets in the city had self-serve check-outs, which were great for people not buying much.

Changing the subject, Morag asked, "I saw your ex the other day,

Isla; what did he want?"

"He comes to see the boys occasionally but this time it was to give me a wadge of cash to get myself some clothes and new shoes for young Cameron – he's got holes in the soles of his school shoes. It's been so embarrassing, but we've not had any spare cash to buy him replacement ones. I'll take Cameron shopping on Saturday. I'm sure that'll please him."

"Did he say how he got the money?"

"Yes. You know he was working as a barman; well, he says they promoted him to bar manager, and he got a bonus from his boss."

"Where's he working now?"

Morag paid for her goods, took her shopping bags, and stood back to let Isla get to the loading area.

"At the Chain & Anchor on Ferry Road. It's quite a big pub."

"I don't think I know it. Is he living in that part of the city now?"

Suzanna knew the pub. In fact, it had a reputation for trouble, with violence spilling out onto the street. Ferry Road tracked all the way from Leith in the city's northeast to Drylaw in the northwest, passing many green spaces and nice residential areas. But the pub was on a run-down part of the road, the neighbouring businesses being a betting shop, a Turkish barber, and some takeaway restaurants.

"Yes, he's got a small flat attached to the bar. Very convenient."

As Isla went to pay, Suzanna noticed her surname on the payment card, McKenzie.

"You know what?" Morag said to Isla. "That bonus must have been a big'un because I saw Jack driving off in a flash car – a big BMW coupe. That can't have been cheap."

"Aye. He says the owner of the bar thinks he's the bee's knees. I just hope he gets more bonuses. I could do with the extra money."

'Interesting' thought Suzanna; she was happy to have been in the queue behind these two women, after all.

CHAPTER 53

"Have you had the police knocking on your door yet, Isla?" Morag asked.

"Why would they do that, Morag?"

"Aye, well... You'll have not heard yet, but young Billy is in trouble with the police. I had to go with him to the police station yesterday."

"What's he been up to then, Morag?"

"I hate to admit it, but he's been thieving from people's homes. The police have charged him with theft."

"But why would they knock on my door?"

"Because Cameron had been with Billy in the pawnshop when he had tried to sell one of the things he'd stolen. They know Cameron didn't do any of the thieving, but when the two boys ran away from the copper, Cameron borrowed a bike for his escape. They said he stole it."

"WHAT! So how come you said nothing before? I'll not have Cameron hanging around with your Billy again. Don't want my kids getting locked up. Can't believe it. Wait til I get my hands on young Cameron." Isla stormed off without looking back, leaving Morag trailing and down at heart.

Suzanna decided she'd best leave the friendly chat with Mrs Boyd. Instead, she walked into the nearby cemetery and found a park bench to sit on. As she ate her lunch, Suzanna reflected on where the bank raid investigation was going. Stevenson and Sutherland were in custody and it looked like they would have the evidence for a conviction. They'd eliminated Wilkins, and now Jack McKenzie was most likely the third man. From what Suzanna had just heard, he'd moved up the list of suspects and was certainly worth interviewing.

She finished her lunch and dialled Angus's number. It rang for a while, then went to voicemail. Suzanna assumed he was still interviewing and decided she'd have a chat with McKenzie, anyway.

Chapter 54

Suzanna pulled up outside the Chain & Anchor. Its surrounding were shabby, with paint peeling from the unmaintained wooden boards, and cigarette ends littered the pavement outside. It was mid-afternoon, and the last of the lunch-time customers were heading out the door. The bar was dingy, the carpet sticky from spilt drinks, and the smell of beer, whisky and sweat permeated the air.

It was empty, save for one broad-shouldered, tall, mean-looking man. He was gathering glasses from the tables, leaving behind the crisp packets and stray, stale peanuts that customers had discarded earlier. The man looked up as she entered, and his expression changed from one of disinterest to surprise and distaste. Presumably, he could sense that she was the Law.

The man didn't carry any excess weight and, from what she could see, appeared to be muscular. He wore jeans and a black crewneck jumper, with the sleeves pulled up to just below his elbows.

Suzanna noticed the dagger tattoo on his right arm. His dark brown hair was unruly and greying at the temples. Thin lips hinted at cruelness. A large nose overshadowed his thin lips, which hinted at cruelness. He had a broad forehead, a large rounded skull and cauliflower ears – probably from playing rugby. 'With those bullish looks, he'd better stay out of a china shop,' Suzanna thought.

"Jack McKenzie?" Suzanna asked, already knowing the answer.

"Who's asking?"

"Chief Inspector McLeod. I need to ask you some questions."

"I'm not in the mood for questions from nosy policewomen, and I don't have to answer your questions. If you want to question me, you'll have to arrest me."

"Well, we can arrange that if you'd prefer to go to the station now, instead of just asking a few questions. I see you've just acquired a 6-series BMW, Jack. I'd like to know where you got the money from to purchase it?"

"None of your business. What's it got to do with the police if I buy myself a nice car?"

"Well, Jack, if you took out a loan, that's fine. If you just answer my questions, I can get out of your hair and let you get back to your skivvying." Suzanna purposely suggested his work was menial, to wind him up. Her phone vibrated in her handbag, but she ignored it.

"Listen bitch. I'm bar manager, not cleaner."

"I don't see you managing much at the moment, Jack. Where are all your staff?"

"They're out-back, cleaning the kitchen and washing dishes."

"Sure, they are. Anyway, you haven't told me where you got the money from for the car – a cash purchase, I hear."

"How would you know I paid cash for the car? Who's been talking?" Suzanna was glad that he'd admitted to buying the car with cash - mere speculation on her part.

"That's for me to know and you to guess. So, where'd the cash come from, Jack?"

"It was a bonus from my employer when I got promoted. He knew I needed a new car and gave me a bonus so I could get one. He's a great bloke."

"So, who's your boss then, Jack? I take it he'll corroborate your story?"

"Sure, he will," Jack responded, thinking he'd better have a quick word with his boss after the copper had left.

Suzanna pulled out her notebook. "Name of your employer, Jack. Address and telephone number."

Jack reluctantly gave the Chief Inspector the details. There was something about this woman that, despite his wish to not cooperate, made him feel he had to respond to her demands. She had an air of authority about her and commanded obedience, like his major back in his Army days.

"Right then, I'll call in on Mr Anderson later." Pausing momentarily, as her mind sorted through her vast database of knowledge, Suzanna spoke again. "That would be Iain Anderson, then?" Iain Anderson owned numerous pubs and clubs, had a sizeable house in the Spylaw area of the city, a Bentley Continental, and went nowhere without his henchmen.

"Aye, that's the man."

"So, when do you get promoted again, Jack, to become one of Mr Anderson's heavies? Surely this job is beneath you? Serving beer and collecting up glasses can't be enough for someone like you, Jack. Don't you miss the buzz of combat, Jack? Miss the adrenaline of the fight, of violence unleashed from your hands when you pulverise a weaker man, Jack. Like you did to your commanding officer before the Army sent you to jail in Colchester, then kicked you out with a dishonourable discharge?"

Jack was huge – barrel-chested, with muscular arms and taller than Suzanna by at least six inches. He looked down at her menacingly, his fists clenched tightly. His face reddened with anger. She'd riled him with her suggestion that his job was bottom rung and reminded him of his love for violence. How dare she talk to him like that?

"Jack, we know you bought the car with cash, and the notes you used were from the bank raid. We've got an eyewitness who saw you in the get-away car just after you took off your balaclava. My colleagues already have your two comrades in custody, and they'll be here in a minute to take you in as well. It's over, Jack, you're going down for this one." She hoped this sounded believable.

"You fucking bitch! Do you think you can take me in so easily and lock me up? I'll not go to jail again." Jack couldn't contain his anger and went to grab her, to push her to the floor and give her a kicking before escaping. But as he lurched at her, Suzanna grabbed his jacket collar, dropped low and spun her back into him, using his momentum to pull him down. She rammed her hips back into him, driving the wind out of him and dragged him lower. Her hands tugged at his jacket and she thrust upwards with her legs as she pulled him towards the floor. He spun over her, doing an involuntary forward roll.

As he came down, Suzanna drove him down, slamming him into the ground on his back, in a classic Ipon-scoring judo throw. His body thudded as it hit the ground and his head bounced off the floor, with the sound of a rolling pin hitting a coconut. On a judo mat with a two-inch rubber cushion, this would have knocked the wind out of him, but onto the hard floor of the bar, the throw shocked his body into momentary immobilisation and knocked him unconscious. She spun him over, took hold of his hands, removed the handcuffs from her bag and secured his wrists to make sure he couldn't do much when he came around. She checked his pulse and breathing to ensure he wouldn't die on her, then called the office at Fettes Avenue.

Chapter 55

Angus arrived at the Chain & Anchor. "Isn't that the DCI's car parked out front?" He hurried into the bar.

"That was quick, Angus. I've just put the phone down."

"We were on the way already. The other two gave him up, so I was coming to arrest him, but I see you've beaten us to it."

Just then Jack McKenzie stirred; he groaned and complained about having difficulty breathing – Suzanna had sat on him to keep him from rising and causing trouble. She stood and Angus dragged him onto his knees, then his feet, while two uniformed colleagues, who had just arrived separately, grabbed his arms to restrain him. "Read him his rights Angus, then take him in and book him for assaulting a police officer."

"What do you mean, assaulting a police officer, bitch? You're the one who assaulted me."

"Look, Jack, if you don't make a fuss, I won't tell your pals just how easy it was for a woman to take you out. OK?"

Jack looked pissed off but stopped complaining and went with the uniformed guys without another word.

Although in her mid-forties, Suzanna was still fit and agile. It had been several years since she'd been on the judo mat competitively – judo was really a young person's sport – but she still trained and hadn't lost the moves. The training sessions always included multiple repetitions of the same throwing techniques – uchikomi, in Japanese. So the techniques still came to her intuitively when faced with a physical conflict. This skill had saved her many times with criminals apprehended when they might otherwise have gotten away.

It still annoyed Suzanna that many of her colleagues' lack of fitness and inability to handle themselves in combat with villains meant that some got away. If she had her way, they'd all be required to do weekly combat-sports training and regular fitness tests.

Angus returned, having seen McKenzie into the car. "What's this about you assaulting him – have you been practising your judo again, guv?"

"Yes. Seoi Nage. Look it up sometime. He went for me, so I floored him, and he got knocked unconscious for a while. He'll be fine; his pride hurt more than anything, although he'll likely have a sore back for a while. The bigger they are, the harder they fall, as they say! But you will need to keep him under observation and have him checked out by a doctor before questioning him or leaving him locked up."

"Boss, you really should have called for backup before trying to arrest him."

"Thanks for your concern, Angus. I tried calling you, but it just went to voicemail. I hadn't come here to arrest him, just to test him. How come you didn't let me know you were on the way here?"

"Like you, I tried but just got your answerphone. So how did your visit result in the arrest?"

"I just challenged him over his suspected involvement in the bank robbery. I made out we had an eyewitness to see how he would react, and he decided he'd do a runner – attempting to take me out in the process."

"We'll not need a warrant to search this place now, as we have probable cause and we're already inside. We need to find something physical to link him to the robbery."

"OK, guv, I'll arrange a search team." With this, Angus hit a well-used contact on his phone and started organising the search.

Suzanna observed him at work. He was an excellent detective. Not just because he helped solve crimes and was good at police work, but because he was so industrious – never wasting time and getting the job done effectively and efficiently. That's why she'd recommended him for promotion.

She didn't like the thought of losing him from her team, and maybe that wouldn't be necessary, but she accepted this was likely to happen. It was the cost of coaching home-grown talent – they deservedly moved on. There were others on the team who were developing well. She'd do all she could to get the best out of them and to help them meet their full potential.

Suzanna left Angus to supervise the search and headed back to the station to write up her account of the arrest.

***

Later that afternoon Angus called Suzanna. "The search team has been through McKenzie's flat and has found nothing linking him to the crime, but they found a small amount of cocaine. Just a self-use quantity."

"Good to know that we have another crime to add to his portfolio. Have the team also searched his car?"

"Not yet, guv. That's next on their list."

"OK; I'll come back and have a look around myself and bring Murray with me, if that's OK? I've finished writing up my report now."

"That was quick, guv. Great. I'll head back to the station. The search team will still be here when you arrive. Happy for you to have Murray to assist. Perhaps he'll learn from you. We'll likely be able to wave at each other as we pass."

"I'll leave the waving to you, Angus. I'd prefer to focus on driving safely."

"Only joking, guv."

***

Suzanna arrived at the Chain & Anchor before Angus had left. He was just walking to his car as she stepped out onto the road. "Ah! Angus. Glad I caught you," she said. "Something occurred to me about what the bank manager said."

Angus tilted his head.

"He said the delivery was late on the morning of the raid."

Angus's head straightened up, and his eyebrows raised.

"He also said that he'd asked his deputy to put the money into the safe. But Bilberry didn't do so, because he got caught up in the routine of opening up and serving customers. And he said he hadn't heard the manager ask him to do it. Well... the late delivery is crucial to their having been a worthwhile sum of money to steal."

"Ah! I see where you're going with this line of reasoning. Perhaps the driver was purposely late. So he could be the collaborator?"

"You got it, Angus."

"I'll get someone to find out who drove that morning and have a chat with him."

"Great. See you later."

As Suzanna and Murray entered the bar, she shared her thoughts with him about the search and agreed on who would search which room.

Suzanna started in the kitchen, opening every cupboard and draw, and looking for anything out of the ordinary, but found nothing. She moved into the bedroom and checked out every piece of furniture in the room, opening draws and doors, then the back of each item. She lifted the rug and checked for loose floorboards or shiny screws – still nothing.

As she turned to leave the room and ask Murray how he was getting on, something clicked in her mind. The clothes in the wardrobe were hanging at an angle, as is common with older shallow wardrobes like many she'd seen from the 1930s, but this wardrobe jutted out from the wall a good distance. She re-checked the wardrobe again and realised that the wooden backing didn't match the wood grain on its rear. There seemed to be a false back to the wardrobe.

She felt around the panelling and found some screws slightly proud, and on closer inspection, noted that the screw slots showed signs of recent abrasion from a screwdriver. Suzanna removed all the clothes and laid them on the bed, then removed her Leatherman multi-tool from her handbag and extracted the crosshead screwdriver. She took out each of the four screws that had glinted at her and found that the panel moved forward easily.

"Murray," she called out, "I've found something."

Murray joined her. "What have you found, ma'am?"

"There's a false back to the wardrobe, so I'll pull it out now. I want you to witness what we uncover."

Suzanna removed the board and laid it against the wall before turning back to the wardrobe.

"You were right, boss. Look at these."

"OK. Looks like we've hit the jackpot. Get the search team back in here with their evidence bags and cameras to record this. The pistol looks like a Hungarian FEG PA-63 – they're quite distinctive. That would make sense because Jack served in the Iraq war and some Iraqi officers carried PA-63s. Chances are that he lifted this from a dead Iraqi officer and smuggled it back into the UK on his return. The balaclava is the same colour as that reported by the bank raid witnesses and the bag looks like it might contain bank notes – we'll find out soon enough."

Chapter 56

Andy sat forlornly in the police cell, his head hanging low. There was a powerful smell of paint from the recently redecorated corridor, but he could also smell traces of vomit, urine, sweat and disinfectant.

'How the hell did I get here?' he thought. I'm going down for this, obviously. Lindi will divorce me. I'll never get a job again and I'll end up on the street, destitute like the other guys I see hanging around the city centre, with cans of high-strength lager, their only friend.

He thought back to when he'd first heard about the opportunity to pay off his debts. The latest credit card statement had been even more of a shock than he'd expected. Just this one card had a £19,000 debit balance, and he had three cards. The debt had built up gradually at first, but he could only pay off the minimum repayment and the interest rate was crippling. The balance just descended into huge negativity, accelerating like a novice skier inadvertently taking a red run, then a black. His debt was out of control and he'd soon crash unless he did something dramatic.

Later that day, Andy had met up with his friend, Charlie. "How're you doing, pal?" Charlie had asked.

"Not good, actually."

"What do you mean?"

"I've been a bloody idiot and now I've got huge credit card debts. I've just not been able to say no to Lindi when she's asked for stuff."

"Tell me about it! I've done like you, but not just credit cards. I owe a guy loads of dosh. Had to borrow it to pay off gambling debts, but now he's calling in the debt and I've got no way of getting it."

"Bloody hell, Charlie, we're both as bad as each other. It wasn't like this when we were in the Army, was it?"

"No, the money was better to start with, and the cheap housing, free uniform, etc, made life a lot easier. At least we're not sleeping rough like a lot of guys who leave."

"Not yet anyway. If it keeps going like this, I'll lose my home. I just don't know what to do."

"There may be a way out for us both if you're interested?"

"Of course I am. What do you have in mind?"

"Well, you know Jack McKenzie?"

"Aye. I haven't seen him in months, though."

"He's had an idea that would bring us together as a team, to do a job that would earn us thousands, quickly."

"You don't mean going to some shit-hole of a place on mercenary work, do you?"

"No, this would be much closer to home and would be a quick win. We wouldn't even have to leave our families."

Andy thought for a minute. "It must be illegal, then."

"True, but it would just be taking back money that the finance industry has taken off us in interest. How much interest have you paid on your credit cards?"

"Good point. So, you're talking about a robbery, then?" "Yes, a bank."

"What, safe cracking and all that stuff, like Oceans 11 and the sequels?"

"Not in that league, Andy. He's talking about a straight in and out, taking the cash they have to hand."

"How much would that be?"

"If they've just taken delivery from a security truck, there could be £100k or more."

"So, more than £30,000 each. It would need to be at least that, just to pay off my current debts." He paused; "I'll give it some thought, Charlie. Becoming a criminal goes against the grain. I've never broken the law in my life, except road traffic laws, of course. Who doesn't?"

"I know what you mean. The only dealings I've had with the law was from a bit of drunken fisticuffs, on a night out. And it wasn't me that started it." He thought for a moment. "Hey Andy, do you remember that time we were on patrol back in Helmand? We came under attack from a couple of shooters, holed up in a farmhouse."

"Aye. I remember. We were exposed when they fired the first shots, and Jon took a bullet in his leg – went down like a drunk who'd just tripped on a kerb."

"Mungo dragged him into cover and did first aid on him, and the rest of us took the bastards out. It was classic, alternating cover fire and running like madmen. They never knew what hit them when the grenade landed at their feet."

"Aye. It was classic, wasn't it? What a team we were."

"You're right there, pal, and we can be a team again, but this time for our own benefit." He paused. "You have a think about it, but don't leave it too long, or we'll have to find someone else to join the team."

Andy had thought about it for a day. He had to find a way out of his situation, and a bank robbery might just be the answer. That had been the start of this journey that saw him now sitting in a police cell, with his life as he knew it, about to end.

***

Owen opened the cell door. "Mr Stevenson, please come with me." He stood aside and Andy walked out. Owen closed the cell door behind him, then led the way. The interview room was as bleak as ever, with no windows and every sound echoing off the hard walls and floors.

"Sit down, Mr Stevenson," Angus said. Andy joined his solicitor, Ms Robinson, at the table.

She leaned towards her client. "Andy. Remember, you don't have to say anything. You can just say no comment. Say nothing that will incriminate you. Understood?"

"Yes. Understood."

Angus started the tape and dealt with the formalities before questioning Stevenson. "So, Mr Stevenson, let me recap on the situation for you. You lied to us about being in Portobello at 9:20 on the day of the bank robbery and you have no alibi for the period of the robbery. We have CCTV imagery that shows you driving the get-away car that we later found in the Leith Docks area. We have a partial fingerprint from the car that matches yours."

Angus paused for breath, then continued. "You were heavily in debt and shortly after the robbery, you paid substantial funds into your bank accounts and credit cards, for which you cannot account. We also have evidence that puts you and Charles Sutherland in your car together just prior to and just after the robbery. And we have DNA evidence linking Sutherland to the get-away car."

"We have a sum of cash and a mask which we found in your house with your prints on, that matches the description of the mask used by the get-away car driver. And... Charles Sutherland has just confessed to the crime and named you as the driver."

Andy's face dropped. He never expected Charlie to grass on him.

"Finally, we have recently arrested Jack McKenzie." Angus paused. "We already have sufficient evidence to charge you with armed robbery, Mr Stevenson. You'll be going away for years. But the judicial system likes to encourage people not to waste court time and to reduce costs. So, if you were to make a statement admitting your guilt and giving evidence against McKenzie – the man who discharged a gun in the bank, endangering innocent people's lives, and who beat up a harmless woman – the judge will take this into account when sentencing you." Andy's solicitor grimaced at the mention of the woman being beaten up by the thug who'd led the raid.

"So why don't you make it easy for yourself, Andy, and tell us how it went that day?" Angus prompted.

The solicitor leaned across and whispered in Andy's ear.

"I'd like to make a statement," Andy stated. "I don't deserve to go away as long as McKenzie. He's a mean bastard. Charlie challenged him about beating up that woman; there was no need for that. We never meant anyone to get harmed in the raid. The guys had blank ammunition in their pistols, so no one could get shot."

"Thank you for being sensible about this, Mr Stevenson. Let's run through it from when you first got involved with the planning of the raid and distribution of the money taken."

Chapter 57

Charlie knew he'd be going to prison for the robbery. He pondered on how it had come to this. His life had been good in the Army, and when he'd been home with Isla and the kids, he'd mostly enjoyed himself – until the more recent times, anyway. It was just over two years since he'd left the Regiment and he'd been separated from his wife for much of that time.

His trip to Headley Court, just after he'd started work as a security truck driver, came to his mind. He'd entered the gymnasium, an enormous room, well equipped with all the latest technology, and sauntered over to a man sitting in a wheelchair lifting weights. "Drummond McMillan... How're doing, pal?"

"Charlie Sutherland. Bloody hell. Never expected to see you here."

"Aye, well, I couldn't be in this part of the country without looking up my best pal. I see you're even more of a short-arse than ever," he jested, as he lightly punched his friend's arm.

Charlie bent down to Drum's height, shook his hand, then awkwardly hugged him. He could feel the muscular power in Drum's shoulders and could smell the saltiness of his recent exertions. He wanted to hold him longer, to say he was sorry he'd been crippled, but he knew he couldn't do that without becoming emotional, and there was no way that he would let anyone see tears in his eyes.

Both men looked embarrassed at their public display of affection.

"So how long is it you've been at Headley Court?" Charlie asked.

"Ten months, now. It will be a while before I get out of here. My arms are getting stronger than they've ever been, which helps with driving the wheelchair around. But I've still got to learn to walk yet."

"That'll be a problem, seeing as how you've got no legs!"

"Yeah. Thanks for reminding me, pal! Actually, they'll be fitting me with prosthetic legs next week. They've been measuring me up and they should be ready soon. They say it'll take at least three months, perhaps four or five, before I become confident using them, and able to walk without someone else by my side to catch me."

"You'll have time to get ready for the Paralympics in 2020, then. Knowing you, you'll not let this inconvenience hold you back."

Drummond's spat back as he responded. "Inconvenience! You've no idea, pal. It's been sheer hell getting this far. You think it's been easy?"

"Hey Drum. Sorry, pal." Charlie's face showed humility, his voice calming. " I never meant to trivialise your situation. Can only imagine how bad it's been. I just meant that you're such a determined guy you won't let this hold you back."

A minute passed before they spoke again. "OK, pal. Understood," Drum responded. "Thanks for trying to be positive. And you're right; I will pull through this and get my life back. I'm not sure whether I'll be able to have sex standing up, though," he said with a smile. "Cheryl might have to be on top from now on."

"Lucky you. Has she been to see you lately?"

"Aye, she was here just last week. But it's normally only once a month because this place is so bloody far from Scotland. Perhaps you could drop in on her when you're next in the area?"

"I will, Drum. She'd be excited to see me, I am sure. Bet she's missing having you around to keep her happy," Charlie responded, hinting at a double meaning to the *happy.*

"You bastard. Don't you go seducing my wife while I'm stuck in England."

"Just joking, pal. You know I'd never try it on with her, even though she is gorgeous. Besides, she'd never betray you, even for someone much better looking than you." Charlie grinned, the banter confirming their continued close relationship.

"You're right. Cheryl's solid as a rock. She'd never go with anyone else. Actually, we get some privacy when she visits." Drum winked at his pal. "It's been fun learning how to do it with me having no legs," he said, beaming. "By the way, how's Isla?"

"I meant to tell you before. We've split up."

"What. You're joking. I can't believe it. I thought you two would be lifers. What went wrong?"

"Ever since I got back from Afghanistan, we've argued about everything: disciplining the kids, how much I drink, how often I go out for a beer, how we spend the money. The climax came about three months after we found out that our daughter, Alana, is terminally ill with cancer."

"Bloody hell, Charlie; that's horrendous news."

"It was an enormous shock for us all. The stress of it just made us argue even more. In the end, we had a blazing row, and she kicked me out."

"Wow. That's so unexpected. I never saw you argue with Isla in all the time I've known the two of you. But I can understand the effect that Alana's diagnosis must have had on you. How are you coping with it, pal?"

"Every day that I'm not with my wee girl is a struggle. I know that her time is limited and every day I'm living away from her is another day of her short life that I'm missing."

"Actually, things had not been brilliant for years. We'd always appeared united and in harmony when we were in public, but as soon as we were back home or in the car, the daggers would come out. Trouble is, she always wants to control me, but I refused to let her so there had been ongoing conflict."

"So, have you moved back into barracks, then?"

"No, I've rented a flat of my own, in Portobello. Nothing special."

"I thought you get a room in the Sergeants' Mess. En suite bathrooms and all your meals cooked for you."

"I did for a while, but that's no longer possible, Drum, because I left the Army. I couldn't face seeing any more of my mates killed or injured in pointless conflicts. The bloody politicians and the Army heads keep sending us into war zones, but they're not the ones who have to patrol places like Helmand Province. They just sit back in Army HQ or Westminster whilst we put our lives on the line or get our legs blown off." Charlie grimaced at what he'd just said and noticed Drum's face drop. "Sorry, pal. That was insensitive."

"Aye, it was. But I know what you mean. We're just pawns in their political game, aren't we? I'm not saying that the British Army should never deploy into combat zones. We do a damned good job when we're there, but sometimes you wonder if it was all worth it – especially Operation Herrick."

"Agreed. I read the other day that between 2001 and 2013, around 400 British military personnel died on operations in that God-forsaken country. I just got sick of it, so handed in my notice."

"Yeah. We lost more people in Afghanistan than we did re-taking the Falkland Islands from the Argies. You'll have not been out long then?"

"No, about four months."

"So, what are you doing for work now?"

"I've just started working for Scottish Security. In fact, that's why I'm down here. I've been training at the security driver's training centre in Hampshire."

"Did you not do the resettlement training at Aldershot before you left?"

"Aye, I did. I took courses in Bricklaying and Carpentry, and when I got out, the Resettlement Service helped get me a job as a carpenter with a firm in Edinburgh. Can't fault them."

"So why aren't you fitting doors and windows in new houses?"

"I was just treated like a junior apprentice. They gave me all the trivial tasks and had me making tea and clearing up after everyone. I had no responsibility, and it was going nowhere, so I got a job as a security truck driver and quit the carpentry job."

"That would have been a bit of a comedown from leading a troop."

"Aye, rather! Trouble is that the courses at Aldershot only provide the minimum of skills and basic knowledge. You can't go straight out and be a professional building tradesman, so you get landed with jobs at the bottom of the ladder – treated like kids straight from school and paid poorly."

"No wonder you left the carpentry job. But does driving a security truck pay well?"

"Not bad, as long as I do plenty of shifts. At least I'm not treated like a kid. They respect my years in the Army and treat me as an equal. In fact, most of the drivers are ex-military. But I'm still not in a leadership position, which I miss. The only responsibility I have is for the truck and the money it carries."

There was a pause in the conversation while the two men gathered their thoughts. "It'll be lunchtime here in half an hour. I'm just going to get showered and changed. Do you fancy helping me with that and staying for lunch?"

"Sorry, pal. I didn't really have the time to stop off and see you. I'll need to be on my way. It's a long way from London to Edinburgh."

"Are you driving it?"

"Yes. Google Maps reckons it'll take about seven and a half hours.

And that's without stopping. So, I'm reckoning about nine hours. So, you'll see why I'm keen to get on the road."

"Too right. Thanks so much for coming to see me. It's made my day. And don't forget to check up on Cheryl for me. Make sure she's all right."

"Will do, pal. You take care. I want to see you running the 100-metre sprint next time."

They both smile at each other, then grasped hands, squeezing to demonstrate their strength and bond.

"See ya, pal," Charlie said, staring straight into Drum's eyes, wearing a serious expression.

***

Charlie snapped back to the present. What a bloody fool I've been. Charlie was a soldier. It was meant to be. But he'd given that up. He wished he'd never left the Army – especially now that he'd become a criminal instead. 'What the hell was I thinking when I agreed to do the bank job?'

He thought about the future. His life was over now. What would his kids think of him? Would he ever get to see them again? He'd never get the chance to take Alana to Disney World in Florida, as he'd planned to with some of the money he'd stolen. And she'd likely be dead by the time they let him out of prison.

When he got out, he'd probably never get a job again and might end up a druggie, living on the streets. He smashed his right fist into the hard cell wall and cursed his stupidity, then sat as the pain from his knuckles hit him and the blood brimmed on the abrasions. Tears trickled from his eyes – tears that no one had seen him shed since he'd been a boy. And then they flowed like a stream after the rains. His sobs could be heard down the corridor, but no one came or asked him what was wrong.

***

As Jack sat in the police cell, he could hear someone crying. 'Soft bastard,' he thought. But it set him thinking about his circumstances. He recalled his three months in The Glasshouse - the military prison at Colchester. This had been the final phase of his Army career – spoiled by his anger and loss of control.

His commanding officer, Major Horton-Smythe, had humiliated him in front of his colleagues after he'd not fully carried out his boss's orders. The ex-Harrow schooled English toff had riled him, and he'd cracked, lashing out at the superior bastard. He'd deserved the punch in the face that saw him fall to the ground with a bloody nose and split lip. But, on reflection, he wished that he'd kept his cool and just taken the dressing down.

They had forced him to leave the Army after being locked up. The screws at the Military Corrective Training Centre, as it was officially known, were evil. They took every opportunity to make his incarceration a punishment, despite their shared dislike of ex-Public-School commissioned officers from rich families, who treated their subordinates as serfs.

Once released from The Glasshouse, he was ready to leave the Army and start a new life. But life outside the military hadn't turned out to be anywhere near as good as he'd expected. And now, here he was, back in a cell and looking forward to being locked up for many years. 'Life was shite,' he thought.

***

"Guv. I have an update on the driver collaboration theory," Angus stated.

Suzanna looked at him expectantly.

"I asked the driver why he was late the morning of the raid and he said he'd had to deal with a flat tyre. But he would say that, wouldn't he? So I also had a chat with the depot manager, and he confirmed the flat. In fact, the manager had helped change the wheel as he'd wanted to minimise the delay. I reckon that line's a dead end."

"Agreed," Suzanna said. "But it still seems to have been hugely risky, relying on the flat tyre to delay delivery. If they'd noticed the flat earlier and fixed it, the delivery would have been on time, the money placed in the safe, and the robbers would have got away with hardly any cash."

Suzanna returned to her office and made some enquiries to put her mind at ease. The results surprised her.

She emerged two hours later and sent Angus off to bring in a new suspect.

***

"Thanks for coming into the station, sir," Suzanna said. "As I'm sure my colleagues will have told you, we have some questions to ask you about the recent bank raid."

The man sat expressionless.

"Let me set the scene for these questions. I found it difficult to believe that the raiders getting away with over £150,000 or just a few thousand, relied on a delivery truck tyre being flat. If they had noticed it earlier, there would have been no delay and the raid would have reaped extraordinarily little money for the effort and the risk."

"So, we checked with the security firm depot and the driver confirmed he'd been late because of the flat tyre and the depot manager concurred with this, so we thought that was the end of it. But it still nagged at me. There had to be something or someone else involved to ensure that late delivery. We questioned the deputy manager, Jonathon Bilberry, and we were satisfied that he'd not had a hand in it."

"I've since spoken with the bank staff again, and when asked specifically, they remembered the driver had knocked on the door. But when Bilberry went to let him in, the key to the door was missing. He had to track you down to get the key. Some would say that was a certain delaying tactic."

The man sat expressionless.

"Further, I note from your statement," Suzanna said, passing him a copy, "that you had instructed Bilberry to place the money into the safe before opening up for the day. Bilberry has no recollection of this, and he said it was normal practice for the manager to lock the money away. How would you explain this, Mr Silverton?"

"Well, he clearly forgot or didn't hear my instructions. I often do put the money away, but it's not standard practice."

"The other members of staff confirmed it has been your habit to place the money into the safe. So, why did you change this practice on the day of the raid?"

Silverton looked flustered. "I had other work to do. And I thought it about time that Bilberry started taking responsibility for the task."

"An enormous coincidence that!" Suzanna paused, giving Silverton time to worry about the line of questioning. "In your statement to DI Watson, you said that when the red light started flashing, you moved into the main office and hit the second alarm button to confirm that the first wasn't a false alarm."

"That's correct."

"But what you didn't say was that you waited over three minutes from the first alarm being hit, to you confirming with the second press. Why was that Mr Silverton?"

Silverton responded sheepishly, "I can't explain it. I'm sure I didn't waste any time on purpose. Maybe it was the shock that caused a pause?"

"I can't see that excuse holding water, sir, given your military training... Moving on: how well do you know Charles Sutherland?"

"I don't know anyone by that name. Why do you ask?"

"Because he was one of the men who robbed your bank, Mr Silverton... Let's be clear: you're saying that you don't know the man who took the money from your tellers, and also delivered cash to your bank on many occasions?"

"No. I don't know who you're talking about."

Suzanna continued. "So, you're telling me that during the six-month period when Sutherland was aboard the same ship as you, you never came across him?"

Silverton looked shocked. "What ship? When? I don't know what you're talking about?"

"HMS Broadsword, in 2010 – during your last tour of duty."

"Do you know how many people there are on one frigate? Chances are that our paths would never have crossed."

"About 200 men and women. It's not such a big ship, Lieutenant Commander, and with your responsibility for logistics and administration, I can't see how you could never have come across him, especially as he would have stood out – being an Army NCO, rather than a Marine."

Silverton sat silently, his face showing the seriousness of the situation. He'd not realised when he came in for questioning that they were planning to accuse him of involvement in the robbery.

"I'll leave that for the moment... I note from my research that on leaving the RN, you joined a private bank in London, 'Somerville and Peacock', and whilst with the bank, became involved in an insurance syndicate. After your move to the Lothian Bank, this syndicate collapsed as the result of a huge claim, and the personal wealth of those involved took a significant hit."

"Even after re-mortgaging your home to the hilt and selling off your car, this still left you with a debt of £27,000. I understand from your boss at Lothian Bank HQ that he recently informed you the bank could not ignore your growing debt, given your responsibility for customers' funds. And they told you to put your house in order or they'd have to let you go."

Silverton sat stony-faced.

"Miraculously, you paid off your credit card debts today. How did that come about, Mr Silverton?"

Silverton's face dropped, and after a pause of several seconds responded, his voice unsteady: "my wife had a win on the Postcode Lottery. £30,000."

"So, how come it took you so long to respond to the question? Surely you would have known the answer without having to think about it. We will, of course, check with the Postcode Lottery." She turned and looked at Murray, flicking her eyes and head to indicate he should check immediately.

"You say you don't know Charles Sutherland, so how would you explain this phone call, made at 08:55 on the morning of the raid?" Suzanna said as she passed him a list with the call highlighted. "It was made to a mobile registered to Mr Charles Sutherland."

"I want a solicitor," Silverton responded.

Chapter 58

"Thanks for some excellent detective work," Suzanna said as they gathered together in the main office. "We've got the four men responsible for the bank raid, and I'm confident the court will convict them because of the sterling work the team has carried out. We've also caught the serial house thief, and my magnifying glass was recovered. A personal thank you for that one."

"Lastly, we've also got the mugger who'd been operating in the city centre for the last few months. A huge well done to Mairi and Zahir for apprehending those two, especially Mairi for volunteering to be the bait and tackling the mugger *head-on*." She smiled as she said the last words. Mairi smiled back, as if to say: "Very funny, boss."

"So, all in all, it's been a tremendous few days' work. Well done to everyone..." Suzanna paused. "When we chose this career, we knew it would be an ongoing battle. We knew it would not be like a war that we could win but would be continuing skirmishes with the enemy – with those who won't accept the rule of law and live within it. But what we do makes a real difference. Every time we catch a criminal, we're upholding society's standards. Every violent person we put behind bars is one less on the street who might otherwise hurt an innocent person."

"I don't say this often, I know, but I'm immensely proud to work with you all. I feel emotional when I think of how professional and dedicated you are to this job. Thank you all for being part of this successful team. Go home tonight with your heads held high."

Suzanna stood motionless as they nodded and smiled. Some mouthed, 'thanks, boss,' before closing down their computers and gathering their stuff.

"Hey, team," Suzanna called out. "I think it's time we had a celebration. If you'd like to stop off at the pub, the first drink is on me."

Smiles lit the faces of the team and they all headed out the door.

As Suzanna was leaving, the Chief Super arrived in the office. "Suzanna. Exemplary result on the bank raid case," he said, sternly. "I've just heard from the prosecutor's office that they're confident of convictions. Pass on my congratulations, and those of the Chief Constable, to your team." He turned and walked away, saying nothing about their disagreement the previous day. Suzanna doubted that clash would have been their last. She just hoped she could hang on until he retired because she knew with certainty that he wouldn't change his interfering ways. At least today, he'd acknowledged her team's success.

***

The pub on Comely Bank Road was typically quiet at this time of day, but the noise level soon rose once all of her team was at the bar, talking boisterously. Suzanna never really felt comfortable in places where men drank pints of heavy, accompanied by drams of whisky. But the bar her team frequented was much more refined, offering as many wine choices as it did Scotch. Suzanna paid for the first round of drinks (sparkling water for herself, as she was driving), then joined the others, who were chatting avidly.

"Hey Murray," Owen said. "You were right about the driver also being ex-Army. Good call, pal."

The discussion continued, with many views about coincidences and gut feelings in police work.

Angus turned to Suzanna and asked, "What was it that made you go to Jack McKenzie's place and confront him? You never said."

"Elementary, my dear Watson," Suzanna responded with a grin. "Once I'd heard that he'd just bought an expensive car, and was being generous with his money, and given the other mentions that we'd already had about him, I realised he must be the third man. It just took a bit of goading to get a response from him."

Angus smiled at the DCI's use of the phrase supposedly used by Sherlock Holmes.

"How did your date go the other day, Angus?"

"Pretty good, thanks. I'll definitely be seeing her again."

"That'll be a change then! You haven't been out with the same women more than twice in the last two years, have you?"

"That's true. I've been shy of getting into a lasting relationship after my last one."

"What happened to make you want to avoid getting into another relationship?"

Angus pursed his lips, as he considered how much to share with his boss, then murmured. "I lived with Erika for five years. It was great at the start. We were madly in love. But as time passed, she became irrationally jealous. Every time I was late back from work, she thought I'd been with another woman. The accusations and violence drove the love away. I had to make excuses to the guys at the station for the bruises and scratches... I just had to leave her."

"Wow! I had no idea, Angus. That's terrible. Everyone is aware of women being physically abused by men, but you rarely hear of men being abused by women. It must have been hard for you, dealing with that."

"Yes, it was. Took me two years before I started dating again. Perhaps you can see why I've kept my relationships casual ever since."

Suzanna reached out her hand and rested on his forearm. “I feel for you, Angus. Being accused of things you’d not done, then abused by the accuser, must have really hurt you. But don’t let that put you off another relationship. There are plenty of women out there who will love you and not abuse you.” She squeezed his arm, then withdrew her hand, smiling as she looked into his eyes.

“Aye, you’re right. Perhaps I’ll find one someday. I appreciate your concern, but I’m fine with it now.” Angus excused himself and went to the gents.

Suzanna wondered if he was all right or whether his excursion to the toilet was an excuse to hide his emotions. After finishing her drink, she said goodbye to the team and headed home. Before driving off, she thought about her magnifying glass’s recent journey. She’d been told that the young scallywag who took it and had been charged with multiple robberies, had mentioned his brother had taken the glass from him. The youth had been knocked down by a car when he’d run off with it – ending up with a concussion and a broken leg.

The man whose car had hit Billy’s brother had been charged with driving offences. What a coincidence that Charles Sutherland had gone to aid Billy’s brother and was recognised by the constable at the scene. If he hadn’t stopped that day, perhaps he’d have not been identified so soon.

Then there was Billy’s pal, Cameron, who was to be charged with theft of a bicycle. It was strange that there had been a connection between one of the bank robbers and the little thief, Billy.

It was extraordinary that Suzanna had been in the supermarket when the boys’ two mothers had been discussing the accident and the thefts and had mentioned Jack McKenzie’s recent injection of cash - sending her to his bar and his subsequent arrest.

Then there’d been a young man called Connor, arrested for the glass’s theft, just because he’d held it in his hand for one minute.

Suzanna's sister would call her superstitious for even considering some magical connection between the magnifying glass and these things, but she couldn't help thinking it had some power over the lives of the people through whose hands it had passed. Just look at how it had changed her life!

Her great-great-uncle's influence, through the glass, had travelled way beyond his grave. Nearly ninety years on, he appeared to still be affecting people's lives. She reflected on her earlier decision to lock the magnifying glass away. Perhaps she should leave it on display and see where fate would lead.

Epilogue – Monday 8th February

Jimmy Boyd emerged from the hospital in a wheelchair, with his leg in plaster. His father pushed him to the waiting taxi, fortunately, a tall vehicle with a sliding door. Jimmy's face was tense as he lifted himself out of the wheelchair and it remained that way as he shuffled through the door onto the seat. His father, Reg, passed him the pair of crutches he'd have to use when they got home and dumped the wheelchair by the wall of the hospital. They'd asked him to return it to the reception but couldn't be bothered.

When they arrived back in Leith, Jimmy struggled to get out of the taxi and stand on his crutches. His father didn't think to offer a hand, but Jimmy would likely have refused anyway, as he was a proud and determined youth. The taxi drove off as soon as he had his money, leaving father and son to walk up the path to their house.

As Jimmy was attempting to step over the threshold into his home, he felt dizzy, then blacked out, collapsing back into his father's arms. Reg panicked. He didn't know how to deal with this situation. He laid his son on the ground and slapped his face. "Jimmy. Wake up, Lad. Jimmy. Don't do this to me. Come on, Lad, wake up." But nothing happened. He took his mobile phone from his pocket but remembered that he didn't have any credit left on it, so rushed inside to call from the landline.

"Emergency services; which service do you require?" Reg told them everything they needed to know, hung up and went back to his son. Jimmy looked so pale. He tried speaking to him again but got no response. Overcome with feelings of uselessness and helplessness, for the first time in years, Reg cried, as his son faded away.

The ambulance arrived 15 minutes later, and the paramedic rushed up, carrying all his gear. He turned his attention immediately to Jimmy, feeling for a pulse – nothing, then checked his breathing – nothing. "Stand back, please, sir," he said to the man hovering over the boy. He pulled out his defibrillator, bared Jimmy's chest, applied the paddles and, when the charge showed it was ready, pressed the button on his paddle. Jimmy's body jumped.

The paramedic checked again, but there was still no heartbeat. He increased the charge on the defibrillator and repeated the operation, but it had no effect.

Reg was in shock. He couldn't understand why his boy lay on the ground with no heartbeat. He'd only had a mild concussion and a broken leg.

The ambulance driver arrived with a stretcher and the medics quickly loaded Jimmy onto it and moved him without pause into the ambulance. "Are you the father?" Reg nodded. "You'd best come with us, Mr Boyd."

The doors closed, and the vehicle drove off with blue lights flashing and sirens sounding.

The paramedic injected adrenaline into Jimmy's arm, checked his vitals again, then tried once more with the defib. He checked Jimmy's heartbeat again, then turned to his father and said, "Sorry, Mr Boyd. He's gone."

Reg broke down and sobbed like a child, collapsing into a vertical foetal position.

***

Morag Boyd sat in the same room as she had been two weeks ago when Jimmy had been brought in after the accident. The A&E doctor came in and sat opposite her. Reg was at her side, but the two younger boys were in school. "Mr and Mrs Boyd. I'm so sorry that you've lost your son. I can only imagine that you're asking yourself why this happened. It was so unexpected. I can't be 100% certain, and we won't know until the post-mortem. But my strong suspicion, based on experience, is that a blood clot from his damaged leg travelled up to his brain and caused a massive stroke."

He let it sink in for a minute before going on. "It's extremely rare and unpredictable. No one could have foreseen this or taken any action to prevent it. I'm so sorry. Mr Boyd, please don't blame yourself. There's nothing you could have done. When the clot reached his brain, it would already have been too late." He paused again. "He won't have suffered. Death would have been quick. Do you have any questions?"

Reg's sorrow turned to anger. "I don't believe you. I bet the hospital didn't do its job properly. Now my son's dead. You lot are going to pay for this. I'll sue your arse off, you bastards."

Morag intervened. "Reg. Shut up. Stop your ranting. The doctors and nurses will have done everything they could for Jimmy. Sit down and be quiet."

Reg lashed out, knocking his wife off her feet. She fell back with a crash as the table and chairs toppled and landed on the floor. Reg stormed out of the hospital.

As he left, a young woman was being brought in on a stretcher, a team of medics around her as they rushed her towards the operating theatre. He pushed past them, knocking one medic sideways momentarily. The medic quickly recovered from the knock, gave a dirty look toward the disappearing man, then instantly returned her attention to the more pressing matter. The patient had lost a lot of blood from a deep wound, and her survival relied on their urgent action.

***

The Chief Superintendent strode into Suzanna's office without knocking, his brow furrowed. His voice was stern as he spoke.

"Suzanna. Dreadful news, I'm afraid."

Suzanna looked up at Ewan Robertson, wondering whether he'd got to hear about her speeding offence and was about to suspend her. 'No, it can't be that. He looks sad, not angry.'

"It's Una Wallace. She's been stabbed. They've admitted her to hospital, and she's in a bad way."

Suzanna's jaw dropped in shock at the news. She recovered, stood, then asked, "What hospital, sir?"

"It's the Western General but there's no point going right now; she's in a critical condition. You won't get to see her until she comes out of theatre."

***

The phone rang in the main office and Caitlin answered: "Edinburgh CID, DS Findlay speaking." She listened intently, making notes, said "thanks, we'll get someone to the scene ASAP," replaced the handset and marched to Suzanna's office.

"Ma'am," she said, then noticed the Chief Super. "sir. Just had word that the body of a woman has been found washed up on the banks of the Firth, near the bridge at Queensferry. Seems to be of Indian descent. Uniform are on scene and they have informed the Coroner." Caitlin sensed that there was something else distracting the two senior officers from the news of the reported potential murder. She paused before continuing, wondering what it could be. "Who would you like to attend the scene?"

Suzanna shook herself out of shock and switched into decisive mode. "You go, Caitlin. Take Murray or Owen with you. Report back when you've found out more, then we'll decide who should lead the investigation."

"OK, ma'am. I'll take Murray."

"Caitlin, before you go. You need to know, Una is in hospital, in critical condition. She's been stabbed. I'll let you know when I hear more." Caitlin's eyes widened at the news.

"Is she going to be all right?"

"We don't know yet. As I said, she's in critical condition. I intend to go to the hospital as soon as she's out of surgery. I'll update you when I hear anything. Spread the word around the team, please Caitlin."

"Right, ma'am. I'll tell the others, then speak with the Coroner and talk with the lads who found the body." She turned and walked away.

"Keep me posted on this washed-up body and any news on Una." The Chief Super said, then strode away.

"Bloody hell! What a start to the week," Suzanna thought out loud. "Here we go again..."

* * *

Free book

Sign up for my mailing list to receive a free copy of The Test (the story about Suzanna's test, taken to win her great-great-uncle's inheritance), as soon as it's ready. Just visit my website: www.harry-navinski.com.

Reviews

As a new author, it's incredibly important to have reviews of my book, so other potential readers have some idea of its quality. **Please, please, please** leave a review on Amazon Kindle.

Want more?

If you would like to know about the next Suzanna McLeod episode or find out about Harry Navinski, check out www.harrynavinski.com.

Reviews

As this is my first published novel, it's incredibly important to have reviews, so other potential readers have some idea of its quality. **Please, please, please** leave a review on Amazon Kindle and, if you can, Goodreads. Thank you.

Acknowledgements

I couldn't have done this without the support of my family, friends, and beta-readers. Thanks so much.

A special thanks to the inspirational creative writing course, by Darren Harper, that I attended at Higham Hall, within the UK's beautiful Lake District National Park.

And a huge thank you to Jamie Salmon for his excellent cover design.

About the Author

Harry joined the Royal Air Force, straight from school at the tender age of just 15. He spent the first half of his RAF career as an aircraft technician and the latter half as an engineering officer. Based in England, Scotland, Germany and Malta, he also travelled the World with the RAF. Harry's first taste of writing came when asked to write short pieces for the RAF Station's magazine where he was based.

Many years later, he created and edited the RAF's magazine for sports and adventurous training, 'RAF Active'. Harry's articles, written from his experience of sports and adventurous activities, included: skiing, sailing, judo, and scuba diving, to name a few. He was also published in the Anglers Conservation Association yearbook and the UK Defence Journal.

After his time in the RAF, Harry spent 6 years on voluntary service in West Bengal (anti-human trafficking work) and it was whilst in India that he made his first attempt at writing fiction. On his return to the UK, he attended a creative writing course and was inspired to write his first novel, *The Glass*. His travels around the world have provided

Harry with a huge source of knowledge and experiences for new books – yet to come – and he looks forward to sharing these.

You can connect with me on:

- https://harrynavinski.com
- https://twitter.com/HarryNavinski
- https://www.facebook.com/harry.navinski.9
- https://www.instagram.com/harrynavinski

Subscribe to my newsletter:

- https://mailchi.mp/33a95762c1c0/harrys-list

Also by Harry Navinski

If you've enjoyed The Glass and would like to read other Harry Navinski books, have a look at these below.

Sign up for my mailing list, if you'd like to hear news about new releases, as they occur.

The Test

There's a mention in *The Glass* that a Victorian-era detective left his estate and a magnifying glass to a relative who, on reaching the age of 18, passed a test he had set. Suzanna McLeod, the great-great-niece of this infamous detective, passed that test to win herself the Glass and the proceeds of his trust fund. But what was that test?

Find out in my novella, *The Test.* This is free to anyone signing up for my mailing list to receive occasional updates. Visit www.harrynavinski.com/books to find out more.

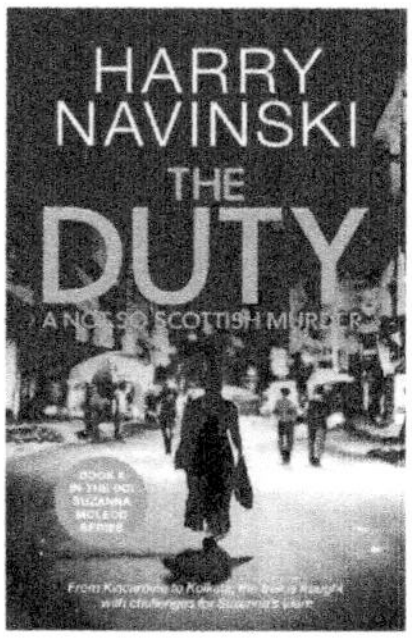

The Duty

The second DCI Suzanna McLeod mystery is *The Duty*,

Edinburgh's top DCI has a murder and a team member's stabbing to deal with, taking her from the Firth of the Forth to the Ganges. Illegal immigration, slavery, and brutality surface as she tracks down the culprits and handles her meddling boss, calling on all her mental and physical talents.

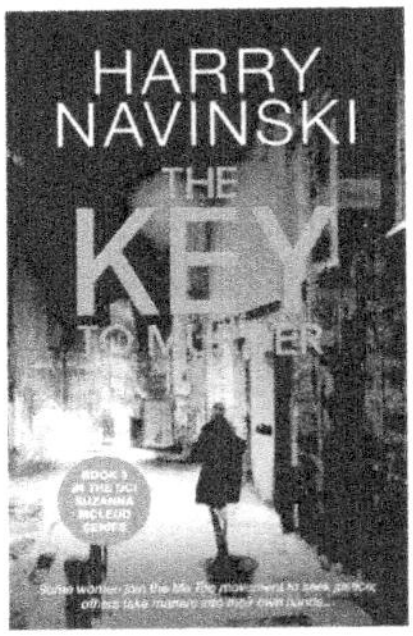

The Key to Murder

Winter arrives early for George White. He was already housebound and reliant on carers, but no one expected the cheeky octogenarian to be murdered. What possible motive could there be? As Detective Suzanna McLeod digs into his past, a darker side becomes evident, and a number of suspects emerge. The investigation uncovers prostitution rackets and sex trafficking. Suzanna's worry is that George's murder could be the first in a series. The chase is on to find the murderer before they strike again.

Printed in Great Britain
by Amazon

19508733R00202